MIRROR OF DESTINY

Other AvoNova Books by
Andre Norton

BROTHER TO SHADOWS
THE HANDS OF LYR

MIRROR of DESTINY

ANDRE NORTON

An AvoNova Book

William Morrow and Company, Inc.
New York

AVON BOOKS
A division of
The Hearst Corporation
1350 Avenue of the Americas
New York, New York 10019

1

THE ROOM WAS long, low ceilinged, and had the unusual attribute of seeming to change size at times—though that may only have been a fantasy of those suddenly entering it. It also would have been unimaginably cluttered had any other mistress been in charge.

In the numerous side cupboards were boxes, crocks, jars beyond any but a very patient numbering. Drawers were meticulously divided by strips between which lay stores of dried herbs, leaf, flower, root and stem, and more precious packets of foreign spices.

Down the long center table marched a line of bottles, of several sizes, each stoppered with a representation of a grotesque head, some clearly non-human, or outright beast—things never to be seen in an honest cottage or its garden.

Though there was the first impression of gloom and over many shadows, after one became accustomed to the long chamber, there was a measure of light. That past all natural laws appeared to gather and hold immediately about any busied occupant of which, on this brisk spring morning, were two and a half—the half being represented by a large shadow-gray cat, sitting on the tabletop as stiff and upright as one of the bottles at his back.

He had something of the air of an overseer and the worker he watched so intently was indeed busy, her head bent a little as if she must keep a constant eye upon the rhythmic movements of one set of fingers.

Her tightly bound braids were of a medium brown and her pale, somewhat too chiseled features expressed complete concentration. For all of that she was young, and the shabby hearthside dress she wore was a dull green, girdled in by a workwoman's belt with loops for various small knives, tools, and pouches. The robe bunched about her but not enough to disguise the fact that her body was childishly slim.

Twilla, apprentice to Wisewoman Hulde, raised her right hand out of a constant circling movement and inspected narrowly the small pads which covered each fingertip. She allowed the disk she had been working on to rest upon her knee and with her other hand worked off each finger a pad now worn to a near vanished thread web. Placing these discards carefully to one side, she reclothed each finger with new pads taken from a store heaped near the table edge before her.

Once those were firmly in place, she returned to her task, smoothing the clear silver face of the disk with a series of motions, which formed a pattern in themselves and which did not vary.

> *"Up and down, out and in,*
> *Sun's path and widdershin.*
> *Power answering to the call*
> *Of flesh and blood and inner all."*

Just such a singsong type of jingle as might girl children voice when skipping rope or bouncing a ball. But this was no child's play and she repeated the words carefully knowing that they were not to be skimped, any more than her hour of mirror polishing each day was to be interrupted by anything—save perhaps a crashing of the house wall about her.

She had been eight years of age—as far as the Kinderhost Keeper had been able to judge—one of the pieces of flotsam which are to be found in a port city even when it is well policed. Then the Wisewoman had come seeking a maid—there were not many in Varvad who would think to apprentice their daughters to such an unchancy trade.

Even at those few years Twilla had learned suspicion, caution, the need for being always self-guarded—the harsh laws of survival. But she had not shrunk back when Hulde, looking like horrow bird in her long flapping cloak, had pointed to her after surveying the five girls available.

There was nothing in the least maternal about Hulde. She was thin, tall, craggy of feature as a man, and her voice had the rasp note of one used to obedience. Yet Twilla had been pleased that it was she who scampered out of the Kinderhost at the Wisewoman's heels, taking an extra skip now and then to keep up with her now appointed mistress.

And after ten years under Hulde's direction Twilla realized very often, with thanks to whatever power might be listening, that she had come here. There had been months, years of testing, but she had learned, how she had learned—as avidly as one lost in a desert might gulp down the water of an unexpected well.

Hulde's trade was not even to be mastered in a lifetime, as the Wisewoman had often said. She herself was still learning, stretching her powers a fraction at a time. While Twilla was yet but a beginning scholar still she had mastered the art of reading, of writing, of memorizing that which was so important. She knew the usage of countless herbs and had attended birthings and soul loosings with her mistress until the ceremonies and skills for each were as a second nature for her—even though she had never tested either truly on her own.

Now what she wrought *would* be her own by Hulde's decree. Some three months earlier the Wisewoman had produced this disk mirror. The reflecting side was dull as a fogged window pane, the back was of a greenish metal and wrought intricately to cover every inch with symbols and hints of creatures which might just be peering out between the swirl of lines which netted them.

To Twilla was given the finishing—the polishing of the upper surface, which must be done with her fingers, each padded with silken pockets seeped in herbal mixtures so that her constant programmed rubbing brought forth scents as she worked, some pleasing and some baneful, but all to be accepted.

She was intent upon her work but not so unseeing and unhearing as to miss the sudden action of the cat who had been watching her with a guardian eye. Greykin had whipped to his feet, facing the outer door which was behind Twilla's stool, his yellow eyes were slit narrow and his tail bushed. From his throat came the low note of a fighter's growl. As if that signaled her, Hulde turned away from the fireplace where she had been methodically stirring the contents of a small kettle. She gave a long look at the cat and then swung the pot away from the full heat of the flames, hooking up its chain, before she too turned to face the door, wiping her narrow, bony hands on a towel clipped to her apron band.

Twilla's own hand stopped in mid-glide down the silver mirror surface. She looked to Hulde and then squirmed around on the stool to face also the outer door. The walls of this ancient house were thick and near all the sounds of the busy port were shut off from its inhabitants. However, Hulde did not need sight or sound, any more than Greykin, to alert them for trouble. Trouble?

Twilla felt a twinge of foreboding. Swiftly she slid the mirror into its bag, drew the string tight and lifted that string over her head to rest breast high on her body. She tucked it way beneath her loose bodice and then shed the polish pads, sweeping all the used ones into a pile and dropping them into a wide-mouthed jar, snapping down the lid of the box which held the unused.

Yet nothing had disturbed them—there was no pounding on the door—

That came even as she wondered about it. Hulde's hand raised and she snapped two fingers to Twilla's surprise. The Wisewoman was not used to revealing any signs of power save when she and Twilla were alone.

The bar at the door obeyed that signal, sliding back, and the door itself pushed inward so quickly that he who had been ready to deliver another drumming of knocks stumbled after it. Then drew himself up to blink as if he had come straight out of day into night. Without any cause the room brightened enough to show the two women their visitor.

"Harhodge," Hulde greeted him by name and Twilla recognized him as one of their street neighbors. Two weeks past Hulde had delivered his son alive and saved his wife into the bargain when all others had given her up to death loosing.

"Wisewoman," he was breathing heavily as one who had been running, "they are coming, sweeping down Gunter Lane, and through Gryfalcon Court. The quota has not been filled this time and they are taking even in spite of the law."

Twilla hunched herself into a smaller self on the stool. There was no reason for Harhodge to give further explanation—they knew.

The maid hunt! For five years now it had swept through the port city—as it did through the countryside and the two other major cities of Varslaad also. Any unbetrothed and able bodied maid was liable to be the prey they sought.

It was a legal thing—passed by the Council in full office, the stating of it signed by the King. Those in the Far Land needed wives; their home country would supply them. Noble born need not fear such a fate, but all below blooded rank, unless betrothed with formal listing at the town hall or some such protection, could be swept away from family, home, all which they knew, and shipped over mountain to wed some stranger out of hand. How this had come about was told in whispers only—the strangest being that the new settlers—whose produce from the land was greatly needed by Varslaad—were in some grave danger unless they were wed: a rumor so unbelievable as to be laughed at—only it never was.

Varslaad, its land torn by the strip mining of those ores upon which all its wealth and safety was founded, needed new productive farmland. There had been riots just last cold season when dispossessed farmers and underfed miners had protested the present state of affairs. And the western land was rich—the caravans venturing over mountain brought such an abundance of grain and other food that people still gathered to see one come in and marveled at what it unbaled and basketed.

Still there was this maid hunt and there were only so many eligible maids—no more than one could be taken from any family—and those daughters of the near-starved farmers and miners were not judged strong enough to make the trip.

"Twilla is apprenticed," Hulde broke the short silence.

"Wisewoman, they say that Skimish has laid notice at the town archives that your Twilla was took from the Kinderhost and that she was never a true apprentice, not having any kinfolk to give bond for her. Also—please, Wisewoman, do not give the blame to me, but there are those who have spoken against you—behind their hands to be sure, but with words which carry—that you deal with unchancy things and that the councilers should have a sure eye set on you. If you stand against them now you will give substance to their shadow."

Twilla moistened her lips with the tip of her tongue. She knew that those with powers such as Hulde could summon would always be feared and even hated by some, no matter how much good the use of those powers might have done. The baker was right—

The girl arose from her stool, moving out a little to face Hulde.

"Master Harhodge has the right of it, mistress. I would not be the cause to bring down all you have striven to do here. I *am* from the Kinderhost and it is true there is none to blood claim me. You know how my kind are thought of in Varvad." She was shaking a little as she spoke that last word. But she held to her purpose—Hulde had given her so much that was good, she was not going now to return that gift with something which would lead to evil.

Hulde raised one hand and beckoned to her so that Twilla came to stand directly before the Wisewoman. That beckoning hand now grasped her own right one, turning it over, palm up, as Hulde bent her head to stare into that palm as if it held some answer to what might happen.

Through that touch Twilla was aware of a sudden tenseness in Hulde's body and then the woman spoke:

"One must go as the power calls—one cannot swim against a current in denial of its force. I had not thought to lose—" She raised her head now and stared down from her greater height directly into Twilla's eyes.

"If it is to be, there is no way of denying it. You have been near Kin-daughter to me, girl, but it would seem my fate line no longer runs with yours. If these come to take you"—now there was a flash of fire in her eyes and her lips drew tightly against her teeth in a half snarl—"then they will discover that they are the ones who may have made a poor bargain. Take that which you wear, use it as the spirit leads you—and in the end it may prove salvation for more than you, Twilla. You are healer trained; that perhaps will win you good standing. Use all you know as best you can."

Sound from outside reached them now, the clatter of thick-soled boots, the rattle of wagon wheels. Hulde raised her hand and pointed to the door behind Harhodge. Without a sound that swung closed, sealing them once more into their own world.

"You have, Master Harhodge," Hulde's tone was formal and its words were set to impress, "come here to ask for a sleep potion for your wife." She took two steps to the long table, her hands now going out in a sweeping gesture above that long array of bottles.

He nodded jerkily, wisps of his straw colored hair free from his cap, flopped near down to his eyes, in which Twilla could see the fast-growing apprehension of one found in the wrong place at the wrong time.

Now a gesture from Hulde sent her also in motion, sliding swiftly around the end of the table to the fireplace where she swung back the waiting pot over the flame and took up the long-handled wooden spoon the Wisewoman had thrust through one chain loop, beginning to stir the mixture as if this was the task she had been set to.

Just as Hulde selected a bottle and held it out into the better light before Harhodge there was another imperious rattle of knocks, one following the other with manifest impatience at the door. A swift streaking of a gray furred body marked the retreat of the cat. Hulde, bottle in hand, went to lift the latch and confront the knocker.

He was hardly of middle height for a man; the Wisewoman could match inches with him easily. Perhaps because of that very fact he bore himself with all the arrogance of an up-country noble new come to town. His lean, forethrusting jaw, was badly scraped of beard, leaving patches of dark shadow which could well mark themselves as the paths of dirty fingers.

His leather jacket was well worn and stained—what could be seen of it, for he was fully accoutered with a stout breastplate and long metal cuffs extending nearly to his elbows. He had pushed his helmet back a little, perhaps to clear his field of sight, and the eyes which swept from Hulde to the other two and back were cold and suspicious. It did not need the addition of that much-creased scarf banding cross-ways on the half armor from shoulder to hip to proclaim his rank. This was undoubtedly the leader of the search-troop.

"You wish? There are many potions for healing—" Hulde's voice had changed oddly, taken on a quiver, a harshness such as age would bring, and also she appeared somehow to shrink—drawing years about her as one would draw a cloak.

"You have under this roof one from the Kinderhost!" he snapped. "She is of marriage age and not bespoken—"

"She is my sworn apprentice." Hulde's voice held now a servile note.

"She is Kinderhost—one without kin to sign her papers—therefore she is not apprentice bound. You, girl—stand forth!"

He was now a step or two within the room and he broke the eye-to-eye wary stare he had kept on Hulde to shoot that order at Twilla.

She took her time as if to emphasize that what she had been doing was of more importance than this—which she thought would be the proper attitude for one completely under her employer's thumb—once more hooking the pot away from the full heat before she turned.

The strutting squad commander swept her from head to foot conveying somehow that his opinion of this particular prey was very low.

"She'll do—"

"As you say, Captain." Hulde bowed her head with deference and Twilla realized that the Wisewoman was playing for time. "She shall be ready upon the summons."

"She'll be ready now!" he shot back. "Tathan." He did not turn his head toward the door, but he raised his voice and that not quite closed barrier was given a push at his summons.

The woman who tramped in was near as heavy-armored as her leader, lacking his breastplate but wearing a double quilted leather jacket, breeches, and boots clearly of army issue. Her hair was cropped short and her features were thick and heavy, her eyes small, yet alert, seeming to dart from side to side to take in all before her with a suspicion as keen or even keener than that of her commander.

"Tathan will go with you, girl. She will see to your gear and you will be bound by her choices. Understand?"

Twilla nodded, allowing herself an expression of fear, which might well lead them to believe that she was most biddable.

"Twilla is healer trained—in part," Hulde said. "It might well be to your advantage, good Captain, if you brought such a one with her healer bag—"

"So be it, Wisewoman. But you will show and tell me each thing so packed and explain its use. Get going with you, girl!"

So urged, Twilla left through the other door. She held one hand to her breast, cradling the mirror against her. There were powers she was sure that Hulde could have loosed against this appropriation of her assistant. That the Wisewoman had not done so was in itself a warning.

The girl led the way up a crooked stair to the room which had been her home, her security, for so many years.

"Warm clothes," she caught a whiff of strong breath tainted with frosale beer, as if Tathan were at her very shoulder. "Strong boots. It's a long hard way, Kinderoffer."

Without answering, playing still the easily cowed, Twilla brought out of the chest at the foot of the narrow bed her winter cloak. From beneath that the garments she used when venturing out with Hulde on their wild herb hunting expeditions. There were breeches of three thicknesses of musil fleece, a jerkin not too different from that worn by her present companion, save it was unstained and smelled of dried herbs instead of old grease and unwashed skin.

Keeping her back turned to the woman, she loosened the drawstring of her dress, having removed her belt with its many small burdens, and allowed the garment to puddle down around her feet. The shirt she had worn beneath she could keep and it covered well the mirror.

As she redressed she glanced about the room. Extra body linen, surely they would allow that. Her eyes touched very regretfully on the slim row of books. No, better not. Like anything from Hulde's house those might be suspect. When she turned once more to pick up her belt, Tathan's beefy hand shot over her shoulder and closed about that.

"You won't be needin' such trinkets where you're going. Witchy stuff."

Twilla let the belt lay, taking a scarf from the chest to twist about her middle and doing it so skillfully that she was sure Tathan had caught no sight of certain symbols embroidered in colors so like the background that they faded nearly into it. She bundled up the linen and turned to her guard.

"I am ready." She had pulled the travel hood well over her head so it overshadowed her face and she did not need to counterfeit the tremble in her voice. In so quick a time she had been shaken free of her small safe corner. Before her lay—what?

Hulde had a small shoulder pack waiting for her. Harhodge had withdrawn well back into the shadows and was biting his grubby nails. The soldier was pressed close to the table, still frowning at the bag.

"Healer's craft," Hulde said. "If you have learned anything during your time here among my pots and bottles, girl, let that show. Remember"—now her gaze bored through the partial hiding of hood and dropped eyes—"what you have learned is to be used for relief and in the spirit of good for one and all. Be blessed by the New, the Full, and the Old." She did not raise her hand, open in the three-fold signing, but under the edge of her cloak Twilla's own fingers moved in that most ancient of patterns.

With that blessing she bowed her head even more, though she thought Hulde guessed that those rare and nearly forgotten tears had gathered once more in her eyes.

"Wisewoman, for all your charity I give thanks," she said and her voice seemed blurred. Then Tathan seized her by the elbow and was turning her toward the open door. She stumbled a little as she crossed the threshold, as if her feet were reluctant to take that step. But against her small breasts she felt the smooth surface of the mirror as if it still drew some strength from her.

THE CLUMSY WAGON jolted from side to side so that those within had to clutch at the nearest handhold at intervals to keep from sliding from the seating benches to the straw bedded floor. Though it was the first month of spring the wind, which thrust in now and then around the raised driver's seat in the front, was chill enough to make the passengers keep their cloaks tight about them.

Twilla steadied herself against a particularly rough bump, but she was unable to keep herself from brushing against her seat mate. The other girl squirmed away as if she wanted no such contact.

They were three days out of Varvad now—this wagon train was not built for speed. And there had been several days before that when Twilla was more or less imprisoned with others swept up in the maid hunt. They were a very wide mixture—even from a port town which was a trade center and drew many strangers and traders.

In this wagon there were six, and in the other two wagons lumbering along, one before and one behind, that number was equalled. From the first time they had been flung together there had been few signs of friendliness among them. They were too mixed a crew.

The girl beside Twilla now, Askla, was a shrinking vormouse of a creature who had wept ceaselessly until her red eyes were near puffed shut and she seemed to have very little strength left in her small body. She was, to judge by her neat if now crumpled dress and bordered cloak, of some family of substance—a minor merchant's daughter perhaps. On the other side Twilla herself was loomed over by a brawny fishergirl, whose sea-stained clothing carried an unforgettable odor.

No tears from Leela, rather a frank curiosity and a hint of defiance in her square chin with the weather-browned skin stretched tightly over it. She looked now to Twilla and her wide lips shaped a half grin.

"Fair shake us to pieces afore we gets there," she commented. "What man is gonna want a sack of blood and bruises for his bed? They'd better make sure of our gettin' over mountain in one good piece for the auction or they ain't gonna get much for this lot!"

"Auction?" Twilla had heard enough rumors the past five days to question that. "I thought it was a lottery—"

Leela winked and then caught quickly for another handhold as the wagon gave a stronger lurch. "Lottery—that's not what Samper says. Oh, they puts names in a bowl—and then they draws—them that is approved for weddin'. But those there pays a stiff tax to git a chance at the wife bowl. So this Lord Harmond he makes hisself a little profit—'less the King wants an accountin' too. One thing they say this lord abides by, though, once one of them dirt diggers draws—mind you, he has to take what his luck has given him—there is no backin' out if he don't take a likin' to what he sees when the names are matched."

Twilla tensed. "What if he does not like his choice after he sees her, or she him?" she asked. And realized that the sniffs from her other seat mate were no longer so loud, as if the vormouse was listening too.

Leela shrugged. Her shoulders wide and strong from seasons at the pull of sails, the casting of nets, the sweep of oars made that gesture doubly emphatic.

"They ain't carin' 'bout that. Samper, he told me as how you gets married to him as draws you and you stays married—'less the green devils get one or t'other of you."

"Green devils?" The fishergirl seemed to know far more than chance rumors.

"You ain't heard o' them, missy? That's why they want us— Luck for me that Samper, for all he's one o' the guard now, comes straight from the Vulkers who be second line blood kin to my people. He's told me a lot, Samper has. And it's worth listenin' to if you want to know what's ahead for all of us, do they get us there still alive—" She grunted at another plunge of the wagon.

"Seems like there has always been trouble over mountain. The first settlers—they was all dirt grubbers as had their land taken away for the uro mines—didn't last long. They got over mountain right enough, and they got their farms started. Then when the caravans came—well, they was just not there—save for a few as had no wits and were wanderin' around like dumb beasts.

"So when the king—he says send soldiers, go a-huntin' for what turned them so. But there weren't nothin' as they could find—just open land and then a big wood as they did not quite want to go in. But their captain he says go. Which was the worse for him, 'cause a half of them only came out again—and they was mind-struck or blind—talking a lot 'bout beautiful gals back in the woods. From then on it was like men was pulled by something, heading off into that place, some never comin' back—others half-witted. Only Lord Harmond he noted something—them settlers who was married and had a woman under their roof to bed—they didn't go wanderin'. So"—she held up her broad, calloused hands—"they began this wife sendin'."

It was very apparent that Leela believed in her story and that to her it was no rumor but an accepted fact. Yet that did not make Twilla any the more eager to be a lottery prize for some farmer, joined to him by a life bond. She was a healer. Let her get to this Lord Harmond—there was no use in trying to convince any underling, on that she had already made her mind—let her get to Lord Harmond and she could argue her worth to any colony in return for her freedom.

At nooning the wagons drew to a stop and they were ordered out, though some of the girls stumbled and complained of cramped legs. This was a dreary land with little worth for the seeing. The low downs about had been leveled by the strip miners until the ore veins were exhausted and only raw earth, with here and there a small struggling plant to supply a tiny patch of green. It was a scene of desolation that struck at Twilla, used as she was to Hulde's respect for all the earth had to offer in the way of free growing things. A manmade desert—she turned her back upon it as much as she could as she chewed on the stale bread and sipped sparingly from the water bottle which was handed around. Even the air overhead seemed to be free of birds. Twilla remembered the difference when she had gone herb hunting from Varvad with Hulde. Around there were still undevastated farmlands, with copses and spring-fed streams to be found—here was nothing.

No birds—but there was one! She brushed back the edge of her hood and looked up, trying to follow the flight of that dot across the sky. It was too high, too far away, already lost.

"Eat up—go to the left to relieve yourselves—" Tathan, who was in direct control of the party in Twilla's wagon, bore down upon them. "You—" she centered in on Askla, "stop that ever-lasting sniveling or you'll git something as will shut you up good!" She swung up a thick fist and the small girl retreated, bringing up against Leela who threw a supporting arm about her.

"Now, then, warwoman, would you knock about the king's own maids? That's what they call us, ain't it? Gives us a dowry too, he does."

Tathan's jaw seemed to shoot out farther, like the snout of a mastiff questing for a good scent of a proper quarry. "You, fish skinner, keep a civil tongue in your—"

But she was interrupted by a hail from the wagon ahead and with a last scowl at Askla tramped off in that direction.

Leela winked at Twilla. But the other girl was sober.

"Best not get on her wrong side, Leela. It is a long ways over mountain and she will have plenty of time to make things hard for us."

Leela's grin faded and she shot a sharp glance at the other girl. "Mayhap you are right. But that one is a bully and all bullies understand is a fist as big as theirs and a good arm behind it. Askla," she spoke to the smaller girl, "there's no goin' back for any o' us—we be in this stew together and must make the best of it."

Askla's chin quivered. "I want—my mother—" It was a thin little wail, which startled Twilla. She saw Leela was watching her over the other girl's bent head.

"Twilla, you have healer learnin'. Can you give her help—else she is going to make herself sick, and I don't trust any nursing from that one." She jerked her head in the direction in which Tathan had disappeared.

"Yes." Twilla flushed. She should have been the one to think of this—she who had prided herself so much on her small skills. Quickly she found a packet in the shoulder bag Hulde had packed for her; a sniff of its contents told her this was what she sought.

"Askla," she said gently, "chew a few of these leaves. Truly this is healer's knowledge and will help you feel better."

The smaller girl, still in Leela's hold, looked at her warily.

"Take it!" Leela ordered and reluctantly she did, mouthing the small ball of dried herbs as the fishergirl watched her sternly.

They were not stinted as to food, but it was coarse stuff—army marching rations, Twilla thought. She searched again in her herb bag and brought out a small container of powder, which she shook over her own portion of the near rock hard bread and then passed to Leela.

The fishergirl eyed it warily and proceeded to take a heavy sniff at its contents. Then her easy grin appeared again, and she proceeded to douse her bread thoroughly with the sprinkling of dull green.

"Good as one can get at the Croakin' Wartoad on a ten day," she approved.

"Askla?" Twilla offered the seasoning to the other girl but she made no answer. Her portion of ration bread was still in her hand and she was staring off into space, for the first time a softening of smile around her small pinched mouth.

Leela surveyed her critically. "Gone to dreamland, that one," she commented. "Here—got to make sure she gets her share when she wakes up." She took the square of hard bread from the girl's hand and tucked it into the pocket of her cloak.

"What you got—" A voice even rougher than Leela's cut in as one of their other wagonmates moved closer. She was wrapped in a thread-bare covering which had a number of ill-sewn patches showing faded contrasting colors here and there. By the looks of her, she came from one of the fringe camps of the displaced landworkers. Her features were sharp, and her eyes sped from one to another of them.

"Scarce seasoning," Twilla explained. "Have some?" The two others who had shared the newcomer's seat in the wagon pushed closer now. One was as neatly clad as Askla under the hood, which covered only half of her head. Her face showed a fine skin and proud features; almost she might have been thought noble born.

She regarded Twilla narrowly. "I know you," she said then. "You were apprenticed to the Wisewoman—she came to leach our yardman when he had the poisoned hand, and you were with her. How did they take you?"

Twilla answered with the truth. "I am from the Kinderhost—they said that I had no kin to swear apprentice oath for me." She recognized her questioner now—the second daughter of the forgemaster. To find one as well placed as she in this company was strange. Surely now this one would have been safely betrothed.

"They threw a wide net, townswoman," Leela commented. "Surely you do not belong with us—hadn't your housemaster betrothed you?"

The girl flushed and the look she shot at Leela was barbed. "I *was* betrothed—he died of the fever two moons ago."

"Ill luck for you." There was a note of pity in Leela's reply.

"Enough!" the one with patched cloak interrupted shrilly. "I am Jass, she is Rutha"—she jerked a grimy hand toward the forgemaster's daughter—"and this be Hadee." The third moved in. "Now, what do you do to that bread, Healer?"

"Season it, as I said," Twilla responded. "Try it if you wish," she held out the jar again.

As Leela had done Jass sniffed the container and then lost some of

her defiant air. "Creep cheese, an' marmint, and—" she looked in-
quiringly to Twilla.

"First of spring vargemt," the girl answered promptly. "You have
herb lore then, Jass?"

The other girl gave a hooting laugh. "I was land bred and land
learned. Yes, we knew something—my aunt she was clever with it—
when we still had the land."

Rutha and Jass used the stuff from the container, but the third girl
shook her head and backed away. She pulled a hand free from the
edging of her cloak and made a gesture in the air between Twilla and
herself.

"Witchery—" she said and turned her back on them all, moving
sharply away.

"Now who is she?" Leela had lost her good humor. "What is this
witchery thing?"

"A new belief." Rutha appeared glad she was in a position to provide explanation. "She is from overseas—serving maid in the house
of one of the Doom Speakers. My father says that they are all mad,
but more and more listen to them when they spout their talk on market
day. Twice her master was taken up for ill speaking by the city guards.
Little did her Doom Speaker help her this time!"

Hadee turned, and with one hand swept back the hood cowl. Twilla
gasped. The girl seemed hardly more than a child, and her head had
been shaved so that only a shadow of hair growth was beginning to
show once more. On her forehead there was a red mark in the form
of a triangle, seeming a part of her pale skin.

Leela drew a whistling breath. "Pray the High Powers, Hadee, that
this overmountain journey lasts long enough for you to grow back
your head thatch. Else he who gets you in the lottery will make you
suffer for his disappointment."

"I go to ravishment at the hands of those who think evil," Hadee
returned. "Surely my sins are great, there is no way I can escape what
lies before." With twitching hands she covered her head and turned
her back firmly upon them.

"Time to mount up." Tathan came swooping down. "In with you."

Twilla looked to Askla and speedily reached out to grasp the
younger girl's arm. She was smiling, staring at nothing they could see.
The sedative had worked much faster and more strongly than Twilla
would have thought possible.

Together she and Leela got her settled between them on the hard
bench as the other three scrambled in to take their places before them.
There were the shouts of the men urging on the heavy beasts drawing

the wagons, and they went rocking off at the unsteady, wearying gait
they had known for a day now.

The constant bump and sway of the wagon kept one alert, mainly to
the task of holding to one's seat. Askla, succumbing to the herb sedative, collapsed against Leela and the fishergirl pulled her slighter companion half across her knees steadying her with one muscle thick arm.

But Twilla's thoughts ranged well beyond the wagon and her companions in travel misery. What she had learned from Leela about the
trials ahead was disheartening. Unless she could bring her talent for
healing to the attention of some one in authority she perhaps had little
chance to escape the lottery.

And the thought of that tensed her body, brought a bitter taste into
her mouth. A healer was never wed, except by her full choice, and
then to one who was compatible to her trade, for one did not stifle arts
once learned and one was under the yoke of sworn duty to exercise
that learning wherever it was needed.

She was no house and field servant to labor for the advancement of
a land breaker and she had a very shrewd idea that that was the prob-
able fate of all of them. As her body swung sharply to the lurch of
the wagon she closed her eyes and reviewed all Hulde had ever said
concerning her own trade.

Hulde was a healer, a well known one. But Twilla knew that the
Wisewoman was more, though her fellow townsmen and women might
not have known that. There was much knowledge to be gained from
the crumbling pages of Hulde's old books. Knowledge which Twilla
had shared, if only in a very small part.

She was certain that Hulde had powers which extended far beyond
the concocting of brews and the making of salves. She could light a
candle with a pointing of her finger, and she had some foreseeing—
though that was erratic. But she was no dabbler in gaining power for
power's sake.

Twilla marshalled memories and reviewed them with strict attention.
She longed for freedom to do some experimenting, but in the present cir-
cumstances that was dangerous. She had not forgotten the fact of that
looming threat, which had pulled her herself away from the Wisewoman—or had it been only a rumor mouthed by Harhodge in warning?

Once more in a sharp mind-picture Hulde was before her, holding
her hand. It was as if Hulde, in spite of herself, had, through her own
talents, been given some order—

Twilla shook her head—guesses were not facts. But the main fact
was that the weight of the mirror was still against her. Again she was

tempted to draw that forth and look at it but prudence cautioned against such action.

The caravan came to a stop well before nightfall. They were within the first foothills of the mountains, but even here the scars of man's plundering were wounds across the land. However, they were glad to be out of their racking prison, sitting about one of the fires as two of the caravan men under Tathan's loud-voiced orders lifted out the benches to which they had clung during the day and brought out long sacks, lumpy with straw, tossing them in the wagons to serve for beds.

There was little talk among the travelers of Twilla's wagon, though the men about their tasks made clamor enough. They were too worn by the ride to do more than huddle down and watch with near vacant eyes the installing of a pot on the fire and the brisk labors of Tathan and another of the warriorwomen in feeding into it first water brought in buckets from a stream not too far away and then slabs of rock-hard meat and blocks of pressed vegetables.

"You—" Tathan had been standing, fists on hips, watching her companion throw this provider into the pot, now she crooked a finger and beckoned directly to Twilla, "stir this, girl. You've had enough training in such from that upnosed mistress of yours."

Twilla obediently pushed her cloak back on her shoulders and took up the long-handled spoon Tathan had indicated, setting to work keeping the now bubbling contents of the pot in motion. The smell was not the same as came from Hulde's nourishing stews and soups. But with Tathan watching, she did not wish to add anything to make the mess more palatable.

In the end they were each given a bowl of greasy, watery stuff, a hunk of journey bread to be softened in it, and a leather bottle of small ale passed along. Twilla noted that only Jass and Leela took more than a sip from that. And she refused her share entirely, content with a cup of water from the cask which had been hung on the side of the wagon.

Overhead the sky was darkening. The mountains looked like crouched things from the fringes of a nightmare. Overhead the stars were beginning to wink into frost points of light. The moon was full and when it arose as they still huddled about the fire, it gave a measure of light, though there were a string of oil lanterns about to ward off the night.

"In with you—" Tathan bore down upon them as they sat near-bemused by fatigue and a kind of hopelessness, which Twilla felt rising like the waves of the sea about them. The warwoman gestured to the wagons, and they got their aching bodies in and onto the scant comfort of those straw-filled pads.

Askla sniffed and then gave a soft, choked sound. Twilla reached out through the dimness and put her hand on the smaller girl's shoulder where she curled on the bed.

"Think on what is good," she repeated awkwardly old, old words which had been said to her in the Kinderhost long ago. "Remember those you love and who love you—"

Askla's body shook under her touch. "I will never see mother again—" her grief-hoarse voice was a rasping whisper.

"Perhaps not so. Lay still—" Twilla hunched up on her own bed place and leaned across to the other. Her hand went from shoulder now to the girl's head, pushing back the folds of her hood, touching her forehead just above and between her eyes. "It is well—" Her words became a croon, so soft that she thought none else would hear. One of Hulde's remedies was the use of will alone. She tried to project into the other a feeling of peace, realizing that this was far different from watching beside the bed of one ailing, but she had very little peace in her own mind to draw upon. However, she sensed that the girl was ceasing to tremble so and in a few moments felt and heard the even breath of sleep.

Leela shifted on her pad sending the straw crackling under her. She tried to keep her hearty voice to a whisper.

"Good for you, healer. That one will have it hard—perhaps more than the rest of us—unless it be that Hadee with her ugly head and whine of a voice. Best we keep up spirits as we may and make the best of ourselves. No man is going to be pleased with a watering jug or an ugly face, and there is no good coming from making the worst of our lot."

"Just so, Leela," Twilla strove to find the proper words for the question which had been forming in her mind. "What if they have among us—for we have not truly seen the others—someone truly ugly? If the man has to take her—what would be her lot?"

The straw crackled as if Leela squirmed again. "One I would not wish for, healer. Be glad you are reasonably fair of face. Me, I'm passable and I have the strength for work. Jass now, she's small but she's tough and she comes from farm stock. That Rutha—she's a different sort but there are men who take pride in having such a wife as other men look after. Hadee—who knows?"

She added nothing to that and Twilla thought that she slept. But Twilla herself fingered the mirror, drawing it out of hiding, a thought so dim she could not truly pin it for examination stirring in her mind. Her fingers, though they wore no polishing pads, moved across the slick surface in the old familiar pattern. At last she tucked it into safe hiding again and settled herself to sleep.

THE CARAVAN ROUSED early in the mornings—they were on their way usually by the first showing of sun rim. They had three days of steady climbing, a fairly gentle incline at first and then steeper where the ill-made road narrowed. At times they were ordered from the wagons to tramp along behind, lightening the loads. On the third day it began to rain, not with the fury of a storm but with a continued steady downpour to turn the whole way and those padding along it sodden.

At least these heights had not been scarred by the eternal mines and there was spring green beginning to show, even in dwarfed and ragged patches. The wind-twisted trees of the heights had been hacked away to clear the trail and their tangles of branches, too small to feed the fires, left to molder and grow strange-shaped lichens.

Twilla kept an eye on those patches of growth, trying to recognize any of which Hulde had made healing use. The supplies she carried in her shoulder pack were certainly limited and, though she had no time nor the proper facilities to prepare any herb harvest, it would be good to know what might be discovered.

Tathan and her even more unattractive assistant guard-driver were ever busy watchdogs. If they walked to ease the draft animals she herded her charges close together and constantly urged them on. Iyt was her assistant. She, when taking her turn at such shepherding, favored them with a monologue concerning the future.

Her words confirmed what Leela had learned from her kinsman.

These would-be brides had little choice ahead, nor had their prospective grooms much more. A man could choose not to take his chances at the lottery—for the girl there was no choice at all.

Oddly enough it was Hadee who challenged that point of view on about the fourth time of the warwoman's gloating speech.

"If we be not to some man's choice," she tugged at her hood trying to keep it from sliding down from her shaven head where only the shadow of down showed the return of hair, "then what?"

Iyt laughed.

"Choice is luck, king's maid. Your man's name goes in the pot and someone draws it out. Does he think you a fright—as you are—then he cannot send you back for another drawing. Lord Harmond, he is a fair man—each draw is final—so you both make the most of it. Better," she raised her heavy voice to include them all in that admonition, "make the best of yourselves and have a sweet tongue at the greeting."

Twilla considered that carefully. Surely they would have need of a healer. She had listened carefully to every scrap of rumor and gossip she could pick up and had heard no mention of such among the new land farmers. If she could prove herself—but Iyt was continuing:

"There was a gal two convoys back—she had had the plague and was cheek-marked from it—looked like a warty toad or nearabouts. The man as drew her was one of the officers—and—well—that one disappeared. Maybe the green demons got her." Her tongue swept across her thick lips as if her words were pepper relish on tasteless meat.

"Green demons?" That was Rutha. "More like—"

"Hush yourself, up-nose!" snapped Iyt. "And don't think that the green demons do not live. You'll see a plenty of their work over-mountain. Get yourself a-near the Wythe Woods and you'll maybe meet one for yourself."

"These demons," Twilla for the first time broke into the conversation. She had had little to say when Tathan or Iyt were about, even to her own companions, feeling from the start of this journey it was better to spend most of her energy in listening rather than in speech.

"These green demons—what harm do they do?"

Iyt raised her hand, fingers curved in a ward sign. "They steal a man's wits, or his eyes, or him! Let a man who has no woman of his own get close to the Wood and he's their meat. Even Ylon, Lord Harmond's own son, he's been demon maimed—blind as if his two eyes were screwed out of his skull. They took some children also in the first days, and a couple of women—but they were all found wandering, wit struck, afterwards. Some, they got back their wits, only

they don't remember what happened to them. 'Cept the children—
those kept running off for awhile tryin' to get back to the Wood. Had
to tie them up, even, until at last the fit wore off them. Yes, a man
with a wry-faced female could well toss her to the demons and none
would know the better.''

A plague-scarred woman who had won her freedom—or had she
simply been put to death by the man she had been forced upon? Twilla
wondered. And these tales of green demons—she had read in Hulde's
books of berries which, when eaten by the unwarned, could provide
hallucinations and affect the mind. Perhaps this Wood harbored strange
growths unknown to those of the coast, unknown even to Hulde's
forerunners.

Surely Lord Harmond needed a competent healer with all this threatening his hard-held domain. But how could she reach him? She had
seen the commander of the caravan only at a distance. He kept himself
and his men well away from the wagons in which the women traveled.
Their guards were all warwomen and she had, she believed, a very
thin chance of gaining any attention—save perhaps a kind she did not
want—from Tathan and Iyt.

On the fourth night they camped in a narrow meadow high in the
mountains. Meeting there a second party from the plains beyond bringing fresh beasts for riding and haulage. The rain let up enough so that
they saw a sullen red streak across the sky and Twilla thought that
they would have a fair day tomorrow when they would make the last
ascent and crossing through the pass.

As usual they were herded to their pallets in the wagons after they
had eaten. Askla said little, she was like some small animal who obediently followed her trainer's orders. It seemed to Twilla that the real
girl had retreated so far within some hiding place that what remained
was close to a shell. Leela had trod upon a rough rock when they had
been herded up to a spring to drink and wash, and Twilla had bandaged
the broken skin and set an herb padding over it. Tathan had come upon
them when she was so busied and had watched.

"Healer, eh? Well, you might as well forget such thing over mountain, Kindergal. Lord Harmond, he don't take to Wisewomen. If you
have any sense you'll toss that there bag of yours in the bushes tomorrow and act like you are—bride bait and nothin' else.''

"But," Twilla was so surprised that she sat back on her heels staring
up at the woman, "healers are welcome—they are needed!"

"Lord Harmond he wants no women shifting theirselves from place
to place, disturbing the peace. There ain't enough females to go
around—and he ain't gonna have someone grab one as is gadding

about when she should be with her lawful husband. You get right out of your head, Kindergal, that you is going to set up like a Wisewoman and be free and easy—because it won't happen.'' She showed yellowed teeth in a wide smile. ''Your Wisewoman weren't no big thing, were she? Let them take you—didn't see her do anything to stop us— did you? Git right out of that head of yours that you are any different from the rest of these here gals.''

She laughed and tramped off. Twilla tightened that last loop of the bandage on Leela's foot. She kept her eyes strictly on what she was doing but her thoughts were busy, though she felt as if they had been badly shaken up.

''Could be, she's right,'' Leela said in a low voice. ''I've been thinkin' that's what you had in mind—git told off as a healer. Most o' 'em never marry do they? Well, what this Lord Harmond wants is wives—''

Twilla had been weighing Tathan's contemptuous warning. Yes, it could be true. She knew herself that Hulde's talents had sometimes been resented, feared even. That was why the Wisewoman had gone to the Kinderhost for an apprentice. Most fathers would not give a daughter to be trained at a craft which might raise her above him in the general order of things. And one of the court nobles might be even more prejudiced—they were used to trading *their* daughters off in various alliances to bring themselves place and power.

So her hope of being able to make her own way over mountain seemed in dire danger. There was—she fastened on a thread of thought—she would have to consider it carefully.

Now that they were back in the wagon supposedly to sleep she was still weighing one peril against another. Not that she was even sure she might be able to do what she was thinking about now.

An ugly wife might find herself a dead one. On the other hand she knew several tricks by which she might defend herself once the lottery was past. The supplies in her shoulder pack were not the most potent she had about her—there were two tiny packets wrapped into the folds of her girdle which were to be counted on. Witless and blind—green demons—also a knowing person might act both of those for temporary safety. But the main thing—

Her pallet was at the far end of the wagon. The waning moon was a thinning slice in the sky. The wane—yes certainly this required the wane and not the gathering of that potent light. She had never tried what she wished to do, was not even sure she had the power. But now it was her last chance.

Hunched up, so that she could see the moon through an open flap of the canvas over her head, Twilla brought out the mirror and set it firmly on her knees, gripping between them that cord threaded through the hoop at its back.

> *"Up and down, out and in,*
> *Sunward, and windershins.*
> *Give now the look to seen*
> *By all save the eye serene."*

She kept her whisper to the merest thread of sound. Her fingers slid back and across the surface of the mirror in patterns they had never followed before—not when she had been at the binding.

And her mind fastened feverishly upon a picture, held it steady, refining it as well as she could. Until looking into the mirror, she indeed saw the reflection she sought. Scanty eyebrows above eyes which looked weak and red-rimmed. A nose so swollen that it near resembled a snout, but the sharpest were those pits in roughened skin of cheek and chin. She had seen enough sufferers of the pocking fever in her time with Hulde to be able to reproduce such an appearance.

Holding the mirror so close that her nose nearly touched the surface, she surveyed her reflection. So far she had succeeded. But it remained—had the reflection worked its spell directly on her? She ran her fingers over her chin—the chin felt smooth to the touch—but then it would—for it was sight alone which must be confused by the change.

And how could that be tested? Wait—pock scars—no, suppose she showed now only the vicious rash of the disease? That might be better accepted. She could induce a measure of fever—they—they might even jettison her here fearing contagion! She looked intently into the mirror again and made the change from pock marks to the reddened lumps that would form such—keeping the largely swollen nose.

They had no healer with the caravan—at least there had been no mention of such, though the girls were kept so carefully apart from most of the group, closely guarded by warwomen. She did have certain drugs which, taken in too heavy doses, would bring about the high fever that marked the outset of the plague. However, to use those on herself would dull her mind, and that she could not have. She did not know how long the mirror change would hold—it might have to be renewed, perhaps even each night.

Could she counterfeit the symptoms of plague well enough to stamp belief in her fellow travelers? With Hulde two seasons ago she had seen one case—strictly isolated when discovered—but they dared not refuse the aid of a healer. Luckily the plague had not spread but she remembered Hulde's treatment—and that the Wisewoman had pressed home the point that once the skin eruptions appeared there was nothing to be done but give the victim certain drinks and make sure that he or she was kept warm and clean.

Their patient then, a trader from the hills who had been found in the fields outside the town, had survived, but he would bear until his death day the skin scoring of the disease.

"What's to do?" Leela's voice was cross. She must have been roused by Twilla's shifting on the pallet, those were so closely set together.

"It is hot—so hot—" Twilla allowed her voice to die away weakly. She had put the mirror into tight safety against her skin but she believed it time to take the plunge into the act with which she must impress those about her.

"Stupid!" Leela snapped. " 'Tis cold enough to freeze the scales off a blackfish. Git to sleep."

"Hot—" Twilla pushed aside the top folds of her cloak. "My head—the pain—"

"Shut your jaws, you back there!" Tathan's harsh whisper was enough to rouse them all. "What are you blabbin' about?"

" 'Tis the healer," Rutha made answer. There was a shifting around as the others roused.

"Hot—so hot—" Twilla allowed her fretful voice to slide up the scale into a sound strong enough to carry through the wagon. "My head— Hulde—mistress—give me to drink of a potion—my head—"

"You, Iyt," Tathan ordered, "light the lantern. That one makes no sense. But she'll learn not to disturb the sleep of her betters!"

They were all awake now, moving to sit up on the pallets, though Twilla judged that more by sound for until the fire snap was set to the wick in the lantern there was no light—even the moon sickle had disappeared from overhead.

"Move—blast you sniveling demon spawn!" Tathan, with the lantern in hand, pushed past Hadee with a shove which sent the slight girl back painfully against the side of the wagon bed. Rutha and Jass had already pulled aside and Leela pushed Askla out of the way. Then Tathan was standing over that end pallet and had swung the lantern well down.

Was it holding? Had she been successful, or had her desire deceived her? Twilla gave a moan and flung up her arm, pushing the cloak hood well away from her face while the light of the lantern shown full upon her.

"By the Fins of Gar!" She felt Leela jerk away. "What—"

"Have you never seen plague?" If Rutha felt fear there was no note of it in her voice. "She claims to be a healer does she not? Who better would be one to bring such upon us? Who knows where she was before we started on this trail? Perhaps it takes a time for the evil to work within one's body before it makes itself known!"

Even Tathan had fallen back a pace. So, Twilla thought with a small spring of self confidence—they *did* see what she wished—she *was* stricken in the sight of all of these!

"Dump her!" Jass cried out. "Get her away!"

There was shaken laugh from someone, near hysteria from fear. Then Rutha spoke again:

"We have been close with her these ten days. She has shared food and drink with us. It is said that so does the plague pass—through closeness and sharing. If we leave her we have not done ourselves any good. She is a healer and carries a healer's pack. If we can get through the haze of the fever upon her she may be able to help herself, perhaps us all, through her knowledge. But," she had crawled partly into the lantern light and was now facing Tathan, "if you value your skin with your commander, warwoman, you will see he has word of this. You have kept us so close that she has not been near others of the caravan— therefore they may not be plague-taken if they keep their distance."

"Call upon your heart power then, that Captain Wasser sees it as you do. Otherwise, gal, we'll all end with our throats slit and the wagon burned about us!" There was actually a shiver in Tathan's last words.

Twilla tensed. Would the common sense Rutha had voiced hold, or would the guards be ignorant enough to follow Tathan's dire suggestion? If that seemed to be coming closer to it she must move fast to undo what she had with over self-confidence done. Hulde had always urged upon her a careful forethinking of any action to do with power— this might be a disaster because she had not really done that.

Her fellow travelers had withdrawn as far as they could to the fore of the wagon leaving her, the lantern now beside her, isolated.

"She's our death!" Jass said in a tight voice.

"You said," Leela ignored the farmgirl and by her choice of words was speaking to Rutha, "that she might carry her own healing—"

"It is possible. But what would *you* choose from that pack of hers if you have it open? We are not trained in herb art."

There was movement. A shadow loomed over her and Twilla was cut from the lantern light by the bulk of the fishergirl's broad shoulders. She turned her head a little.

"Leela?" she dared suggest, now, that she had moments of consciousness—she must do what she could to carry out Rutha's sensible suggestion.

"Me!"

"Drink—please—"

The shadowy Leela turned her head and spoke over her own shoulder. "You there, Iyt—hand down the water bottle—"

"And have the plague slobber on it?" countered Tathan's lieutenant. "Are you mad fishergirl, or just dull-witted?"

"Leela—" Twilla allowed herself a fraction more voice, perhaps enough to reach Rutha, upon whose good sense she might well have to depend. "I am fevered. In the pack—the twigs tied—in—in green threads," she made her speech as halting as she thought she now dared. "Break into water—give—"

She felt rather than saw the other jerk the precious healer's pack around. The lantern light shifted as that was moved to a better position for the rummager.

"Found 'em!" Leela announced triumphantly what seemed to Twilla a breath-holding time later. "All right, do we git that water, or do you answer to the captain when he asks why we ain't doin' what we can?"

"Warwoman," Rutha's clipped city speech was as sharp now as if she gave orders to some dull-witted maid servant within her own walls, "do we wait for our deaths or do we do what we can?"

"She be sick—how does that one know what is to be done? We don't come to more water until midday tomorrow and if she fouls what we have—"

"You know the use of that sword you wear, do you not?" demanded Rutha. "To each their own talent. If a healer can heal others then she has the knowledge to also heal herself. Here—if you can—pour a portion into the cup and let us see to it!"

There was movement in the dark wagon and Rutha must have prevailed, for Twilla caught sight of an edge of a cup within the lantern light and saw Leela thrust into it the small twist of twiglets. Not a remedy for fever but something to depend upon in times of stress to clear the mind for straight thinking—and she certainly needed that now.

She pulled herself up a fraction so that her bespelled face was well seen. Twilla braced herself on her arms, not expecting these who were well aware of the plague ravages to aid her. But Leela was still beside her and held out the cup from which there now arose an aromatic scent. She could sip, and then drink until the twigs were exposed and the liquid all inside her.

Now there were sounds from beyond the wagon. Tathan had gone for her superior and it sounded as if more than one of them was returning. Then a man's voice sounded from outside.

"You'll keep your distance—get back from me, woman. We cannot leave any behind. We are pledged to a number and those we deliver, even if we have a wagon load of bodies to make up our score. As soon as we are over the pass news will be sent ahead. But you will move out in the morning in your proper station, understand. You—none of you are to come near any others. We'll stack supplies and you can pick them up as you come. You say that this one claims to be a healer and has supplies—all right try her own treatment on her if you can. But—by the Horns of Ramu, woman, you and all with you keep your distance."

If Tathan raised any dispute to that they did not hear it. Then she clambered in over the driver's seat.

"You heard the captain," her voice was sullen. "We takes our chances and there'll be no dumping. He had the right of that—we bring in our full score. Didn't Robeen last season bring the body of one as fell to death at the crossing? Had to prove they started with full number. All right—what do we do?"

She sounded oddly at a loss, much of her loud-voiced authority seemingly stripped from her.

"She came a little out of the fever," Rutha answered. "Told us what to do. Fill that cup again, Iyt, we may well need it."

"Who you speakin' to, smartmouth!" growled the woman. "How can you be sure she told you true?"

"Better to try something than wait for the worst to strike us," returned Rutha. "Here you are, Leela, see if you can get this down her. You know," another shadow joined that cast by Leela, "it is odd that such illness can do to one, she—perhaps it is the swelling of her skin, but she looks almost like another person."

Twilla thought it time to make a small recovery. "Thank you, Leela," she said in a near normal voice as the fishergirl held out the second cup. This time she pulled herself into a sitting position and took it into her own hands, swilling the leaves in the rusty water from their carrier.

"Last year—there was plague—a merchant—"

"A stranger from the north," cut in Rutha, "yes, the council were much worried. But—he recovered did he not? Yes, and it was your Wisewoman who cured him!" she ended excitedly.

"Yes, Hulde had a great knowledge—I have some, but only a little compared to hers. What I do now—that is of her learning." And in the light of the lantern she deliberately not only swallowed the contents of the cup but chewed away on the sodden leaves it contained.

"Stay apart from me for three days," she said, spitting that cud of leaf into her hand. "If by that time the blisters on the skin have run their full course—then I think you have nothing to fear. But I shall make it so. Leela," again she appealed to the shadow who had drawn back at her warning, "go you through the pack again. You will find a small box which is marked with the sign of a flying bird. I shall not touch it so there can be no fear of any of you. Take out the paste you find within and roll it into small balls. Then let each one of you take one. You will feel drowsy—you will wish to sleep. And this you must do. Since the caravan would move on leaving us to be last it will not matter if we do not arouse at the first horn call. Tomorrow you will still feel tired but by the next sun all should be well. This Hulde uses in times of danger—"

Danger for some highly nervous patient who must be calmed before hard treatment. It was powerful but not dangerous and would give them sleep, take them through the first hours of their present fears.

"Wisewoman's messes—" began Tathan, but again Rutha interrupted.

"Are better than anything your captain offers us," the girl returned in a clipped voice. "Twilla, if we come out of this I will indeed speak well of healers."

4

FOR THREE DAYS now they had been the tail of the caravan winding up, through the pass, and so out of the world they knew and into the unknown. Twilla had come to the end of her supplies of the mild sedative she had used to calm her companions. Since none of them had developed any sign of the plague they lost some of the rigid tension which had gripped them all on the first morning they had pulled out to be last in line.

Though they were anything but forgotten by the captain. One of his men appeared—at a prudent distance—each morning for a report on Twilla, on the chance that any of the others had so begun to suffer, on what supplies they would need. And since the report remained an ever satisfying one Twilla lost little by little her apprehension of what might await them now in the matter of ostracism over mountain.

She had allowed herself a gradual recovery, though one far more speedy than would have been normal for a true plague victim. By trading on her healer knowledge and the awe that her wagonmates were beginning to display for that, she succeeded in getting them to believe that indeed it was Hulde's discoveries of yesterday year which served her apprentice so well now.

Twilla had urged upon them the warning that they were better out of the wagon as much as possible so that at night they now lay in blanket bags (against the chill of the high regions) beside the fire. Tathan was undoubtedly convinced that no one was going to strike

away from that fire into the unknown—they were too far now from
any possible settlement or outlying farm—even if those living there
would dare to offer them refuge.

Rutha and Leela had become Twilla's nurses. Odd partners that they
were—educated merchant's daughter, unlettered fishergirl—they
shared an intelligence which did not need the nudging of book learning
to awaken. Both of them, when they decided Twilla had reached a
stage of convalescence wherein company would not be amiss, began
to ask questions about herb lore.

She had dragged out that small book with its very tiny crabbed
writing, meant to seal as much to a single page as possible, which
listed herbs and the remedies for common ailments such as might visit
any household during the seasons.

With a stick she drew on a cleared space of soil the outlines of leaf
and flower shapes and drilled her listeners in what to look for. Lord
Harmond might not want wisewomen, but he could not deny to any
woman the right to care for her own household and kin.

Askla listened also, but it was plain that she had yet only a child's
interest, one quickly broken as she tired. Jass took a word in the pro-
ceedings now and then, sometimes scoffingly, but she was more attracted to Tathan and Iyt. The latter had been telling tales of battles,
of the green demons and of great doings ahead and the once farmgirl
listened with an awe and interest surprising to discover in one land-
born. As for Hadee—the serving maid from overseas—she registered
aversion to anything Twilla said, declaring loudly and long, that all
such knowledge was of the dark and those who followed it would be
possessed by the blackest of spirits. It had been difficult to get down
her the pellets Twilla prescribed—only under the dire threat of Tathan's fist had she gulped them in.

At night they slept—and Twilla was free to further her own plan.
She held to it doggedly. Surely a combination of a haggish face, and
her supposed service to the caravan would impress Lord Harmond, set
to uphold customs as he was.

With moonlight and mirror she wrought as might an artist painting
some masterpiece. The red marks on her face had become quickly
eruptions—enough to repulse even friends. Rutha had asked over and
over if there were not some healing she could bring to them and Twilla
answered only that the disease must run its course and that the breaking
of those eruptions and their draining would bring relief and a far step
toward health again.

The night after they had crossed the pass, after Rutha had shared
around the last of the sedative paste, Twilla waited tensely for their

sleep. Then she sent into the heart of the mirror the full of her concentration. The change in her eyes—they now seemed smaller and red-rimmed, the eyes lashed thin and pale—could well have been left by an onset of a severe disease.

The badly swollen reflection of her nose she pondered over. None of them had commented upon it, not even Leela with whom Twilla had been closest since before she began this mage labor. She could hope that, in the shock of her illness and the plague mask, they had truly forgotten what she had once looked like. No, she did not believe that she need lose that added bit of ugliness.

Now she concentrated on the skin, erasing most of the outer signs of eruptions, bringing in their places the beginning of pock marks which left her cheeks with a scaly, almost ragged, appearance. She surveyed the result of her efforts for some time, the dying fire giving her light enough for a critical evaluation, then she slid the mirror back into concealment.

There was one more obstacle ahead. Surely the outlanders had *some* form of medical attention, even if Lord Harmond had set his will against healers. There were men who could set bones, perform rude surgery and the like who traveled with an army. If such a one was sent to inspect them Twilla thought her disguise would hold. She would not have been so sure if she faced such a one as Hulde.

Before sunset she was to be proven right. The long line of the caravan had crunched the trail down from the heights. Before them stretched wide the new land. There were lesser heights to be crossed and those hid and revealed, hid and revealed what lay ahead.

To the south, stretching as far west as eyesight could reach was plains land. Twilla making her first attempt at walking beside the wagon, Leela solicitously beside her, thought she could also see evidence of man's coming there in suggestions of fenced fields and a small blot or two, which might signal the planting of a farmstead.

However, to the north there was no light and openness. Rather, like a shadowed fortress looming over the country, stood a dark blot, which covered all which might lie there.

That—that could only be the forest—the dreaded territory in which lay the mystery which had been so fatal to those who had attempted to learn any secrets it hid. She studied it carefully. Such a huge and thick stand of wood as to blot out the land was unknown in Varsland where delvings, slashings, and the ever-present demands of humankind had been known for untold years. Trees in the east were, as it seemed herded by man, orchards bloomed and bore to order and were pruned, and otherwise bent to the will of the owner. Even the few firs which grew in the yet unstirred corners looked small and thin as if they hoped to be overlooked and forgotten.

In that dark blot yonder man had set no bonds—though bonds might have been set—against invaders. Twilla could not measure the height of the trees crowding into that dark mass, but she guessed that they must indeed be tall—large enough to awe an easterner. Yes, in the shadows of such, any nervous invader might well see demons.

Rutha seemed to pick up her thought— "Demon land," she said. "It has an uncanny look to it anyway—such put stories into the minds of the unknowing."

"Hullooo!" The ringing call from ahead brought the wagon to a halt and those tramping by it to attention.

From below, cutting between them and their sight of the last wagon ahead, came a small mounted troop. These reined to a halt a goodly space away, save for one man who approached them with an air of caution.

"You there!" he raised his voice in sharp command as he drew near, swinging from the saddle but still remaining by his mount. "Stand forth— They say you carry plague!"

Meekly Twilla, Rutha, and Leela who had been on the tramp, drew themselves into a line to be joined by Askla, Jass, and Hadee from the wagon. Tathan passed the reins of the team to Iyt and joined them.

Still leading his horse as if he needed to know that was at hand and he might mount in a second and be away from them, the man came forward. He was wearing mixed-dress Twilla noted, as if he were half townsman, half guard.

Of middle years, his face was as browned as that of a soldier and he had keen eyes which he swept along the line of waiting girls and warwomen.

"All of you here?" he demanded.

"All," Tathan answered stolidly. "Six king's maids, two of the troops—so we set out of Varvad and so we still be."

But his attention had already centered on Twilla and held.

"That one—" He jerked his thumb toward the girl but took no step closer. "She bears plague marks—"

"She heals," Tathan answered with a note of defense as if some skill of her own was in question. "She be a healer and was able to doctor herself—also us lest the plague spread. We are here and she is walking as stout as any landdaughter—as you can see. Her looks may be spoiled but she has talent—"

Twilla was surprised at Tathan's words. She had not expected backing from the warwoman, and yet it would seem that their guard was striving to make some point in her charge's favor.

"Healer." The man repeated that with something like a snort. "She is a king's maid as the rest. Our Lord does not hold with such, as well you know."

"Mine was not the selection, Learned One," Tathan returned. "I am a guard only but what I say is the truth. She healed herself and we stand here now with no plague marks on us."

"Nonetheless, you will keep your distance, not entering the High Keep but camping where you are shown, until we have our Lord's word on the matter."

Now he did mount and on horseback made a sudden turn and rode straight for Twilla, Leela having to scramble swiftly out of way as he came up beside the girl. Using his riding whip he caught at and flicked away her cape hood staring down at her with eyes which were narrowed and searching.

"Marked you are—" he commented. "But you have healed. Well, I do not envy your bridegroom."

With that he wheeled his horse again and rode on, the rest of the squad falling in behind him. While they were kept to the slower pace of the wagon. And it was well into dusk before they reached that level land, which had been in their sight for most of the afternoon.

The sun was still far enough up for Twilla to sight that dark dot which spiraled upward from the looming shadow of the wood fringe to the north. She lost sight of it as it climbed. Then she became aware of a wind-skimming, wide-winged bird which dropped from out of the sky to hang over the wagon as it trundled along.

By its spread of wing she judged it to be larger than any bird she had seen overmountain—and it seemed able to glide with few beats of wings, keeping at the same distance above them. That this was what she had seen rise from the ill-omened wood she was oddly sure. There were stories in Hulde's books about ancient powers which could harness the animals of the field, the birds of the air, to their service. It would seem that now they might be spied upon. But she said nothing, drew no attention of the other to that airborne company.

All she had been able to gather of rumor and report was that those who kept away from the forest had not been troubled by any attack, and the road they were following now curbed well to the south of that blot. Yet, as twilight grew and they traced the guiding wagons ahead by the lanterns, each bobbing from their high poles, this cruiser of the winds did not leave them.

Now they could see ahead the outline of buildings with lights here and there. And the first wagons of the caravan were very near the gates. Their own passage was so slowed by the orders to keep well to the rear that, when darkness fell, they could only see the few winks of lantern light pass through a strong stockade.

Once more a rider came pounding back toward them and with a circle of arm and a shouted order sent their wagon from the road, bumping across the open land until it finally came to a halt under those walls but not within them.

Just as they had through all the weeks on the trail Tathan and Iyt set about loosing the beasts to graze and ordering a camp to be set. Rutha sighted the pile of supplies which had been left as usual and these they brought into a fire, which here was set in the encirclement of a brazier as large as a full washing bowl, fueled with lumps of thick black stuff new to the girls.

It smoked and smelt and was far inferior to the wood they had used during the journey. Twilla, coughing as a sudden puff of air brought that smoke to her, could begin to understand why the plains settlers would want to glean in the forest.

It was too dark now to sight the bird above. But there would be the beginning of the new moon tonight. She dared not try to strengthen her spell by it—the waning was what she needed. But when they settled on the pallets in the wagon her hands were curved about the mirror tightly. And it seemed to her that there was an odd warmth from it, even when she lifted it away from close contact with her flesh, also as if it caused some friction, except there was no movement, save that which followed her own.

Had she been irresponsible, foolish in believing that she could escape the net set for her? She stared down into the mirror surface, dark to her sight, and thought of Hulde. She herself knew so very little— some of a healer's skills, yes, but little enough of the powers she was sure the Wisewoman had easily dealt with. It only remained that she was waiting upon time and would see what would come. And that aroused an impatience which ate at her.

Would her play with the plague be enough to make an impression on the Lord Harmond so he would see she had a different value for him and his people? She could only hope.

The sound of a horn aroused them to crawl out of the wagon in the dawnlight. They could see more of the Keeptown now. Unlike the cities of Varslaad there was no stone wall here. Rather blocks of what looked like packed earth, which had been set in place and then perhaps fired into a solid mass reaching well above the top of the wagon.

Nearby, the gate showed a ponderous expanse of heavy wood,

barred and thickly reinforced with metal. While above the top of the wall showed one square tower, which was at least three stories high, as well as the roofs of other buildings.

The gates swung open and a party from the town, both mounted and on foot came toward them. As had been at the meeting in the mountains they stopped several lengths away allowing only one of their company to advance.

Twilla tensed. A healer of some sort she had expected but not one of the long discredited priests of Dandus! How such a one had found his way into this new territory was a mystery—unless the strange ills seeming to spread from the forest, must have induced some stupid councilor that they must have here one of the Twilight learning.

Hulde's kind were a kin to the earth and its bounty, striving ever to tie their patients to the aid of nature. The Dandus priests believed that mankind were greater than nature and need make no concessions to any other form of life. They were very few now, mostly stationed in a single shrine in the capital, and they recruited their order—at long intervals—from only the noble born.

This man now stalking toward them was as far from the beliefs by which she lived as the earth itself was from the sun now rising. If Lord Harmond favored the Dandus followers there was indeed no chance that he would listen to one with the wise talents.

"Where is this plague bearer?" he snapped almost before he reached them. His rust-red short robe was like the blot of a fast drying bloodstain.

"Here—you—" Tathan turned swiftly and caught at Twilla before the girl, still staring at the priest, could move. The warwoman pulled down her hood with her other hand, exposing Twilla's head to the full light.

What did he know? Had the followers of Dandus also powers which Hulde did not? Could he sense what she carried, sniff out mage too?

He was directly before her now. A gloved hand shot out, caught her chin in a painful grip, turning her head first right and then left. Dropping his hold, "Let me look upon the others."

Tathan had them already lined up and he went down that line making each girl uncover and looking at her intently, staring into eyes, even pinching cheeks. At Hadee he stopped short.

"What manner of female have we here, warwoman?" he asked sharply. "Why does she come shorn like a lop-ear ready for the butcher's knife?"

"She was maid to one of the Doom Sayers from overseas," Tathan replied. "They named her daughter of sin when her master was taken for his treason talk—so they served her before the maid squad took her.''

The Dandus priest grimaced. "You, outlander," he nearly spat the words into Hadee's face, "know that we do not listen to such ravings as your people use to pollute the minds of sensible men. You will forget what you have been taught, or your man will take a rod to your back, with the full approval of our Lord, who does not take kindly to females who do not know their proper place."

He turned away from the line of girls and once more approached Twilla. "And you—they prate of your skill saving your own life and warding these. There are no healers here save those signed to Dandus. Think on that and make it plain in your mind. You will be as any other king's maid, fully subject to the man unlucky enough to win you—with a face such as that you show to the world there will not be any welcoming mate here—though mate you will!"

He turned away from her and for the first time since he had arrived Twilla allowed herself a deep breath. She had expected to be recognized, for a dabbler in power, to be denounced. Yet that had not happened and somehow she believed that she had passed some stout test successfully.

Once more within the wagon they now passed through the gates and down the packed earth of a street, until they pulled up before one of the buildings close to the tower of the center keep, where they were ordered with their small bundles of belongings into the company of the other girls who had traveled with the caravan and who had already settled in.

At least they were well fed—there were fresh vegetables, meat, some fruit—that new to them. There was a bathing place where they were able at last to get all the dust from their bodies and hair. Twilla kept to herself and the others again edged away from her as if some ill fortune might rub from her to them. Thus she was able to conceal the mirror. When their trail worn clothing was taken from them she hid it under a towel. Then she slipped its cord quickly over her head as she pulled on what was provided. There was a chemise of a coarse yellow-white material and over that a full-skirted dress with a laced bodice. All their new issue was alike—of a dark brown shade not unlike the color of the dusty road they had followed for so long.

Apparently there was to be no chance for any girl to enhance what looks she had. So clad Askla suffered as did Hadee, Jass took on the likeness of one of those small city birds that nested in house eaves. Only Rutha and Leela were eye-catching as their height and general assured carriage made them noticeable. Hadee presented as nearly a hopeless sight as Twilla was sure she did.

For three days they were so pent, and small quarrels among them, harsh words and sneers were common as they mingled with those who had arrived before them. It was, Twilla understood, largely because fear of the unknown rode them. No one explained more of the coming procedure than they had picked up from the talk of the caravan and none of them looked forward to wedding a man of whom they knew nothing and living tied to this unknown and ill-omened land.

On the morning of the fourth day Tathan and three others of her service descended upon them. They were allowed to take their bundles, but they were lined up and marched two-by-two out for the first time outside.

There were those gathered to see them as they went. Remarks were made, a few in that line were greeted with whistles and others brought boos. Twilla specially heard remarks strong enough to bring the red of fever back into her cheeks had she not known what she was doing and held to it.

Her hope of consideration as a healer had been quenched by the Dandus priest. But if the man who got her by lot was enough turned away by her face she still had a small hope of perhaps a respite until she could somehow win her freedom. It was a very poor and slender hope, but it was all she had to cling to now.

There had been a platform arranged before the Keep wall and in that a chair, which had some pretense of being one of state, sat a man in half armor with a noble's brilliant cloak swept back from his shoulders.

He was of early middle age and had the weathered face of one often afield, in contrast to the few city nobles Twilla had seen. There was about him now a certain air of impatience as if he wished the matter which he was to supervise over so that he could be about some more important business.

He was flanked by two officers, and a stout man wearing such a robe as a prosperous merchant of Varvad might own.

Before them, on a tripod, was a bowl of metal. While the space about the platform was crowded—though mainly with men—Twilla caught sight of a few women on the outer edges of the throng. Nearly all wore the drab clothing of the landtied.

The girls were now herded into a single line and by some chance Twilla was at the end of that. Whether that was a good omen or not she could not tell.

THERE WAS SOMETHING shaming in this whole procedure—as if they were female beasts being put up to auction in a marketplace. Was this done deliberately, Twilla wondered—meant to enforce upon any rebel among the brides that her wishes or needs were nothing at all—only the fact that she was a female so able in some strange way to protect one of the men waiting impatiently here from whatever ill fate might reach out from that north lying wood to attack.

There appeared to be a delay of some sort. She saw Lord Harmond shift in his seat, the beginning of a scowl drawing his heavy brows together. Meanwhile, the undertone of mutters and murmurs from the waiting crowd were growing into fragments of impatient speech. Someone, Twilla gathered from the few words she caught, was still missing from the assembly.

Lord Harmond turned his head a fraction, and the officer on his right instantly leaned down to capture what his commander was saying. He saluted and turned to the stairs on the opposite side of the platform. However, before he had descended those a young man pushed through the crowd who gave way hurriedly to allow him passage. He, too, showed a stormy face but he stationed himself at the very fore of the assembly and stood like one preparing for a bared steel encounter. It was very plain that he was not there by any choice of his own.

Lord Harmond stared bleakly down at him with one of those looks so well used by superiors to subdue those beneath, and then he snapped his fingers and the warwomen at the head of the straggling line of girls set hand on the arm of the first of the "brides" and pushed her up the three steps of the platform.

She was one Twilla did not know. As Jass she was small and thin and the bundle she clung to with both hands was wrapped in an old patched piece of quilt. Another perhaps from one of the community of displaced farmers.

At a sharp gesture from Lord Harmond she turned to face the crowd below. Her eyes were not for them but on the ground, and there was the stain of shame on her cheeks.

Lord Harmond leaned forward now, inserted his hand into the bowl and brought out a finger-long strip of what looked like coarse leaf-paper.

"Carterer Ewon of Twin Streams—"

He read that aloud. The crowd had already fallen silent so the name echoed out over the marketplace.

"Here, Lord—" A man of middle years pushed through the massed men to come to the steps on the other side. He climbed them, shedding his cap on the way, bowed low to Lord Harmond and then in a stride was at the side of the shrinking girl, catching at her arm and turning her around so that together they faced the King's viceroy.

"Bear witness," Lord Harmond was very evidently repeating a formula he had uttered many times over, "that Carterer Ewon takes as his bride, by the grace of our lord, the King, this maid and let no gainsay their bonding."

Ewon made a clumsy bow, and his grasp on the girl brought her ahead of him as he urged her toward the stairs up which he had come. While the warwoman on the other side was already sending up the second victim.

So it went. There was no consenting on the part of the maids and apparently the men were used to abiding by the chance of the name pulling. Sometimes the matching was a grotesque combination, sometimes it was youth with youth.

When her own small circle of trail comrades came to be so disposed of Twilla paid even closer attention.

Leela went to a brawny, wide shouldered youth who looked to be her match in physical strength. Askla was prey to a man perhaps old enough to be her father. Rutha was claimed by a man in a better style of dress, perhaps some townsman or even retainer of the lord.

The one taking Jass was clearly a farmer of small means. When Hadee was pushed forward there was a murmur from the crowd and

Twilla gathered the fact that this one was certainly considered no bargain.

Then Twilla herself was urged forward. The man in civilian clothing at Lord Harmond's side was frowning now and the murmurs of the crowd were growing louder and more disparaging. But Lord Harmond paid them no attention. Rather he pulled forth the last of the strips from the bowl. And when he read aloud the name there was a complete hush over the assembly.

The young man who had been so late in arriving jerked as if he were a horse to which the spurs had been suddenly applied.

"That hag face! No!" His face was flushing and he made no move toward climbing to claim the choice fortune had made for him.

Lord Harmond did not rise from his seat, but the look he turned on the young officer promised wrath to come. When he spoke his voice was icy and carried a note of command which was not to be disobeyed.

"All know the law, all will abide by it—no matter what his station may be. You will do as all others here have done, Captain; accept the bride which fortune has decreed for you."

"No!" He had turned and was pushing his way out of the crowd where voices were being raised. Lord Harmond nodded once more to the officer beside him and he was quick on his way to intercept the younger man. Meanwhile Lord Harmond turned his attention to Twilla, looking her up and down. There was a twist to his lips as if he had sipped at a sour wine.

"We keep the law," he said. "No man, even *if* he be my son, can refuse the lottery. You are of my household now, and you shall conduct yourself accordingly. Take her to the tower chamber," he added now to Tathan who had come to the top of the three steps at a crook of his finger.

Lord Harmond's son! Twilla kept a tight grip of her bundle as Tathan hurried her down and around the end of the platform toward the gate into the Keep itself. What triangle was she involved in now? The Lord was determined to keep the law—if his son was in such disgust of her what might he do? She found her heart beating faster as the warwoman hurried her along.

Wedded by force to some field man she might have had a chance for escape, but she believed now that she had little hope of such. Lord Harmond would make sure that the marriage would take place—he could not favor his son over any of the others in the lottery, for the sake of both his own hold to the law and the matter of discipline.

Unlike the rest of the buildings of the town, which had been constructed of fired clay, this was of stone which must have come from some distance—though it had none of the feeling of age about it which one was aware of in the buildings of overmountain. And there was the smell of newly cut wood as well as the odor already imprinted on a building housing a number of people.

Tathan pushed her toward a steep wall stair, narrow enough so that not more than two could share a step, and then came to the second story of the tower where two doors opened off a narrow landing. The warwoman set hand to one and then gave Twilla another push sending the girl into a chamber which was bare of all but a bed, a chest, a rude table and a pair of stools. Certainly there was no luxurious living in Lord Harmond's establishment.

For a moment Tathan stood, hands on hips looking the girl up and down. Then she gave a coarse laugh.

"Good that you be a healer, girl. His whip to your back will give you plenty to heal. Young Lord is not going to take kindly to being bond to such as you, and Lord Harmond, he won't let him slip the leash. He has said too often there be no changing of the choices. Captain Ustar didn't want no bride to begin with but they's talking again about trying to get house timbers from the woods, and them as goes after such will have to be protected. There ain't anyone in this keep town, gal, as is going to envy you even if you got a lordling out of the lottery."

She snickered and went. Once the door had closed behind her Twilla just got to one of the stools in time to save herself from a fall. Her whole body was shaking. The mirror—she had used the mirror and she wore the brand she had asked for in her reckless folly—she was not even sure she could undo it. Certainly not for a space, for she needed to build up her inner strengths. Also, suppose she showed her natural face—the Dandus priest would be after her at once. If Lord Harmond trusted such a one he would be the first to condemn the mage-learning Hulde taught. She was caught.

She wrapped her arms about herself feeling the near bruising pressure of the mirror as she pushed it tight against her breasts. At any moment she expected Ustar to break in upon her and——Do what? She remembered the story they had told during the trip of ill-favored women who had disappeared—conveniently for their bond husbands. Though she hardly believed that they would dare kill her out of hand in the Keep—for one thing Lord Harmond would not allow his son to so evade the law he himself so rigidly enforced.

She stooped a little farther and fumbled with her pack. There were tricks with herbs—but she had not been driven to that last extremity as yet. Though she believed she had the right to defend herself if her life was threatened.

What she did choose were a selection of the last remaining bits of that mind clearing substance she had called upon when she first started this mad action.

She had no water in which to steep them, rather she chewed two of the sprigs. Her mouth was so dry that she found it difficult work.

Then she forced herself to make a clear-eyed survey of the room. There were hooks set into the wall and from one depended a weather cloak. From another a belt which glittered even in this subdued light and was plainly meant for feast-time wearing. Hurriedly she got to her feet, but even before she laid hand to it Twilla knew that the sheath was empty of knife.

She turned to the chest and tugged up its heavy lid. Clothes showing touches of fur—probably for the cold season wearing. A tunic richly embroidered to match the elegance of the hanging belt. Plainly this was indeed a noble's wardrobe.

Carefully she searched to the bottom of the chest hoping to find some possible weapon—but there was none. The windows were covered by oiled skin so that the daylight was dimmed and there was no looking out. Nor could she free a corner of that. She turned back discouraged as the door opened without any ceremony and she moved hurriedly to face whoever had come upon her so.

It was a man she had not seen before. Certainly not Ustar, nor his father, nor that officer who had been on the platform. Yet he had the air of the well-born. Until, looking closer she could see that his clothing, good as it had been, was now dingy, soiled, stained with food droppings down his jerkin and in the creases of his shirt showing between the loosely laced jacket.

He moved oddly as he came forward, as if each foot that he advanced sought solid foundation before he put his full weight on it. His head was up, his face framed by a mass of ill-kempt dark hair, had a curious set expression and his eyes—His eyes stared straight ahead as if he could not see her at all! They were wide open, a dark blue which was near to gray and the pupils appeared overlarge as if he were in the dark.

In the dark! He was blind!

She must have made some sound, for with the quick awareness of one who had learned to depend on a second sense, his head turned sharply in her direction—like a hound who heard the sound of a distant summoning horn.

"Who is here?" His demand came quickly. Now she saw his nostrils expand as he drew several deep breaths, a hound now turning to scent as well as sound.

His whole attitude was that of one wary as if his walk through dark days was ever under threat.

Twilla found her voice. Judging by his clothing, as ill-used as that had been, he was someone of importance so she gave him the address for a noble.

"I am Twilla, Lord, one of those brought overmountain for wedding—"

Rather than a smile, the movement of his lips now was a wolfish grin.

"Bride? Then my father has done as he threatened—saddled young Ustar with a bride! He would carry out that plan of his to meddle with the forest again and is making sure this time his heir will not be rendered useless."

She did not know how to reply to that. He sniffed deeply again.

"What manner of bride dowry did you bring with you, Twilla? I smell—" He paused a moment and then added, "Herbs—yes, but not the ones for the scenting of body and clothes. So—what do you deal in?"

"Though your Dandus priest denies it," she was taking a chance now, "I have healing skills—with me is the healer's bag my teacher gave me at our parting."

"A healer!" Now he gave a guttural laugh. "It would seem that fortune guides my steps this day. What can you do for blinded eyes, healer? I am an unman here, a useless mouth, my heritage given to my brother because of these!" His hands raised to his face, clawed as if to tear those staring eyes out of their sockets.

"Did it come upon you as from a blow?"—she had heard of such cases—"or were you ill?"

She came to stand before him looking up at those changeless discs of gray-blue.

"It—" He shook his head as if he were trying to order some thoughts. "It is a curse—and how it came to me I do not remember. That is truth!" He ended fiercely as if he expected her to scoff at his story—perhaps others had.

"Let me see," she used the soft voice such as she summoned when dealing with the ill whose body's betrayal frightened them.

At first he drew back a fraction but then stood fast as she put a hand to his shoulder and urged him forward to where was the best light in this dim room.

"Sit down," she had guided him until his knee was against the chest and he obeyed.

To all appearances his eyes were normal save for that fixed, open-lidded stare. She could see no redness, no encrustation of the lids, nothing as a guide to the few eye troubles in which she was trained.

"How long has it been so for you?" she asked.

"How long?" His voice raised a note or so higher. "Long enough, healer—and past. A blind man cannot reckon time—we see no day nor night—all is alike to us. I only know that I went forth with a scouting party into the Demon's Wood and was lost there from the others. When I came forth again I was as one drunk, babbling of what did not exist—and blind. So they brought me back to a father who has no use for one who is maimed, true son or not. Lucky for him he has Ustar—which satisfies his need for blooded kin to rule after him.

"My father, you see," he continued, the bitterness coloring his words ice cold, "has been promised rulership over these lands. He need only establish a productive community here and he is the king's voice, not to be gainsaid. A lordship with none to envy him as they might were he to aspire to such an honor over mountain where there are many jostling one another for the king's full attention. My father is a man who heeds the law—" He paused again.

Twilla had picked up her healer's bag and was rummaging for a certain phial.

"Therefore a maimed son is now an outcast, and a second son will wed that he may fulfill the quest his brother botched."

She was measuring drop by drop a clear liquid onto a small puff of well-cleansed fleece. As she counted the drops with one part of her mind she was arranging in another two lines of words to awaken the power.

> *"May light be brought—*
> *As ever taught."*

With the sodden pat of fleece she delicately swabbed his eyes, making sure that they were closed, yet not so tightly that the moisture of her treatment did not reach the eyes themselves.

Then, with care she stepped back from him and brought out of the hiding the mirror. If this blindness was indeed some foul ensorcellment the rumors would have it she had this other test.

"Open!" she ordered, wanting quickly to be done and the mirror back in hiding.

He did, his straight stare unchanging. She swung the mirror directly up before him and looked at its surface. Because she was expecting some such she did not gasp at what she saw.

There was his ill-shaven face, his wide mass of hair and—across his eyes a concealing band of silvery motes as if he were half masked with a thick gauze.

"Sorcery," she said.

For the second time he laughed. "You need not read it so, healer. Has not the Dandus priest already seen the taint in me? And what have I in answer to mage curse—or what have you? I am demon-struck, I can only be thankful that my wits have returned to me and I no longer babble—or should I be thankful? Not to understand misfortune is perhaps the better. And death now the best of all!"

Twilla wet her lips. She was trying to remember any bit of Hulde's lore which covered such ensorcellment. But the nature of the spell which had set it must first be known—and where could that be learned save from the one who has done the casting?

"You remember nothing of what happened to you in the wood?"

"Do not raise that question again!" he half snarled. "They have thrown it at me in one form or another for what seems near a lifetime now. No, healer, I do not remember! If I did perhaps I would still be able to wage some form of battle on my own behalf. None of us know what lies within the wood—only this—that a man who is wed can venture there. One who has no wife to bed comes to a fate like mine or worse. For that also there is no answer. The Dandus priest would have it some demonic dark outside even his wide knowledge."

Twilla raised a hand and brushed back a long lock of hair which had swung down over those unseeing eyes. To such a man the loss of sight would seem far worse than a clean death, that she could understand.

"There—there is nothing you can do for me?" There appeared a crack in that harsh shell he had built around himself.

"Not with herbs, Lord. Not with such small learning as I have. But I swear that this is not of the body but of ill wishing, and for that there can be a remedy."

"Where do I seek such?" His head was up, that harshness was back in his voice again. "Among the demons of the Wood? They will show me no mercy—but perhaps you do have the right of it." He stood up and turned toward the door as if he knew this chamber well enough to cross it without mishap. "Perhaps an accounting with demons would be better than to live like this—un-man that I am—"

He was out of the door with two swift strides and slammed that behind him before Twilla could answer.

TWILLA, HAVING PUT her herb bag to rights again, once more seated herself on one of the stools. The light was growing even more dim, and she was hungry. Weddings such as she and Hulde had attended as guests had been very different.

There had been feasting and laughter, dancing, joy in a new beginning for two lives. But there had been no degrading lottery there, no reduction of any girl to a thing which a man needed to keep himself safe from some invisible menace. Even if the bonds had been arranged by the two families the young people had always known each other and she had never heard of a girl being pushed into some uneven match willy-nilly.

She wondered what was happening now to her late companions. Most of the men at the lottery had plainly been from farms, and some of those might be situated some distance away. Perhaps they were already trudging back to those shelters with their "brides" beside them like beasts bought in the market.

They were wedded—and that by the will of Lord Harmond and the formula he spoke but— Twilla drew a deep breath. That formula had *not* been spoken over her. The unwilling Ustar had not been brought back to stand with her before his father. That could mean that she was *not* bound to him!

Though what good did that do? She was very sure that sooner or later she would see Ustar and that his father would make very sure he was married and that marriage consummated so that his second son would be safe in the proposed venture into the demon woods. Therefore there was no escape, only a breathing space.

She drew out the mirror again and peered into it—the surface was dim in this light and those window skins would keep out a scrap of moonlight. Yes, the face she had designed for herself and which would probably be her undoing still stared back at her. The red splotches had faded into deep pocks. Her eyes were still small, red-rimmed, weak looking with lashes scanty enough to hardly show at all, and the swelling of her nose—she looked not unlike one of the young sows in a farm yard. Truly a face to frighten away or disgust any man. And she feared now she was going to suffer for it.

She was debating on trying to assuage her hunger with some of her herbs when she heard the bar on the door rattle and a moment later Tathan clumped in, setting a tray down on the chest top.

"Eat up," the warwoman leered at her, "a maid needs strength for bedding. Though that may be yet awhile. Lord Ustar and his father are not of one mind concerning you. However, Lord Harmond will win in such a dispute. You'll be brought down before the company, the bond given and then"—she now grinned widely—"you'll have to greet a very unloving master." For a moment she hesitated.

"I have heard things of wisewomen, mind you. That they may have powers. But the Dandus priest will be sure you don't summon such. His sort do not take kindly to yours. Best not try anything that that one can catch upon—it will be the worse for you. Eat, and be glad that you were remembered when the bowls were filled tonight."

She tramped out, and Twilla heard the bar slide back. She edged her stool up to the chest and investigated the contents of two bowls and a tankard. What she wanted and needed now was food.

However, as she dipped into a thick mixture of root vegetables and small blocks of meat (nothing which required the aid of an eating knife, she noted—she had only been provided with a spoon) her thoughts turned to that earlier visitor.

He had come into the room as if he expected to find it empty. Had she been allotted the chamber which had been his? And she was not even sure of his name—only that he had suffered the curse of the woodland and as a result was seemingly an outcast in his own home.

Now that he was no longer before her with his infirmity to hold her attention she began to remember things she had unconsciously noted and only now drawn to mind. It was plain from the disorder and spotting of his clothing that no one had paid attention to his comfort and appearance for some time.

But he had made some attempt to shave and she knew enough of the customs of the nobility to realize that that had been a clinging to a small detail which asserted his caste. Landsmen, merchants of the lower class might go bearded but those with any pretense to good birth showed their faces proudly to the world. And in spite of the ragged appearance of missed stubble and some cuts he had achieved at least that much—a goodly feat when done by touch.

If he had been able to give full attention to his appearance he would be, she realized, a far from ill-looking man. His features much resembled those of Lord Harmond but were not set so sternly. And he was younger than perhaps she had first guessed—perhaps there was not more than a year or two between him and Ustar, which might indeed make his present maiming an even more bitter thing to bear.

Ensorcellment—yes, Hulde had spoken of such matters during Twilla's learning. Though there were fast rules for those who would follow the Wisewoman's path. One did not summon any calamity to another unless one was willing to pay a price oneself. Her own fancied disfigurement was aimed only at herself, it injured no one else—therefore she would not suffer any return of an ill-power backlash.

But Hulde's learning was circumscribed by what she herself had managed to amass over many years of study and experimentation. Her own mentor, the Wisewoman Katerna—long since dead—had clung more closely to a healer's studies, and what Hulde had learned of other powers she had had to ferret out for herself and had imparted only in bits, and with much warning, to Twilla.

This ensorcellment born somewhere in the dreaded woodland might be utterly new, not obeying the laws Hulde dealt by. There such ill wishing could be fully released, used without harm to the sender. Twilla shivered, her hands going to the mirror, pressing it so tightly its rim bit into her skin. She had only this for any major power, and its abilities she had only partly explored.

She shoved a little away from the chest which formed her table, her appetite suddenly gone. Though she put out her hand to take up a slice of bread and pinch it between her fingers, a childish habit she thought she had forgotten.

At least they had not scanted her on the food. And it was a noble's feast compared to trail rations. But she did not lift the cup on the tray to taste its contents, which were dark and had the odor of thick wine. To a healer, such was something to be indulged in only after dire physical exertion. One must not muddy one's mind with such potions.

Or perhaps the "brides" were expected to become so bemused that they would not offer even token resistance to the demands of their new masters. For a moment she caught her lip between her teeth and considered a new thought.

Within her stores she had that which would render the senses far duller than any drink, except that it be offered in a far greater quantity than had been offered here. Could she escape—her inner self if not her body—in such a fashion when Ustar came to carry out his father's wishes?

No, that was the coward's way—and beneath the will of any wise-woman. There were certain times when one might indeed use what she carried, not only to lose keen senses, but even life itself. However, she thought that she was not yet driven to such a state. Once more her hand pressed the mirror and it seemed that her answer came in a wave of disgust against her own dark thoughts.

The room was very dark now—she could see no candle, no lamp, and when Twilla tried to move again she bumped against the bed. Now she felt her way along the wall until her outstretched hands touched the wood of the heavy door.

She had seen no latch—and she had heard the drop of a bar on the other side when Tathan had left. But still she had hoped that she could apply some lock upon her side so that no one else could come on her unaware. There was nothing. But still determined to have some warning she pushed the stool on which she had been sitting, having found it in a wide sweep through the chamber, against the door.

The wood of its rudely chiseled legs had made enough of a scraping noise when she moved as to assure her that that sound would alert her, even if she missed the slippage of the bar without.

Having done what she could, Twilla felt her way back to the bed, moving clumsily and barking her shin painfully against the side of the chest. She heard the rattle of the dishes from which she had fed, groped her way using the edge of the chest until she came to the bed.

It would seem that the dispute between Lord Harmond and his second son was a long one. She had not been brought forth as Tathan had promised, to have that bond placed upon her in the company of those within these walls. Thus she wondered what pleas Ustar was raising on his own behalf. Not that it would matter in the end for Lord Harmond was duty-bond to honor the law and see his son wed as fortune decreed.

Twilla settled on the edge of the bed. There was a small measure of light now showing at one of the windows as if some torch or lantern had been set alight not too far away. But it was not enough for the mirror.

Suddenly she was aware that the inner tension of the day had worn hard upon her. She wanted to sleep, needed to.

On impulse she pulled at the mirror cord, working it around on her throat so that she could slip the mirror itself under the thin pillow her hands had located.

"Sunwise, darkwise—" Her lips shaped the words rather than pronounced them aloud.

> *"Power that lives be aguard.*
> *"Creeping evil thus barred.*
> *"Moonwise rise in me*
> *"May I safe in slumber be."*

Rhyme of a sort, if hardly better than that of a child playing with words. She laid down on the bed and now slipped one hand beneath her head, rubbing her fingers about the surface of the hidden mirror.

Perhaps it was only because she had so longed for it, but it seemed to Twilla that her fears lessened, were gone. Instead there arose in her a new strength of purpose, body, and mind. Accepting that as the truth because she must believe so, she closed her eyes and slept.

Mist, silver mist, a mist which whirled and blinded, made all which lay before an unknown path. Still she pushed on and the mist reached out hungrily for her but could not quite engulf her wholly.

Such a gauze of mist she had seen. Dimly memory moved, presented to her mind a picture—a mask of mist laid across the upper part of a gaunt and drawn young face, a mist which blinded!

The mist appeared to close more tightly about her. She held something, which chill shrank from, a glowing disc—a cold light—moonlight—not suntouch. The encroaching mist drew back. Twilla felt the lash of unseen, unheard anger. An anger which was so rooted in contempt it was twice as potent. But the anger—the mist—could not prevail.

Twilla awoke. No mist—only the darkness of the small chamber. Yet she was as certain as she would have been had Hulde herself told her that in this night she had been discovered by something which was beyond the common understanding—something which was clearly inimical. But, oddly enough, she felt no fear.

To fear the unknown was prudent, perhaps, but this unknown had a foundation in an emotion she could put name to: anger, contemptuous anger. And she was equally sure that the dream, if dream it had been, had not been forced upon her by any power within these walls.

It was nothing summoned by a Dandus priest. They certainly did not dabble in such visions—rather foul nightmares to punish.

The blind lord! Twilla sat up suddenly, jerking the mirror from under her pillow to strike against her shoulder. If that dream had been born from his mind—No, he would have no reason to so try to reach her, enmesh her in an ensorcellment like his own bitter one. She had done him no harm—unless his reason was the crooked one that he wanted his brother to fail even as he had done, and so would use her as a weapon in that wise.

She heard it now—not from the door, which gave upon the interior of the Keep, but outside. A sound of—yes, it was like the beating of air by great wings. At the same time she heard a shout from below as if some sentry had been alerted.

But though Twilla now strained to catch any sound which might give her knowledge of what might be happening without the noise of the wings—if wings those were—ebbed. Though the clamor from below grew stronger.

Before that had died away there came another—a warning. She heard a sound from without her door now. That which might have been the bar was hurriedly pushed from the hooks which held it. Then the door itself was sent flying inward, with force enough to send the stool she had left as a warning scraping across the floor.

Light streamed also enough to make a silhouette of the one who pressed in. The blind lord—surely it was he.

Twilla slipped from the bed, taking a moment to put the mirror back into hiding. She reached his side just in time to save him from coming up against the chest.

Though his face was in the shadow, she did not doubt that he was in search of her. And she was made very sure of that when his arms swung out with the speed of a man used to battle training, his hands closing upon her upper arms as well as if he could see what he would capture.

"What would you do?" His words were near spat into her face. "What ill webs do you weave here?"

He was shaking her now with such vigor as to send her head rocking dizzily on her shoulders.

"I—do—nothing—" she got the words out, near breathless from his handling.

"You lie! I—I saw—for a breath of time I saw—webs spun of mist—and—and I remembered!" There was exultation cutting through his first anger. "She enwebbed me, but I won free—now she has sent you to spin me prisoner again!"

"No." His shaking had grown more and more of an attack. He had shoved her back until the bed struck behind her thighs and there was no escape. "No!" The prisoning hold on her arms, bruising in its intensity, kept her bound. Now she gave a savage twist of her own, striving to break that captivity. The mirror slipping from her loosened clothing came out of hiding, was between their bodies.

He pressed in against her as if he would crush her with his greater strength. The mirror was caught fast between them, its reflective surface against his chest.

"What—?" He gave a short cry, cut off as if a hand had fallen over his lips and then he dropped his hold, so suddenly she fell back on the bed, drawing back from her as if she had become a fire to sear him.

Twilla caught once more at the mirror, pushed it into hiding. He had withdrawn well away from the bed and was now fully revealed in the light from the corridor.

His dark brows were drawn near together, his jaw set. He had the look of a man facing odds which he could not understand but which he would not surrender to.

"I have done nothing," Twilla found her voice, was glad to hear the words issue levelly from her lips. "I dreamed—of a mist—but it was none of my weaving."

His head had turned a fraction, she felt rather than saw that fixed stare of his useless eyes was on her, as if he was fighting for sight, for the need to learn—

"Mist—" he repeated. His hand went uncertainly to his head, rubbing fingers across his forehead. She saw him sway and was quick to move, reaching his side and steadying him until he reached the bed and dropped down to crouch at its edge, his head now forward and hidden in his hands, supported by elbows planted on his knees. He was shivering now, his whole body quivering as if he stood bare in some icy winter wind.

Twilla leaned forward, laid her hands first on his tangled mop of greasy hair and let them rest so while she pulled on healer's strength. Then her fingers slid down toward his hunched shoulders and she worked at the knotted muscles until she heard a sigh out of him and he raised his head.

"I do not know who or what you are," he said slowly as a man working out some puzzle, "but that you mean any harm—that I will not believe, healer. There is that in you which is different—I have heard of the learning of wisewomen—some speak them fair, some believe like the Dandus that they are ones who open gateways to evil.

But sure as my name is Ylon and I am son to Lord Harmond, I am certain that you do not bring evil here. Or—''

Under her touch his body suddenly tensed once again and he shook his head. "No!" Though to what he gave that denial she could not tell.

Suddenly he shifted around on the bed so that he was half facing her, his face again most wholly in the shadow.

"You are in danger, healer, worse than you know. To speak ill of a kinsman is a fault against the blood. But listen now—'' His hands once more swung out until they touched and then gripped her but not painfully as before, rather as if she had stumbled and he was drawing her back to safety.

"Because I am blind—an un-man—rift of my kin standing, they no longer pay attention to me. I have become as a wall, a hound, something which has no thought or feeling.

"Ustar believes himself shamed by you, he has held out against our father as I would not have believed that he could do. But his anger is not turned toward our father, nor toward the laws which bind him to what he will not endure—he hates *you*."

Twilla shivered. There was such intensity in his warning that it aroused all the fears which had dwelt in her since she had stood on the platform below.

"He will kill me," she said trying to keep any quaver from her answer.

"No. Clean death would be one thing. This night I have heard him plot something else—'' His voice trailed away as though he found it very hard to summon the words to complete his message.

"The Dandus priest?" That she had also feared since she had seen the man outside the town walls. What fate did such fanatics bring to those they had so long tried to vanquish?

"No," the word came in a low voice hardly above a whisper. "The Dandus priest wants his place here well-assured, he would not lend himself to any action which would counter my father's well-known law. No, what Ustar intends is something foul, something which calls upon the very core of House Blood. One of the House cannot wed a used woman—''

"A used woman?" For a moment she did not understand, and then her face flushed though there was no one to witness that rise of blood from shame and anger.

"There are always fewer women sent here for wedding than there are men in hunger." Ylon's voice was toneless, as if he used tight control to keep it so.

"Those who are to establish the landholds, a few of the townsmen, are summoned to the lottery. Soldiers are not men of homes and families for the most part. Even though they would be sought by the demons if they went wood venturing, there are only a selected number and that very small which are allowed bride taking—it is considered an honor and much sought for.

"However, in any force there are those who are never far removed from the animal, who would have no chance under my father's eye to ever hope to be chosen for the lottery. And to many of these a woman has become a much-longed-for but unobtainable trophy. They would be willing to risk much to allay certain hungers of the flesh.

"It is with such Ustar deals. He plots even now. Once those have had their will of you—and the gaining of that would be a monstrous thing—you would not be taken as bride by any man. How could he be sure that any child you bore was not conceived in rape?"

Twilla's shiver grew stronger, almost to equal those which had racked Ylon earlier. The mirror—was there any way the mirror could save her from this? Or—or must she resort to those potent herbs she carried to take her into oblivion?

"What must I do?" she asked aloud, but of herself rather than him.

"It is rather what I *will* do," he answered, sitting straightly now as if he had called upon inner strengths. "I believe that you are truly a healer, you have shown me"—he paused and then continued—"somehow you have shown me that I am not a useless thing. This night—the mists—when I came to you it was as if some greater will cut through those webs and I was again a true man. Therefore I shall act as one. I believe—I truly believe—that the Wood holds a secret and I shall never be free until I discover it. It is my intent now to return there—"

Twilla put out a hand to lie over his. She could understand, if only a little, what that decision must mean for him.

"You have heard of the danger waiting there," he continued—"Blasted wits, blindness—complete disappearance. Yet you have such strengths as I have not touched before. In the Wood you would be free of pursuit—by those here."

"How—" she was beginning when suddenly his hand moved under hers.

"Be quiet," he breathed, getting to his feet. He started to move across the small room toward the door. She threw herself off the bed and pulled away the stool to give him clear passage but he was not going out, instead he took his stand behind that half-open door and now she could hear the tramp of boots up the stair without.

7

THE DOOR SWUNG slowly closed and so the light from without was cut off. However, there was certainly no way of returning the prisoning bar without into its hooks. Whoever was coming would know that the room had been visited.

Twilla backed away until she stood with her shoulders planted against one of the hide-shrouded windows. Did she hear more than one pair of footsteps outside?

Then the door was sent open once more with a violent shove which must have slammed back against Ylon. There was light in abundance now for he who tramped in was holding a lantern. From him came the sour smell of that poor ale which these outlanders fancied. His face was flushed and he moved unsteadily.

He swung the lantern higher so it fully revealed Twilla. Now he scowled and then spat noisily so a fleck of his spittle spotted her dress.

"Sow-faced trash!"

Twilla tried to slide away along the wall, away from his advance, but he moved quicker than she thought possible from his appearance of being well drunk. The lantern fell to the floor as he dropped it and then one of his hands tangled in her hair and, with that painful hold, he pulled her toward him while with his other palm cuffed across her face with exploding force.

For a moment the room whirled dizzily and she could not see

clearly. Then she smelt a foul breath as he drew her by that hairhold closer to him.

"Bride—" His voice was almost a cackle, as if laughter and rage fought for supremacy in it. "We shall see—bedded you will be, trash, but not by me. You will have a man, yes, more than one—and they are lusty fellows. Give you a dance they will. And they are waiting—so come along, sow-faced—for your bedding!"

His hand was still fast in her hair dragging her head down and around so that she could not see. She struck out vainly only to be rocked again with one of those bone-bruising slaps.

"No use in fighting—"

Then his voice ended in a gasp, the hold on her hair was loosened and she jerked away. Ustar crumpled to the floor, his head striking with an audible crack against the edge of the chest. He lay unmoving, face up with the bulk of his brother looming over him.

Twilla had regained her senses enough to make two quick moves. She rounded Ylon to once more shut the door and then caught up the lantern to set it on the floor to completely illumine Ustar's body.

The way his head lay, her breath caught in her throat. She was on her knees, striving to find a pulse in the throat.

"Get up—coward—" Ylon advanced the toe of a worn boot, thudded it home so that the body rocked under Twilla's touch.

"Don't—don't—he—I think he is dead!" She still strove to find a pulse. Now she was pulling at the strings of Ustar's jerkin, trying to bare his breast that she might seek a heartbeat.

"Dead?" The word sounded hollowly over her head.

"I can feel no heartbeat." She tried to calm herself, remembering the teaching of her craft.

"Then—" That voice still held the hollow note but there was a spark of urgency in it. "You must get forth from here! They will believe that he came to you and by chance you killed him."

"But—but you can tell the truth." She looked up from the body into the face of the man standing over her.

"Of a surety I can," he laughed. "I can spin the whole tale—and they will say that my wits wander again as they did before. But you will suffer for it nonetheless. My Lord Father will not take lightly to losing his second son. No, you have only one hope, Twilla—and that is—"

His hand groped out and down, touched her hair but with none of the rage which had left her scalp smarting.

"You must get out of here," he said.

"How? Perhaps they have already heard—"

"There is no keep designed by one who has grown up in the feuding country over mountain," he said, "which does not have its secrets. I can show you a path out—and then—then, Twilla, it will be your own choice. They will hunt you but they will not enter the Wood."

She sat very still under the touch he still kept on her.

"What of you?" she asked.

"Me? What does it matter? I am already flawed past any usage to them—to myself—"

"No. Listen!" She reached up to catch his hand and used it to draw herself up so that their bodies touched. "Listen," she cried for the second time, trying to impress on him what she had come to believe. "In the Wood lies the source of the ensorcellment which holds you, for I swear by the Three Faces of the Moon that you are ensorcelled. If you seek out the Woods again can it not be possible that you might gain back what you lost?"

She heard, felt, him draw a long breath.

"I am a blind man, we are far from the Woods. You can hide and dodge and have a chance—with me as a burden that will not be so."

"You have the power to get us free of this place, you have said that. And the countryside is open to my sight—that can serve for two out there. You have this night saved me from horror—do you think me so poor in spirit that I will not repay such a debt?"

Then she was aware of movement in the body of the man she had thought to be lying dead at her feet.

"He is alive, I must tend to him—" Her healer instinct took over, but when she would have knelt again Ylon fast caught and held her.

"Not so. We have little time. Alive or dead Ustar will be the death of you. That is a truth I can swear to."

His hand loosened and then caught again in the bunching of the skirt about her waist.

"You cannot go forth wearing this. At first sight any wayfarer would have the hunt up after you. In the chest—take what you need and change into it—quickly."

Twilla felt she should protest but the vigor of his orders now drove her to obey. From the chest she tumbled forth a pair of breeches, a shirt, a jerkin, all of an earth-brown shade. Pulling off the dress and heavy petticoat beneath, she kept her chemise but dressed hurriedly in what she had found. The clothing was too large, but a sash swathed twice around her middle kept the breeches in place and though the jerkin was too wide in the shoulder, too long in the sleeves it would have to do.

Once reclad she looked again at Ustar. Then she knelt beside him, looking in each ear for any sign of blood which might signal a badly cracked skull. On impulse she pulled the cover from the bed and put it over him, but she felt a guiltiness of betrayal that she did no more.

"I am ready." Twilla hefted her depleted shoulder bag of herbs. Ylon had already moved to stand by the door, which was open a crack. It was plain he was listening.

"Are there any coming?" she ventured in a whisper as she joined him.

"Not as yet. Leave the lantern—that will provide a beacon for any and they will try here first." He pushed her ahead of him out of the door where the faint light of another lantern down one flight of stairs gave some light.

Ylon stooped, picked up the door bar and slid it into place.

"Now!" He held out his hand and she put hers into it. His grasp tightened as he drew her with him to the stairs.

"We can hope," his whisper was so faint she could barely hear the words, "that Ustar has seen this place cleared for a space that his foulness can be accomplished without interruption. As captain of the guard he would be obeyed."

That descent from step to step, pausing now and then to listen, so tensed Twilla's body that she began to feel the beginning of cramped muscles.

They reached the ground floor and there was no challenge. Doors remained shut. There were lanterns burning here and there but no sign of any others under this roof tonight. At the foot of the stairs Ylon turned to the right entering another room. The dark was thick but he moved confidently through it, drawing her with him. She only hoped that by keeping her so close to him he was making sure she would not stumble over any piece of furniture. She had always heard that with one sense being at fault the others would compensate and perhaps that had become so with him.

"Stand!" again a whisper. "Wait." He loosed his tight hold on her and she heard faint sounds of movement, at last a creak as if some protesting door had yielded. Then he came back to her.

"We must descend here," he told her. "There is a ladder only. I shall go first, you feel for each rung with your foot before you put weight on it. And I shall guide you."

She heard a faint scrambling noise and then the whisper—

"Ready!"

Going to her knees Twilla felt before her. The rough floor was splintery and hurt her hands, but then those caught on the edge of an open space and she drew herself toward that. To see with one's fingers she discovered was one of the hardest tasks she had ever attempted. But she found the ladder at last, and, trusting because she must, she began the descent into a well of complete darkness.

Then she felt a light grasp on her foot, even through the soft and too large boots she had taken from the chest. Oddly that touch steadied her, broke a little the net of apprehension which had drawn so tightly about her.

Then his body backed hers as her feet once more came to rest on a floor.

"Wait," his voice was a little louder, "I must close the passage door aloft." She heard the creak of the ladder rungs under his greater weight, then a noise from above before he rejoined her.

His body brushed against hers as he descended once more. Her hand was caught again in his linking grip.

"The way is narrow," he warned, drawing her after him.

Narrow it was, Twilla speedily discovered when her healer's bag was caught and swung back so she had to shift it into the crook of her arm. The smell of damp earth never sweetened by the touch of sun hung about them. She felt it more and more difficult to get a deep breath as they slowly advanced, her shoulders scraping wall and moldering wood supports first to the right and then the left. But his hold on her remained tight.

This journey through the dark made Twilla realize a little what it might be to lose one's sight. Yet here Ylon walked with the ease of one knowing just what he was doing. Was it true that he would be in danger if he remained? She did not know the customs of nobles. Could it be that his father would offer his son some hurt—after he had heard his story? Yet Ylon seemed very sure he would not be believed.

"The way slopes," he warned her.

They were going slowly enough and she felt tentatively ahead before she took a full step.

"There is water," he added. "Shallow, we must walk in it for a space."

His grip on her had not loosened. She gave a gasp as her next step did take her into running water. Though it did not rise any farther than her ankles. She felt the pull of a current but not one strong enough to threaten.

At least here the air was better as if the flow of the stream brought with it a recent memory of the outer world.

Ylon's guiding hand drew her to the right and their way was marked by the sound of splashing. His pace had slowed again and Twilla had a sudden fear that he might have lost some memory guide, which would bring them out of here.

"Here!" There was a note of triumph in that, and the girl was sure that he had been nourishing that same fear.

"There are two steps up," he told her.

She found the first by ramming her toe painfully against it. Then his firm grasp drew her up, even as it had guided her down that ladder. She had no way of telling how far they had come by that boltway. Were they out of the village yet? Beyond the wall? Was it still night?

Her sense of time seemed lost to her and she began to worry about the fact that they might come out of this way in full daylight, visible to any who might be watching.

"Steps again," his warning came. "I must go to open the outer door."

When he dropped her hand Twilla felt suddenly lost. She had not realized how much she had come to depend upon him, how great her trust had grown to be. And these were really only the first few steps of the journey they must make. Once in the open it would be up to her to be responsible for their going and her own self-belief wavered.

"Climb—" The word brought her to feel out. There was no ladder here, rather narrow steps cut into the earth, hammered hard to be sure. However, the edge of the first under her groping touch crumbled a little.

Then—there was light—blessed light!

She could see the steps plainly even though the bulk of Ylon was partially between her and that goal. Daylight—so they had outworn the night.

Twilla found herself, after she had climbed, in a space so small that she was crowded hard against Ylon. The light was half shattered she could see now by a netting which had been interwoven with grass and vines. So deeply anchored was that growth it was as if they were now locked in.

Ylon felt along the frame which supported the matted barrier. Then he set his shoulder to it and crowded her yet farther as he heaved it outward, catching his boot in a tangle of vine to fall face down.

Twilla pushed at him, squeezing at last into the full of the day. She did not rise to her feet but squatted there, peering up and around.

They had come out on a bank above a river, perhaps one which had given birth to that streamlet through which they had waded. She did not remember sighting any river on her journey here, but her view of the town had only been from the east—and they may have won westward in their escape.

She dared to raise to her feet and turn slowly. Then she gave a gasp and ducked down sending Ylon, who was up on his hands and knees flat again, sputtering curses.

"The wall—it is just behind us! Any sentries there can sight us!" She shook him. "Maybe they already have."

He managed to free himself from her and sit up. "We are on the river bank?"

"Yes—yes!"

"What do you see in the water?"

She could not understand what he meant. What did one expect to see in the water? Still he must have a good reason to ask her that.

The river had a definite current, certainly much swifter and stronger than that of the hidden stream. On its surface there was showing what could only be storm wrack. Here and there a sapling toppled from its bankhold to bob along and provide an anchor for floating brush. To cross that she thought would be dangerous and she said as much.

"It flows south," he commented brushing his hand across his shrouded eyes as if he would impatiently clear them. "We head north. This season brings storms and no one tries the river way. Therefore we can hope that we have already passed out of their reach."

His hands were busy now twisting at one shirt sleeve.

"Have you a knife?" he demanded.

"No. They took it from me."

"Tear—!" His voice was hot with impatience as he worked with the sleeve until at last it did part and he pulled loose a strip. "You also—"

Twilla did not yet see his purpose, but she had begun to believe that he had something in mind. She worried at the sash she had bound around her middle to keep her large clothes in order and when she had torn a piece from that she thought of something else and brought out of her bag one of the linen house caps which had been part of her limited allowance of luggage.

"I have a piece of scarf," she told him, "and a house cap."

"Good!" But he was still frowning.

"Now!" He continued pushing away from the battered framework which had concealed the inner way down the bank. "Is there some flotsam near enough for you to reach?"

She dropped her bag beside him and, on hands and knees, fearing any moment to hear some cry from the town wall, she edged along the water's lapping. The flood had risen to engulf a large strand of reeds and was nibbling at the bank. She found what she hunted just when she thought there was nothing.

One of the floating bushes had caught in the tangle of the reeds and she could just reach its earthy roots. She gave a cautious tug. Luckily her find was small enough to yield to her efforts. She could not drag it all the way out of the water but she could edge it along back toward where Ylon squatted on his heels. His head turned as if he could see her, but rather, she believed he was depending upon his hearing.

When she had explained what she had he handed her the strip of shirt, and her own bits of cloth.

"Wedge them well—make it look, if you can, as if one of us fell in and the other was lost trying to aid—" He laughed. "I'll die a hero yet—in spite of all their talk."

She did the best she could, hoping her efforts would paint the proper picture for anyone near them. Then wiping her wet hands across the folds of her breeches she came back to him.

"The Wood lies to the north does it not? Yet this current bears to the south. How are we going to travel it?"

"How far along is the day?" he asked her in return.

At first she thought that it must be well into the afternoon but the sun was hidden and there was a massing of clouds. It would appear that a storm was gathering, and she reported what she saw.

"Storm? It would seem that some power is in our favor! There is a ferry well up toward the north. They tried to build a bridge some time back but it was storm riven. If it will rain now and we can reach the ferry it will be on this side as there are the unbreakable orders—it must always be ready for any scouting squad."

"A ferry? There is a ferryman, then—"

"In a storm he will be under cover. We need not get directly across." Ylon was speaking slowly as if with every word he saw another point of some plan become clearer. "We get aboard and loosen the anchor ties. The current will carry us—downstream, yes, but with all this debris afloat we can make it to the opposite bank. While those in search will believe the boat broke loose of its own accord—if they are not satisfied with our other false fate."

It sounded like a plan too full of holes to Twilla. On the other hand she had nothing better to offer and to remain here was to put all their past efforts to no avail.

"Wait for the rain!" Ylon's head was up, he was drawing deep breaths of the rising wind. "This has the feel of one of the great storms."

So they waited and the day grew darker and darker. There was the roll of thunder and then the cracks of lightning lashed across the sky. The rain came—in vast drops pocking the river, soaking the two of them to the skin. It was her turn to lead and Twilla fastened the same kind of unbreakable grip on his hand as he had kept on hers, battling against the storm wind trying to warn him of all possible snares along the uneven ground.

She was not used to such fury as this storm seemed to be able to gather. The river, now and then she glanced at it, each time with more foreboding. To trust themselves on a ferry to that—almost she could believe that Ylon remained part troubled in his wits.

Find the ferry they did at last. There was a light in the small cottage there but they made a careful detour, coming down to the small departure wharf. River water was already sloshing over it and the ferry was tugging wildly at the anchor rope.

Somehow Twilla got Ylon on to the plunging, whirling boat. They could not get any wetter than they were, but the spray from the river dashed at them. Ylon broke from her hold before she could catch up with him and was pulling his way toward the end of the boat where the anchor ropes still held. He began to fight at the knots and, gasping at the fury of the airborne water around them, Twilla followed.

It would seem that once more touch served in place of his eyes. Somehow he had mastered the lashing, and the boat plunged out from the small dock into the full fury of the river.

Afterwards, Twilla could remember very little of that wild ride. They were twice nudged by floating debris with nearly enough force to send them over—yet still they remained unsunk.

It was the last of those masses of bush which served them well— for it shoved the bobbing boat toward the opposite side of the stream. Then, out of the storm's gloom, there arose a pillar rooted in the rage of the water.

Their craft struck nose against that and was flung away. It tipped and they were thrown into the water but Twilla's outflung hands grasped reeds, held grimly, and she found the strength to drag herself up into the hold of that water-logged vegetation. She looked around quickly. There was a shadow floundering into the same reed bed and she forced herself to inch back, catch at spongy leather where it covered Ylon's shoulder, and lend what strength she had left to drag him a little closer to safety.

Together somehow they gained the crumbling clay of the bank and with clawed fingers fought their way up, to lie exhausted under the ever beating of the rain.

8

TWILLA MADE A feeble effort to try to win to her knees, only to slip back and lie, breathing hard, until her head fell forward on her crooked arm and a darkness which was not storm born overlaid her.

Pain roused her. Ustar's hand in her hair—he would have her to his will— She choked out a cry and tried to strike out in a feeble defense.

"Up! Up with you! The water climbs, it will have us again!"

Water—yes, about her was the wash of water tugging at her legs, striving to reach hold of her hips. That painful grip was not in her hair after all but centered on the nape of her neck as she was being dragged forward, the reeds whipping viciously across her face.

Somehow she got her hands out, caught at those same reeds in the hope of protecting her face. Then, finding them stiff-rooted, expended what was left of her strength to use them to haul herself on. The grip on her neck loosened.

There was a darker blot before her and then a lash of lightning revealed that she was fumbling with her hand against the wall of a bank, which arose abruptly to tower above her.

Another body beside hers, scrabbling also at the cliff. Half dazedly she remembered—Ylon. The water lapped behind them, their legs were still awash. By sheer will Twilla won to her knees, reaching up along the now unseen surface of the bank seeking a handhold strong enough to support her weight. Her outflung right hand struck a hard lump embedded in the rain-slicked earth and she caught at it as well as she could.

Somehow, as might some poor half-drowned beast washed out of its grazefield, she found strength enough to claw her way up to roll over the edge of that drop and lie on her back her face up to the beat of the rain. Then her body was given another shove, pressing her painfully against what felt like stones, as Ylon landed almost on top of her, his greater bulk carrying him on.

Twilla was content to lie where she was—too spent to care whether or not they had at least defeated the clutch of the river.

"Up!" He was crouching beside her, pawing at her arm and shoulder, his fingers slipping over the rain-slimed leather of her jerkin. "Cover—find cover—"

Cover? Here? He was truly wit-struck this time. But he would not leave her alone, going so far as to dig in his fingers so strongly that they bruised her flesh.

He pulled at her with a fierce grip, dragging her up against his own body. In the darkness she could not see his face but there was a note of anger in the voice, which exploded nearly in her ear to deafen out even the sound and fury about them.

"By the Brazen Throat of the Thrice Dead—up with you!"

Somehow she answered his pull, his appeal and was half-tugged, half-risen to her feet. But once there she shook and wavered like a sapling with roots undercut.

Once more a lightning flash showed the world for an instant. His head was turned away from her now, though his hold kept her tightly steady against his body. He was looking inland, away from the river. Though—what could he see—or sense—or hear—? She could not think of any guide which might come to him in the midst of this fury of wind and pelting rain.

"Come!" He seemed determined, dragging at her and Twilla too weak to fight him off. At least the ground under them appeared level enough as she flung out the arm which was not prisoned against him in a wide sweep before her—hoping so for a warning against any obstacle.

Sodden grass twined around their feet so that they went at wavering pace. Then that outflung hand of Twilla's cracked painfully against a barrier. Her fingers slipped along what appeared to her the top rail of a fence.

"Fence," she braced herself enough so that Ylon was prevented from crashing into it.

"Guide—"

She was able to catch his meaning from that half-choked word.

Drawing him on a step or two she shifted to loosen his hold on her and catching up his now free hand she set it on the rail. He stood for a moment as if undecided which way to take and then turned resolutely to the right, pushing by her.

Twilla felt for the same guideline and with her other hand linked fingers in his belt. Thus they fought against the push of the storm. The chill of the wind was caught and harbored by their drenched clothing. Twilla was shivering and she realized from her healer's training that they were indeed both threatened now with a death from exposure unless they could find shelter. The fence might be a false guide, but at least it was something they could travel by.

She plodded on. Her feet were numb now, and it was getting to be more and more of an effort to raise them for another step. Ylon halted suddenly so that she was brought up against him.

"Corner—" The wind had died a little enough she could hear and a moment later bring her battered wits to understand. They had found a corner of the fence.

Ylon swung at a right angle and she followed. Slowly she began to realize through the burden of misery which enclosed her that the sky was beginning to lighten, the wind was dying, and the rain did not strike them so heavily.

She could actually see the fence—at least for a short way ahead. But there was something else—a dark bulk of what could only be some kind of building—perhaps a shed, as it did not look as large as any farm shelter. She jerked at Ylon's belt, pulling herself closer to him so that her voice might carry.

"Something—shelter—"

His head went up. "Where?"

"Just ahead—on the other side of the fence."

The thought of getting out of this fury seemed to give them both new strength. Their pace quickened. Then they reached that structure. The light had lifted even more. Twilla could not see any sign of a door, but there was a shuttered square above her head which might be a window.

"No door," she reported to her companion, "maybe inside the fence."

His hands tightened on the top rail, there was only that one line of wood, below it was an untidy jumble of packed earth and stones. With Twilla's guidance by hand and voice he got over and she followed awkwardly after, her shivering making her doubly clumsy.

The structure itself was of the same stone-earth construction and had begun to suffer from the watery fingers of the storm. But they rounded the side to face a wider opening, with no door to stand as barrier.

"Sheep huddle!" Ylon said.

The animal smell had reached her also and Twilla could see in the growing light there were animals even now sheltering there. Shepherd—would there also be a shepherd on guard here?

"Shepherd?" she ventured.

Ylon's head was bent a fraction as if he were listening. She, too, could hear the fretful sounds made by the flock. Apparently they were not finding their state hardly more pleasant than that of the newcomers.

It was light enough now certainly for anyone inside to be able to easily sight the two of them. The rain had slacked off. Clouds were breaking with sullen slowness. It was dark in that shelter, yes, but all she could sight was the movements of the milling sheep. That and some stacks of what might be last season's hay against one wall.

"We would be challenged by now," Ylon might have been speaking to himself more than her. "In—the beasts will do no harm. In fact they might give us both warmth and cover."

Twilla chose a path for them along that wall where the hay was roughly stacked, and, once they were well into the shelter, she urged Ylon down on that as the sheep scattered away from them, pushing now together at the other side of the huddle.

It was not until she allowed herself to down into the musty smelling hay, the sharper scent of fresh dung in her nostrils, that Twilla realized she could push her body no farther. This must be the end for now.

"Have they been shorn?" Ylon forced her to stay awake with that question.

She knew little of sheep but now she noted that he was right in his guess—these had been recently shorn. Which meant they had been turned into summer pasturage. And it might well be that, if there were no predators here, they had been left largely to themselves. The huddle would provide them with shelter against the storms and if the landsman was shorthanded this was the best he could think to do.

"Free pasturage then." She felt the tension go out of her companion. "There will be checks from time to time but no continued guardian. We may rest in peace—"

He was pulling at the hay about him, thudding it down into a kind of nest. "Down with you," he ordered when he had finished.

"You—?" she stammered, so tired she could hardly mouth the word.

"I—yes. Now down."

She pulled at her wet overclothing, shedding it as best she could, noting that he was following her example. With only her chemise still about her, covering her shivering body and hiding the mirror, Twilla burrowed into the hay and was almost instantly asleep in spite of her aches and shivers.

Sun reached in to wake Twilla. Their woolly companions of the night were gone, though they had left behind them pungent memories of their stay. She steadied herself up on one elbow to view the outer world. It was as if the fury of the storm had never swept over it.

There was a light snore not too far away, and she quickly turned her head. All she could see of Ylon was the back of his head, hay stems having caught in the tangle of his black hair.

Trying not to awaken him Twilla crawled out of her musty covering. Her clothes lay in the huddle in which she left them and now she went to work smoothing them out, striving to wring out the dampness. She mourned the loss of her herb bag. There were potions in that she could have shared between them which would have stayed off any but the most severe chills.

She swallowed experimentally and had to admit that her throat was sore. To put on the wet clothes again—

> *"Come all you bold lads as want to be free.*
> *Get you a ship an' learn the paths of the sea.*
> *There're maids in a plenty wherever you roam.*
> *Besides those who wave sing to bring you home!"*

Twilla clasped her wet jerkin to her in a fierce grip. That voice, cheery as it was, had come from close by. Were they coming to see how the flock had survived the storm?

Quickly she pulled the mass of her clothing closer and heaped hay over it. Then brushed a tuft over Ylon's head before she sank back into the dried stuff to shiver and watch.

The newcomer had only to come a little closer, round the side of the huddle perhaps and they could be sighted.

> *"Oh, love the waves high, swing with them low,*
> *Where these are true waves the sea doth go.*
> *Where the sea goes, so does my love.*
> *All is well—"*

"Drat! By the snaggle-teeth of the Seventh Shark—what a mess!" The song was forgotten and there was exasperation in that comment. And it was uttered just beyond the wall of the huddle. Only that was no man's voice. No! Twilla lay very still, her thoughts racing. She knew that voice now—Leela! But what had brought Leela here?

Though the fishergirl had been in part a supporter during their travel over mountain, there was no reason now that she would not betray them.

Twilla tried to remember something of the man Lord Harmond had so callously joined to Leela. He had been young, she recalled, tall and broad of shoulder, so that beside him even Leela had seemed small and feminine. A landman certainly, therefore under the Lord's rule.

There came a scrambling noise now followed by a thud. Then around the edge of the huddle Leela did stride into view. She had taken to trousers, which were tucked into high farm boots, and her arms were bare to the shoulder since the smock over the upper part of her body was sleeveless. Her sun-bleached hair had been gathered back and secured with a twist of cord. Yet she did not have the appearance of a farm drudge, rather her air of independence remained as strong. Leela had manifestly come to good terms with her fate.

She stood now with her back to the huddle opening, her hands on her hips, staring out over the field beyond.

Twilla had unconsciously clasped both hands over the mirror as if that might raise some defense against discovery. Perhaps it could if she only knew more.

"No—I will not—" There was an eruption out of the hay as Ylon sat up, his face wearing a battle snarl.

Leela whirled about and stood staring open mouthed. There was no chance to remain hidden now. Twilla wriggled up beside the man and caught at him, shaking him awake out of the evil dream which had betrayed them.

"You!" Leela strode forward toward them. "What are you doing here, healer?"

She seemed honestly surprised. Then her attention went to Ylon and her eyes narrowed.

"Who is here?" he demanded in turn.

"This is Leela who came over mountain with me," Twilla told him. She looked to the other girl. "He is blind—"

Leela's hand came up and her fingers made the complicated warn off sign for bad luck.

"A blind man—they mated you with a blind man?" she asked.

Better face this with the truth. They were already discovered. But there remained the very faint chance that Leela could be persuaded to let them go—unless she feared for her own safety when the hunters came, as they well might.

"They would have mated me with Lord Ustar, Lord Harmond's

son," she returned. "He was not minded, as he said, to take a sow-face to wife. There—" She drew a slow breath—would the full truth influence Leela to her side? She could only hope so. "Therefore he was ready to turn me over to the guard—to use as they would do that his father would not force him to mate with damaged goods. This"—she put her hand out to touch Ylon's arm—"is my Lord's other son who met with the wrath of the forest demons. Yet he came to my service and brought me out of that danger Ustar had planned."

Leela had blinked several times as Twilla spoke. Now she gave a laugh. "Healer, always you do something to surprise one. So you have come out of the town, but where are you bound? There are only a fringe of farms and"—now she frowned—"those on them want no quarrel with my Lord. They will deliver you up at first meeting."

"But you will not!" Ylon made that statement as if he believed it.

"My Lord," she looked in his direction, "I fared well in the lottery. My man is one I can welcome to my bed and we shall do well together. But this forced mating is a thing of beasts rather than people. Though fortune might favor some of us, yet your lord father has condemned others to misery. Had the brides been given more chance in the matter he would have drawn in fuller nets in his fishing. I know Twilla and what she says is a black use of power against the helpless.

"However, I shall not let you draw my Johann into this. Which means that I do not welcome you here."

"We do not ask for refuge," Twilla said then. "Lord Ylon has saved me from evil, now I pay my debt—"

"How?" broke in Leela.

"We journey to the Wood. It was there that this ensorcellment came upon him. I am healer enough to know that it is no distemper of the eyes from which he suffers but rather a curse laid upon him. I was apprenticed to Hulde and some of her knowledge is mine. Thus we would seek out the source of Lord Ylon's disaster and there learn what we can. Also, I do not think that Lord Harmond's men will come hunting us within the Wood."

"The demons will!"

Twilla shrugged. "Demons are unknown, the evil of man is plain. I am willing to take my chance with demons rather than return to Lord Harmond's hold or be hunted down by his soldiers."

"Well, the choice is yours. Always, Twilla, you have thought different thoughts from the rest of us. So you would go to the Wood. What need you to get you there?" She asked that briskly as if she were a marketwoman bargaining behind her stall.

"Clothing—" Twilla answered promptly. "We were in the river and need that. And any food you can give us."

"We shall see." Leela diasppeared to return with a leather pouch plumply fat. She tossed it to Twilla. "I came out to walk the walls and see what harm the storm may have done—that is for my nooning. Johann is in the far meadows at the plowing and will not be back until sunset. As for clothing—I shall see what can be done."

With that promise she strode away. Twilla opened the bag. There were thick slices of brown bread bound together with cheese. She pushed one of those into Ylon's hands and began wolfishly on another.

"She is a friend?" Ylon made a question of that before he set teeth in the slab of bread.

"I think she spoke the truth," Twilla said. Did she really, or did she accept Leela because she had no other choice?

They had finished the supplies the fishergirl had left and Twilla had spread some of their clothing out in the sun as best she might, hoping that it could go unnoted. The grimy brown and gray of its coloring were not too far distant in color from the earth walls of the huddle.

It seemed to Twilla that Leela had been gone a long time. Had it all been false and was the fishergirl now sending some message to the town? She sat on a tussock of the hay and withdrew her mirror from hiding, not knowing what way it might be an aid but drawing comfort from rubbing her hands across its gleaming surface.

"Mirror Light, Mirror Bright—" She shot a glance at Ylon. He was lying back in the hay, his well-muscled body bare except for under-drawers, one arm over his eyes. He might be asleep but Twilla was not sure and kept her invocation to the thinnest of whispers.

> *"Mirror light, mirror bright,*
> *Lead us in the path a-right.*
> *By all the power that in you be*
> *Let me now our future see."*

Childish rhymes; but those seemed always to bring a response. As this jingle did now, for the surface she looked onto clouded and there was first a misting and then something to be seen through that silver dotted mist—a wall of trees. It had come and gone again in a flash but she was sure she had seen it. Thus the forest was to be their goal— and she knew that there was no longer any choice.

9

EVENING WAS DRAWING in fast and as soon as it grew dark enough they must be on their way. Leela had at least proved her sympathies in this much, Twilla thought, as she hefted again the sack of course food, and considered what now covered her body (in voluminous folds, to be sure) and Ylon.

Leela had returned just as Twilla's impatience had won near to the snapping point. She had with her a roll of clothing which she admitted freely were discards from the wardrobe of Johann's father who had died the previous fall of the flux. She stated frankly that she could only furnish them with such discards as Johann would not miss for she made it plain that she had no intention of sharing with him the facts of what she was doing.

"What he don't know," she had said, flipping out patched shirts and a couple of working smocks, "the better for him. He is a good man—I would not put him to the test of standing up with a lie to Lord Harmond's men."

With that they could all agree. Twilla had to make what alterations she could so that her share of the thoroughly dry clothing would not envelope her to hamper movement or drag on the ground. But the coarse shirt and over-smock fitted Ylon well and his sprouting beard was that which would be worn by a landsman.

Leela was in haste to bid them goodbye.

"Johann will be home from the fields. I must be seeking any more breaks in the pasture walls or he will wonder what I have done with myself today. Healer, I wish you and the young lord the best of fair winds and smooth waves!''

Twilla made a sudden move, reaching to hug the bigger girl, standing on tiptoe to kiss her on the cheek.

"May the Fortune of the Three be with you always, Leela," she said none too steadily.

Ylon moved in beside her, his unseeing eyes staring a little to Leela's left. "Landmistress—" His hand was out, and somewhat timidly Leela raised hers so that their fingers touched. His grasp closed about those, and he raised her hand to his lips in the salute that a noble born gave to kin maids. "Landmistress—you have the blessings of one who has little to give. Save that he will hold this in memory all his days and should fortune favor him in the future, then he will see that favor touches also upon you."

Leela flushed, and then gave a sound near a giggle. "Lord, I be no kin to such as you, but I come of honest folk and the teachings of the hearthside are always share the catch with those who go in need. Now," she swung to Twilla, "you remember the way? Johann's land is the last worked hereabouts—they are too frightened of the Wood. There should be a moon tonight for the storm seems to have driven out its force."

"Go with good," Twilla raised her hand in the sign she had so often seen Hulde give when saying farewell to one healed and in good strength again.

They still had to wait for sun setting and that gnawed at Twilla. Even dressed as landpeople strangers wandering this thinly settled country would arouse curiosity, challenge.

Ylon had thrown himself once more on the hay bed. Perhaps he was able to sleep that time away. Twilla could not. She longed to draw forth the mirror and yet there was that within her which was a warning.

They ate again of that dark bread, though this time with a scraping of a berry jam across to give its tasteless dryness flavor, and drank from the leather bottle Leela had brought. As the dusk closed in Twilla slung the cord of their food bag over her shoulder and arose.

"We go—"

He could not have been truly asleep as he shoved up at once in the hay and got awkwardly to his feet. Twilla linked hands with him for guidance and they set off in the direction Leela had pointed out.

There was other life haunting the dusk-darkened land. Small things which squeaked and ran as the two of them climbed back over the huddle fence and set out across another stretch of rough ground. There were sky flitters also, swooping and giving eerie cries, and a number of insects—ones which fastened avidly on all parts of their exposed skin. Twilla longed for her herb salves and found this hard to endure.

Luckily the land had been well-cleared, only twice did they have to circle small copses of trees and tangled brush. Then ground growth was taller here, perhaps it was not pasturage to be toothmown. The thick stems caught at their feet, seeming willfully to entangle them as they went.

By Twilla's reckoning there should be a quarter moon this night. She could already see the bright sparks of stars and pick out that which would guide them north. As always she was grateful for the bits of knowledge Hulde had had her study.

But it was not until they were well on their way that she saw that other dark line cutting across the horizon—the edge of the wood. It was far more foreboding than the walls of Lord Harmond's town— threatening as even the port castles at home had never seemed. From this point one could not see individual trees only that black shadow thick enough to stand out even in the faint moonlight.

"The wood—" For the first time Ylon broke the silence with which had appeared to wall them apart after they had set forth.

Twilla shot a glance at him—how did he know?

He might have read her unasked question. "It calls—" he added. Then he stopped, brought her also to a halt since their clasp still united them:

"Lady, if that which struck me mindless afore strikes me again— leave me! This I do not ask—I order. For I cannot remember what I did when that fit was upon me, and I may be of greater harm to others than myself."

"You only fear that," she said slowly. "Since you cannot remember you do not know what awaits us there."

He laughed harshly. "Whatever it is it has not used me well—I would not have the like happen to you! It is my order and you must obey it—if I turn strange—leave me!"

She made a small sound which he might accept as assent if he would, but she determined that it would be for her to judge what she would or would not do. Now she pulled at his hand.

"It must be close to midnight, let us rest and eat. I cannot judge distances in the dark—we may still be far from our goal."

His head was up and he was facing straight toward that dark line. It was almost as if he were listening.

"Well enough," he agreed.

They hunkered down where they had halted, in the middle of that tall grass, which near topped Twilla's head when she was sitting. Ylon, she noted, still faced the direction in which they had been going, as if he could see what lay before.

She shared out more of the bread and broke apart a lump of strong smelling cheese into as equal shares as she could manage, setting both in his hands.

The insects in the grass seemed not so aggressive here, perhaps the late night was not their time of hunting. Twilla had lifted the water bottle to take a sip when a hooting cry sounded loud enough to startle them. Flask still in her hold she looked skyward. There was certainly movement there. The stars she had been watching were blotted out, then returned to view, as if large wings had cut across their field of light.

Again that cry, much stronger and closer. She longed for even a staff for some protection. The flying thing swept over them, turned and was gone, back she was certain toward the waiting wood.

"Anisgar—"

Twilla turned quickly to her companion. "What?" she demanded. She had never heard the word before.

But Ylon's hands were at his head, over his sightless eyes.

"I do not know!" There was almost a child's fear coloring those words. "By the Favor of Word, I can't remember!"

His hands balled into fists, she could see dimly. Now he leaned forward and beat down the tall grass before him with sharp blows as if he were in battle against some mortal enemy.

"Anisgar," she repeated, striving to remember if she had ever found such a word in any of Hulde's old books. But she was sure she had not.

Now she moved closer to Ylon, caught his shoulder. He was shivering even as he had when they had come out of the icy clutch of the river.

"It is gone," she said with what calmness she could summon.

She heard him draw a great ragged breath. Then a moment later he spoke. He had regained control. "Again—memory—after a fashion." It seemed to the girl that he was striving hard to make light of his distress. Perhaps he was shamed by it.

"To remember, even in part," Twilla observed, "is a good sign. Hulde dealt with all manner of ills and once a man was brought to her who had a bad head injury. It was thought that he would never again regain his wits. But he did—little by little. There came flashes of memory and those stayed so that he was able to repatch it—"

"So you have knowledge of such, Healer," his voice was normal now. "Then you will not be fearful of—of what might happen to me again?"

"Are you fearful?" Twilla asked.

For the first time his head turned in her direction though she could not see his face.

"A man of war is not supposed to know the touch of fear," he answered obliquely, "or so we are told. I was once a soldier— What I am now is unman, as my former comrades would name it. So perhaps I can be also a coward—yes, I fear."

"And yet you go to face what you fear," Twilla replied, "and that, I think, no one can name cowardly."

"I go because I must! Because I can no longer live as unman. So, let us be on our way that I may find out for myself just what or who I now am."

She hurriedly shoveled what was left of their food into the bag. He had already taken several steps forward and she had to hasten to catch up. Once more they linked hands and moved on toward the forest fringe.

The sky was lighting into the gray of early dawn when that black mass before them spread so far as seeming to encompass all the world ahead. Twilla could make out individual trees now. But such trees as she could hardly believe the earth had strength enough to support.

Far taller than any tower she had ever seen, wide in girth to the point it would have taken several people, just touching fingertips to encircle, they presented an awesome barrier. There was also a kind of ragged fringe along their roots, masking any way into their stronghold. That was formed of brush, brighter green of leaf than those the forest giants bore. Here and there a breeze-tossed spray of flowered vine gave a hint of stronger color.

What Twilla felt was not fear, she believed, but rather awe. These trees were like another race, living a life of their own, secret to those who were like her, majestic as kings seldom were, proud as a wise-woman who had won a battle with death.

Again Ylon had halted of his own accord. His head up, his sightless eyes on that new world before them. Wind was rising, there was a singing of leaves—but no sound of bird. And to them wafted a strong scent—pine, Twilla recognized, and flowering locust, other perfumes she could not name.

She did not glance back at the open land they had crossed—that seemed to have no meaning now. It was what lay ahead which counted.

"I—come—" Ylon pulled his hand free of her grasp and plunged forward straight at the half wall of brush.

He had moved so quickly that he gained a good lead as he ran straight for the brush, which seemed to Twilla to form a near solid wall. Before she could come up to him he had reached that barrier—and—was gone. Yet there was no opening he could have broken so quickly. Twilla was aware of warmth against her skin, under that unwieldly bulk of clothing.

The Mirror—power answered power. And one of the tricks which could be raised by power was glamorie—the seeing of what was not and yet seemed to be tangible. She dragged the mirror from its hiding place by the neck cord and held it up to face that spot in the seemingly solid mass of growth into which Ylon had vanished.

Nor was she greatly surprised now to see reflecting on the gleaming surface not brush and briar but an open way. Toward and through that she confidently walked, her head bent a little to see the surface of the mirror she held out to face the woods in order to guide her way.

If the trees had seemed overawing when sighted from a distance they were doubly powerful in effect as they aisled the path she had found. There was a thick carpet of other seasons' leaves underfoot, soft enough so that her feet sank into it a little. Here were towering ferns like coarse green lace, the very trunks of those overshadowing giants were also green with the velvet of moss.

She could see a scoring of footprints in that leaf carpet though Ylon was nowhere in sight, and somehow she felt reluctant to call out. She could only follow his trail and hope that he had not come to any crashing disaster in his wild rush back to this perilous place.

Since she did have such a trail to follow now Twilla slipped the mirror back into hiding. This was a thing which was hers alone and until she knew more of how it might serve her she would not share with—

With whom?

There was a silence here in the deep tree shadow which there had not been out in the openlands. She had heard no call of bird, no buzz of insect—saw no movement among the ferns which could suggest that she was not alone. But she was sure that she was watched, and by no friendly eyes. There was a trace of menace, which grew the sharper with every step she advanced.

Nor was the way ahead clear. A mist appeared to twirl about, thickening, thinning, sometimes seeming as dense as a sea fog, to blind and bewilder her. Just at the farthest range of her ability to hear there began sounds which were like whispering of voices.

She had been in the tamed woods over mountain, herb hunting with Hulde but she had never encountered there this feeling of being cut

off from her own kind. Yet she kept resolutely following the scuffed
leaves.

The mist was thicker, a curtain hung between this tree, only to
dissolve and wreathe that. Twilla kept most of her attention for the
trail she followed, beginning to believe that that also was a form of
glamorie meant to bewilder and confuse any intruder. Then like a
curtain it was drawn to one side and she stepped into a clearing—
where at least the heavy branches overhead did not roof it so completely and the green gloom of the wood was lightened. Ylon stood
there, his arms hanging limply at his side, breathing in gasps, his head
turning from right to left and back again as if he strove to pierce the
curtain on his sight.

"Ylon!" Twilla pushed forward.

He paid no attention to her and before she could lay hand on him
there was another shifting of the mist on the other side of that clearing.

Out of the embrace of the floating wisps stepped a woman. She was
tall, delicate of form, long of limb, with a slender throat upholding
proudly a head from which streamed hair as dark as night, interwoven
with chains into which had been set small green gems which appeared
as bright as newborn stars. More gemmed chains formed a wide collar
about her throat, and heavy cuffs about her slender wrists. For garments she wore a robe of the same green as the gems, fitting closely
her body near to hip line so that her small high breasts were clearly
outlined. From that hip line the skirt swirled out yet seemed almost to
have a life of its own, always in movement about her thighs and legs.

Her face—

Once in one of Hulde's books Twilla had seen a representation of
something akin to that perfect mask. Her brows were delicate lines
like wings—slanting upward on each side toward her temples, and her
mouth was somewhat full of lip but well-shaped. She was surely the
most beautiful woman Twilla had ever seen.

Beautiful and powerful. So strong was the assurance with which she
bore herself that one could well believe that she ruled some dominion
in her own right and owed homage to none.

As she moved toward Ylon his head stopped that swinging, and he
faced her as if he truly saw through his clouded eyes. A perfume as
rich as her jewels and garments heralded her coming. And for Twilla
she had no attention. Her sight was centered on Ylon, and her mouth
moved into a smile, which had Twilla believed more than a hint of
malice in it.

"Well met, Lord Ylon!" Her voice carried almost the same whispering note as the breeze might stir from the leaves overhead. "So you have returned."

She appeared to glide rather than walk and now she was directly before the man, staring him up and down, her expression one of distaste.

"And in what a state you come! Lord or beggar—which are you, traveler?"

For the first time Ylon spoke. "Lotis—" There was recognition in that—and, Twilla believed, something warmer. He might be truly bedazzled as any landboy by some flower woman from the city.

"Lotis—Lotis whom you fled. Ah, Ylon, you earned our anger for that. We believed you well content—with your lot—with me—" She was mocking him now and there was that in her voice which stiffened Twilla. Ylon might be bedazzled but to this one he was only prey—to be used how and when she wished.

"Yes, you must learn your place again, Ylon. You have come to us and therefore ours the judgment. It is your good fortune that we do have a use for you—Come!"

She snapped her fingers as one might summon a hound and Twilla hoped that the bedazzlement did not hold—to ensnare such a man was evil, and that evil had come with this one she believed. Her hand went to the mirror, pressing it against her breast.

The woman had turned and was gliding away and Ylon went into action, falling in behind her.

"No!" Twilla could not understand that sick feeling which gripped her on seeing him so obedient to such a one.

He raised his hand and bent her fingers away from her hold on his smock sleeve, exerting enough pressure as to bring a pain-born cry from her. Nor did his head turn in her direction.

The woman laughed. "Well, little drab, did you think that you had found a fit mate? Know you that this lord's son will get to his knees and lick my shoes, should I require it. We of the Folk set our spells well. This one would be dead, save that he does have a purpose which he can serve. As for you," she stared at Twilla and that perfect face twisted in a sneer. "Though we play games with your kind I do not think any of our men will find you to their taste—"

"No?" Lotis's stare shifted from Twilla to a point over the girl's shoulder. That one word question had come from a deeper voice. The girl looked around.

As Lotis, this newcomer was clearly one of another blood and kind. He was taller than the woman, and there was nothing willowy about his broad shouldered body. However, his hair was of the same black and was confined with a band set with the same glitter of green gems. Those also formed the larger portion of a belt about his narrow waist, confining a short overjacket also of green. This had hanging sleeves lined in a red as rich in hue as the green and those bared arms on which metal cuff bracelets heavily gemmed. His breeches were of the same green as his coat, and even the calf-high boots he wore echoed that shade.

"I called—this one came." Lotis showed teeth in a near snarl. "He is my meat according to our custom. And you cannot gainsay that. Have the pig-faced slut if you will! I take what is mine—Come!" Again she snapped fingers to Ylon who had stood during that exchange as if he had heard nothing of it.

Again she started off and he obediently fell into place at her heels like a trained hound.

"She has no right!" Twilla spoke her thoughts aloud rather than address the man.

"Unfortunately she does," he returned. "His bonds were spun by her and only she can break them, which Lotis will not be inclined to do. She is a highly possessive woman."

Twilla scowled at him. "You think to make me—like that—?" She waved toward Ylon just as one of the swirls of mist came up to cloak his going.

He was looking at her intently as if she were some strange object he had found, one he must study closely for reasons of his own.

"I cannot. You have a power which is not within our knowledge. You are the one our messenger sensed coming over mountain, and again in the hold of the tree slayers. No, our nets cannot, I believe, hold you. But you were led here for some purpose— Are you then a new weapon our enemies have forged for our undoing?"

He spoke calmly enough but Twilla sensed that this was not one she would want to cross. To deal with him truth might be the wisest course.

"Those at the Keep count me no friend, rather a quarry for their hunt."

"And that I believe is the truth." Suddenly he smiled and she could understand how this one could bedazzle any of her sex that he wished to draw into his net.

"I am Oxyle—see let us share names and thus give a weapon into the other's hand."

She remembered Hulde's teaching—a name was a thing of power— it could be used against one. "I am Twilla," she answered promptly, "sometime healer—apprentice to a wisewoman."

He nodded. "Even as I thought. Well, Twilla, will you accept hospitality we offer as we would to kin?"

If she did so there might be hope of getting Ylon free again. She did not know why that was so important to her but it was.

"Yes." She held out her scratched and grimy hand and his closed swiftly about it. The mist swirled up, cocooned them in and she had a sensation that they were in flight.

10

THAT SENSE OF flight lasted for only a flash. Then the walling mist was gone in a puff. They were no longer in the same forest clearing. What fronted them was such a tree as made the awesome giants she had wondered at earlier no more than saplings in girth and height. It was wider than the Keep tower by far. Oxyle had dropped his hold on her and now advanced to stand at the foot of that giant among giants, so eclipsed by the sheer size of the tree as to have appeared to have shrunk to far less than his own inches allowed.

There was another swirling of mist to one side, which gave way to reveal Lotis and Ylon. The woman flashed a venomous look at Twilla.

"So—you are caught now by ugliness," she addressed Oxyle. "I wish you the joy of your bargain."

Though she had spoken to the forest man her attention had not left Twilla and now her eyes seemed to narrow, her full lips thinned to show the tips of white teeth.

"She is not—"

"No, she is not," Oxyle replied. "You are over-swift in any judgment, Lotis. Because you have had success with your present prize, do not believe that all those coming into this land may be of the same kind."

Lotis's hand rose so suddenly that Twilla saw that movement as a flash. In the air between them now swirled out a flutter of something which might be a light scarf borne by a strong wind, it was heading for Twilla—perhaps at eye height. Her own hand went to the hidden mirror.

The spray of silvery motes never reached its goal but rather halted inches away from the girl's face, twisted vainly in coils as if it battled some barrier and then dropped—was gone. There might have been first surprise in Lotis's stare but that was swallowed up by rage.

"What are you bringing among us, Oxyle?" she demanded fiercely. "These dirt grubbers have found themselves a new champion? Is that it? But why do you play their game?"

"I play no games," he answered curtly. "This one who has taken refuge here has power—and not one we can measure."

"Taken refuge," she caught him up, "you meant rather sent to cause mischief. The Council shall—"

"Shall be informed in due time," he replied. "Now let us see to the comfort of our guests."

He passed her as if she had ceased to exist and stood directly within touching distance of the trunk of the great tree. Perhaps he made some sign or muttered some charm, but Twilla neither saw nor heard such. However, there was a parting of the barked surface before him and from that streamed forth a light which was not unlike that of the fullest extent of the moon at the year's height of that power.

The forest man turned to beckon Twilla forward and, refusing to show any wariness before Lotis, she went, so that she passed into the source of that radiance only a step behind her guide.

She was not—Twilla shook her head as if to free it from the silver cobweb of sorcery, which had not bound her.

It was plain that she was no longer in the forest—nor could she be in a tree, no matter how large, for she was standing on a ledge of green and white crystal which magnified the light and sent strange rainbows upward from below. And below—below was what was truly another world!

The light was soft, less fierce than that of the sun, yet it dazzled the eyes as it was reflected back from the smooth green and black-veined boles of other trees, these of a height which might be that of a thrifty and well-tended orchard.

From the ledge there was a short flight of steps leading down into this new world. Those mists which had appeared woven through the true forest in the outer world were here also so Twilla could not gauge how far the land below stretched away for there was no sighting a horizon.

She took the steps with care. Oxyle stood awaiting her at their foot and then led the way along a path. But such a path! This was not beaten earth, round cobbles, dull gray gravel—rather it was like a stream of small gems, all afire and curling on among the trees to vanish in the sweep of mists.

The trees themselves— Twilla drew a deep breath of wonder. Their leaves of many shades of green gave the appearance of having been most skillfully carven from jewels. And fruit of glorious, glittering color hung among them. It was a dream of some vast treasure house such as even the King could not imagine.

The King—Lord Harmond—those from over mountain. Her own world snapped back into her awed mind. If they knew, guessed even, that this was here—what a looting would follow! No wonder the forest "demons" took jealous care of their own.

There was life among the trees also, things with wings rainbow hued, which flitted from bough to bough, along their way. Some dared to swoop down and hold for a moment or two to Oxyle's head or shoulders. They were like butterflies—yes, as to their brilliancy of their wings they were. But those slender bodies—human in appearance, no longer than her middle finger, startled Twilla anew.

Oxyle seemed to pay no attention to them even when they perched on his shoulders. But if they were free with the forest lord they were not so with Twilla. Several had first swung in her direction and then veered hastily away as if they feared she might strike them out of the air.

A few continued in escort even as they emerged on the other side of the orchard of gem fruit into the open and saw before them, half veiled in mists which appeared thicker here, a building of gem veined walls, graceful towers, only momentarily revealed by the mists—as far from the grim stone of the only palace Twilla had ever seen as she could imagine.

There were other of the forest people there, some lounging at ease on the grassy banks of a silver bright stream, over which arched a bridge giving access to the castle. They were clearly interested in the newcomers, rising to meet them.

"Ha, Lotis," a woman near as fair as the one she addressed moved forward. She, too, favored green for her robe as did most of those in that company, but her gems were clear drops of rainbow moonstones, the rarest of stones in the other world. "So you have again your foundling." She laughed. "And a sorry sight he is, my dear. You should keep your possession in better order. Faugh, he stinks." With another laugh she pinched the tip of her flawless nose and walked about Ylon at a short distance.

He stood still, his face empty of all emotion, the seeming blindness of his eyes having now settled in turn once more over his wits.

Twilla did not know why anger came to life within her. She only knew that these women with their jeers were cutting at one helpless and alone. It was as if they were teasing some poor trapped animal. And the man who had struck down his brother to save her, shared with her all the peril of that journey by storm and river, was no animal!

"We have someone else." Now it was a man who drew toward Twilla. "An invader female, eh, Oxyle? Well—one cannot say much for their tastes. No wonder Lotis and the others have such an easy time with invaders. They must be very tired of seeing such faces—"

He came with an insolent stare closer to Twilla, giving her the same degrading inspection as had been turned on Ylon. But he halted suddenly. The sneering half smile vanished from his face. He surveyed Twilla from head to foot and back again and then turned his attention to Oxyle.

"What do you bring among us?" he demanded, coldly hostile now.

"Yes," Lotis raised her voice shrilly. "You may well ask, Farsil. It would seem that the dirt scratchers have perhaps found a new weapon and we have been betrayed by that ever-present curiosity of our Chief in Council—ask him why he dares to bring a wild power here!"

They were encircled by the forest people now, and Twilla saw faces both beautiful and handsome take on the masks akin to the fanatical countenances of the Dandus priests. How strong the influence of the mirror might be she could not tell. She had trusted Oxyle but if all these strange beings were now to unite against her what could she hope to do in defense?

"Twilla!" Startled she looked to Oxyle. "Give me your heart hand—"

Heart hand? At that moment she was not quite sure of his meaning. But she remembered the old belief that the third finger of the left hand offered passage to the heart. Thus she lifted that and allowed him to take a firm grasp of her wrist and turn her palm up.

"Karla—read!" That was an order.

Another woman drew closer. Unlike the others her robe was almost dull in shade, akin to the darker leaves of autumn, and her jewels were red and yellow. Though she showed no signs of age as to hair or face yet, Twilla believed that she was the eldest within this group.

Now she inclined her head and looked down at Twilla's dirty hand in much the same way as Hulde had done before they had parted many tens of days ago. She even pursed her lips a fraction as the Wisewoman did when presented with a problem she must bend her full knowledge and ingenuity to solve.

She extended an index finger but did not quite touch Twilla's flesh, though she moved it as if she traced the lines showing there.

Then her head came up and there was sheer astonishment open to read in her face.

"Moon power—" she said with an explosive breath. "And for us— no danger—perhaps something else—But—" She looked now to Twilla. "Take care, moon's daughter, that when you wield you do so with thought."

A murmur ran around the circle of the forest people and that same astonishment Karla had shown was on most of their faces.

Oxyle released Twilla's wrist. "Do you question now why she stands here?" he demanded.

Lotis was scowling and did not add her voice to their quick chorus of approval. It was plain that what Karla had reported put Twilla, at least momentarily, beyond the malice of Ylon's mistress.

Twilla sat on such a softness of piled cushions as she had never known in her life. Even here, within the castle, there was always that floating mist which parted now and then so some treasure within the room showed clearly, only to be veiled once more.

It had been Karla who had taken over her guidance from Oxyle, led her in through those massive gates and through halls and corridors, showed her a pool on which there floated masses of fragrant petals, set out for her use jars of soft herb-scented cream, banished her rough and travel-stained clothing and brought out a garment of a hue which matched old silver.

That clung around Twilla's thin body now, so soft to the skin beneath that she might be wearing nothing at all. She had taken what precautions she could to conceal the mirror and once more it was in hiding against her body. But Karla, having shown her all the delights of this palace, had left her to herself.

Now Twilla was combing her hair, shaking away the petals of the bathing pool which had caught in the loosened locks, which she had already toweled as dry as she could with the large squares of scented cloth piled beyond the pool, seemingly for that purpose.

She lacked the jeweled splendor of the forest women but for her this robe was rich enough. Ylon—her thoughts turned to him. He had still stood like a hound in leash when Karla had drawn her on.

Twilla frowned, more at her thoughts than the pull of a damp tangle her comb had found. This—this slave Lotis had made—held— It was not the man who had brought her out of the keep, shared with her the struggle on the river and what went thereafter. Then, in spite of his blindness, he had been a staunch support, someone to rely upon. What was he now in Lotis's hold? She grimaced—feeling both pity and shame, and a small quirk of anger.

She rebraided her hair with busy fingers while she thought. So this was what the forest women could do to a man of the invaders! She had not heard of any woman from the farmlands who had been so enticed and netted—was it only the men that they feared enough to attack? And why was a man with a mate immune to their sorcery? She knew so little.

They seemed willing to accept her for now—because of Oxyle and Karla—though she knew that Lotis would stir up trouble if she could. Her face—what if she were to release the mirror mask? Would that have any effect on their hostility—or increase their now lulled suspicions. Perhaps the latter. It would be prudent to keep what secrets she could to herself. In knowledge there was always strength and in concealed knowledge arms for the future.

Karla suddenly appeared within a swirl of mist and Twilla's inward wariness increased. It would seem that these forest born could travel so unseen.

"Moon daughter, there is food—we await your company."

But Karla did not use any mist to place them among that company now. She walked, quite as any lady of the household might, back through the corridors, which in themselves were enough to make a visitor lag and stare. For there were niches in the walls, bordered with frames of gems, and in each stood a figure—some human in appearance, some grotesque, but not to the point of being frightening—rather awakening a need to know more of them.

These also were continually veiled, revealed, and veiled again by the mist. Twilla shook her head, bewildered by what her eyes reported. So they came into a large oval room. Here the very walls were of metal—well polished silver for the most part, but with here and there a panel of fire bright copper on which spiraled lines of symbols. Benches with thick quilted pads of rich green stuff, were at each side of a long table. At the head was a chair which had the opalescent gleam of a pearl-bearing shell. Oxyle arose from that as Karla ushered Twilla in and came toward her, his arm raised a little. Guessing at the honor he would pay her Twilla self-consciously placed her fingers on his wrist as she had seen once one of the Highborn do when led into a merchant's shop in the town.

There were others there, a gathering of colors, glinting gems, voices among themselves seemed to have a singing quality. And, as Oxyle brought her to sit at the top of the bench on his right, there was also Ylon.

Though he was dressed in green, the livery of this strange court, his face now bare of the straggle of beard, his hair in order, he showed no fellowhip with those about him. Rather, he sat staring straight ahead, his eyes still with the blankness of non-sight. Lotis was beside him and even as Twilla slipped on to her designated seat, the forest woman leaned closer and her hand went up to pat Ylon's cheek as she might have done to some pet. But her eyes were on the girl and Twilla found the menace in them easy to read. Lotis was making very plain that Ylon was truly hers.

At her touch he appeared to shiver, but he did not move. Twilla wondered if he were not as much a prisoner as if he sat there in bonds.

"To the branch, to the root, to the trunk, to the crown, may the land bring forth the tree, and the tree shelter well the land. As it has been since the beginning, may it so be!" Oxyle had not reseated himself, instead, he had picked up a silver goblet from the table before him and held it breast high.

Those about Twilla reached for goblets also and she realized that this was a toast which perhaps to the forest people had the solemnity of her own race's casting a drop over the shoulder in honor to the Three in One. Nor could she see anything but goodwill in those words. So she picked up her own goblet and watched for a clue.

Oxyle drank and all those others, including Twilla, immediately raised their goblets to do also. Even Ylon had put forth his hand uncertainly, felt carefully until his fingers touched the goblet that was his, and raised it to his lips.

There seemed to be no other ceremony to their dining. The covered plates down the length of the table were unlidded and she saw fruit and cakes though there seemed to be no meat. However, what she helped herself to proved to be provider that was satisfactory not only to allay hunger but so tasteful as to satisfy all one's needs.

It was not wine in the goblets, she discovered, rather a liquid much thinner, almost like water, but sweet, giving the drinker a feeling of renewed strength. All of the meal was so far removed from the coarse food which had been provided since she had left Varslaad that she relished each bite, finding herself chewing at length to savor the flavor.

That hum of conversation which she had noted on her arrival was to be heard again. Twilla did not recognize this speech, which seemed almost closer to the twitter of birds than words and phrases. But she applied herself to clearing her plate, more interested at the moment in satisfying her hunger.

Ylon sat with an empty plate, his hands not in sight. With a flash of understanding Twilla knew what held him so. He was ashamed to fumble, hunting food, perhaps overturn some dish. And that spark of anger in her flared the stronger. When Lotis beside him, or the man on his other side, made no move to help him, she refused to remain silent any longer.

"Lord," she spoke directly to Oxyle, gaining his attention at once, "you serve one guest well within your halls, why must another go hungry?"

That murmur died away and faces turned in her direction, then eyes slanted to Ylon. Lotis was smiling straight at Twilla as if daring her to carry the attack farther.

"Lord Ylon you say is in some way captive to this Lady of the House. In our world even the lowest of servants goes not hungry when master and mistress dine. Is there then no house honor among you?"

Oxyle's eyes glittered nearly as brightly as the gems in the band about his brow. He looked at Twilla but she could read no anger in that glance. Then he arose, and walked down the room behind the bench on the far side of the table. Reaching where Lotis sat he leaned forward across her shoulder, by his gesture shoving her somewhat aside, and caught up from one plate some cakes, which he placed before Ylon, from another he selected a cluster of berries.

"He who labors goes not empty of plate, Lotis." His words were seemingly impersonal but Twilla thought she caught the hint of reprimand which lay within them. "You have chosen to call this man, by our own laws though he becomes then yours, you also have duties toward him—"

She spat like an angered cat. "Listen to your ugly wench, Oxyle, and you will come to regret it—"

How much farther she might have carried her tirade they were not to know for one of those thicker twists of mist gathered nearly at Oxyle's elbow and when it cleared a man in green and red dress stood there.

"There is black trouble," he announced even as he became fully visible. "Young Fanna found iron—"

Oxyle tensed. Then his hand fell on Ylon's shoulder. With the other he beckoned to Twilla and she hurried to join him.

"You have said that this one can aid us, Lotis—and have done so many times. Now he will prove his worth!"

The mist swirled in about them even as Ylon had been urged to his feet by the grip of the forest lord. They were encompassed by it and again Twilla felt that being not of the world and time she knew.

Whimpering much as an animal in pain might make startled her and aroused her healer's instinct as the mist cleared.

They were out under trees again—in the forest. Before them was a tree with a fresh-hacked gouge in its trunk. At the foot lay an ax, but twisted in a painful curl was one wearing the forest green and as he writhed Twilla was able to see his face. Though she had seen no children among the assembly in the castle this sufferer was plainly much younger in age and still one of the tree shadow dwellers.

11

TWILLA WAS ON her knees beside the twisting body.

"Help me!" she demanded, not looking up to see whom she was calling upon. Her healer's bag—long since lost. What did she have to offer now?

It was Oxyle who joined her, his hands on the shoulders of the boy, turning the young body face up so she could see the damage. Twilla winced. She had seen burns before, stood by Hulde and watched their treatment or even done the soothing herself in these last few years. But these blackened wounds on the hands, seeming to spread even as she looked, to strike up over those thin wrists and into the forearms, were worse than any brand-caused wound she had ever sighted.

"You are a healer—what do you say to this?" Oxyle's voice, for the first time, was sere and cold to her.

Twilla made an uncertain swing of her hands, again she had tried to reach for that bag she did not have.

"Burns—" She leaned closer. The boy's eyes were closed, he no longer made any sound, except that his breath came in ragged pants. "Butter—ease all— But where do I find such?"

Obviously not here. The hands which had sought the missing bag were now at her breast. The mirror—but—such a small chance—and in using it she would be betraying her own defense.

The boy shifted again in Oxyle's hold and gave a faint moan, before his head fell limply to the side. Yes—unlike the nature of true burns those marks were climbing his arms, eating at his flesh!

She brought the mirror out of its hiding place.

"Lift him," she ordered, "across my knees—"

With Oxyle still holding the sufferer's head his body was settled as she ordered, so those twisted and blackened hands and the changed flesh of the arms was directly before her.

Twilla steadied the mirror. The reflecting side of the disk must hang directly above. Yes, in this fashion—still high enough for her to see that reflection clearly in all its horror. She drew a deep breath and then another, willing her world to contract, to exist only on what she saw in the mirror.

She had managed change for herself—but that had been illusion only. What if what she could raise now would be only illusion also? Doubts weakened—she fought.

Into the mirror she forced her full will, see firm healthy flesh, no sign of those searing burns, that blackened skin flaking away to show raw cracks. Flesh unmarked, unseared—

She felt the lift within her, coming from some depths she had not known she sheltered. It was like fire also, but cold—clear— The mirror glinted now, and its bright surface was shining as if the full moon hung overhead.

> *"Power to heal, power for need,*
> *Power to enter, power to seed."*
> *"Let the power come to call*
> *Grow and flourish—tree tall!"*

Another of those jingles but the best she could summon. The mirror was very bright, but its surface no longer reflected. Instead there dripped from it points of even brighter light which it hurt her to watch but she knew that she must—illusion—or power indeed?

Those specks dipped down, like roots growing even as they watched, seeking soil in which to shelter and grow. But she did not follow their descent, her attention was on the mirror.

Twilla swayed. It seemed that her very life force was being harnessed to what she did and yet she held. Dimly she was aware that, even as Oxyle half supported the boy, someone had moved in behind her, was bracing her now trembling body.

"Grow"—she gasped— "Show.

"All well above, and below."

Those roots, what she could see of them were penetrating the blackened skin. No longer were they cool, clean silver, rather they were tainted with a greenish yellow. The mirror shook in her hold as if it would escape what was now drawn toward it, but Twilla kept it steady. Just as that sturdy body behind her, the hands which had come to hold, kept her also as she must be.

The mirror was fighting her, striving to twist and turn, escape what was climbing. Grimly Twilla held. Was she now stilling forever any power which might hold therein—pushing the power she did not understand past what it could control? She could not tell but her stubborn will held her to this.

The greenish roots were being absorbed back into the surface. That no longer shone. It was smeared, filmed. Twilla cried out. The fingers which held the mirror, there was a burning— Whether she had succeeded or not—she could no longer hold. Out of her grasp skidded the mirror and, with its going, she was so utterly drained that she wilted as might a plant pulled from its rooting.

Strong arms around her, a body behind hers holding her steady. She could see only dimly, as if the brightness of the mirror had affected her sight.

But the body supported across her knees stirred and was drawn away from her. Twilla blinked and blinked again, somewhat clearing her sight. However, she was too weak to move, though she forced out a shaking hand toward the mirror now so dulled, as if centuries had worn across its surface. It was heavy, so heavy she could barely lift it, and—dead—dead—

Weakness, the knowledge of her loss, brought tears. She was crying. A hand raised to touch her cheeks, coming over her shoulder, leaving its hold about her. Fingers calloused from sword play drew down her skin.

"She has given much. What have you taken, forest born?"

Ylon's voice, no longer that of Lotis's hound—now that of the man who had shared peril and river death with her.

"We give her our blessing for Fanna—Fanna has not died the iron death!"

Once more Twilla blinked, forced the last of those foolish tears from her eyes. Facing her, holding the boy much as Ylon was holding her, was the forest lord. And those hands which had been seared into crooked claws, were clear, unblemished, though the boy was limp against Oxyle's shoulder.

With shaking hands Twilla brought the mirror close to her once more. She found her wide spread fingers stroking its surface even as they had done for so long, once more polishing, smoothing what appeared wholly without light.

Laying the boy down upon the leaf carpet Oxyle got to his feet. Now he spoke to Ylon.

"Iron is yours. Take it out of our land so that no more may be so entrapped."

When the young man would have moved Twilla caught at him. "NO!" And then she looked up at Oxyle. "If that ax be poisoned, you shall not ask that of this man."

"It is not poison for one of his kind. They deal in iron and it does not turn on them. Only for us it is suffering and death. Lotis claimed the life of this one so that he might serve us so—taking away that which would be death."

"Yes." That was Lotis, though she was not in the line of Twilla's sight and the girl was too wearied to turn her head to look at the other. "Get you to the iron, bondman, and see it out of our wood! Let the so-gifted one see to herself, she has done well enough before." There was raw spite in that.

"Let me," Oxyle had come to their side and now knelt, steadying Twilla. She felt Ylon move away. But she caught at the Forest Lord and drew herself up to her knees, turning so that she could see Ylon now on his feet, his hands outstretched. The tree where the ax head had sliced was to his right as he blundered forward.

"To your right." Twilla's spurt of anger gave her a remnant of strength. She clawed at Oxyle bringing herself wavering to her feet.

"He cannot see!" She pounded one fist against the Forest Lord's arm. "May the Blight of Pagorn be upon you—he cannot see!"

"For me he will." Lotis had glided up behind Ylon. Now she thrust him forward until he brought up heavily against the gouged tree. His hands ran down the trunk until they fell upon the ax head. As he lifted something else came with it, a brown dagger, its hilt a mass of green stones, the gleaming blade snapped across.

Ylon had the iron free. Lotis moved again giving him another shove. "Out with it!" she ordered. "Out of our land!"

Twilla strove to free herself from Oxyle's hold and then she turned on the Forest Lord.

"He cannot see—he serves you and you allow this?"

Oxyle looked at her strangely—almost as if he knew a pinch of shame and then he gave another order:

"Vestel, lead him to the fringe. See he has a clear path."

As the man who had summoned them to the site hurried to obey, Lotis fronted Oxyle and Twilla.

"He is mine! By custom I claim him, and would you question the rites and elders, Oxyle? Leave me my bondman or else you will need to go up against the Five Laws yourself."

"Will he not serve you better," demanded Twilla, "if you give him back his sight?"

Lotis's beautiful mask of a face drew into a haggish grimace.

"Look to yourself, dirt slut! What I do with my property is none of your concern. Also—" Now her scowl smoothed into a sly, evil smile. "I think you are no longer armed against—me!"

She raised her hand so swiftly Twilla could hardly mark its motion and throw. There came a sparkling dart seemingly born out of the very air itself.

The mirror—the mirror lay now at her feet, still dull, diminished. She had no shield—if the mirror had been her shield before.

She was whirled aside, Oxyle's hold sending her out of the path of that bolt so fast that she stumbled and fell to her knees. She groped out, found the mirror and drew it toward her.

"This one," the chill was back in the forest lord's voice, "is kin-saver. Hold that in your mind, Lotis—there is to be no spelling raised against her."

Lotis laughed. "Ah, so the swine-faced beauty is for you, Oxyle? A perverted taste. But—since you have claimed her, take the slut into your service."

"Not so—she has taken all of us into hers!" he countered. "Fanna lives because of her powers. Can you match that?"

"Faugh!" she whirled, the full skirts of her robe flying out as she turned away. However, Twilla thought dully, she had not admitted any defeat. Why the woman was so set against her—Ylon? Could it actually be, in spite of what Oxyle had told her, Lotis's hold on Ylon was not as secure as she had thought it to be? He had come to her—the mirror turned in Twilla's hands as she sought the cord to restore it to its place about her neck again—he had come to her, sustained her with the strength of his body as she fought that battle with death. And certainly Lotis had not wished that.

There was a murmur which was not the wind in the tree leaves, that mimic of faraway voices which the forest held. Twilla looked around. Behind her were gathered others from that company which had sat at the feast table. One of them, a woman wearing a robe the silver of frost-touched wood, her gems crystal, knelt now by the still unconscious boy, her arms about him, his head against her shoulder.

She was singing in a voice so low Twilla could catch only the quaver of the tune—no words. And as she so sang she rocked her body back and forth a little as if she held in her arms some child she would soothe.

Oxyle had gone to the gouged tree. He stooped and picked up the broken dagger.

"The boy drew his own peril upon him. He strove to master iron with this. He has paid dearly for his foolishness—let none remember it against him. Musseline," he came to the woman with Fanna, "call him into wakefulness—we would know if the poison has left him unmarked. As a mother summons, do."

For a moment she looked mutinous and then she nodded. The tune she had crooned became louder with a faster beat. Fanna's eyelids fluttered, opened wide. He was staring up into the face of the woman who held him.

"Mother—?" He made a question of that word. Then suddenly he raised both hands and stared at them.

"I was caught—" The shadow of fear still was on him. "The tree cried out in pain and I would have helped—but—I still live."

"You still live," she answered gravely. "It was because Moon daughter drew out the poison of those from away."

He shifted a little in her hold and looked wonderingly at Twilla where she still sat limply; the mirror was on its cord but still within the grasp of her hands.

"It—it is a thing unknown—" he said. Again he shifted in those arms which cradled him. "Moon daughter, there is blood debt between us. Mighty is the power you summon—great are you in its service."

Twilla shook her head slowly. "I did what was to be done. I am a healer, and a healer turns not away from those needing her."

There was a crackling of brush behind to their left and all of them looked to where Ylon came back at his slow and cautious pace, Vestel at his elbow. Lotis also pushed forward. However, he seemed, in spite of his set stare, to look beyond her to where Oxyle stood as if he could truly see the forest lord.

"But," one of the other men of that company pushed forward now, "who set the iron to our boughed brother? The wound is fresh. Did you not sight them beyond the trees?"

"Only marks of their going," returned Ylon's escort. "The tracks of one of their carts."

"You hold this border, Vestel," Oxyle said to the man. "What barrier was set here?"

"A monger." Vestel clicked his fingers even as Lotis had done to summon Ylon. But what came lumbering out of a twist of mist a little beyond was such a thing as might inhabit a nightmare.

It was taller than any man of that company and yet it did not stand fully erect. Rather it stooped a little, its demon mask of a head clamped against shaggy pelted shoulders, its long arms a-swing ready to seize. Its barrel of a body and thick legs suggested strength enough to crush such prey as it would choose. Reddish wild eyes showed in the caverns of its skull sockets.

Spittle dripped from its half open jaws, where tusks showed yellow-green. It gave a guttural grunt.

Once more Vestel clicked fingers and the hellish thing was gone. Illusion, guessed Twilla, and yet she could not altogether be sure. Did illusions leave such a stink behind to foul the air? However, had that appeared she could well believe that any plain dweller would have taken to his heels—if he had not been totally frozen in place by fear.

"Effective," commented Oxyle, "but the invader got in one blow. Slow—Vestel—too slow."

"Yes," the other agreed. "Too slow. That shall be seen to."

"We leave you to that task," Oxyle commented. Before Twilla could move he was on her, drawing her up against him as the mist curdled about them.

Then they were back in that feasting hall where the table still bore most of its burden of food and drink. But Twilla wanted only to rest, to rest and perhaps forget, if sleep was given to her, that what she still clung to might now be dead of any power and she left defenseless among a people she did not understand and could fear—if she let herself.

They might have guessed her state for Karla came to her, putting an arm around the girl's shoulders and drawing her away, back down those treasure-walled halls, seeing her at last established in a chamber where there was a bed formed like a well-open lily, fashioned of some pearl gleam material, into which she crawled, the petals seeming to close a little as if in protection around her worn body.

She dreamed she was back in Hulde's room of many mysteries, sitting on her stool, polishing her mirror. Greykin watching her with great eyes. And she was singing again that childish rhyme as her fingers moved without ceasing:

"Up and down, out and in.
Sun's path and widdershin.

Power answering to the call
Of flesh and blood and inner all.''

Only when she looked down at her work she saw only a dull platter-like piece, there was no answering life in it.

She called to Hulde, fear rising in her. But there was no answer. Greykin yawned as if this was no affair of his.

Twilla turned again to the polishing, first as fast as she could move her hand, and then, remembering Hulde's often repeated warning of haste making waste, she set herself once more to follow the slower rhythm of her jingle.

Somehow she was sure that what she held was not truly dead, the fault lay in her not this focus for power. She had overstepped the boundaries of her learning, tried too much. Would it ever answer to her again?

"Up and down, in and out—"

She could feel the heavy beat of a heart set pounding by growing fear. No—that she must control, even as she controlled the movements of her fingers.

"Hulde?" She called as she had always done in her time of need.

There was no answer. Greykin yawned once again and then looked straight at her as if in reproof.

No, the mirror was her magic, had been since Hulde had given it to her and only she could deal with it. Once more she set her hand to the slow even strokes of the polishing. Her fingertips burned, there were no protecting pads on them now, yet she still kept to what she must do—

Do? There was nothing to be done. Around her now enfolded darkness even as the mists could enfold the forest people and she lost touch and hearing also—finally lost herself.

12

SHE DID NOT return to Hulde's safe world. Though the darkness about shifted as if it had taken on the powers of the forest mists. Twilla sensed menace in that shifting. She could no longer feel the mirror or was aware of her own body—only that which was the inner part of her was now threatened.

Something as beastlike as that illusion set to guard the Wood prowled about in that dark. Moon—mirror—she sought them both with all her strength. The dark shifted again, pushing in upon her first on one side and then the other. But for all its slavering hunger it could not reach her.

Twilla made a great effort, reached—for the body which seemed gone from her. A hand—she envisioned a hand, a stretch of fingers, the wrist from which it sprung, the arm of which that wrist was a part, the shoulder—She was back—back in her body!

Now she opened her eyes. Above her was a puzzling pearl-lustered curve, she blinked at that but it did not vanish. Then memory returned and she pulled herself up in that flower bed, looking out into a room which was carpeted with the thick green of what might be moss, walled by entwining screens of ferns.

Her fingers rasped on a light cover which was over her and had now slid to her waist. She flinched at sudden pain and looked down. Her fingertips were raw, skin broken, with small clots of blood.

There was a weight resting on one knee near that hand. The mirror.

It was no longer blank, dead. Nor was it the bright silver she had always seen either. Instead it gleamed now with a coppery glint as if the substance of it was co-mingled with her blood, brought so to a brazen state.

Twilla was wary of the change—afraid at first to touch it. When she nerved herself to that she found that it lived again, though the throb which answered her held a different beat, heavier.

Raising it she held it to view her own face—her own face? Or the face she had drawn upon herself? One she was not sure now she could ever banish again.

There was a reflection there, but clouded, showing no more than a faintest of shadows. Instinctively she rubbed her fingers across the mirror surface and winced at the pain in her abraded flesh.

The passage of those had left traces of blood which sank instantly into the coppery shine. Blood was a mighty source of power, to be used very sparingly. The Dark called upon blood to feed it. Had she taken a misstep down the Left Path which Hulde had so often warned her against doing? Even if the blood so shed was her own and not that of any sacrifice—?

Trembling Twilla hung the mirror once more in its place and pulled herself out of the cupped embrace of the flower bed. She felt as weak as if she had walked all the way over mountain, and when she tried to stand she had to hold onto the petals at her side. She knew hunger too, like a gnawing in her middle, and her mouth and throat felt as dry as if she had not drunk in days.

As if it had been known that she would waken so there was a table not far away on which were set out a goblet in the form of the same pearl white flower image as the bed, a disk which might be formed of leaves chipped from emeralds.

Twilla lurched a step or two, reached a stool set beside that table and dropped heavily upon that seat. Her hand shook as she picked up the goblet so that its clear contents swished back and forth, slopping over to spatter her fingers and she had to steady with the other to bring it to her lips.

It was that same drink which had refreshed her at the feast. Now it seemed even greater as a restorative. She gulped it down, so fast some of it dribbled across her chin. But even as she felt it descend her dry throat she knew a strengthening renewal—it might be some much-trusted concoction of a healer's brewing.

With half of it down her she was able to sit straight, reach with a hand which no longer shook for the cakes on the plate. They were crisp and flavorsome, and she ate with a greed new to her until she had cleaned the plate, emptied the goblet.

Once so refreshed Twilla felt herself again. But she remained seated, glancing about the chamber. There were no windows to break the fern screens nor was there any door. Beautiful as it was, this place could be as much a prison as that rough-walled cell in the keep.

With care she forced herself to open memory wide. All which had happened since she and Ylon had fled the invaders' village she tried to recall in detail. However, had not Oxyle named her Kin-saver?

Lotis—

That flick of memory might have been a summons for a section of the wall screen pushed to one side. However, she who stood there was not Lotis but Karla.

"You are yourself once more, Moon daughter—" the forest woman said—not a question, a statement she seemed to know was the truth.

Twilla opened her mouth to assent to that, and then remembered the mirror. What powers this other woman might possess she could not record, but if she herself was to claim more than she could summon it might well be dangerous for the future.

"I am restored in body."

Karla had come to stand before her. "Those who drink of the forest's life," she made a small gesture to the goblet, "find it good. But one is more than body—Moon's Daughter—"

"Moon!" Twilla caught up that word. "Have you any check upon the moon, you who live beneath the trees? Does it wax, does it wane, hangs it in full glory now?"

"It begins to wane. We are not blinded to the night power. If you would see, come—"

Twilla arose quickly but she was not to follow Karla down one of those corridors, rather the mist swirled in and again they were transported in the strange way of this other race.

When the tendrils of the mist again released them they were in a far different place than that luxurious chamber where Twilla had rested. This chamber had walls of rock and in its center was a pool. Overhead was the open sky—a night sky—and in the pool shimmered indeed the disk of the full moon, so bright, so easy to be seen in all its glory as Twilla had never looked upon it before. It might have been drawn nearer to the earth it encircled at this spot alone so that the strange markings, which dimpled its surface, were plain for any eye to see.

She fumbled to bring forth the mirror. There was no reason to try to keep it hid since she had put it to use to save Fanna. The sullen coppery surface of it looked dirty, flawed, when she held it out over the water. Then, because she could only grope and test, strive to find her way through that which she did not understand, Twilla turned it over so that the brazed, blooded surface it showed might reflect the glory in the water.

It cast no shadow upon the moon reflection there, she was a little surprised. Sing—but what song would draw the virtue of that reflection up into the smirched mirror?

> *"Silver bright, in the night,*
> *Give freely of the light.*
> *Let blood and pain*
> *No longer stain—"*

Child's words, a child's rhyming, but all she had ever been able to summon for spell singing.

She did not rub her sore fingers across the surface now, for she would have had to withdraw it from the moon in the pool to do that. Rather she turned the mirror itself around and around, spinning it first right then left and then back again.

Into her need for what must be done Twilla poured all of her strength. Nor dared she look at the mirror's surface, rather she kept her attention fixed upon the pool.

There was an odd sensation beginning, a tingling in her hands. And—out of the air about her sounded a contented whir like the song of a spinning wheel.

She dared look now. The brazen stain was gone—silver bright again. Had the moon in the pool pulled from it the poison even as it had drawn that death from Fanna? How could she tell—she had so little knowledge.

With a cry of joy she clasped the mirror once more tightly to her and looked at Karla with shining eyes.

"Healed!"

The forest woman nodded. "Are you not a healer? Why do you then doubt what can be done when it must?"

"You—helped." Twilla arose from her knees. "You—have power, like Hulde—you have it."

Karla smiled. "To each her own talents, Moon Daughter. Ours lie with the Wood and within the Wood—yours draws nourishment from a different source. There are ill powers also and those have come into the land—those of your blood have brought them hither. Though they do not know as yet just how much harm they can do—"

"With the iron?" Twilla interrupted.

"That and perhaps other things. We can only wait and see."

They entered the mist again and it bore them away from the moon chamber. When it released them they were in a corridor. Instead of the walls bright with niched treasures and jeweled banding, these were plain of decoration. As they went they passed three doors. Each had no sign of latch or way to open, each was dust-marked, and on each there was inlaid a symbol in red and black, something oddly threatening when one looked upon it.

Karla must have noticed Twilla's curious glance at each as they passed, for now she spoke:

"Time has a way of turning upon itself as a serpent coils. Once we faced another danger—not from over mountain but within our own holding. We won a victory then—at a cost. What you see are in truth set there to remind us that even though we won, we also lost. For in no warfare is there ever a true victory."

She said no more as if it were a subject that made her uncomfortable. A turn to the right brought them out of that corridor, through another wandering swirl of mist into the same bright luxury which seemed to make up the living quarters of the forest people.

They came by such ways out of the castle and into that land of gem flowers and trees and the small flitting spirits. A number of those sped toward them as they came into the open, encircling them and Twilla could hear faint high-pitched sounds which must mark speech. Though they looked human as to form, except for their wings, she believed that they were of a different species altogether.

She impulsively held out her hand and one of the spirits, a female, landed on tiptoe. The tiny body had some weight, but it was very light. Twilla's fingers had curled up a little unconsciously though she was careful not to try to grasp the creature. The winged one reached up and touched one of Twilla's abraded fingers. She turned her head a little and shook it as if to signal pity. Then she whirled about and was gone with a flash of rainbow wings, two of her companions taking off as swiftly after her.

There were forest women seated on cushions in the open. One held a book as if she had been reading aloud and the others sat with busy hands. Before each was a short trough of some green stone and into these they were pressing seeds taken in what appeared to be set order from the circle of bowls set within reach. They looked up to beckon and Karla went to join them, Twilla following somewhat uncertainly after. She still felt ill at ease with these women. Though none of them except Lotis had shown any hostility, still she knew that she came from those they bitterly resented and hated, and it was hard to believe that they would accept her presence willingly among them.

Karla dropped down beside the reader and then made an urgent motion for Twilla, which she could not overlook. But she settled herself outside their circle. However, no sooner had she done so than the flyers gathered once more about her and three of them—surely the three which had left so abruptly—reappeared. Each embraced an armload of leaves almost as long as their slender bodies. Twilla caught a familiar scent—Ill Bane—the herb so precious, the answer for so many ills. Wonderingly she placed her injured hand on her knee palm up. Straightway the three came down around it, twisting the leaves between their tiny hands and then rubbing the half pulp on her fingers.

Ill Bane—she could feel the virtue of the herb as they so carefully anointed her fingertips. Ill Bane was so rare that Hulde had only a few brittle bits of dried leaves which she guarded above all her healing harvests. And this was fresh—perhaps other herbs could be found— Her healer's bag, long gone, and without it she felt that a portion of herself was missing; it might be assembled again.

The sprite had taken half-pulped leaves from her two companions and carefully anointed all the fingers. Twilla cautiously raised her other hand and held the index finger out to the flyer as she had done with the last leaf, letting its mangled remains drift down to Twilla's knee.

"Heart thanks to you, small healer," Twilla said softly, feeling somehow that full voice might seem a roar to those small ears.

The sprite looked up at her, gave a brisk nod, which in its way reminded Twilla strongly of Hulde. Her lips parted and Twilla caught a very high trill of sound, far beyond her powers to hear in full. Then a small hand was laid for a moment on the finger she had held out, bringing warmth which was fleeting as the sprite took wing.

There was another sound now, a murmur from the gathered forest women. They were all giving her full attention, their tasks forgotten for a moment. It was Karla who spoke so that Twilla could catch words.

"The Asprite wish you well."

Twilla turned her injured hand around. Some of the bruised leaf pulp still clung to her skin. The feeling of heat and dull pain were gone.

"I am indebted," she said slowly. "They used Ill Bane—that is very rare and hard to find. In my country it is a treasure. I have lost my healer's bag, with it went what I have to serve my talent. Tell me, are there other herbs to be harvested here? Feverbanish, sleep giving, those to heal and those to cherish the weak?"

"You have another healing tool—" Karla looked to where the mirror again hung against her body. "What need you of leaves, roots, flowers and their like?"

"I would deal with what I know best until I learn more," she answered with the truth. "Can the ills of your people be ended as this was done?" She raised her hand, palm out, so they could see that the redness had gone from the fingertips even as the pain had been drawn out.

"We have our healing, yes. Perhaps in a little it may be akin to your herbs, Moon Daughter. Darsia," she spoke to the woman still holding the book, "such things are more truly of your knowledge."

The woman regarded Twilla level eyed. There was neither welcome nor rejection to be read in her beautiful mask of a face.

"Time and enough for many things," she said ambiguously.

There was a stir of those who had been listening to her. Now they handled spindles, ready to draw thread from masses of substance over which played rainbow lights that appeared to have no true color any more than water of a forest pool.

"How goes the hunt?" one of them asked suddenly giving a graceful twirl to her thread.

Darsia spread the book flat on one knee, pressed her hand flat on the open pages, and closed her eyes. Her lips were moving but there was no sound, if she read in this strange way Twilla had not the ability to understand.

A moment or so later Darsia opened her eyes. Now there was a faint emotion on her face, a glimmer of frown.

"The dirt diggers have come to the river," she reported. "Our illusions cannot hold there. But what they do I cannot understand—they wade out into the water, scoop up the sand and gravel and shake it back and forth in pans—"

"What do they do, Moon Daughter?" Karla demanded directly of Twilla and once more she was the center of their attention.

She must accept that in a manner of her own Darsia was seeing some new threat of invasion. But—scooping up gravel, wading in the river—at least they were not threatening the trees—but what *were* they about?

"This is something of which I know nothing—" she was beginning and then interrupted herself. Last year she and Hulde were up in the rolling hills to the north of Varslaad herb hunting, and they had seen a man and woman—wearing the rough clothing of the miners. But they had not been digging—they had been squatting to shift through the sands of a small stream which wore its way down from the mountains.

"They hunt gold!" She could not be absolutely sure of that answer, but it was close enough to what she had seen with Hulde that day. "The mountain waters bear down with them much which has been loosened up above where men have not gone. The heavier pieces of such—stone and the like—sink to the bottom of the stream," she was recalling, trying to make clear what Hulde had told her. "And in some streambeds there are uneven places which catch and hold rolling bits. If one delves therein and shifts well, there is gold—even rough gems to be found."

"Gold!" Karla fingered the stuff of one of her own heavy bracelets. "In these from over mountain, these delvers in the dirt, is there also such a hunger?"

"A great hunger," Twilla nodded. "Gold is highly priced. The King claims all such finds for the crown, but those finding are given also awards—so they seek the farther always."

"And illusions cannot abide over running water," Darsia said sharply. "The guards watch but how can a barrier be set up across the river? This is a matter for the Council—perhaps the greater assembly. Moon daughter, it would appear that the greed which eats at your people will never end. They would assault the forest, now they would break our lands in another way."

"I am Varslaad born," Twilla answered steadily. "But I was apprenticed to a Wisewoman, and I have no liking for what is being done here over mountain. There are others of like mind, but I fear they are few—"

"We want none such here where we have fought for our peace and freedom!" snapped Darsia. She closed her book with a sharp crack.

What she might have added was never to be said—though Twilla wondered if her fragile standing with these women might not have been speedily broken by some heated words classing her with those in the open lands.

Oxyle appeared on the castle bridge and something in the speed with which he strode toward them caught their full attention.

"Darsia," he came straight to the seated woman still holding her book, "there is a shadowing—where and why?"

13

DARSIA FINGERED THE right-side edge of the closed volume she held, there might have been some mark there for her guidance for she opened it and once more held it flat with palm pressure while she hunched above it, eyes closed.

"Spelling—" she said.

"Who and why?" demanded the forest lord.

"Lotis, but she has barriers. I cannot read beyond those settings."

"She has the outlander with her?" again that came swift and sharp.

Darsia took longer to answer this time. "I think not. There is no feel of him."

"Where?" Oxyle added a third question.

"Far ash, broad oak, three pines—" Her eyes remained closed, yet she might well have been reading that off the pages her hands covered.

He stood, looking beyond her now. "That is border land," he said slowly. "Has her bondman made it to freedom again? Well, we shall see!"

He passed Darsia in two long strides to stand over Twilla. "Blood can call to blood," he said. "If she plays tricks with this lordling then perhaps you can sniff out which ones."

And the mist came at some unuttered call to encircle and enwrap them both.

Once more they were in the forest of her own time and world. And on the very fringe of it. She saw that the trees were not so set in threatening barricade and immediately before them, beyond a thin curtain of brush, was indeed the open land.

Twilla had become so used to the dimmer light which was a part of the true forest, and of the hidden land it concealed, that the full blast of a midday sun half blinded her for the moment.

Of Ylon there was certainly no sign, and if Lotis was near she kept in concealment. But out in the open there was something moving.

The grass was tall but it wavered and fell before the determined forward push of a child. A girl child with a reddish braid bouncing on her thin shoulders. Her face was freckled and she stared before her intently as if she searched for something of great importance.

Then she leaned forward and Twilla saw her straighten up in triumph again, clasped in her hand a brilliantly scarlet flower of gem brightness in the light. The child laughed and held tight to her trophy, then advanced some steps to pluck out of the concealing grass another such find, this as golden as the other was red.

The third time she found a flower Twilla realized that this path was bringing her straight into the woods and she understood the meaning of that—a trap—Lotis had baited a trap and was drawing the small girl in.

"Stop her!" She caught at Oxyle's sleeve, gave it an imperative tug.

"I cannot." His eyes were ablaze. "Lotis has set the spell, only she can break it. Like to that laid on your lordling this is of her weaving and only she can stop it. Long ago this was decided so and the *law* holds—"

The child had another trophy, she had thrown out her freckled arm to push aside the bush. Already the shadow of the forest touched her.

Something arose in the air among the trees, twisting as might a frond of the mist. As that passed out into the sun it appeared formed of flashing motes. It passed well above the child's head as she stooped to retrieve another flower, then dropped down behind her and was gone.

However, of Lotis there was no sign, though Twilla was sure that that shining thread of cloud had been of her weaving. Nor did the child seem aware of what had happened. Only Twilla, watching so closely, saw that shimmer a short way out in the open and she guessed that it formed a barrier—either against the child's retreat or for any who would come in search.

Suddenly the child stopped short. She was already into the shadow of the trees, and she looked up and around her as if she had awakened from some sleep. Her small face became a mask of fear. She must have realized that she had entered a place which had long been forbidden to her.

Lotis was not going to entrap this one! Blind her—twist her wits—Anger was hot in Twilla, sending her out into within touching distance of the child.

"Little one—"

Her voice must have broken through the paralysis of fear. The small girl dropped her flowers, turned toward Twilla. Then her eyes went even wider, she shrank back away from the healer.

"No—no!" Her voice shrilled up into a scream. "I will be good—no!"

Before Twilla could grasp her she threw herself to one side and into the edge of the brush, her arms out as she frantically pawed at branches which left red scratches on her sunburnt skin as she fought her way in the other direction.

Mist swirled—she was caught up—gone! Lotis had gathered in her prey.

Twilla turned upon Oxyle. "What will she do with that child?"

"Bind her to what she wishes. It seems that the lordling is no longer so tightly tied to her, he has shown signs of rebellion. She wants a more pliable servant—"

"Do you not realize," Twilla spoke then in a tone which she hoped would make a deeper impression than any of the threats and demands she longed to throw at him, "that by entrapping a child she has stirred up far more rage against you all? Even an animal will fight to the death for its cub. Lotis has brought down on you now what may be your doom.

"Let me go—tell me where to track her—the child must be freed—returned—as quickly as possible."

"True—all of what you say is the truth. However, you know nothing of our ways, Moon Daughter. We have a geas set upon us so that only when the full Council meets and there is an accusation brought and answered, can any one of us interfere with another's spelling. That Lotis has passed the border of good judgment—that is so. And she will be made to answer—"

"When?" demanded Twilla. "After she has blinded that child, twisted her wits as they have told me you are able to do with those who invade your land? Time—"

"Time—" He nodded and there was a shadow on his face. "Time is both a friend and an enemy—and can serve either for good or ill."

"If she had only not run—"

"She looked at you and saw what she thought to see here—a monster."

"What?" Twilla stared at him, open mouthed, so astounded that for a moment she could not find any words.

"Have you forgotten your own powers, Moon Daughter? What face do you wear?"

"My face—?" Her hands flew to her cheeks. Ugly—the ugliness she had drawn upon herself. She had thought to make herself repulsive enough to disgust—perhaps it also was such as to frighten.

Slowly she felt for the mirror, drew it forth and looked into its again shining surface—and saw. Yes, she had wrought well, very well. Though she had not the rampant horror of that boundary monster illusion she did not—even to herself now—look human. It was as if her visioned face had, during the days and nights she had worn it, developed stronger and rougher lines—truly a child afeared to begin with would flee from her.

And if she were to be able to confront Lotis, find her with her prey, Twilla did not doubt that the forest woman could use her own beauty to deepen the ensorcellment which was a part of the binding of those so stolen.

The need for that near beastly mask was gone. She did not really know why she had still clung to it. Or rather she did—because the inner fear pricked at her that she had not the power to undo what she had so swiftly and ignorantly done.

Twilla was lashed by the need to follow Lotis, but what good would that do if the child still feared her.

Oxyle had taken a step or two away. He was frowning, but his attention was no longer for Twilla, rather upon some churning of his own thoughts.

"Come—" he said as if he suddenly remembered that she was there. "The Council must know—"

"Wait—" she said quickly. "Where has Lotis gone?" She must have some direction, for certainly she was not going to leave the child in those hands.

Oxyle shrugged. "To any number of places," he returned. "She has what she wants and she will see that it is prepared for the use she wishes. Come!" That last was an abrupt order.

She was well used now to the swirling of the mist, that momentary journey through any space. And she had no choice but to take it.

The castle hall. After the brightness of the sun brightened meadow the light seemed dim. Oxyle had left her, going swiftly to that table where they had feasted. He sketched a gesture in the air and there sounded a rustling as of breeze-swept leaves.

Let him to his council if that is all he was empowered to do. Twilla was not bound by these Laws of theirs though she was certainly not sure how much she had to call upon in the way of attack and defense.

She swung up the mirror again, stared deeply into it. Not to see her mask of ugliness but something else—that cave-like chamber in which she had caught the moon's splendor. She might not be able to summon mists to waft her hither and thither but perhaps she had a guide of use.

There was a flicker across the silver expanse. She was already walking toward the far door of the room, out into the hall of treasures. As she went the flicker deepened, took on more substance. Setting all her dependence on it, Twilla passed from one corridor to another, twice going down unembellished passages which had those sealed and symboled doors.

Time ceased to have any meaning, she might have paced so for hours—perhaps even longer—there seemed to be no end to the inner maze of the castle ways. As Hulde's room, the inside was far greater than it might at first seeing be.

The mirror flashed as a lash of lightning, blindingly brilliant. Then Twilla rubbed at smarting eyes before she could make out that she stood again in the moon chamber. Though the orb must be missing from the reflecting pool now since it was day without.

Missing in its entirety, no, she saw as she drew near. But it was a moon on the wane—diminished from its full splendor. A waning moon—she had used such to set the pattern that she wore. Could that also release it?

Twilla crouched beside the pool. This time she did not hold forth the mirror to reflect what lay in the still water, rather she held it before her face. With all the strength she could summon she strove to look upon the mask she had wrought and destroy it.

But there was no change—ugliness—it held. Twilla began to shiver. Indeed she had sealed herself into a trap with her recklessness.

Her eyes—they were not small, red-rimmed, near hairless of lash; her nose—it was straight not swollen into a sow's upturned snout—there were no pock marks on her cheeks. What she saw was—NOT!

> *"Time will sever, time does wait*
> *She who dares can question fate.*
> *Let all be as once it seemed,*
> *This I see only dream."*

She pulled the words out of hiding in her memory, raised her voice and sang them imperatively as she would have given orders to some companion ready for battle.

Twilla heard the ripple of water as if the pool was rising to answer her. But her eyes clung to the mirror.

"Ill done, well begun
Born under moon, worn under sun,
Break the mask that cloaks me
Let moon charm answer me!"

Was there a troubling of that reflection? Twilla's breath caught in what was close to a sob. Yes—oh, yes!

The pock marks were gone, her nose—her eyes—she lacked the beauty of the forest women but she was no longer one a child would run from. A child—Lotis—and the child—!

As she lowered her trembling arms Twilla caught sight of the pool. There was no moon! She might have wiped it through its waning into nothingness. For a moment she felt a coldness in her. So much—so much she did not know! Had she once more taken a reckless stride without thought?

But there was a need—the child—

Twilla got to her feet clumsily. Even as it had been when she had treated Fanna so now that exhaustion weighed upon her. Still she could not stay here.

When she turned slowly around examining the walls of the moon chamber she could see no doors. Karla had brought them here and taken them out in the mist. She had entered somehow with the aid of the mirror. Therefore—surely the mirror would take her out!

That was the side—she must have come through somewhere there. Twilla walked purposefully toward the blank expanse of stone, the mirror outheld with its reflecting side toward what seemed solid rock. And she walked through.

Once back in the corridor she leaned against the nearest wall panting, the mirror sliding from her grasp to hang dangling from its cord looped now around her wrist. It was even darker here—there were no traces of the light mist which fought shadows elsewhere. But she remembered the way she had come and now she forced herself to stand free from the wall and retrace her path.

She had transversed several of the maze passages when she lost that trace of memory. Slowly she brought up the mirror, tried to focus on it a mental picture of the great hall. But the mirror remained obstinately blank—not even her own features showed there now.

There was nothing to be done but to try her luck at guessing and that she set to. It was at a cross passage where she was offered three ways that she finally realized she could go no farther and slumped, to sit with her back against the wall, her head resting on her hunched knees.

A sound disturbed the half stupor she had fallen into. Steps, slow ones, almost as uncertain in their rhythm as she herself felt. Twilla raised her head.

Ylon! He was edging along, his hand out against the wall as a guide, the strained look about his sightless eyes which she remembered only too well. Twilla scrambled up.

"Ylon!"

He stopped, his head came up as he faced her.

"Twilla—Twilla!" He moved outward from the sustaining wall his hands outheld as if to feel for her. She hastened to grasp the nearest.

"I am here—though I do not know where 'here' may be," she said with a shaky little laugh.

"These are the twist ways," he told her. His hand had turned in hers so that now he grasped her wrist in a tight hold.

Now it was his turn to laugh, though his was a harsh, rusty sound. "Lotis makes good use of these upon occasion."

"Lotis! Ylon—she has taken a child, a little girl, drawn her by ensorcellment here. Oxyle will do nothing. He says that it is some law of theirs. But can they not understand that the taking of a child makes matters worse? I do not think that that will not be followed up."

"A child! She dared—that!" Certainly he was no longer the blank faced bondman she had seen obeying Lotis, subject to her whims. This was the man with whom she had come out of the town.

"We've got to get her free—that child! Ylon, where can we find them? Oxyle would not tell me."

"No!" His wrist grip was enough to bruise her. "She would use you—she has power—greater power than she allows even her kin to believe."

"Ylon, I have power also," Twilla spoke with a careful spacing of words, determined to impress what she said upon him. "I saved Fanna—remember? His own people could not do that. I am a healer— and there are many kinds of power."

He was frowning. "I heard—a strange story— You carry some talisman they say which they do not understand. They fear iron above all things because it is truly poison for their kind. Yet your talisman defeated the death brought by iron. If you have such power why—"

She could guess what he would say, "Why did I not use it before— back at the village—at the river? Because"—she drew a deep breath— "it is a tool I do not know how to use, I can only guess and if my guess proves to be wrong—then I believe that never can it be put right. It was Hulde's gift to me but she said that I must learn its use by myself. I think that she meant I had—somehow put a part of me into it as it could answer only me.

"But, Ylon, for the child we must try—''

She tried to free her hand from his grip, but it was like a fetter holding her.

"Ylon, can you find our way out of here?" she tried another question. To her joy she saw him give a slow nod.

"I wondered why the bond raised. Yes, I can find a way—but, Twilla, do not deal with Lotis unless you are sure of your weapon. She is different, I think, from the others. They, those I have had contact with, are not as twisted of purpose as she. It is with them as it is with us, each has his or her own kind of spirit, is able to choose good or ill.

"They are, you must understand," he had swung around, towing Twilla with him by that hold he kept on her, "akin in some strange way to the forest. Any destruction within it—the felling of a tree, the pressure of an uncaring boot to crush a plant, is to them as great an injury as a sword thrust through the body can be to one of us.

"They have been fighting a war of protection for the Wood, their way of life. To them our kind are a great and abiding threat. And the weapons they use are strange and sometimes beyond belief of our race.

"Those who harm the Wood, would raise ax to a tree, grub forth a bush—they are inviting attack in return. Until our people understand this—''

"But a child! And she was not near the Wood when we first saw her." Swiftly Twilla told of that hunt for the bright flowers which had drawn her into Lotis's reach.

"Foul!" His lips twisted as if he would spit. "They have few children themselves, and surely they hold them high because of that. Thus Lotis is daring— She may think that to take such a youngling she can change her, shape her as a potter shapes his wares, so that she will be forgiven her deed because she has added to their company. Though that would be a new way of thinking than any Lotis has shown—at least to my knowledge.''

"She—she made you seem like a—a hound at her call.''

There was a dull red flush on Ylon's cheek. "To her I was—a hound, yes. She enticed a man and made him less than a servant, for a servant is not under such commands as can be laid here. I do not think that even Oxyle knows what lies in Lotis's mind, what pattern she weaves in secret.''

14

"WHAT DOES SHE desire then?"

Ylon had quickened pace and Twilla, in spite of her fatigue, had to match that because of his continued hold on her. Once more he was running fingers along the wall. Just as she asked her question his touch passed from the stone to one of those sealed doors.

He gave a small exclamation and swung that guide hand away.

"Another—" he muttered. "Trap? It must be so. But why set here? Surely Lotis does not look forward to so protecting *all* the corridors—"

"Trap?" For a moment Twilla forgot her question concerning Lotis. "That is a door—sealed. Karla told me. There was a war long ago and some ancient enemy sealed away in those portions they may still hold."

He paused, took a backward step so he was again opposite that stretch of what appeared to be wood scrawled over with long-faded signs. Very gingerly he touched it. To Twilla's amazement his finger appeared to sink straight into the seemingly solid slab.

"What do you see?" Ylon demanded.

"A—a door—flat within the wall—it has symbols on it. There is no latch, no seeming way to open it."

"A door?" He thrust his questing finger deeper until it was swallowed past the second joint and then jerked it back.

"Something soft enough to yield to my touch. But let them have their mysteries—we are fast caught in our own tangle."

He started on and Twilla returned to her earlier question. "What does Lotis want?"

Again Ylon gave that grating laugh. "I think sometimes even Lotis does not know. She tried me as a tool—or a weapon. Now she will do the same for this child."

"Unless we stop her!"

"That we can is another question," he returned.

They had come to a place where the passage they were following now split in two. To the left the way held the same dusk as masked all the stone walled ways, to the right was a gleam of light. Ylon had paused again, his head swung to the right and she saw his nostrils expand to catch some scent. In a moment she also picked up that faint hint of fragrance such as had no place in these gloomy ways.

Ylon seemed as certain here as he had been in their night's journey out of the Keep. And undoubtedly he had his own guide; they were heading toward the silvery light. She caught a glimpse ahead of what could only be a flutter of that mist which used its trails to cloud and then uncurtain the way beyond.

The walls here were also pierced by niches in which stood figures. But there was something subtly unpleasant about these, all humanoid as they were. Beautiful forms still hinted at hidden misshaping, there were sly quirks of lips, a sidewise leer of eye.

Ylon no longer held to that wall as a guide but strode confidently forward, and the mist drifted toward them in long trails.

He came to a halt and wheeled to the left, to face a doorway. At the same moment that mist came down upon them, as might the net of a fisherman hurled at a school of his prey. Ylon's hold on her hand loosened—was gone.

Though they stood nearly shoulder to shoulder Twilla could no longer see him. He was enveloped—hidden. Yet, though the mist curled about her, sifting, nearing, she was not totally caught by it. Tendrils reached out for her, touched her body and slipped away again. Those might have been roots seeking earth to nourish them but finding only stone.

The fragrance was thick, so strong now as to seem rank, filling the air to stifle breathing.

"Ylon!" She dared to call his name. That pillar of mist beside her spiraled around furiously and was gone. While the portion of it which had tried to enfold her whipped back and forth until the girl could almost feel that rage embodied in it.

Ylon was gone. Twilla could not help but believe that in some fashion Lotis had reached out for him again. But there remained the door before her and this one did have a latch. Lotis's quarters? Twilla could but try and see.

She had more than half believed that she would find some barrier when she tested that latch, but it moved easily so she pushed the door wide to look within.

What she viewed was a room not unlike that in which she had slept and dreamed. Here also was a bed fashioned to form a well-opened flower. The colorful hangings on the walls—these were not ferns but blossomed vines massing together.

And—on the bed lay the child. Of Lotis there was no sign. Twilla advanced with caution. Surely the forest woman would not be so easily robbed of her new bond slave! Unless that mist which had removed Ylon had been meant to also pursue her small captive.

Why the mist had not engulfed Twilla also she did not know, save that perhaps the mirror was once more serving her, not as a tool, a weapon this time, but as a shield.

Twilla crossed to the bed. The child lay with closed eyes. She was smiling, and now and then she murmured a word in a whisper—

"Pretty—" Twilla heard. "Pretty flowers—pretty lady. Good drink—"

Drugged! But how deeply? The child suddenly rolled over in bed and her eyes opened so she looked straight up at Twilla.

"Pretty flowers—give Wandi pretty flowers—"

"Yes," at least the girl did not appear to be so deeply sedated that she could not move, "we shall go—" Twilla held out her hand. "Go to look for the flowers."

The child did not shrink from her this time. In so much the mirror had served her well. Wearing her over-mountain face she must look much like any of the landwomen Wandi knew.

Wandi scrambled out of the petals readily enough, took the hand Twilla held out without hesitation. Twilla was tense, waiting for Lotis to appear. This was too easy—far too easy—she could not believe that the forest woman would not rise to stop them.

However, she brought Wandi with her into the outer hall. The mist? Would that be Lotis's weapon—a coiling mist to enfold Wandi and take her as it had Ylon only moments earlier?

Abruptly the fragrance which wafted out of the room as they left changed. There came a whiff of stench, stomach-churning foulness. There was sound also—a scrambling—a heavy padding. The mist, which had hung there waiting for them, thinned. What came through, scuttling toward them was a monstrosity, not as large as that illusion which was set on border watch in the forest, yet carrying in its smaller form the same looming menace.

Wandi screamed, twisted her hand free from Twilla. She turned and ran blindly, so fear-possessed that she had only flight in mind. Only she had not headed back into the room, rather she was flying down the passage toward that dusky maze of other corridors.

The six-legged thing gave a leap, one of its clawed legs swung out in a blow promising to rip Twilla from breast to knee.

Illusion! It must be illusions. She backed, her hands fumbling to free the mirror. The thing leaped again—and vanished in the middle of that leap. Twilla could hear faint screams now—Wandi had found her full voice and it sounded as if the child had been truly driven out of her wits. Twilla followed, running. Again she heard sounds behind, looked over her shoulder at a second apparition. This was offensively humanoid and the worst for having taken that form. A skeleton-thin figure, showing a skull face half eaten away by some loathsome disease. As it came it sputtered threats.

Once more Twilla made herself stand her ground and hold out the mirror shield. The stench of decay encircled her as might a reaching of the mist. Then—that, too, was gone. However, she had lost time. Wandi must be very far ahead now and she could not be sure, once the passages began to divide, which one the child would choose to follow.

She ran as best she could wondering if she dared call the child by name, or if she did so she would alert more crawling menaces.

Twilla came to where the corridor had split before. Which way? Had the child gone straight, the way Ylon had led Twilla, or taken the other way? She made herself stand and try to pick up some sound to lead her.

Yes! Wandi screamed again. Had the child confronted some other monster in the dark, sent to herd her back? Twilla whirled into the side passage and ran, mirror in her hand. Then she saw ahead a wall cutting off the way. Wandi had reached that point, heading straight for the barrier as if she could not see it. In a moment she would crash headlong into the stone!

Only she did not. She vanished. And, Twilla racing up, saw then ahead one of those symbol marked doors. Wandi had plunged through it—even as Ylon she seemed to find it no barrier. Twilla followed, though her eyes told her that she was going to hit a solid surface.

What she did plunge into was, as Ylon had reported, a kind of jelly fluidity which slowed her but did not prevent her entrance. Here was a dark far beyond any dusk of the outer ways.

Now she dared at last to call, knowing that if she could not find Wandi in this dark they were both in danger.

"Wandi! Wandi!"

Twilla took one careful step at a time into the dark.

"Wandi—?"

She stopped short. That had been an unmistakable whimper from ahead—and not too far away.

If she only had some measure of light! Was that wish a command of the power she could not believe she had mastered? From the mirror spiraled a fine haze, far less than the corridor mists, but it was a weapon against the dark.

She swung the mirror back and forth, striving to see the way ahead. Again the whimper came and this time from a point to her right. Part of that very faint light showed a rough-edged hole rather than the well built other ways.

"Wandi?" she called.

"Here—" The word was choked forth amid heavy sobs.

Twilla moved in the direction from which it had come, under that rudely chiseled archway into the unknown.

The haze did not reach far. Twilla was fearful of becoming lost if this passage was like the mazes she had wandered through in the castle. However, she had not yet sighted Wandi and must keep on.

"Wandi—?" she called again.

Her answer was a whimper from somewhere still ahead. The haze showed walls which had not been smoothed but were pocked and ridged. Once, when her hand with the mirror swung closer to the right, she saw a gleaming stream of what might have been slime—perhaps marking the pathway of some creature of the dark. Only that stream was not any normal slug or snail trail—this was as thick as her wrist and she did not want to think about what might have crawled that way.

Then she was nearly bowled off her feet as a small form burst out of the dark and threw itself at her, clasping arms about her waist.

"Wandi!"

"Get me out—out—" The child's voice held the shrillness of hysteria. "The things—they'll get us!"

"The things are gone," Twilla hoped that she was right—that there were no more monsters. To meet such in the dark would heighten their power to frighten. "Come—yes, we shall get out."

Twilla slipped the mirror cord over her head so it rested on her breast and the haze seemed a little stronger. Perhaps her eyes adjusting somewhat to this complete gloom made it seem so. She had to unhook Wandi's clutching hands and then gathered the girl close and turned to go back the way they had come.

She kept on because she must, because she could not believe that she was lost, when she had made only a single turn beyond the door. Yet there was no jaggered edged arch ahead—and she was certain that she had come far enough to sight that.

"Please—please—get us out!" Wandi's small body, pressed still close to hers, was shaking. Twilla felt her own rise of fear.

"Yes." She fought to control her own uneasiness, to reassure the child. "We shall get out." Only the haze light brought into sight no arch—only a continuing rough passageway. Twilla was forced to admit to herself that there was surely some warding sorcery here.

The air about them was dry and something, probably their own passing, stirred up dust which set them both to coughing.

"I'm thirsty—" the child said. "Please—where is out?"

"We shall find it." How long wondered Twilla could she keep up the pretense that she knew where they were and that there would shortly be an end to this?

There was only one thing to give her hope, the light from the mirror seemed to become more intense as they went. She could see now perhaps three or four feet before her. Save there was nothing to see but the endless rough wall on either side and the dust sanded pavement underfoot.

Not until that light caught something which gave back a wink of reflection. Twilla paused and turned a little to the left, so that the full light of the mirror could center there. Anything which was more than just the rough stone might be of importance.

What her turn so illuminated brought another scream out of Wandi, clutching at her, hiding her face in Twilla's bedraggled skirt. The older girl gasped, frozen in place for a moment.

There was a face there—and that glint had betrayed an eye, her turn another as well, in addition the surface of a sleek, lolling tongue, curling out of a full fanged cavern of a mouth.

Her surprise held her there long enough for her to realize that this was no monster apparently halfway through a solid wall, rather a mask of such. Placed as a warning?

As Twilla studied it, her fear now under control, she saw that it was carven in bold relief and that it formed the head of a boar—but such a one as certainly was never seen over mountain. The carving had been done with such skill that mask-head had a pseudo life when the haze touched it.

"Wandi," Twilla gathered the girl closer. "It is not alive. Someone has made it out of the wall stone. Remember the Harvest Dancers—the masks they wear?" She did not know if that custom had been brought over mountain but where there were landsmen and farming, generally the harvest festival was one of the great feast days of the year.

"—get us!" Wandi's voice was muffled. She continued to keep her face hidden in Twilla's skirt.

"No—it cannot!" Somehow she must get through to the child. She remembered only too well those stories of the mind-blasted who had come out of the forest. If Wandi was driven too far by fear—what could she do with the child?

She moved a step or so toward that mask on the wall, dragging Wandi with her. Then she worked to loosen the grip of those small hands, striving not to use hurtful force.

"Wandi—" Twilla went to her knees, the heavy dust of the way rising around to cling to her clothing, skin and hair. She held the child and turned her toward the wall.

"Watch!" she ordered. Twilla let go her grip with one hand and raised that to catch the end of the dangling tongue.

Wandi was looking, her eyes wide in a pale face.

"It is only stone," Twilla urged. She pulled herself up, and now drew her hand along the carving which so closely and cleverly resembled the creature's bristly pelt, from between the ears, down the snout, venturing into the mouth as if to count the teeth, landing once more on the tongue.

Wandi gave a heaving sob. "Not real—"

Twilla nodded with relief. "Not real—only a made thing. Wandi, you live on a landholding, do you not?"

The little girl was still staring bemused at the carving but she nodded.

"And when the fields are early sown," Twilla called upon what she knew of farm affairs, "do not the birds come often to try and eat the grain?"

"Yes—"

"Then what does the farmer do?" Twilla encouraged her.

"We make a dancer." Wandi's breathing had slowed.

"Yes, you make a dancer—out of clothes no one wants anymore, and you make a head with straw for hair."

"And we paint eyes—big and black—and a mouth—" Wandi's hands came to her own face, linked fingers in the corners of her lips and pulled them in a wide stretch.

"Your dancer must be a very good one," Twilla applauded. "Now I believe that this is a dancer, too—"

"No fields here," Wandi was quick with the denial of that.

"True, but perhaps this dancer is put here for another kind of warning. Not for birds—"

"For us?" Once more Wandi reached out and caught Twilla's robe.

"It has been here for a very long time," Twilla attempted to evade a direct answer to that. "There may have been those very long ago whom this dancer was set to warn. But we are not birds—and we know he is not real."

"Lady," Wandi looked straight up into Twilla's face, "how do we get out?"

"That," Twilla could do nothing but share the truth, "we must discover. If there is a way in—there must be one to let us go. We have only to hunt for it."

"I'm thirsty," Wandi said.

"Yes, that too we must find—water. But oftentimes streams run underground and we may discover such." To hearten another was one thing, to believe one's own self what might be vain prophecies was another.

They started on, leaving the boar mask on watch behind them. It was shortly after that that the passage they followed split into two. Each had an arched entrance, but the face of one of the arches had been smoothed and as Twilla held up the mirror she saw there a carving—lines which might be script of a sort she had never seen. The other way was bare of any such directions and she decided that perhaps that with the symbols was the most promising.

This one, after their first few paces in, did not run straight but wound about, though there were no side openings. After one such turning Twilla gave a gasp of relief. Ahead was light—not the brightness of day—but at least far greater illumination than the mirror offered. Catching Wandi's hand she urged the little girl on at a faster pace.

They could see now another opening through which speared that light. Then they came out onto a ledge. Before them spread a cavern so long and wide that Twilla could only faintly see the hint of walls. Those near were overgrown with lichen and it was that which provided the light.

The strangest thing of all was that immediately below there was another forest—stunted and crooked, but still a forest. Only these were not true trees or even large shrubs, but rather upstanding rows of what seemed to be giant gray fungi which had a velvety look.

There was something very unnatural about those lumpy growths.

Twilla had no wish to approach them closer. Luckily they did not reach the wall of the ledge, there was a wide enough path there to follow. Surely at one end or other of this place there would be another way out. While from the ledge itself there descended a rude stairway, narrow steps cupped into the rock.

"Come—follow—me—watch each step," Twilla warned as she started down that crude stairway.

15

THE AIR IN this place was oppressive, and there was a moldy under-scent which was unpleasant. Though it did not carry the heavy stench which warned of monsters. Twilla was very careful as she went from step to step, having no desire to set hand to the wall over which sprawled the fuzzy, luminous growths. Luckily they did not have far to go.

Above all she knew that they must find water. The passage dust left them with flayed throats and an aching need to drink. Nor could they go without food either and how long they might have to wander there she had no guess.

"Lady—" Wandi pressed close to her again as they came out on the level flooring of the cavern. "I don't like this place—"

"No, but we shall find a way out," Twilla tried to put to her answer an assurance she herself did not feel.

She had become more and more aware of a rustling sound, almost as if those lumpy, fungi growths *were* trees and there was a light breeze at play among their leaves. Now there was something else—a ripple of sound which she seized on with new hope for that could be a steady flow of water—and it lay still ahead.

They worked their way along the walls, keeping as much distance as they could from the growth. Then they sighted a narrow break in the barrier they followed. It was low but around it the stone was bare as if the wall growth did not like the moisture which arose here—for moisture it was. A stream came through a narrow crack to cross their path, flowing to the right out into the fungi forest, though those misshapen bulbous growths shunned its brink.

"Drink—" Wandi loosed her hold on Twilla's grimed and snagged skirt and was on her way until the older girl caught up and grabbed at her.

Who could tell what lurked in the water in such a place? They must take all care.

"It may not be good water," she explained. "We must make sure before we drink."

The stream was hardly more than a thread compared to the river she had fought. They could, both of them, she believed jump across it. Twilla went to her knees and scooped up a palmful of the water. It was icy cold against her hand and clear enough.

She had only one test she might make and whether that was a true one she did not know. But she lifted the mirror in her other hand and held it as steady as she could, dribbling what she still held of the water onto its surface.

The silver surface was clear under each drop. Could she be sure that that meant that this water on flow through such a place was indeed harmless?

Raising the mirror to her mouth she tipped it. Though most of the liquid on it dribbled down her cheeks and chin, enough got into her mouth and she could detect no taste at all.

"Give me!" Wandi clutched and tugged.

"Yes. But you must drink so—as I did," Twilla explained. Once again she had cupped water onto the mirror and held it steady while the child half lapped at the very small portion. It took them some time to satisfy their raging thirsts and they were forced to do it in hardly more than sips, one at a time.

"Good!" Wandi squatted back on her heels at last. The dust had washed from the lower part of her face from her exertions and there were splotches in plenty down the front of her shift dress.

Twilla hoped the child was right. She turned up the hem of her dress striving to find a fairly clean portion and with that she polished the mirror dry. They had found water right enough but they had no means of carrying that bounty with them. And now that they had come to a halt she began to realize how tired she was.

There was no way of measuring how far they had come, nor even how long they had been traveling. But that they could keep on without any rest—of that she was not sure.

It was a temptation to remain here, by the bounty of the water. She got up and went along the stream to its entrance in the wall. That was hardly more than a horizontal slit. She did not believe that even Wandi could squeeze through without having to duck under water. That was not their door to freedom.

However, the stream had an exit also and that might be better suited to their purpose. Right here and for a space of a number of paces its flow was straight. Then it curved in a manner to bring them closer perhaps to the end toward which they had been heading. Very well, they could keep to the source of water and still explore.

"Lady—" Wandi was trudging behind her. "I'm hungry—please, get us out of here."

"I am trying," Twilla returned wearily. "We shall go this way, beside the water—"

"My feet hurt—I want to sit down!" Wandi's voice had developed a distinct whine and Twilla could not fault her for that.

Yes, they must find a place where they could rest. Eat? There were certain fungi which were not only palatable but esteemed by the cooks over mountain. However, looking around her, Twilla could sight none here which were familiar. She shrank from approaching those trees to break off a bit.

The curve in the stream continued and the flow of water itself widened. It was shallow but if they crossed it now they would have to wade. On either side the fungi kept their distance.

For the first time Twilla noted that they grew in distinct rows as if this was some monsterous garden which had been planned for a purpose.

Wandi gave a cry which deepened into exhausted sobbing. When Twilla turned the child was sitting on the ground, her hand clasping a bruised knee, rocking back and forth. Clearly they were close to the end of their strength.

But—not too far away was the rise of another wall, at right angles to the one which had guided them on their descent into this place. Between them and that wall were none of the fungi growths, except in one place where there was a mound of the stuff, not tree-shaped but with queer slender lengths protruding from it at different angles. And some of those showed small glints, even in this subdued light.

"Just a bit farther, Wandi." Twilla helped the little girl to her feet. "We shall go across the water—to that wall. See?"

Lending support to her companion the girl did splash through the water and approached the strange heap of fungi. It was different from the "trees" in another sense. Whereas those were uniform dark brown, this had a shimmer of other colors, very muted but distinguishable enough to be sight as a glimmer of gray, a line of red, a rolling patch of blue.

As they made their way cautiously past it Twilla saw the true shape of one of those projections. Fuzzed as to outline it might be but that was the hilt of a sword.

The thought of a weapon was heartening. Telling Wandi to remain where she was, Twilla advanced to the side of that heap. Having sighted the sword hilt she now was sure she made out a pole ax, what might be parts of other weapons.

Gingerly she reached for the sword. As her fingers closed about that hilt the fuzzy covering of it sloughed away. The feel of it was greasy, highly unpleasant. But she kept fast her hold and pulled. She might have been trying to free a weapon embedded in stone.

Nor could she bring herself to touch or handle what else might be hidden there. Disheartened she returned to join Wandi. The little girl had again slipped to the ground and was crying, rubbing her hands over the eyes.

"We shall rest," Twilla said. "And then we shall feel stronger. Come—" Once more she supported the child, drawing her along until the wall of the cavern was at their backs. Wandi curled up, her head on Twilla's lap, and was quickly asleep.

But Twilla, though she ached throughout her body, could not relax. She was surrounded by too much that she distrusted. At last she took the mirror in both hands.

The silver surface reflected her own face, the dust grimed skin, her eyes filled with weary shadows. Without knowing that she did so she thought of another face—Ylon—but not under the mist which so blinded him. Rather as she thought he might look were he totally free of all Lotis's bespelling.

Did she really see that face form in the mirror? She was not sure— But—Yes! And those blind eyes were turned upon her—seeing somehow through the mirror to her!

She found herself whispering—not the jingles which had released the mirror power before, but rather telling all which had happened since he had been drawn from her side before Lotis's door—

She had nearly done when that face, which had grown more and more alive and clear to her, flickered and was gone as if a finger on the mirror surface had wiped it away. But—there was another shadow form there, one which deepened, took on substance. Then she was looking to Oxyle for only a second before he, too, vanished. That sense of fatigue which overcame her whenever she used the mirror was back and she could not fight it. She was only aware that she laid on the rock of this place, Wandi curled beside her, and then she slept.

How long Twilla lay in the depth of an exhausted slumber so deep that no dreams could invade Twilla did not know. But she came groggily awake, to realize that someone was pulling at her, screaming out in her very ears. She struggled up balanced on one elbow.

Wandi shook her.

"They are coming—Lady. They will get us!"

They? Bemused, Twilla looked. She could see nothing at first except what had been there when she had fallen asleep. There was—movement!

The first row of the "tree" fungi were indeed so close to the stream bank on the opposite side that they might well topple in if they ventured farther. No longer were they standing in an ordered pattern but were moving, slowly but surely, toward the water—toward Wandi and her!

She swung up the mirror, but it was dulled again. If those—those *things* reached them—! The thought of being struck down by such was sickening. Twilla stumbled up and headed toward that pile of weapons. The sword would not yield to her, and anyway she knew nothing of defensive sword play—a healer did not war.

What else then? The pole ax took her eye, and she grabbed at the shaft of that. At least it was long enough to aim blows from some distance, and she had handled an ax enough in the land over mountain splitting firewood to have some idea of a proper swing.

Twilla braced her feet and put both hands to the shaft giving a mighty heave. It was fixed. Steadying herself Twilla tried again. As she leaned a little forward to get a better grip the mirror swung out.

There was a flash striking down into that fungi-cemented mass. Where that struck the cover curled away. Twilla staggered back, the pole ax free, the sudden release of the weapon nearly sending her against the wall as she fought for balance.

"They—Lady—they come!" Wandi's shriek sounded as Twilla swung around, the freed weapon at ready. But—how long could she stand up to this company? The mirror had blasted this weapon free for her use, could it turn now against the things splashing through the water of the stream?

Twilla did not have time to change weapons, she must make do with what she held. The fungi tree things plodded toward her—the first one in advance of its fellow by several strides.

Twilla waited until she could be sure she could reach it and then swung her weapon. The cutting blade of the ax jarred against the upper portion; it did not cut in and she knew a moment of horror at that failure.

Then—there was a hoarse scream, louder, deeper than any Wandi could utter. From where the ax had fallen without apparent harm there was a splitting now. Flacks of the brown fungi covering were falling, breaking free. The thing had stopped its advance. Its fellows, which had crossed the stream, closed behind it, wavering back and forth as if unable now to carry out whatever purpose had sent them at the girls.

More and more of the brownish stuff sloughed. However, there remained an inner core—a core which was different from the coating. A figure which was hardly more than a skeleton was left. Only this did not fall to earth. It raised two arms and made a beckoning gesture, urging on those which followed it.

For the second time Twilla used the ax. Not at that skeleton which was continuing to cry out frenziedly but at one of the newcomers. The touch of the metal began another transformation.

The girl drew a deep breath. That skeleton thing—and its fellow—made no move toward her, only beckoned on their companions. They might have been in some way urging her to give them release. Because there was nothing else that she could do, she used the ax again and again. Her arm was aching, and still they came and she could not stop. Until at last the very end of that company stood within reach of the ax blade and then she could lean on its pole panting and looking with wonder at those now ranged before her.

They were not true skeletons, but pitifully thin. All of them were smaller than she and they turned wizened, wrinkled faces in her direction. The first two that she had freed had fallen to hands and knees and were creeping toward her. When they saw her gaze turn in their direction they gave cries and groveled, head down. It was plain that they meant no harm.

Twilla was aware of a change in the scene about her even as the fungi forest had come to life. To her right the edge of that pile of imprisoned weapons was now free. And, having paid homage, the first two figures lurched in that direction and pulled with more vigor at what had been piled there.

There were swords bared in the light as more and more of their fellows joined them. She saw one drawing on a mail shirt hardly bigger than Wandi might have worn with comfort. She and the child had backed away, Twilla leaning on the pole of the ax, watching in astonishment these small beings so busy around the weapon pile from which the last of the fungi had disappeared.

One of them broke from the crowd, so busy at claiming arms and armor, and approached her. A mail shirt hung on his thin frame, but he had belted on a sword and carried in one hand a plain helm. Facing Twilla he gave a low bow and then pointed to where the mirror hung on her breast.

It was no longer dimmed and the silver of its surface seemed to flash in answer to his gesture. He laid the helm on the rock at his feet and made gestures suggesting one holding and looking into the mirror.

Twilla slipped the cord from around her neck and looked into the surface herself. What she saw was not her own reflection, rather a small, wide shouldered, bearded man, a face of vigor and in its way distinction. Swiftly she reversed the disk and stooped a little so that this creature before her could also see. He gave a great cry in which she heard a note of joy. Those still busied at the weapon pile looked up, then spoke to each other in a hoarse guttural speech she could not understand before they surged forward again just as they had done to meet her ax.

The one who was now staring intently into the mirror was changing. This time he was not losing bulk as he had when he had shed the fungi covering, rather he was gaining. His body thickened, putting on flesh, and then he showed now to the world the same face Twilla had seen in the mirror.

There was a voice raised in what might well be a shouted command. It drew attention back to that place where the weapons and armor had been mounded. There was only trampled dust to be seen now—only that and something which was enough to rivet sight.

A staff much like that of the pole ax now at Twilla's feet lay uncovered. It did not hold the gray sheen of the blades and mail which had been piled over it. Rather was dullish red—or tarnished gold, she could not be sure which. Surmounting it was a large knob or carving.

There was a single one of the wizened once captives still remaining, as if he had held himself aloof from the scramble which had armed his companions. Now he strode purposefully forward and picked up the staff.

Then—even as the mirror could do upon occasion—that took on life. From where his hand grasped the shaft red-gold came into gleaming life. As he upped it Twilla could see that it bore the head of a boar, as cunningly fashioned from its tusked snout to its up pricked ears as had been that on the wall of the passage.

He who held it was changing now, and this was no sorcery born of the mirror. His crooked back straightened, his head was proudly aloft, the hollows which showed bones filled out with muscle. He was taller than these others, matching Twilla in height, though below the stature of the forest people, or even most men of the invaders.

Instead of a mail shirt the bits of rag clinging to his own shrunken body drew together and became whole even as did the flesh underneath. Unlike the one who had gazed into the mirror his face was clean of hair, his features finer cut as if he were indeed of another race.

Holding his boar-headed rod as if it were some symbol of office he came toward Twilla. Before him the others gave way, forming an open aisle as courtiers might make room for a king.

He came to a halt, shoulder to shoulder with the warrior who had first regained his face from the mirror.

The boar-headed staff made a slight dip in the girl's direction and Twilla, in return, inclined her head as a sign of respect. Certainly this man was a person of higher authority.

Then he spoke—not in the guttural, deep-throated speech she could not understand but in the language of the upper world, though strangely accented:

"You are not of the trees, nor is that one," a small gesture indicated Wandi standing wide-eyed beside her. "How came you here—and why?"

"We came by chance, being lost in the ways—and why—because we were hunted."

There was a moment's silence as he appeared to be thinking that over.

"Prey to those of the trees?" A murmur ran around those who had gathered in to circle them.

"This one—" Twilla touched Wandi's head as the little girl once more crowded closer to her. "She was taken—she must be returned— to those of her blood."

"How did you come into the long sealed ways?" Now he had another question, and Twilla was aware that all of them were alert. Perhaps those he headed could understand the upper-world speech even if they did not speak it.

"Wandi ran through one of the sealed doors—I followed," Twilla replied. "Then we found ourselves lost. Can you return us to the forest?"

"If you are not of the tree people—and they hunt this one—then why do you want to go back into their hold?"

"There are others—others of Wandi's kin nearby. There is a good chance to win from the forest and free her to them."

"But you," his eyes swept downward from contact with hers to touch on the mirror, "are you then one for power with those?"

"No, if they could find me they would be my enemies. But the child must be sent back to her kin. And the tree people—only one of them would hunt me down. I stand in neither company—that of the fields, nor of the Woods."

"It has been long, perhaps very long," he commented, "and we must learn more before we speak any words or make promises we cannot recall. Now, since you have proven that you can break the timelock as you have done for Gorum here, will you do so for the rest?"

"Gladly." Again she might be being reckless—too quick to judge. Yet without the aid of these newly awakened from sorcery she was sure she and Wandi could not find any door to the proper world again. "Let each come forward in turn," she readied the mirror, only hoping that its power would not be exhausted again before she had finished this matter of time transformation.

Come they did, lining up to move before her, each one trading eagerly on the heels of the one ahead to face that disk. And the changes continued. They were much of a kind, these prisoners from the fungi. Short, broad-shouldered with well-muscled arms which were longer than was necessary, so that their great fists hung on a level with their knees. Their legs were short but very sturdy and, small as they were, they gave off the aura of impressive strength.

Those who had been revived to what must be their proper state scattered, splitting into bands of three or four, each commanded by one who looked somehow to be older than his fellows. He with the boar standard watched silently.

Once more the drain of the power was on Twilla. She had to fight to keep her hands from shaking as she raised the mirror anew now. And she was barely able to hold it in place when the last of that company stood before her.

As he turned away restored, Twilla's legs suddenly gave out under her and she fell to the ground, the weakness she had tried to hold in check overcoming her.

16

TWILLA WAS NO longer truly aware of what was going on around her. Then Wandi's hold was on her again as the child shook her.

"Lady—they bring us food—"

At the same time she was aware of an odor she had almost forgotten—that of meat which had been roasted. She lifted her head groggily. Coming toward them was one of the small warriors carrying in one hand a platter of what looked to be time-darkened silver from which threads of steam arose, and in the other a goblet oddly curved as if it were fashioned of some beast's horn.

He placed the platter and drinking horn on the rock within Twilla's reach and sketched an awkward bow, backing away still facing her as might a court servant.

There was an eating knife balanced across the plate beside the portion of meat and Twilla used it to carve at the hunk which gave off those mouth-watering smells. She freed a finger-sized portion—it was hot but not burning—presented that to Wandi on the point of the knife before cutting a piece for herself.

The meat had a curious texture between her teeth, it was unlike any she had tasted before. However, she was hungry enough at the moment to seize upon a rock and chew it if it seemed to be edible. And Wandi was apparently relishing the food as much as she did.

"Go slow—" Healer's knowledge awoke in Twilla. One did not

overfill at a single meal after a long fast without dire results. "It is not good to eat too fast—too much."

Wandi had already finished her first portion, her hand was out for another. "Hungry—" came that near whine again.

Twilla made sure that the second cut she made and gave to the child was smaller. She picked up the drinking horn, sniffed at what it held— a darkish liquid. What might serve these underground dwellers might not be as good for those from above. She put a fingertip cautiously into the stuff sloshing back and forth, a little for her hand seemed still inclined to tremble.

The water! Now as she had tested the water! Twilla flicked several drops from her fingertip onto the surface of the mirror. There they showed a yellow-brown tinge, and there arose a faint odor not unlike spice. But the mirror seemed unchanging. She could only hope that was a verdict affirming her guess of harmlessness.

She dared to taste now. Like the meat it was different from anything she had savored before. Tart but not enough to catch in the throat, and, as she swallowed, a warmth arose in her middle.

It might be too hearty a drink for a child, yet she herself was feeling a renewal of strength from only that one cautious sip.

She held the horn out to Wandi. "Only a little—"

However, Wandi made a face after a first sip and pushed it away.

"It tastes funny," she declared.

Her hunger a little appeased and feeling far more alert and strong than when she had first awakened, Twilla now looked about her.

Where that fungi-disguised force had stood there was only a stretch of bare rock. However, for some reason the whole cavern seemed much lighter. Not too far away three of the warriors were assaulting the wall from which they had scarped the lichen coating.

Twilla could see that what they uncovered was a doorway fast sealed with a panel which fitted so well that only a marking line made it visible. There was no latch or bar. But deep graven into the stone above that portal was another representation of the boar's head. This did not jut from the rock as had the one in the passageway but rather was far more akin to a flattened mask. Save that the small eyes on either side of the snout glistened.

Behind the workers stood the standard bearer. There was a tense line to his unarmored body as if in expectation of important action upon which might depend much.

As the last of the cloaking lichen was slashed away and the door fully cleared, the work party stepped to one side allowing their leader free passage. He moved forward to stand directly before that latchless door.

Gripping the staff of the standard with both hands he raised it higher so that the head at the top was directly facing the wall mask. And then—

Twin beams of light speared forth from the standard head, struck full upon those gleaming eyes in the mask. They began to ripple as if some power coursed along them but not steadily, rather in juts.

Twilla absently eating as she watched was fascinated by what she saw. Here was another kind of power. As with the mirror it must be focused—what was its source? Certainly this could not be moon-fed when so far underground.

There was a sound, sharp high—one which was a sudden stab at ears and as quickly gone. The sealed portal shimmered, then Twilla witnessed a webbing of cracks spread across it. Those cracks grew greater, the substance which separated one from the other crumbled, broke, fell as gravel-sized rubble.

Out streamed a reddish light to bathe the priest leader who still stood, standard aloft. The boar light flickered, was gone, as the pole slid through his grip. He was leaning on the staff a little as a man very tired might lean on a traveler's aid.

Around where she and Wandi sat there came movement. From all corners of the cavern the others of the fungi prisoners drew in. Some of them seemed to be carrying what looked like freshly butchered meat.

Now he who had opened the gate glanced over his shoulder to Twilla.

"Power carrier, power mistress, it is time for us to enter Ragnok which was ours—was long lost—and now ours again. We give you and the child free passage, for we of the Makers and Doers pay all debts."

He did not move and Twilla guessed that he was waiting for her and Wandi to join him. Since there seemed to be no other way out of this place, and she was sure the small people wished them well, Twilla was willing. She could perhaps draw on that debt he had mentioned to get them eventually to open another door one into the other world she and the child had lost.

The red light was tinged with gold. It might have shown as the glory of a summer sunset. Taking Wandi's hand, though the child dragged back a little as if she was afraid, Twilla walked confidently forward.

What they entered so was not another maze of passages but rather— as the forest people entered their stronghold through that mighty tree— another world indeed.

Twilla could see no source for the light—it just was. What it showed was a stretch of country pushing on and on into a hazy distance her sight could not pierce.

Right before them lay a gentle slope downward, and that was covered with a matting of growth, brown, yellow, pale green, spotted with patches of paler flowers which were, in contrast to their foliage, near as bright as the jeweled fruit of the forest.

She heard from behind cries, cries which blended into the rhythm of a marching song, though the words she could not understand. However, her feet answered to the beat. It was a song of triumph, of victory over odds—a song of return to a homeland.

There were no trees in this land. Here and there stood tall monoliths of rock, rock veined with crystals which flashed as their party moved past. Perched on some of these were lizard-like creatures equipped with skin flap wings. One such took to the air and wheeled about them. Wandi shrank closer to Twilla, her hand hold tightened. The creature came in a circle to the priest-leader and settled on his shoulder. While he reached up with his free hand to caress its bobbing head.

The downward slope led to water. But not the small stream of the fungi cavern. This was a full river. Could it possibly be the same as entered the forest above, here running underneath the ground for a space? If so, perhaps this would provide them with a road out.

On the other side of that there was what could only be a hall, in its way to match the forest castle. There was something about it which awoke wonder in Twilla—though it was but a mighty pile of stones of various colors, patterned with crystals. This was somber and projected a feeling of sadness. The company with her may have been touched by that emotion also, for the song of their triumphant return slowed, and then died.

Around the hall there were no signs of life except for the flying lizards, some of which appeared to have found quarters in the upper reaches of that building. The great door, in the wall facing them as they came to the river bank could be seen clearly to hang a little open. This was a deserted place.

One of the small war band, whom Twilla recognized as he passed her, as the one who had first asked her to use the mirror for changing, pushed ahead of all down to the very edge of the riverbank. He carried a pole ax—perhaps the same one she had used in defense—and now he thrust the shaft of that into the flow of the water.

It struck some obstruction before it was very deeply sunk. He pulled the weapon out as a dripping length, shook it above his head. At the same time his beard-ringed mouth opened and a sound very vast for such a small man, roared up from his throat.

"Hullloooo!"

A number of the winged lizards took to the air, circling back and forth across the river. However, there came no other answer, though it was plain, Twilla thought, that the shouter had hoped for one.

He did not turn back toward them, but, staff in hand, sounding out of path which he took step by step, he plowed into the current. A ford of sorts Twilla guessed.

The carrier of the boar standard followed him, beckoning to Twilla and Wandi. It was true, the girl discovered, there was a hard ridge not too far under the surface and although the current pulled at them until she took a tight grip on Wandi, there was firm enough footing to bring them across.

Yet since that summons had been uttered by the first in line there was no other sound from any in the band. That vague melancholy Twilla had felt when she first looked upon the hall deepened.

They came up to that door ajar and she could see that it had been designed as a proper height for her dwarfish companions. The taller priest had to bend his head, as did she, when they passed within.

The interior was totally unlike any castle or keep of her knowledge. For they shuffled down a short passage, dark but with the call of light ahead, until they came out into a mighty chamber, which perhaps occupied the whole center portion of the building. At roof level there were open spaces where the light poured down.

Each of the four walls was broken by openings. There were flights of steep stairs which led from one floor to the next, each feeding into a balcony running completely around the center court. There were four stories of such. Some of the doors opening onto the balconies were less guarded. Some entirely open almost like merchants's stalls.

Over all hung that awesome heart-deadening silence. They all seemed bound in place by that, none venturing away from the others to explore, until the priest made the first move.

He did not hurry, perhaps he did not want to have some suspicion or fear confirmed, but he crossed the open courtyard to one of the larger cubbies. Not exactly knowing why, Twilla followed, drawing Wandi with her.

There was a measure of dust on the pavement, mounded here and there into small dunes as if winds might venture here now and then to shift this debris of what must be many seasons. Within the cubby there was a small fire-blacked hearth. And by it was clearly an anvil—though too small for any human smith to put to the test. Along the walls hung various tools Twilla could not recognize, but she was able to put name to an assortment of different-sized hammers laid near the forge.

The priest stood by the workplace, looking around him slowly. There was a stricken expression on his face. Whatever should be here was not—for him.

"Long gone—" He used the speech she could understand. Then his features set in a stern mask and she could actually feel the hate and sorrow radiating from him. Swiftly he looked back to the others, only two of which had ventured into the forge.

In their guttural tongue he gave what might be an order. The party split, some of the men ran for the steps which would take them up to the balconies, others scattered, to invade the other hall floor apartments. They had found their voices, for many were calling as they ran or climbed.

Wandi tugged at Twilla. "This—this is a hurting place—"

The oddness of that observation centered Twilla's attention. It was true. The sadness she had felt was growing deeper. Now she wanted out of here as one might want out of a tomb in which hopes as well as bodies had been laid to painful rest.

She dared to break the silence here which had fallen when the priest had sent the others out:

"Wise one, what has happened here?"

He gave a small start as if his thoughts had been well away but there was now set anger in his face.

"This is our Great Hold. When we were tricked by Khargel and caught by his dark-spun magic we were on the march—for still we believed that we could find a common ground with those above. We had lived in peace with them for many lifetimes. There was trade between us, times of feasting. Then came Khargel. He was one filled with greed—instead of trade he demanded tribute. I have heard it said that he used certain ores we worked for strange purposes of power.

"Some of those ores are deadly. We do not touch them nor go too near the earth and rocks which hide them. He set a geas on three of our blood without our knowing what he did—and they mined what he wanted—and they died.

"We sent a mission to the upper world, a protest to their Council. Our kin were ambushed and killed. For even among his own kind there were murmurs against him and suspicions that he dabbled in forbidden things and our tale might have brought a judgment on him.

"There came then a message that those of the forest would meet and hear us out. I"—he hesitated—"have power but it is not theirs. I felt there was great danger, but we had already in place all the safeguards we knew.

"There were not warriors waiting for us," his anger was very apparent now, "rather dark power. We were changed to what you first saw us. And—here—who knows what demon tricks were pulled? Our women, our children—they are—not!"

"I have not heard of this Khargel among the forest people," Twilla said slowly. "They have talked of a Council which is responsible for their laws. The leader of that is Oxyle."

He shook his head. "Not a name I have heard. But—woman of power—who knows how long that imprisonment has held us? Those of the forest are very long-lived—but they can be slain. Perhaps there arose those among them who were not pleased to be Khargel's bond-kind. Tell me, you are not of their blood—how did you join with such—and why?"

Twilla told him the story as swiftly as she might and he listened closely asking no questions until the end:

"So you who come from far away are a threat to those who were in their time threat and doom to us—?"

"The invaders are a threat to this land," she returned. "Their homeland they have pillaged. If they find what they deem treasure here, then they will do the same here. And before I came into the maze there had been word that this perhaps might already have begun."

"In what manner—"

Twilla spoke then of the men panning the river gravel. At her mention of what those searched for there was another change in the priest.

"So they think to thieve from the People! It was given us from the beginning that our talent was to work with metal, making things of use, things of beauty, things of war, things for peace. That is our life and it shall not be taken from us." The staff of his standard arose a little from the floor and he brought it down again with a force which made a piece of metal jump against the next to give forth a sullen ring.

"This is something we must think on, woman of power. You say that these distant-born thieves are of your kind—that she"—he pointed to Wandi—"is of their blood. What would they pay then to get her back?"

Twilla gasped. She had not thought that her being open with the truth would lead to a suggestion that perhaps they would both be used as hostages.

"Wiseman," she kept her voice level, but her hand had gone to the mirror in her breast, "where—or what—were you and yours before I came into these ways?"

"Yes, the debt is ours. What would you do with this child then?"

"Return her to her people. If they have discovered that she was enticed into the forest they will declare open war—'' Twilla was sure of that.

"As above, so below," he said. "In spite of all which now lies between tree and rock, one cannot prosper if the other is destroyed. We were linked from the beginning. Khargel could not destroy us for that would have rebounded on those above and they would have withered also. Instead he bound us with his sorcery. But—what happened to our women? To the families we left here when we marched out to be entrapped? That we must learn—learn and pay for!" He shook the staff he held and Twilla was not surprised to see small flashes from the boar's eyes.

"If this Khargel was responsible certainly some of the forest people would know—"

He swung on her suddenly. "Or you, woman of power. Look upon that focus of yours and tell me—where are our kin?"

She had flattened her palm over the mirror, a small protection. However, she did not know what he in turn could summon up. Nor did she have the least idea how she could answer his demand.

"I—I must see a face—" she groped wildly for some excuse, "I cannot focus unless I have a face and I have never seen your women."

He was tapping his staff impatiently against the floor. Would he accept her answer? She believed it to be true.

"To have a face—" he repeated. Then he turned and went to the open door of the forge. Once there he gave a halloo which was echoed around the great room without.

One of the small warriors came on the run and the priest gave him some order which sent him pounding away again toward the far side of the courtyard.

"Perhaps we can find a face for you," the priest said. "Come—"

They went back into the larger chamber. There were benches there and he waved Twilla and the child to one, seating himself on another, facing them. At a scrambling run his messenger returned. What he held caught the golden light and shimmered until there appeared to be a coating of haze around it. The priest took it and, by the way he handled it, Twilla guessed how great a treasure this was. For a long moment, he leaned his staff against the bench to leave his hands free while he turned it around as if he did not want to surrender it now to any other touch.

What at last he held out to Twilla was a figure. She had marveled over those she had seen in the hall niches of the forest palace. This was of the same high handiwork. She took it gently from the priest and held it at eye level.

A woman—not with the sharp-cut features of the forest kind—but possessing another quality which was closer to Twilla's own kin. There was something in that small, beautifully molded face which reminded her of Hulde. The figure did not resemble the squat, thick figures of the warriors but rather the larger, more slender body of the man who sat before her.

"This is Catha, my sister-mate, for I am Chard, Master Craftsman— We are the last of the powerful trained ones among our kind, unless the Great Power favors us with a child—" His head drooped and he pounded his fist on the bench beside him. "Catha—" his voice was almost a sob.

Twilla did not know what could be done. But try she would. Again the brooding loss and sadness of this place closed in about her. The girl placed the figure against her body, slipped around a little on the bench to give it room. Now both she and the representation of Catha were facing the mirror she steadied into place.

> *"Lost is lost, found is found.*
> *Such is true what ere the ground.*
> *Let she who sleeps now be found.*
> *Above, below, all around."*

A limping verse like all the others she called upon but she hoped helpful to what she called upon. The small figure's reflection in the mirror was very clear. Then that haze drew in, thickened, as might one of the mists of the forest kind. Also from vibrant red-gold it bleached in color, becoming duller and duller. What she could see now was a finger of rough rock set up as if a marker. Rock—?

She repeated the word aloud and Chard was with her in a moment, leaning over her shoulder. However, already the reflection misted— was gone.

He gave a small cry, reached out as if to take the mirror from Twilla and then shrank back.

"There was only a pillar of rock," she told him in disappointment that she had not been able to serve him better. Rock could mark a grave—was that the meaning of what she had seen—that Catha was entombed somewhere?

"Khargel!" His voice made an oath of the word. "But there must be some knowledge—somewhere—above!"

"Oxyle—" Twilla polished the mirror once more with her palm. Was the ancient trouble between these people and those of the forest so deep that answers could not be found? She had found Oxyle sympathic—but certainly there was old enmity here. However, one could not be sure until one tried.

"Chard, you will need someone to bear your message to those above. Will you let me go—with Wandi? I shall swear any oath you ask that I will do what I can to discover what happened to Catha and the others."

"Swear—by that—blood oath!" He pointed to the mirror.

Blood oath was powerful—it could unite old enemies, bind together strange allegiances. Such a swearing was a matter for warriors usually.

He was watching her intently, warily, as if expecting her to refuse—to assure him that his suspicions of all from above were correct.

Twilla laid the mirror flat on her knee, shining side up. She had the knife with which she had cut their meat and the point of that was sharp enough to serve. A pricking of her first finger was deep enough to bring a drop of blood. Holding her hand above the mirror she allowed that to drop. It hit and spattered a little.

"By the blood which is mine, by the power which answers to me, this do I swear—that once I am above again I shall carry to Oxyle, to those leaders among the forest clans your message. If you in turn will offer truce to hold council with them. Will you swear to *that* Chard?"

He reached for his standard, slipping the shaft around, until the boar's head faced her, was inclined a fraction to loom over the blood-spattered mirror. Twilla was certain she saw those eyes blaze gold and then red. On the mirror the blood faded, it might have been sinking into the metal.

"Well enough," Chard said. "Remind those proud upper ones that all metals answer to us. Not only their beloved silver, our gold—but—iron." He pronounced that last word with the emphasis of a threat. "Now, you and the child must abide until we discover the swiftest passage, one which will serve us best. Until then rest and wait in patience. A good blade cannot be forged in an instant's work."

To that Twilla was willing to agree. Though she had eaten and rested some in the fungi cavern she still found her strength lacking and the far seeing of Catha—or the rock which now stood for Catha, had taken its toll of her.

They were escorted by one of the little men up the stairs to the first of the galleries, onto which living quarters opened, and then ushered into a room where there was a pallet of fur and padded grass wide enough for the both of them. Thankfully Twilla allowed herself to trust and, with Wandi beside her, stretched out to sleep.

"Lady—"

Twilla wanted to twist away from that voice but now she was aware also of a hand on her shoulder shaking her a little. She opened sleep-weighted eyes. Wandi still kept her hold.

"Lady—there is food—"

The child pointed to a low table on which was a tray bearing two bowls wrought cunningly out of metal in an oval shape. Each was patterned with intricate designs which might have been from some long lost script. Beside those were spoons as fancifully fashioned, for the ends of the handles were tiny boars. Both bowls and spoons had the sheen of precious metal and when Twilla felt the weight of the one she picked up she was sure it was of gold.

The contents were a stew. She thought she tasted a hint of herbs she had once known, but the meat was strange though not unpleasant. And certainly she was hungry enough not to quarrel with the portion offered her. Wandi sat cross-legged on the floor by Twilla's knee, scooping busily out of her bowl.

There was a finely wrought flagon, made in the form of one of the winged lizards, though many times the size of the living model, and two horn cups, mounted on tripod feet of what Twilla was sure were a boar's fighting fangs. What meaning that upper world-animal had here she could not understand but manifestly the species was of vast importance to the under-people.

There was water in the flagon, someone must have noted that Wandi had refused the earlier drink at their first meal. Twilla poured into both goblets and drank from her own.

A sudden memory arose—did they not say—those from over mountain—that if one ate or drank from stores unnatural one was thereafter linked to another world? Yes, that had been repeated twice in one of Hulde's books. Well, she had eaten of the bounty of the forest people, and now this—doubtless in the future she might have reason to test the worth of that warning. However, she could not go thirsty nor hungry when there was that to drink and eat just because of some old tales.

There had been one other warning in those accounts. Obscure they had been, for the strangers involved in them had never been clearly identified. That other warning had dealt with time—time which was less in one world, faster in the other. Tales of people who had wandered into the fringe of alien powers and then broke free—to discover that what had seemed a few days to them was a lifetime or more to their family and friends.

However, all that was legend, even Hulde had sworn that such accounts existed without proof. Those who had ventured in the forest and returned mind dazed or maimed—as Ylon—there had been nothing said about any great lapse for them.

Ylon—Twilla carefully set the goblet back on the low table. Ylon's reflection in the mirror—the surety she had had that somehow he had seen her.

But that thought was swept away by a tapping on the door of the chamber and Twilla arose to answer the summons. Not Chard as she had expected, rather again the first of the fungi host whom she had loosed. He bowed and beckoned, speaking in that grating language she could not understand. However, there was no mistaking his gestures, he wanted her to follow him.

With Wandi keeping close beside her Twilla went. Now, when she stepped once more out on the gallery she found that a change had come over the great hall. There was life, busy life. Not one but two forges were being worked and the clang of metal on metal echoed loudly. She saw groups of the small people carrying boxes and bags, heavy enough to make them grunt when they shifted the weight of them a fraction. Some of those bags were dumped at the forges, and others into what must be store rooms.

Twilla was not escorted to the descending stairs but rather along the gallery, passing the doors of many quarters, until they reached the far end of the hall. There, centermost in this gallery was a much wider entranceway—surmounted by the boar mask. There, a guide stood aside to allow them both to enter.

She found Chard seated cross-legged on a floor pillow, one of the small tables before him. That was covered with piles of flat plates, metallic in origin and close covered with script patterns. Some had been plainly pushed aside impatiently, two had skidded off onto the floor, but others held his full attention.

He appeared to shake himself free of some preoccupation when they entered and arose to bow with the same ceremony Twilla might have met with above ground in the forest.

"It has been very long," he burst out. They might have been in the middle of a discussion. "Long." There was a slight droop of his shoulders as if he had taken up some burden.

Then he shot a question at her. "You heard no word of Khargel among the over people—no mention of his name? Or of us and our fate?"

"No, I saw doors in the castleways sealed tightly and with symbols on them. All that I was told is that they walled away ancient enemies."

"Yet you and the child came through such a door—"

"Wandi was greatly frightened and threw herself at one, it let her through, I followed to find her. Yes," she remembered Ylon, "one of those bond to the forest was with me earlier. He touched such a door and his fingers sank within."

"So, and why do you think that you, the bond, this child, could enter where such ward spells had been laid."

"I can only believe, Wiseman, that I was able to do so, and these others also, because we were of different blood and kin and therefore such wards had not been set for us."

"Yes!" he nodded, "they did not try to bind you because you hold power. The child is not yet sealed to them, but even the bonded one you mention was able to pierce one of Khargel's sorcerous wards.

"I have had speech with my people in full assembly," he added after a moment's pause. "Because you freed them they give you a measure of trust. Because you have given *me* blood oath I trust also. Now, we have been at work all through our land. And this much we have learned—you are right, those of your race not only tried to plunder the forest, but they want metal. They have brought in special workers trained to search for such. We have our own guards and those Khargel did not meddle with—perhaps he believed that with us safe locked in spells there was no need to do so.

"But there are now men striving to come upstream to search out those mines which are our life, even as the trees are the life of those above. The forest ones have their power, we have ours—for example iron is no threat to us as it is to them. I search now," he stirred the metal plates before him, "for answers we need. If it is true that Khargel is no longer master in the forest, there are those there who will heed warnings and—perhaps need support—then we must speak together.

"There is also the matter of our women—Khargel's further sorcery. I have persuaded those here that you and the child are to be freed— shown a way out of the under which does not go through one of the doors. Speak with this Oxyle—if he is head of the Council now then his power is high. Tell him it takes two to bargain but there is a chance that both may benefit. Will you do this?"

"I will."

Her promise set in action a flurry of activity. She and Wandi were supplied with boots which came thigh high for the little girl and well above the calf for Twilla. She discarded a portion of the full-torn skirt of that robe of which she had been so proud so that it was knee length. They were given a pouch containing strips of dried meat interwoven with roots for food, and Twilla was also equipped with just such a pole ax as she had used in the fungi cavern.

Chard accompanied them down to the river where they were joined by another of the small warriors.

"This is Utin, he will be your guide to the borders of our land. Beyond that you must trust your own knowledge." He hesitated and then added:

"Woman of power, I believe that you will deal fairly with us. It seems that perhaps a darkness as evil as that raised by Khargel may be descending upon us. I have not the power of foresight—that was the gift of my Catha, but I have my night fears."

"I am but one," Twilla answered. "And my influence may be for very little. But be assured that what I can do that I shall."

He raised his staff a little as if in salute and then they followed Utin. For a time it would seem that they would not take to the water, only walk beside it. The boots were clumsy and rubbed Twilla's feet, and after a while Wandi complained that she wanted to take hers off.

Utin set a brisk pace in the lead and he did not halt, only grunted some warning when they lagged a little behind.

There was no variation of the light here, no coming of dark. Twilla could not reckon time but at length she stopped, knowing that Wandi could not keep up. The child had been hanging on her for some time, without a rest. She seated herself on the ground Wandi flopping down beside her. Utin turned and growled at them but Twilla shook her head and pointed to their feet trying to make some gesture he would understand. He gave a final grunt and went a little away from them down to the river, staring into the flood as if he were looking for some lost treasure there.

The grass before them moved, heaved upward, gave room to a form. Huge, far larger than any of its species she had seen over mountain. A boar which must stand as tall as Twilla's shoulder, small red eyes fastened on the girl and with a large front hoof it pawed the ground, tearing loose chunks of tough grass.

Always it had been said that the wild swine of the unsettled places over mountain were the most dangerous of any animal man might try to hunt. They were wily, showing a frightening cleverness, an ability to turn upon a hunter when least expected. And this was the epitome of any boar she could imagine.

It grunted, tossing its heavy head. There were threads of spittle spinning out from those great tusks set in both upper and lower jaws.

Wandi whimpered and cowered next to Twilla, shaking with fright. The older girl had already put hand on her pole ax though that she would have the skill and strength to stand up against such a creature she did not know.

Utin moved, setting his small body in front of the two he guided. He was grunting also, sounds so like those the boar was making Twilla could believe that he actually spoke some beast-like language.

The boar's attention swung to Utin, those red eyes intent upon the small man. For a long moment they stood so in confrontation. Then the heavy, bristled head tossed.

Utin turned his back on the creature and returned to the girls. He made an emphatic gesture ahead—it was plain he wanted them on the move.

For a moment longer Twilla centered her attention on the boar. It had not approached closer, simply snorted, and once more impatiently dug into the ground.

Chard bore the semblance of this creature on his staff of power, she had seen the masks elsewhere. There was certainly a tie between the under people and the boar. Utin showed it respect but did not seem alarmed at its presence.

He was gesturing again, more emphatically and Twilla arose. One arm about Wandi and the other gripping the pole ax, she moved as their guide signaled. However, they were not free of the boar.

Snuffling and grunting it fell in behind as they went. The rank odor of its kind was strong on the air. Wandi still whimpered but she did not try to evade Twilla's hold on her, matching pace with the girl.

However, they were not to be easily rid of the new, four-footed guard. A guard, Twilla was sure the beast must be, cutting off any retreat into the innerlands.

Since the creature showed no signs of attack she believed that as long as they followed Utin they might be able to go without interference. Now, rising a barrier for them ahead, was a cliff which stretched up and to either side without apparently any end.

The rock which formed it was banded by outcropping, rich, easily mined, ore deposits of more than one metal. Such riches as the over mountain lords had never chanced upon with all their delving and wracking in their own land. Let one of the king's overseers set eye on this and there would be the inpouring of an army in an attempt to secure such a source of wealth.

The river cut into the cliff but the water did not fill that passage completely. Utin stopped, letting them catch up. Behind, Twilla was well aware, that the boar still followed.

Their guide pointed to that cliff opening through which the water flowed and made signs that Twilla and Wandi were to take that path, though he made no effort to lead the way any farther.

Twilla used the shaft of the pole ax to sound for a bottom. She discovered, after several such thrusts, that the water covered at least two levels. Near the bank there appeared to run a way which would give them good footing but not rise higher perhaps than the boots with which they had been provided. Then there was a sharp dip in the bed and there the water was much deeper.

Utin waved at them impatiently and behind she heard the boar give a significant grunt. It would seem that both their traveling companions wanted to be rid of them.

"Walk behind me," Twilla told Wandi, "hold to my skirt and try to step where I have gone. Do you understand?"

The child nodded vigorously. Twilla raised a hand to Utin and said a word of thanks which undoubtedly he could not understand. Then she stepped onto that side ledge and headed toward the cavern through which the river flowed.

For a space the light from behind them gave some chance of seeing, but the darkness grew thicker the farther they advanced. Luckily their underwater path seemed to have no break. After some moments of travel along it, Twilla felt more at ease.

They went on steadily, Wandi crowding closer against her as the dark increased. Twilla wondered about using the mirror light here but there were too many unknowns ahead. She had no wish to weaken any power she might well need later for a defense.

There were no turns in the river, it ran as straight here as if it had been purposefully cut. The water was cold and gradually Twilla's feet, in spite of the boots, grew numb. She worried about Wandi, not sure that she could carry the child should she be unable to keep on by herself.

However, it began to grow lighter ahead promising that they might soon win into the open. Abruptly the rock walls vanished and they were free. Though there were still barrriers on either side, these of earth with above sentinels of tall trees. The green stirring of the forest reached here though, Twilla saw none of the floating mist which marked the aisles between the trees elsewhere.

Here were signs on the crumbling earthen banks that at times the river must reach a much higher level. She kept watching to find some way of climbing out of the cut.

At last she discovered a place where a tangle of roots was exposed and, boosting up Wandi, following close behind, Twilla made use of that as a ladder.

The forest gloom was not as thick here as open sky stretched about the river. But in which way she should now head Twilla had no idea. If she struck into the full dusk of the woods she would still be lost, not only lost but perhaps prey for Lotis. She had no guide back to the castle.

While, on the other hand, if they kept on beside the stream they would eventually reach the plains and there she might be able to leave Wandi with some land family. Though she herself must keep under cover.

Judging by the sun it must be midday. There was a chill nip in the air and she shivered.

"Where are we now?" Wandi stopped short to demand.

"In the forest. Your own land must be ahead and we shall go in that direction—"

They had not gone far before the forest murmur of leaves was pierced by other sounds—the ring of metal against stone, voices raised—

Cautiously Twilla pushed on. There had been a landslip here and one of the great trees, its roots undermined, had fallen, just missing choking the water flow. About that men were busy, hacking with axes, orders being shouted as the great limbs were chopped free, to be hauled downstream by laboring teams of sweating horses.

The invaders! Twilla crouched down. She studied the men below.

They were under the command of a burly man in landsman's clothing, but, even as she settled into hiding, she saw another small party coming upstream with one of the horse teams to get another limb.

Ustar! There was no mistaking the leader who was followed by two armed men. To get away—that need tore at her. There would be no chance to parlay with these if Ustar was in command.

Wandi moved suddenly. Before Twilla could catch her she was at the bank sliding down to the fallen tree waving both her arms and shouting at the top of her shrill child's voice.

"Da—here I be, Da! Da!"

The working men stopped, were staring upward to the child now dancing in a frenzy. Then the burly man who had been giving orders shouted in turn:

"Wandi—Wandi!"

He threw himself forward, arms outstretched.

Twilla drew a deep breath. Wandi was free—and there was no need for her to remain here. Moving first on hands and knees so she might not be sighted from below, she pushed her way well back under tree shadow and then ran blindly, thinking only of Ustar sighted below.

TWILLA GASPED FOR breath, a sharp pain pierced her side. She realized slowly that her fear had very little foundation. Ustar had seen her only with the mirror face, he might not be able to recognize her now. But even then, had she been discovered by those workers below, what explanation for her presence would she have been able to give? No, it was best that she was now beyond their reach for she was sure that they were not going to follow her into this dreaded territory.

A second thought was daunting. She was undeniably lost. For her there were no landmarks, no guides. She had no idea of how one could reach the glade of the Great Tree. One forest aisle was like another and the drifting mist made more confusion.

Trembling with the effort of her run from the river cut, Twilla dropped at the foot of one of the trees, the great outspreading root tops above the ground forming a support. She fumbled with the food packet the under people had given her and tried to wrench free a mouthful of the stuff. Its taste was unpleasant, oily, but she continued to chew and then make herself swallow the mess.

She had no idea how well patrolled the forest was—whether she could hope to encounter someone of its people—perhaps a guard such as had reported to Oxyle. Certainly they must have some watch upon the river cutting and the men working there.

However, for the present, she was content to remain where she was.

To get up and wander fruitlessly again was beyond her present strength.

Perhaps she dozed a little, she never knew, but suddenly she gasped and coughed. There was a waft of putrid stench in the air. She looked up to see, lumbering out from between trees, just such a monster as had been on patrol on the opposite end of the forest.

Though she knew it to be illusion, unable to harm unless one surrendered to the waves of fear it broadcast, still she clawed her way up to her feet, using the ridges of the roots for support.

The thing was so real! She could see it, smell it, hear clearly its growls. Twilla almost feared that she might even find it solid substance if she touched it. And, if all her senses so betrayed her, she would be its meat.

Mirror—she felt for the mirror. It could also show what was not and perhaps she controlled some form of illusion to counter this. She held the disk up with hands which shook a little as the thing strode purposefully toward her, dripping mouth wide, claws reaching.

"You," she summoned up words to be spoken by a dry tongue, "are not. You are not!"

Its fetid breath puffed at her. One of those clawed appendages scraped along the roots among which she sheltered. The thing snarled, made a swipe in her direction.

"You are not!" She choked back her scream and said those words like a chant of protection. "Not—not—not!"

But it was! There was no hazing out of that haired body. Was it possible that there *was* such a creature and the forest people summoned for their own needs an illusion of a thing that did live?

She steadied the mirror. At least it was not appearing yet to close— bring her down with those claws.

Twilla drew a deep breath, strove to hold to control when all her senses reported that this was real, that she was its prey beyond hope of escape.

"You are not!" She cried out in what might have been a scream had she not fought for control.

The thing grinned. Its small eyes gleamed. But it did not advance. Instead it squatted down, its thick lower limbs folding under it. Now it threw back its great head and from that fanged muzzle broke a howling.

Twilla cringed in spite of her efforts to believe that this was all illusion. If the thing had been created to patrol the forest perhaps it had also been set to take prisoners of intruders—those which did not flee when they first sighted it. Then—sooner or later one of the warders would—

Mist swirled behind the monster, thickened and from its core stepped Oxyle. Twilla gave a little sob of relief. The forest lord snapped his fingers and the monster, never taking its eyes from Twilla standing at bay, snorted and growled.

"Off!" Oxyle ordered as he would speak to a hound.

The thing growled again, shaking its head from side to side, but it was regaining its feet, though giving the impression that it did so reluctantly. Then it turned to face the forest lord, and snarled again.

Oxyle merely pointed a finger at it. Uttering a cry of protest it shambled away, back into the wood shadows from whence it had come.

"It—it was real—" Twilla said in a shaking voice.

"That one, yes. But how came you here, Moon Daughter? And where have you been?"

She was shaking, slipping once more into that pocket among the roots. Where had she been? So long a story—

Twilla pressed the mirror to her, feeling something of comfort as its hard substance filled her hands.

"In—in the innerways—the sealed ways. There was the child," she tried now to set memories straight for reporting, "in Lotis's chamber. I brought her out—there were monsters—and those *were* illusions," she added sharply. "But Wandi ran—and she went through one of the sealed doors—I went after her." She paused. Tired as she was and shaken as she had been during her confrontation with the monster, she found it hard to marshall the whole story.

"You have then been," Oxyle said, "where no one has ventured for a thousand seasons. And what did you find—? No, this is a story which deals with hidden things and you shall tell it to those who have reason to know."

He held out his hand, coming forward, and she scrambled up to take it. The familiar mist closed to cocoon them. She held tightly with her other hand to the mirror.

Once more she stood in that land where the jeweled trees bore their fruit and before them was the castle. Oxyle had continued to hold her hand and now he drew her on into that place of many treasures, bringing her to the hall in which stood the feasting table.

However, there were no feasters there now, only five of the forest people. Karla was there, and two other of the women—one she recognized as the mother of Fanna. Though she did not remember the two men. All of them faced around to stare as Oxyle led her forward.

"We have been summoned," Karla spoke first. "We are in council, Oxyle. Now what have you to tell us? And the Moon's Daughter, where has she been?"

"In Ragnok—I think—but she will tell you."

Someone drew a breath which might have marked a stifled protest. Oxyle drew Twilla to that chair at the top of that table, handing her into it. He took his place beside her.

Holding the mirror, because somehow that gave her comfort, Twilla told her tale. Several times there were muttered ejections from those who listened. One of the men made as to speak when she told of freeing the fungi-bound warriors. Fanna's mother shook her head slowly when Twilla spoke of their coming to that great hall to find it deserted.

Her mouth dried. There was suddenly a goblet before her and she sipped that same sweet, watery drink she had first tasted at the feast.

She told of her bargain with Chard, of the departure from the hold. There was another stirring when she spoke of the boar which had so suddenly appeared to trail them to the riverway. Then she related what she had seen, the invaders working at the downed tree, of Wandi's going to the man who must have been her father. Twilla drank more deeply a second time, and she felt the rise of energy within.

"That is the full story," she ended.

"Khargel!" The man next to Oxyle shifted on the bench. "But— that is a tree life away! Khargel and his works have been long swept into the shadows!"

"Rightly," snapped Karla. "We have a darkness to remember from those days. But their women—"

"And their children!" broke in Fanna's mother. "Where are they? You saw a rock," she spoke directly to Twilla—"nothing else?"

The girl shook her head.

"In this their priest lord is right," the third man said, "we now have a common enemy. If those from the open lands work their way up river, hunting that metal they seek, they will win into the heart and, if the old stories are true, also as the Moon Daughter has said, those of the underways are not harmed by iron. Therefore they would be allies worth having."

"If they are willing to deal with us," Oxyle said. "Remember the sentence Khargel passed on them—though we have long refuted him and all his works—yet these have suffered in person from his powers. We will restore their women if we can. But what sorcery that Dark One wrought are leaves of another season. We can meet with them and with goodwill on our side—if they will accept that we come in good faith."

"There are still those among us," Karla returned, "who play with power wantonly. Lotis enticed this child into our lands—and have we not had trouble ever since with determined efforts of those outsiders to win within? They ride the fringes and the wardens must be ever on guard. That the child had been returned—perhaps that will aid us in a little. For Lotis had not had time to bind her.''

''Yet she has raged ever since,'' commented the third woman. ''The more so after her bondman went—''

Twilla straightened. ''Lord Ylon—what has chanced with him?'' she demanded sharply.

''It would seem that Lotis had him not so tight bond as she thought,'' Karla answered first and there was a certain satisfaction in her voice. ''He disappeared—''

''Through one of the doors,'' Oxyle cut in. ''He said that he had farseen you and you were in need.''

That reflection in the mirror! So it *had* drawn Ylon into the under world. But she willed her hand to cease shaking as she emptied the goblet.

''Show me the door,'' she said.

Would the dwellers beyond allow a second intruder—treat him as fairly as they had her? She had no way of answering that, but she did know that she could not let him wander below if there was any way of helping him.

''I have told you all I know,'' Twilla continued. ''Now—'' she looked to Oxyle, ''show me where he went.''

She was aware of some protests but she kept her attention fixed on the Forest Lord and at last he nodded.

''If this be your will—so be it.''

Once more the summoned mist whirled them to one of the darker corridors, Twilla recognized this. It was where Ylon had guided her after their chance meeting—bringing her to Lotis.

The mist gave some light, but there was another source of illumination. Before one of those closed doors were set out in a triangle three tapers, the flames of which burned blue and wavered as if constantly caught by wandering drifts of breeze.

Behind these stood Lotis. She did not look at them, perhaps she was entirely unaware of their arrival. She held in one hand a short branch which supported a single leaf at its tip and with that she was drawing a pattern in the air. Faintly blue were those lines which shone for a moment after the branch passed.

What she might be doing Twilla was not certain but that it was not for Ylon's good she was sure.

Oxyle took a single stride forward. His hand lashed out to interrupt the sway of the branch, bearing that earthward.

Lotis snarled, her mask beauty drawn into a grimace which promised ill. She whipped up the branch again, this time as if she would lash Oxyle across the face with the supple length of it.

Twilla went into action. Since Oxyle had broken part of the pattern of the sorcery wrought here she could do her part. She kicked out, sending the candles flying, their flames sputtering out.

Lotis swung on her with that threatening branch but Oxyle caught at the woman's arm.

"You have broken the oath!" His eyes were blazing. "What foul games have you been playing?"

She laughed and that sound was like the screech of some evil bird. "I deal with my own, weak of heart. It is time that we have true leaders of the older ways! Would such as Eudice—Serana—yes, and Khargel—have let these outlanders live? The land can be roused—"

As she spoke she was backing away. Now she raised her branch wand in both hands and snapped it, throwing the pieces straight at him. The mist whirled, enclosed her, and she was gone.

Oxyle stared down at the upset candles and the broken branch. He now wore his own mask and it was one Twilla would not wish turned upon her.

"So—" he spoke, his voice was soft but there was another note in it. A beast aroused to its defense might utter a growl which had much the timber. "So—"

It was their quarrel Twilla thought, but something Lotis had been doing here was a threat to Ylon. Now she moved to the door.

"Ylon went this way?" she asked.

For a moment Oxyle stared at her as if he did not know who she was, so closely caught he was in thoughts of his own. Then he nodded.

Before he could speak or move, Twilla gathered her strength and plunged through that door, feeling again the jelly-like resistance which gave easily before her push. Once more she was in total darkness and with no guide as to the path ahead.

She held up the mirror. This time that thin haze of light did not answer. An outstretched hand found the rough surface of a wall and touching that she went forward slowly. Perhaps it was Lotis's meddling which had deprived the mirror of its light power here. Twilla felt the burden of uncertainty as she slowly paced through the dark.

It was always dark for Ylon—it would be until he won his freedom from Lotis. There was a fear which went with the loss of sight—she felt twinges of it now. But still she went, though ever more slowly, one hand rubbing the surface of the mirror hoping to summon some faint answer.

She took another step and there was no solid surface, so, overbalanced, Twilla plunged forward, striking painfully against rock as she fell, until she landed on rubble which added to her bruises. The girl could not move at first. Slowly she stretched arms, legs, tested for broken bones. Every movement brought pain but she still had control over her body, she was not injured to the point of being helpless.

If she had fallen here—what of Ylon?

She called his name, then listened with all her might for any sound of a moan or cry in return. Still on her knees, the rubble painful against the press of her flesh, Twilla swept out hands, searching for any body which might lie here.

There was nothing. Even if he had been injured he must have dragged his way on. She got up and went on, one step at a time, searching and now and then calling out. But it would seem that she was alone in the darkness.

She turned to the slope, down which she had come; there were no handholds she could trust. If she dug her fingers in, the stuff scaled off and shifted down. There was only one path and that she had to follow. But her fall had been a sharp warning. She went even slower, sliding a foot ahead with care before she planted any weight upon it.

Time had no meaning, there was the dark, there was the path, and she had to take it. Her caution saved her another mishap as she came up to a barrier against which her foot stubbed with force enough to bring a cry of pain out of her and turn her slightly.

Light! Very faint and distant, but still light! Twilla gave a gulp which was almost a sob. She turned toward that distant promise and struggled on.

After another age of shuffling she came to the source of that light, a slit in the wall—whether it was meant for a door or not she had no idea but she could pull herself forward into—through it.

This was another such cavern as the one in which she and Wandi had found the ensorcelled under men. There was activity here not too far away. By the grayish glow from the lichen-curtained walls she sighted a party of the small men. They were gathered around a bundle on the floor. Twilla edged forward.

She could see more clearly now. There was Ylon! But he was enmeshed in a silver net like a trapped animal. One of the small men approached the prisoner holding out a sword.

Twilla scrambled along the wall, ran toward Ylon and his captors. She must stop this!

"No!" she cried out as she ran unsteadily. The mirror was her only weapon and she held it in both hands.

At her cry the captors, startled, turned to face her.

"No!" she gasped again. At least that one with the sword had not yet struck any blow. Mirror—if the mirror would only answer her!

She lifted the disk. But Ylon moved within the netting. It tore, fell from his shoulders, away from his body as he stood up. While, with startled cries of their own, the under men retreated. But Twilla had already recognized one of them.

Utin! At least he knew who she was, perhaps on demand he would take them to Chard.

She spoke his name. He stood where he had been, though his fellows withdrew, the astonishment in their expressions as they looked at the now-free captive plain to read.

If she only spoke the underspeech! But perhaps he would recognize his name when she called him:

"Utin!"

"Twilla—?" Ylon turned his head to stare in her direction, that seeking look on his face. "Is it you?"

"Yes," she was beside him now, then moved again to stand between him and the under-men.

"Utin—" she said that name firmly and then added another "Chard!"

If he would only understand and the priest leader be summoned. She had fulfilled the mission he had given her—or at least in part. She could tell him that the Council would be willing to listen to him.

"Chard!" she repeated more loudly.

Utin spoke, a guttural roll of words. One of the others took off, running across the cavern. Had he sent for the priest leader, she could only hope so.

Now he edged forward until he could pick up a dangling end of that silver net. He pulled it across his forearm testing each portion as it came into his hands. It was plain that he was hunting some fault which had made it break under Ylon's struggles.

But Twilla's attention was for Ylon now. "They have not harmed you?" She surveyed him, looking for any sign of a wound.

He was smiling as if they were wholly out of danger.

"Caught me like a fish," he said lightly. "But it certainly was a flimsy net. You—you are safe? The child—?"

"Back with her own. It is—" she got no chance to add to that for the messenger was trotting back and, behind him, Chard was certainly in sight.

"They bring their leader," Twilla told Ylon hastily. "He knows me—I am sure he will listen to me."

She was still standing before Ylon and would continue to do so as long as the members of that company still held swords, and several of them did.

"Wisewoman!" Chard's accent could not distort his words. "You come again—and you have this bond one—" He regarded Ylon with a shade of disgust.

"This is my friend—he came seeking me—so I must seek him in turn. He is of my blood—"

"But bound to the forest!"

Utin gabbled a sentence of some length and now Chard looked puzzled.

"What power has this one?" he demanded of Twilla indicating Ylon. "There was laid upon him the binding to hold. He is not of forest blood yet he stands free! What are his powers?"

Twilla shook her head. "I do not know. But do you bind those who are not your enemies?"

"Did you not yourself tell us that those of his kind would bring trouble to us? They move up the river even now. We have set the guards but they may have powers we do not know—as this one seems to have. If we have a captive of their kind we can discover what will work the best against them."

"Experiment with me," Ylon commented though he did not seem upset by that.

"Lord Ylon is no enemy of yours," Twilla stated flatly. "He is bound to the forest—but perhaps not so much as he once was."

"They have taken his sight, if not his wits, after their own ways. Certainly he hated them for that. And in hating the forest he would gladly lead in his kind for vengeance."

"Sound-enough reasoning," Ylon commented, "if it were true. I know not who you are who wishes to pass judgment on me, but you can do no worse than my own people have already done. When I first returned to them with the forest doom laid on me they held me in fear and would have none of me. Those of my blood kin turned against me. Then did I not return to the forest—though not for the purposes they must believe—and that will fan their anger against me the hotter. This is a wide land—if a truce could be made—"

"Who is this Wisewoman? She speaks of under- and overground

coming once more to friendship, now you suggest that these of your own kind might be enticed to council.''

"Stranger things have happened," Ylon returned.

"We shall see. For now you and the Wisewoman will abide with us until we know what should be done.''

19

ONCE MORE TWILLA was escorted through passages but this time Ylon strode beside her, and she had taken his hand in hers. He walked with confidence as if he could indeed see the rough rock walls around them, their hangings of the luminous lichen. Then they reached the center of the underground with before them the hall. This time there was no feeling of abandonment. But rather an assembly of workers bent on many jobs, some at forges and the others delivering the raw material for their hammers or on other errands.

Twilla walked a careful way with a low murmur now and then for Ylon's guidance. And at last they reached those chambers which seemed to be Chard's own. Small flying lizards had whirled almost dizzily around them as they went. One almost landed on Twilla's shoulder and then sheered off at the last moment.

Ylon ducked his head, he must have caught the warning sound of wing beat. Twilla swiftly explained their escort. But the creatures did not follow them any farther than the door leading into Chard's first chamber.

"Rest—" The priest waved his hand toward low stools with padded leather seats and Twilla steered Ylon to one, dropping down beside him on another she had pulled closer.

Chard himself no longer was faced with the piles of inscribed metal plates Twilla had seen at their last meeting. But there was a worn look about him as if he had indeed been busied for hours at tasks which could not be postponed.

"Wisewoman," he said, "we perhaps did ill in letting you go before—Our eyes and ears along the river report that those coming up stream have been laboring hard to clear way one of the great trees brought down by the sinking of the earth. Already these have completed their mission—that which was the body of the tree has been drawn away.

"However, the invaders have not withdrawn. There are those who are still searching for our riches in the river gravel, and those who lurk and slink about, venturing slowly upstream. They have found the road by which you and the child dared the current."

"Wandi—" Twilla replied. "Her father was among those who labored—she went to him."

She hesitated and then added: "However, perhaps that was for the better, under lord. Those of my kind love their children well. Knowing that one had been taken by the forest spells would only rouse them to greater efforts."

Chard regarded her intently. "Had she been indeed under forest spell she would remember nothing upon her return. But this one does, of that I am sure."

"So Lotis failed this time!" That coming from Ylon broke in to startle them. There was a note of strong emotion in his voice. "Just as she is failing to hold my bond." Ylon smiled then, a wry quirk of lips.

"Of this Lotis I know nothing," Chard replied. "As all the forest women she has her powers. But—" he had turned that searching gaze on Ylon now, "you may not feel bonds, outworld man. Perhaps she means to let you run a little for her own purposes. Only—" now he held up his hands, setting fingertip to fingertip and eyeing them both, "the netting did not hold you."

"You believed it would?" Twilla wanted to know.

"Yes. In the old seasons before we were left in our own bondage such was a defense against those wanderers who came over mountain. There were never many but they pried, and spied, and some of them had knowledge of the nature of rocks and the treasure which such can hold.

"We trapped them—those that the forest did not take in their turn. And silver bonds held, for it is our silver work which can stand against cold iron which your people can use without hurt, even as our smiths can handle mage-forged silver—while the forest ones cannot. Silver is of our power and we turn to it when we must.

"You were trapped." He addressed Ylon directly. "Yet you stood free when it suited you to do so. This can only mean that a forest bond still with you allowed this. Therefore, outman, do not believe yourself free, it may well be that your tree mistress holds you only on a longer leash.

"Thus—" Chard continued after a moment as if he wanted that thought to sink well in, "you may also be eyes and ears—for those above. Though perhaps I should not say eyes—"

Twilla tensed at that strike against a maimed man, even as she had days ago striven to offset Lotis's malice at the feasting table.

"And I—" she asked swiftly, "am also now an enemy? You have said that the freeing of the child has brought ill—that was my doing."

"You have given blood oath—" the priest replied. "And that oath lies upon your own power, you will diminish that if you break your word—not only that—" he was the one to smile now—a none too pleasant smile—"surely you are learned in the rules of power—if you use that which you can summon against another, and that other," he suddenly reached behind him and brought out the boar-headed staff, "has a defense—the very force of your ill-used attack will turn on you!"

"I have done what I said I would do—I carried your message to Oxyle of the Council—"

"Yes? And what does that one say in return?"

"I do not know. For I learned that Lord Ylon," she put out her hand and laid it on Ylon's, "had gone into your dark ways in search of me. So—fearing disaster—I came after him."

She remembered the strange ceremony she and Oxyle had interrupted, that Lotis had been engaged in, and swiftly she added:

"Lotis of the forest was busied with things of power at the threshold of that doorway through which Lord Ylon had gone. We broke her spelling."

Chard had rested the staff on the low table and now he shifted it around, leaning forward and peering into the eyes of the boar. He uttered some words in that guttural language of the underworld. The red eyes glittered, and, to Twilla's amazement appeared to blink slowly, breaking the steady glare of the yellow-red gems again and yet again.

Chard's face grew taut. His own eyes appeared to hold some of the same baneful glitter as he raised them to stare at Twilla.

"Khargel's spewing—his poison lives still! So the taint there abides! Then, for all our need, there can be no truce between above and below! Your words have been wasted—"

"No," Twilla was quick to return. "Oxyle broke Lotis's spell. He has no wish to follow the old pattern which made trouble here and aloft."

"Then let him prove that by giving us back our women!" Chard thumped the staff down on the table.

"If," it was Ylon who interrupted, "there is a struggle for power in the forest—then cannot your taking Oxyle's side be advantage to both of you?"

Chard threw up his hands in an impatient gesture. "Words! Of what use are words without deeds to back them? Listen, bond man, if this Lotis is bringing ancient foulness to life again—then we shall move in turn. And this time—well, perhaps that which Khargel held in the past has lost some force through the walling of time."

Twilla took the initiative. "Let us return and repeat your words to Oxyle. Remember, I am bound to you by oath—which, as you pointed out, will bring me only ill if I try to break it. This Lord," she again pressed her hand on Ylon's arm, "is eldest son to the leader of the invaders. Though they cast him out when his sight was taken. Therefore he can well advise us as to what defenses we may need against them. Oxyle is already aware that they are stirring once more. And the fact that they have ravished one of the great trees to their purposes, even though it is fallen, will give them courage. By your favor let us return above."

Chard frowned. "You ask much, Wisewoman. If this Lord is whom you say then he may well be an excellent hostage— Unless," his eyes narrowed a little, "the forest has indeed marked him forever. If that is so I do not think he would find favor with the invaders now. But—" he paused, "if he is also the prey this Lotis seeks we do not want him in our hall. Perhaps Oxyle can find a better use for him— bait for some trap he would set for Lotis."

"Then we can go?" Twilla asked firmly.

"I play a wide game," Chard spoke as if to himself. "But sometimes the chances offered by fortune are true. Yes, you shall return. But know you, and tell this also to this Oxyle, I do not believe that his kind shall again find us easy meat. And let Oxyle also remember who holds the river holds the way to the heartland. If we fall—that the trees also will find iron laid to their bark."

At least they were given some hospitality for Chard ordered food and drink for them, set aside in another chamber. Twilla made good use of her portion. Meals had been so scattered in the past few days that she was never sure when she might have opportunity to eat again. Ylon matched her appetite. She was done first and she played with her tankard of water, pushing it back and forth, and trying to sort out her thoughts. He spoke first:

"What manner of place is this?"

Twilla was startled and then remembered, only too swiftly, that for Ylon all the world was a mystery until explained or explored by touch. Swiftly she described the great hall which was the center of the underworld.

Ylon listened and at the word of the boar he frowned a little. "These undermen were seemingly bound away from life until you broke the bespelling which held them. Still that hoofed rover has been seen— Though we laughed at such reports thinking them born of forest madness. How then was such a creature unleashed if its masters were enspelled?"

His voice had risen and now his hand fell away from the goblet and curled into a fist. "We stumble from one mystery to another. There is no end to what may be everlasting entanglement!"

"There will be no end," Twilla agreed, "unless there are some cool thinkers—among your people, Lord Ylon, among the forest ones, and among Chard's."

Ylon leaned a little forward, as if he was straining now to see her face. "You speak of 'your people' to me, Healer. Do you then say that we two are no longer of the same blood?"

"I say that I have nothing in common with those of the settlements," Twilla returned flatly. "I was taken and brought to this land by force. They tried to bend me to their will—" she hesitated and then continued. "That they did not, I have to offer thanks to you. I have no roots in plains, forest, or here beneath ground."

"Therefore," Ylon cut in crisply, "it may well be that in the end you shall be a deciding factor. I was raised a man of arms, Healer— perhaps in an opposite fashion to your training. My teachers spoke of force, not mediation, for that was their creed. And it was mine until—" he paused for a long moment, "until," he lifted his hand to his eyes, "I learned how helpless and hopeless one can be for all training and hardening. You were taught to heal even as I was trained to wastage and hurt. We must listen to another voice now or we shall all be lost.

"My people deemed me no better than a shadow in their rooms when I returned to them. Therefore they spoke before me as they would before a halfwit who knew little and would remember less. My father has been promised full authority over this land—if he can bring it under permanent settlement and, as younger son of a younger son, there lies in him a great pride of blood and a need to rule. Perhaps if it can be shown to him that there is also a gain from more peaceful ways—'' His voice died away.

"Would he welcome a truce if the forest offered such?" she asked when he did not continue.

Ylon shrugged. "How can I say? For near two seasons I have been a nothing, reduced to charity under his roof. Ustar is now his right hand and my brother is first a man of force—and perhaps nothing else. Nor does my father take kindly to any advice. The Dandus priest—'' his mouth quirked as if he tasted something evil, "he was sent—and by those who have little wish to see my father rise in the king's favor. My father gives outward acceptance to him because it is the king's will, but the fellow dabbles in trouble. He is a fanatic as nearly all of his kind are—he would, I think, like to see the old ways of the Far Calling return."

Twilla shuddered. "No!" she protested. "Such are the acts of darkness and surely none would see them return. There would be outcry— the people would truly rise then!"

"The Dandus priest has those who listen—how many are moved by true fear when it is set upon them? He has powers also."

Twilla's hands were on her mirror. There were so many different powers, and certainly she was only groping to learn the extent of that which Hulde had set upon her. Of old the Dandus priests were the stuff of nightmares. They enforced rule upon much of over mountain until the last of the Gardlian family of kings had brought down their head, losing his own life doing so. That they had been creeping back during the recent seasons was a threat. But in time all forget the ills which once were.

"This Dandus—he feeds them fear and hate of the forest?" she speculated.

"How else? To such a one any unknown power is a threat to himself."

Then—how fortune had favored her that in their meeting he had taken her for a healer, had not sensed that she might be more! Twilla wondered if the mirror itself had provided her with armor at that moment.

"You think he will stand against any truce?"

"He must, being who and what he is. That we shall remember if or when this leader gives us back to the forest."

They were summoned at last by Utin who seemed to be again the chosen guide. But once they were out of the great hall they did not turn toward the river with its hidden road but went directly back to the cavern wall.

Utin grunted and struggled until he achieved some words they could understand:

"Look—well," he ordered. "This be true way."

Twilla saw a shadow behind a swinging curtain depending from the lichen above. The small warrior held that to one side and showed them a narrow portal in the wall and Twilla caught Ylon's hand explaining what must be done and leading him through. Utin scrambled after them as they came again into dimness which deepened ahead into the general dark she had found here.

Utin pushed past them and gestured for them to follow. For a wonder this passage appeared to run straight with no side ways—which she could see as Utin produced a glimmering ovid he carried, held a little before him, on the palm of his left hand. In his other she noted, with a fading of confidence, he held one of the broad bladed swords bared and ready. What dangers did he expect?

They tramped on. This way had one quality which had impressed her in the forest. There was a feeling of something just beyond her range of sight or hearing which was astir. And that roused a wariness in her.

Utin had slowed his rocking gait. Under his ridged helm his head pointed forward and he began to swing back and forth that source of light, as if he looked for some traces on walls or flooring.

There was an actual sound which broke through now, a slithering noise as if something was being drawn along the rock of the passage floor. Utin stopped short, turned his head to look back.

"Bad—" he grunted out the word.

Ylon's nostrils expanded. Now Twilla caught a whiff of the same odor. Part of it was of the rottenness of evil decay, but—there was something else—a hint of heavy fragrance she associated with Lotis. But here?

Were they about to face one of the illusions which the forest woman used as her weapons? There was certainly movement beyond in the thicker darkness where Utin's limited hand light barely touched the fringe.

"Ssssss—" A hiss, and from Utin in return a guttural cry.

"What is it?" Ylon's hand jerked in hers, there were lines of strain about those eyes which would not serve him.

"Something out of the dark—"

But Twilla had no time to say more. The thing looped forward. If one had fashioned a giant worm from the field soil, one with the girth of a large tun, then this might be it. One pointed end wavered in the air, though Twilla could not see any indication of eyes. But there was a gaping hole of a mouth, fungi white against the darkness of the rest of the body. From that issued a thrumming note which scaled upward as the thing drew its slimy length forward.

Another illusion? But Twilla also remembered the forest creature above which had been real. She drew Ylon's hand up and put it to rest on her shoulder, moving a step in front of him, her mirror held steady in both hands.

The worm thing uttered again the whispering sound, and the pointed head struck with arrow's speed and skill at Utin. Stolid and thick of body as the underman was he eluded that first attack and struck in return, his blade sinking into the creature's body. But when he jerked it free again there was no sign of any wound mark where it had struck. The worm had withdrawn a little, its pointed forend wavering back and forth. Was it more cautious? Twilla thought so.

Then, once more, with near lightning speed, it lunged! This time that point struck Utin and the underman uttered an audible grunt. But the gaping mouth had not caught him. He staggered back against the wall. The worm reared.

Its attack was not now for the underman, but at Twilla. From the mouth frothed yellowish liquid and the foul odor of that flood caught at her throat. But she did not drop the mirror. That pointed forend swayed back and forth before her as if some wall stood between the thing and its prey and it now sought access through that barrier. The stuff it frothed forth spattered wide.

Twilla gave a small cry as the heat of a glowing coal seared her skin. She could believe that the creature was now spraying poison. The girl edged back, pushing against Ylon.

There was no blaze from the mirror. But some drops of that discharge touched its surface. Curls of smoke arose, intertwined. Then they began to glow, not with the clear silver she had seen echo from the mirror before but the pink of watered blood which deepened to a more fiery red.

Now those loops reached out, wreathed the crawler point—closed. At the same time Utin sprang. He struck the creature from the side as it was ennetted by the smoke. Now he held his sword in both hands and he brought it down across the twisting back of the thing with a force which was well apparent to the eye.

He was tossed aside by the writhing of the coils, crashed against the wall and slid down it. Only this time there was evidence of a wound—a gap. From the net of smoke, holding the thing in spite of its now wild writhing, there ventured a thread which spiraled down, entered into that hole in the thick rolls of flesh.

Ylon's hand dropped from Twilla's shoulder. He moved to one side before she could hinder him and was groping until he found Utin, swinging up the limp body of the underman.

Twilla could only hold—hoping that the mirror was the weapon which they needed. The lines spun from the thing's spittle when the disk faded, but the creature snapped the forepart of its body aloft and back and then lay rolling on the rock as if it would crawl but could not.

Was it dying? They could not edge past it now for the coils still rounded and beat. And if they retreated it might come after them.

"What happens?" Ylon demanded. She could feel his body against her tense. His head turned from side to side. He had laid Utin down but stood over him plainly ready to bear him away if that could be.

"It is wounded—I think." Swiftly she described what had happened with mirror and the threads seeming born of the worm's own poison. What had been told her—that evil could be turned back upon itself if the defense was strong enough.

In the limited light provided by the fallen ovid Utin brought, the body was still quivering and pulsing. The headpoint raised once again, and from the creature burst a cry which was more than the hiss of its attack—a shriek against the coming of death. It beat against the ground, drew in upon itself—was still. Though Twilla yet eyed it with caution. So it had not been any illusion spun by Lotis after all. Yet she was sure she had sniffed that betrayal of fragrance. Did the forest woman somehow know the secret of the under ways? But how could she have come through the doors so long sealed against passage?

Twilla drew a deep breath. She was sure that if the worm was not dead it was past further attack. Though to squeeze by it into the way beyond—that was another thing. And there was Utin—with the under man injured they should take him back to their people.

It was Utin himself who answered that problem for them. He sat up, lifted his large hands to his helm and strove to wrench it off.

Having freed his head from the iron piece which had been so tightly jammed down upon it, he rubbed his hands across his forehead and then shook himself all over, as might an animal emerging from deep water.

With a grunt he pulled himself all the way up. He did not at once shake off the help Ylon stooped to offer him as he stood staring at the body of the worm. Then he turned his head and looked to Twilla. With his hand he made a gesture she took for a salute.

"Arpse—" he mouthed, repeating the word twice as if to make sure she understood. After that he did loose himself from Ylon to waver forward.

With deliberation he kicked at that eyeless head and then stood back watching. There was not even a quiver in the hulk of the body now. Then, slightly more steady on his feet, he made for the wall against which he had crashed and picked up his sword again before he also stooped for the light.

"We go back?" Twilla gestured.

Utin shook his head. Instead he pointed forward with the blade and set out to edge around the worm on into the unknown. They could do no more than follow, though Twilla took great care to avoid the patches of slime the thing had spat and see that Ylon did not come near them.

It was when they got at last past the dead that they realized how great in size the thing was. Like the trees of the forest it was out of all nature.

Utin gave it a last contemptuous kick when he reached the end. And they did not look back.

The way continued straight and that persistent undercurrent of only half-sensed sound Twilla had noted before again took up. Then they faced a flat surface in which there was no opening—but there, above the level of where a door might be, she saw again such a mask of a boar as she and Wandi had come across on their wanderings.

Utin sheathed his sword and took position straightway before that. He raised the odd lamp, positioning it carefully so that its strongest beams went straight into the mask. Under that light the thing looked as alive as if the boar of the inner meadow had furnished a trophy to hang there.

Eyes gleamed in the head, and the light reflected also from the great tusks. There came a grating and suddenly there was a doorway outlined there. The outlines grew deeper, the barrier to that way was opening slowly and ponderously. Utin gave a jump backward as it came to a full swing.

"On—" he waved. "On—" It was plain he was impatient with them. But he was standing aside—he did not move to follow his own suggestion.

Twilla still held to the mirror with one hand but now tightened hold on Ylon again and drew him forward. On they went out of the grim darkness of the underworld into a dusky form of light.

She had no more time than to realize that they must be back in the runways of the forest when two tall men drew in upon them, one from either side. They held what she had seen in Lotis's hand—boughs with a single leaf at the tip. Those were pointed directly at them.

20

IT WAS PLAIN that these two did not face them with any thought of goodwill.

"Go!" The one to Twilla's right made a sharp gesture. Ylon stood a little free of her, facing the speaker. There was straightness to his jawline and Twilla sensed that within him the anger born from his helplessness was stirring. However, she was wary enough of what those branches might evoke to catch again at his hand and draw him along.

Both of their guards fell in behind as the girl explained in a few words to her companion that they were under that restraint. She began to fear that since her second passage into the underground the climate of the forest had drastically changed.

There was no move to transport them via the mists, instead they were urged along the network of passages, mainly of the undecorated kind, a maze she feared she could never retrace. Then once more the splendor of the treasure halls burst into brilliancy around them as they came into the great hall.

There was again an assembly around the table but it differed from the one Twilla had last seen. Oxyle, Karla, Fanna's mother, Musseline, and one other of the men were gone. In this room Lotis sat firmly in the great chair. There was another woman Twilla had never seen before, plus three men, but it was plain that Lotis was in command here.

She smiled as Twilla and Ylon were urged up to the foot of the table.

"So the far farers returned," she observed. "To your place, bondman." She clicked her fingers in that degrading way she had done before.

Ylon did not move. Lotis's smile was abruptly wiped away. Her large green eyes gathered fire in their depths.

"You will do my will!" She uttered that as a master bringing a rebel servant to heel.

However, Ylon remained where he was. His sightless eyes were centered in her direction but except for that maiming he stood as if he were truly his own man again.

Lotis's wide gaze narrowed, it switched from Ylon to Twilla, and then she had a hint of a smile.

"So you have been playing your own games—healer," she made of that term a name of defamation. "You believe that you can use your skills—yet here he is still blind."

"Yes," it was Ylon who answered before Twilla could summon words. "I am blind, Lotis. But bond still—no—I think not!"

Now her mouth worked and her hands enfolded into fists struck together on the tabletop. "I will deal with you later, bondman. As for you"—once more she gave Twilla her attention—"your meddling has cost us dear. That changling I would have made sure of to our gain you freed to her kin and they are able to pick her thoughts and learn what they must not know. Then"—again her fists struck the table—"you have broken the restraints laid long ago that those below not rise to trouble us. We had a taste of their ambitions, their deviousness, and then we had indeed a leader who could see where their rebellion might lead. He took proper action—they were not—until you summoned them again. Unfortunately for us in the passing of growth time some of our kind have grown weak of will. We shall not let them in any way break the ancient laws.

"These two," she said now to the guards who had brought them here, "you will see them into safekeeping. They call you Moon Daughter—dirt woman—" Lotis continued. "Be sure that our knowledge is very old, and greater than any power an outlander can summon. Yes, you have a power of a sort, and so do others among your kind—or they believe they have, and, as long as it suits us, they may think so. But with you we shall certainly deal when it is time!"

Twilla could not see any good in challenging the forest woman now. She must discover, if she could, what had happened to Oxyle, Karla and the others she had held in a measure of trust. Had it proven true then that Lotis had tapped some of the knowledge which had brought that Khargel to rule long ago?

"Well, do you remain silent, dirt woman?" Lotis's smile curved the perfect line of her lips. "You shall have time to think of what you have done—creeping among us as a spy for those outer ones. Yet I believe, from what has drifted to my ears, that you are not well rooted there among your kind either and may find yourself a sapling brought down in the first of the season's storms. Anyway—we have no time for this now—take them!"

Once again they transversed the hallways. It seemed to Twilla as they went that the ever-present mists she had always known here before were less in number, thinned in substance, as if somehow those had been weakened, sapped. They came to a door and one of their guards stepped to it, drawing his branch down its surface in a crossing of lines. It opened and he nodded. Twilla, hand in hand with Ylon, went through, turned quickly, only to see there was no longer any door but rather what appeared to be an unbroken wall of rock.

The room in which they found themselves was smaller than any of the private chambers she had seen, and there was none of the magnificent furnishings of her former quarters. Also the light began to fade as the door closed upon them. The chamber did not fall into complete darkness—she could still see a pallet-like bed place in one corner, a trio of stools. But there were no fine carpets or cushions here. It might be cleaner and of a good standard compared with the city dungeons, but it had the same feeling as those prisons.

"So," Ylon spoke first, "Lotis has her power—she has worked for it long, she must relish it."

"I do not understand how Oxyle defeated her by the door if she has become so strong." Swiftly Twilla outlined what she had seen of the breaking of that bespelling. "How did she gain a victory over him—over Karla—for Karla has knowledge." (She remembered well that visit to the moon reflection pool which had cleansed and restored her own focus for power.)

"Lotis," Ylon had found one of the stools by knocking against it as he moved and now he sat down, supported by elbows set on his knees, his shoulders hunched as if some of that strength Twilla had sensed in him, was cracking.

"I was bond to her. You cannot understand what that means, Healer. For a while she was all a man could long for in his life. She was—his life when she desired. Lotis ruled me as if I were an empty pot into which she poured what she willed, and stirred as she pleased.

"Somehow I cannot remember how—I managed to break free—to

leave the forest. The men I had once commanded found me staggering brain bemused—blind. Slowly my wits returned but my sight did not—thus I was of no use to anyone. Then—with you, I returned.''

He drew a heavy breath which was near a sob. His face continued hidden from her.

"Again returned that binding—I was her—thing! But also something within me awakened, fighting for life. I think, Healer, it was partly of your doing. You could not give me back my sight, but since we came out of the Keep I have gained back a portion of my manhood, so I managed to do what must be done.''

Twilla remembered his downing of Ustar, of their battle with the river flood.

"You were a man, you are a man!''

"Perhaps." Now he raised his head, turned it a little toward her. "By fortune's favor that which had been awakened in me grew even when Lotis claimed me again. And then''—there was a kind of eagerness in his face—''there was the matter of the iron and I knew that in one thing I had power greater than any of the forest. That brought a further loosening of the bond hold. I do not know whether she found me too difficult to control without effort she did not want to expend— or perhaps, in her contempt, she was not even aware that I was slipping from her. She had already determined on bringing under command someone younger, whom she could mold as she pleased.

"Thus she summoned the child. Though she did it against the intentions of her own people. In these past few days she has become very sure, very confident. And she has long wanted power.''

"However," Twilla said softly, "she has no longer control of you.''

"Only my eyes!'' Those words rang through this small chamber as if he cried out against all the injustices he had known. "I am a frighting man who is now no more than a child. She has robbed me well.''

Twilla settled on the edge of that pallet which had been placed on a ledge jutting out of the rock wall. She was trying to find words to answer him when Ylon continued:

"A woman fights my battles. You stood before me when that horror of the underways would have downed us. Even the dwarf made a better showing—''

"No! It was not me—not truly me, Lord Ylon. I am a healer, no worker with power. My mistress gave me an ancient thing and told me only to make it truly mine through certain labor. As I did. Even yet I know not how much I can command. While to use it to any extent brings a weakness to me. If Lotis wishes to challenge me she is the better armed for she has all her people's learning behind her.

My mistress was only an explorer of ancient learning, she longed to know, but she was not adept. And I am even less than her.''

"Yet so far you have survived well," Ylon said. "You cannot claim you are maimed."

"Still—" Twilla was beginning. Then she stiffened and her hands went instantly to the mirror as they always did when such only half understood warning came upon her.

There was a curdling in the air, movement, and then opaque streamers, not the shining of the silver mists, only a dimmed shadow of such. On impulse Twilla raised the mirror to face that disturbance. If Lotis had sent one of her monsters to them, then perhaps this would be again a defense.

The surface of the mirror cleared to bright silver. There was a small spray of motes in the air before it. Why she did so, Twilla did not know, but she gave the disk a twist, almost as if it were a spindle for the spinning of thread. Now spin it did—sending out threads of silver, needle thin but striking toward that troubling in the air. There they struck and clung. The glitter born from them spread across the muddy surface. In a moment or two what Twilla saw was a true whirl of the travel mists. Out of the embrace of that stumbled, nearly to fall, Karla. Ylon must have sensed her coming for he was on his feet, and when her body touched his, he supported her.

The forest woman was gasping. There was a dusky tinge to her normally ivory pale face, and she wavered in Ylon's hold.

Then she found her voice: "Moon Daughter—to you my thanks. That cursed one has rewoven that what has been untouched since the first sapling arose from the earth! May she be swallowed into the Maw of Grippar! Even Khargel did not so twist that which is our lives.''

Twilla helped her to sit on the bed. Karla continued to gasp for several breaths. Then she straightened a little.

"What news have you brought back from the underworld?" she asked. "Has that one managed to foul again any hope of effort?''

"Chard fears that the invaders may follow the riverway within. His people prepare certain guards—" Twilla described the nets.

Karla nodded. "As of old—yes, those entrapped very well the out-mountain people who strayed into our land many seasons ago. Even after the sundering and Khargel wrought his will below we had still a supply of such. But their virtue weakens with time and they fall apart. So they weave such again? That is good hearing—we have had little enough to make us hope.''

"Chard will only act with you," Ylon spoke up, "if you release their women and children.''

Karla clasped her hands together and stared down at those entwined fingers.

"So we would have agreed—"

"But not now?" Twilla interrupted.

"Lotis has made her move—and so far she has gathered others to her following. We did not know—we were ever bound by our *law* that one does not question the powers of another—though that was what brought us trouble before long ago. Lotis has somehow discovered knowledge which was sealed and bound after the destruction of Khargel. She"—Karla waved one hand now in the air—"you have seen her power—she keeps us who have not sworn themselves to her service from the mist travel. Oxyle has gone searching in the unused ways for where she has made such discoveries. With him stand the strongest of our empowered. It may even be that they have been entrapped by some snare long forgotten, for we have not heard from them.

"Lotis has spoken against you, Moon Daughter, saying that you are one sent by the invaders to weaken us and bring discord. She has stated again the warnings that the underworld are our enemies and that you have moved to release their fighting men and artificers to lead another attack. And—Moon Daughter," she twisted about to face Twilla as if to read an answer in the other's expression as well as hear it, "the invaders do have a power—something we did not dream of. In some way Lotis has tapped this—perhaps because power is ever drawn to power—and she—we believe, those of us of the inner council she has driven into hiding, that she makes a common cause in some way with this power. What power is it, Moon Daughter, that your race have and Lotis can treat within this fashion?"

"The Dandus priest." Ylon had not reseated himself and now he took a step forward, looming over both of the women. "The old stories—the warnings—yes, those Dark Ones had their strengths which they kept jealously secret. Such a believer might well think that he could gain his will by causing dissension here—and if he is truly in touch with Lotis, perhaps he has!"

"So," Karla accepted that. She sat straighter and her expression was one of determination. "We draw from the forest, it provides our strength, if Lotis meddles with that which is not grown from this soil, then she disputes all which is our birthright. Let those tricked and teased into following her realize that and they will fall away. For it is she who has truly betrayed.

"How powerful is this outer world magic, Ylon?" Twilla noted that Karla addressed him by name and not by the contemptuous "bondman" used toward him earlier.

"Who knows," he replied. "Once the Dandus rule was tight upon my land—and mistake it not—it is a vicious rule! Those of my blood died horrible deaths to break it in the end. Here—should it be able to draw upon a new source—who knows?"

"Moon Daughter, you hold power," Karla gestured to the mirror. "What can you summon?"

Twilla bit her lip. What *could* she summon? If she only knew more. Lotis was long skilled. She shuddered away from the thought of what the Dandus priest might use—those tales were too dark to hold in memory.

"I do not know," she spoke the truth. "You, of all, Karla, must guess that I am one who holds a weapon of which I am unsure. But I can only try."

"Can you find Oxyle? We must have him and those with him—if they *are* entrapped as we fear, perhaps they can be freed. Only with the real council in office can we reply to the under people, enlist them on our side."

Find Oxyle? Twilla lifted the narrow cord from around her neck and settled the disk on her knees. She thought back to that time in the underworld when she had been able to raise Ylon's reflection on its surface by sheer willing. And she asked:

"Lord Ylon, sometime since—when I was lost in the under ways— was there ever a moment that you were strongly aware of me—almost as if I called upon you for aid?"

"Yes," he returned simply. "I—I cannot say that I saw for that has been taken from me—but, yes, in a way I saw you as you are in my mind."

Karla looked from one to the other of them as if she were avid to learn what she might.

"And you were not linked with power," Twilla was really thinking aloud, now exploring this idea. "But Oxyle *is* one empowered. If my thoughts were carried by the mirror to you—then—"

"Then," Karla broke in with a fierce note in her voice, "you can so communicate with Oxyle! Do so!" That was a command.

Twilla stared down into the mirror.

"Give me now sight of mind—" she sought the words which she believed might empower her strongest strivings.

> *"Link with power of other kind.*
> *"Let us see whence they have sped.*
> *Where strong power is truly led."*

Oxyle—this was the shape of his face, the odd slant setting of his eyes, the curve of his mouth. He was coming into being on the mirror surface. Hazy—too hazy. Twilla fought to make the reflection clear.

Then, as if some obstruction had snapped, it *was* clear. Not only clear but those green eyes were staring at her—seeing—she was sure of it.

"Where—" she began that thought and then quickly stopped for the reflection had quivered as if only her entire concentration on that one thing alone was all which could hold it so.

The lips in that so clear reflection of the Forest Lord moved.

"Yes! Yes!"

Twilla was partly aware of Karla's weight against her shoulder. "Yes!" Karla's third word was near a cry of triumph.

Still, in spite of all her efforts, Twilla could not keep to that peak of hold. The reflection quivered, was gone as Twilla weakened, sank in upon herself on the bed.

"So there we search!" Karla was on her feet.

"The mirror power worked?" asked Ylon. He looked in Twilla's direction as if he could see her shivering body. He was at the bed, then his arms were about her holding her fast, as if he would pour into her a portion of his own body's strength.

"She has done as you wished," he spoke over her head in Karla's general direction. "You have what you want of her—what next, my lady?"

"We go in search," snapped the other. "Unless you choose to await Lotis's pleasure here."

"There is no door—now," Twilla spoke wearily. "Do you call your mists for us, Karla?"

The woman stood very still. Some of the exultation faded from her face. She half raised a hand and then dropped it to hang by her side.

"She has warped the mists. It was all I could do to raise that poor remnant to reach you. We have to go on foot. As for the door—that is a matter of illusion and already you know the way to deal with such, Moon Daughter, as you have before."

Ylon did not move, he still held the girl closely.

"And what do we find beyond your illusion?" he demanded. "Twilla is wearied, she cannot risk another pull upon her power."

Karla hesitated there. "There may be guards. Lotis is not one who trusts without a second warding."

"So, we find guards," Ylon repeated. He loosed one hand of its hold about Twilla and it went to the front of his journey-worn jerkin.

When it came forth again his fingers were curled about the hilt of a dagger.

Karla hissed, drew away.

"Iron!"

"Just so," Ylon returned. "The underpeople use it without fear. This is of their forging. I need not even strike true, need I? A touch only—"

"Yes," she was shivering.

"This time I hold a weapon and one which is greater in these halls than any power. Is it your will that we go follow fortune beyond?"

Twilla returned the mirror cord to its place about her neck.

"It is better to act than to sit and wait for what one is not sure of," she replied. "Yes—Karla, do you know where we go?"

"Oxyle—yes. The words I was able to read from his lips. He is not trapped, but he needs us. He has found the place of old knowledge."

"Then," Ylon arose, drawing Twilla up beside him. She was glad of his support for the mirror weakness still held her. "Let us go."

Karla walked purposefully forward straight at what Twilla saw as an unbroken wall and Ylon followed when she took her own first steps still beside him.

She aimed the two of them directly behind the forest woman, though at the last moment she could not help but shut her eyes as it seemed they were going to slam directly into the stone. When she blinked again they were out in the hall.

There was a cry and one of those guards Lotis had set upon them came in a rush, his branch wand ready.

Ylon had dropped his hold on Twilla and swung around. Now even the fainter light in the corridor showed clearly what he held at ready— the dagger.

PERHAPS IN HIS amazement the guard had not been able to stop the downward lash of his branch. Ylon might be lacking one major sense but he had been without sight long enough to refine those which remained to him. The swish of the branch through the air was answered by a sharp upward and outward thrust of the dagger.

Wood met steel. There was a flash of light, and the guard went stumbling back. With a cry he threw from him what remained of his power weapon, for that was alive with a dancing flame seeping from the point of contact with Ylon's weapon.

His scramble of retreat brought him against the wall of the corridor and then he rebounded, taking off as if he believed that wisp of fire still reaching for him.

Ylon laughed. And there was a new note in that. It seemed to Twilla that he stood straighter, his head was held higher. "So," he said, "this hound still has teeth!"

Karla moved a step away. "That one will raise the alarm," she said. She was looking at Ylon and there was a shadow of uneasiness in her eyes. "Without the mists we have far to go and those I dare not summon now."

"Then let us be on our way," Ylon returned. But he did not return the dagger to hiding, keeping it in a tight grip—now and then moving his wrist so that the blade performed some slash in the air. Perhaps he was pulling from memory warrior knowledge. Karla kept well ahead, glancing back now and then at those threatening gestures.

Twilla gave up all hope of trying to keep track of the ways they transversed. One passage curled away from the other. Sometimes they came to one of the treasure-walled halls and then Karla proceeded with care. It was in the second of such crossings into the brighter light that they met others for the first time.

Four of the forest people appeared to be advancing with the same caution that they themselves were using. And of those four Twilla could name two—there was Fanna and his mother.

Before Twilla could retreat, urging Ylon with her, Karla hailed the others.

Musseline looked beyond Karla to Twilla.

"So you reached them, sister?" She moved forward. "But there are searchers in the ways—and Lotis has brought in darkness we do not understand. And Oxyle—"

"Oxyle has been successful," Karla told her, "we go to him now. He has found the source of that which Lotis bends to her will."

One of the men accompanying Musseline nodded. "Well enough, then we go also. For now we do not know who is friend, who is another hand for Lotis."

Their party so increased they made a hurried trip down a section of the lighted passage and then into a narrow side track which led them again into the dusk of the other ways.

Twilla lagged a little. She had been without rest for so long, and her mirror calling had eaten into what was left of her reserves of strength. Then Ylon, as if he saw that she was faltering, moved up beside her, his arm closing about her, lending her support. She wondered a little that he seemed to be able to keep the pace without any wavering. The strain which blindness set upon him, the fact that he must depend largely on the aid of others to travel at all, must be near as sapping as the mirror was to her. Yet he strode in even paces, a rock strong to her aid.

Karla and Musseline were exchanging news and, from the bits she overheard, Twilla gathered that indeed the forces of the forest were split. Some held neutral, withdrawing to their own places of refuge, refusing to side with Lotis or be hunted down because they held to the council that had been.

The interference with the mists had startled, even frightened, some for they had so long accepted such powers as natural and understood. It had in a manner crippled those who might have taken a stand earlier against Lotis, separating them from each other and from sources of their own powers.

Still Karla kept on and the rest followed. Twilla lapsed into a strange dreamlike state wherein the walls flowed by her as if she was being borne along by the river current. She found herself blinking, fighting to keep her eyes open, for a fog was closing in around her.

However, she was shaken out of this when Karla suddenly halted. They had come into a very short passage and before them was one of those unseamed walls which did not promise any entrance.

Karla raised her hand and gestured, ending by pointing at the wall immediately before them. There was no change that Twilla could see. Again Karla went through her series of gestures and this time Musseline echoed her.

"It is warded," one of the men said. "Warded by other power."

Twilla felt a sudden tug at her arm and she blinked at Fanna.

"Other power," he repeated, "power you can break, lady?"

She fumbled with the mirror. But as she raised it she saw a dimmed surface. She had drawn too much in her search for Oxyle. Bemused she shook her head.

It was Ylon who spoke up. "This is forest power?" he demanded, as he gently put Twilla to one side.

"It must be so," Karla replied. "But the sealing does not answer to the proper spell, though this is the way Oxyle went and he must have passed this. Perhaps Lotis indeed set a trap. Of us all Oxyle has been the only one able to confront her."

Ylon held out his left hand to the woman. "Show me where this passage must be."

She shrank from him as did the others when they sighted the bared weapon in his right hand. "What would you do?" one of the men demanded harshly.

"Iron is your greatest fear, is that not so? Could any of your spells hold against it?"

Karla's surprise was as open as that of the man who had spoken.

"To use that against spelling—" she said slowly.

"We need some answer," Musseline nodded. "Iron is our bane of body, can it not also be our bane of power? Show him, sister, where the door lies!"

Staying carefully away from the weapon, Karla came to his left side and with a light touch on his arm guided him on until he was within touching distance of the wall. Then she caught at his hand, lifting it up and drawing it in a straight line across the stone several inches above their heads.

"So!" she said.

"You must guide me," he ordered. "Keep your touch well from the blade—but guide!"

Her hold shifted gingerly to his other hand and she again drew that line, pushing his fist, fast closed about the dagger hilt, closer to the wall until Twilla heard the faint grind of the steel point against stone.

And—as the double-held dagger moved, a dark line appeared there. Down to the right stooped Karla, the tip of her tongue showing between her tight lips, drawing Ylon with her until the point reached the rock under them. Another line.

Now the forest woman pushed to the left and made a second descending journey for Ylon's guidance.

There was truly the outline of a block which could be a door now before them but there was no sign of how they were to open it, for there was no visible latch.

Ylon continued to front it, his sightless eyes in a set stare as if he could plainly distinguish what should be there. Then he shouldered Karla back. He might have been fronting again the guard who had threatened him as he went into a part crouch. His weapon moved out in a sweep which crisscrossed with flashing speed the space between those lines.

Once again came a burst of light. This time so intense that Twilla cried out and covered her eyes, not sure for a moment that she had not shared Ylon's fate and her sight had been riven from her.

She heard in turn cries from the others. Blinking hard she stared ahead and slowly (too slowly she thought) clear sight returned.

Where there had been only the outline of a door a square of light beamed out to encompass all of them. Through that reached a tendril of that silver mist which had been swept from the ways. It seemed to beckon them in.

Twilla took grip of Ylon who had not stirred from his place and urged him on, the rest crowding behind.

The light ahead pulsed in a heartbeat pattern, and its birth seemed centered in a single artifact in the middle of what was a round chamber. A tree stood there, trunk, branch, twig, leaf, a miniature in form of the forest giants yet not much taller than Ylon.

That trunk, branch, twig, and leaf, though seemingly of silver, were not opaque, and through each flowed in rhythmic surges, a green fluid. Whether it was alive in some strange way Twilla could not be sure, but she swayed as that pulsing light lapped about her. Her skin tingled, her very hair stirred with a throbbing beat. Here was power such as she had never faced.

There was a cry from those who had followed them in. Karla, Musseline, Fanna, the forest men, all had gone to their knees and were
holding out their hands as if they might so draw to them that strength
which this tree symbol was whirling outward with steady pulse.

"Frosnost!" Karla cried out. There was awe, exultation, breaking
the mask of her general expression.

"Frosnost!" echoed the others, making that cry ring through the
chamber.

"What—!" Ylon retreated a step and Twilla spoke hurriedly to
explain what stood there. His head swung from side to side slowly as
if he were denying what she had to describe.

One could watch forever that play of the green gleam within its
silver prison. No! Twilla caught herself up short, and she felt for the
mirror. This was high power, it could well enchain those who yielded
to it. She was not one with those on their knees worshipping the tree.

Instead she made herself break eye contact with the thing, survey
the chamber in which it was planted. Planted—for there was no longer
any rock surface under her worn boots, and it was plain that the trunk
of that wonder arose out of that earth.

Nor were the walls, she looked from side to side, of stone here
either. There was instead a brown-red irregular surface—like—tree
wood—a tree which had been hollowed to provide a hiding place.

Those walls in turn were covered in neat netting of shelves, all of
which were filled. There were boxes, almost crudely shaped from still
barked wood—a heavy limb must have been cut and hollowed to make
such. And there were small figurines.

Her attention was first caught by a lumpy monster form. That was
the creature which had menaced her in the wood, the one she had first
believed to be an illusion. Next to it—the abomination loosed upon
Wandi and her when they had fled Lotis's chamber—the first monster
and also the rotting lichen which followed. There was drawn up here
an army of nonhuman, horror-born things.

Yet the array of monsters gave way to something else as her gaze
traveled along their lines, here were creatures of another cast altogether, as fair to the sight as the others were foul. She recognized a
representation of the asprites who had brought her healwell, and ones
as entrancing. Nor was she surprised to find numbered among these
the winged lizards of the underland.

At one point the circular wall was broken by a narrow doorway and
near that stood a table, a chair fashioned of age-polished, entwined
branches pulled up to it. While on the table lay piles of ash-gray leaves,
each patterned in green with a flowing script beyond her translation.

She was not given much time to add to her knowledge for out of that silver of door came Oxyle, and he was followed by Vestel, the border guard.

"Frosnost!" again that united cry from those who had come.

Oxyle made a wide circle around the tree as if it were well not to approach that too closely.

"How did you open the door?" he demanded of them at large. There was excitement plain to read in his pale face.

Ylon's head swung around until he was facing the forest lord he could not see.

"With this," he answered simply and raised his hand. The blade of his weapon flashed almost as vividly silver in this light as the tree.

"Cold iron!" Oxyle laughed. "So there was an answer to her seal-spells which we had not thought about. This," he made a gesture which indicated all which surrounded them, "is Wood heart—where roots Frosnost—which Khargel held and sealed. It was lost until Lotis pried and called on strange powers. Even then she could not have broken into this stronghold had it not been for outland magic," now his gaze was bent on Twilla and there was a challenge in his voice as he demanded:

"What strange skills have your blood brought into this land, Moon Daughter? Lotis has long sought power—but she could not have gained what she now holds unless it was fed from elsewhere. She has been here, she has scavanged and thieved, she has thought to seal it against us, capture so we who were able to trace her here. And that she did—only because she drew on strength we do not know. I ask you again, Moon Daughter, what being of power now strives to blot us out?"

"The Dandus priest." It was Ylon who replied before Twilla could summon words. "And do not ask us, Lord Oxyle, what power that one can summon. His kind once ruled a dark dynasty which brought my people groveling before all their mage kind. Their power is founded on blood, on fear, on all which hides from the light of day. When my father was sent to this land, the Dandus priest was made a part of his company by a will my father could not deny.

"I will swear, by whatever oath you ask of me, that my father does not willingly dabble in the slime of such shadows. But how much control that priest exerts I do not know. When those of our blood before us cleansed the land of their evil most of those who stood for the light died. And it became a thing forbidden among us to keep any knowledge of what those of Dandus had, least fools be tempted to try to revive what had been stamped out. There were still priests of Dan-

dus, but we were assured that those among them who had the great
powers were safely gone from this world. It would seem that our teachers were wrong. I tell you truthfully, Lord Oxyle, I do not know what
that one now in the outlanders' company can summon.''

"So, you have brought more than men of greed to threaten us. You,
Moon Daughter, what does your power?''

"This much I can also swear to—by blood if it need be—I have
no touch with the dark. The Dandus priest is my enemy; when I was
brought here he made it plain. Over mountain my mistress was of the
circles who once fought the dark. The learning I gained from her was
that of healer and uniter, not destroyer. And—''

She spoke very slowly now hoping that each word would have
meaning to arrest the forest lord, to turn his thoughts to what might
be done.

"Lord Oxyle, I have been twice with the undermen. They have no
love for the invaders who threatened them even as they do you. Now
they labor on certain weapons of their own. Perhaps their powers and
yours united can stand fast now. Once more they make you an offer—
free their women and they will make truce with you.''

"Free their women. Another secret of Khargel's. We have been
searching—'' he waved his hand toward the table with those piles of
leaves. "Lotis rummaged here. I think she would have destroyed some
things to keep them from us, but Frosnost protects its own. Yes,'' his
shoulders sagged a fraction. "We would be willing to make a common
cause—those of us who have not fallen to Lotis's glamorie. But where
does one hunt for a secret? And time is now our enemy. There was
news that they send over mountain strange weapons, fearsome and
unknown to us. When those arrive they will not linger about the use
of them.''

Ylon gave a sigh which perhaps only Twilla clearly heard. "I think
not,'' he agreed.

"Then,'' the forest lord straightened again, "we shall do what we
may. In this chamber lies knowledge which has been kept since the
great tree itself was but a seedling.''

Karla and Musseline moved a little closer. "Point to where we begin
this hunt, Oxyle. There are five of us, and—''

"Myself and Vestel,'' Oxyle agreed.

Thus there passed a time which Twilla could not reckon. Oxyle and
his companion had brought packs of food and drink with them not
knowing how long their search might continue. Since Twilla and Ylon
could not aid in the examination of those fluttering leaves the others
were fast turning out of the boxes and sorting out in piles on the floor.

She and Ylon went into the room beyond where there were some rolled sleeping mats and stretched out side by side.

Sleep came quickly and it was not dream-disturbed—at first. Then Twilla was aware of passing out of the safe soft dark which had welcomed her into another place.

This had the gray of dusk, the gray of death, and ashes. Yet not too far away there stood, pillar tall, a flame. It was not of honest scarlet as a fire should be, rather a strange yellow, and around it curled oily black smoke. It must have been near as tall as one of the forest trees for those at its foot looked very small.

In spite of her will Twilla was forced toward that flame. Those who moved about the foot of its pillar were human of body as she could clearly see for their bodies were bare of any covering. They capered, jiggling from one foot to another, on the move around the base of the pillar. But there was another who stood so close to that sick flame as to be enwrapped now and then with a fluttering wisp of the oily smoke. And his cloak she saw clearly—the Dandus priest.

Whether she witnessed something now taking place afar, or whether this was a dream born out of her fears she could not tell. The priest raised his arms high. That smoke gathered and coiled around him. The dark stream spiraled upward. When the girl raised her eyes to look, she saw that it formed a sooty finger pointing out and out and out— though toward what it might point she could not see.

"Twilla!" The gray place broke open. There were hands about her, she was being held close to warmth—the human warmth of another's body. Only then did she realize that she had been so chilled in that country of the dead. "Twilla."

Opening her eyes she saw it was Ylon who held her, his blind eyes wide open and centering on her face. Those sightless eyes! More than the warmth of his body heated her now rising from a growing core of rage. Lotis—Lotis and evil! There must be some end she herself could bring to this. She was, she discovered holding the mirror very tightly as one held to shelter in a storm.

"Twilla?" he asked again. "You were crying out—"

"Dreams!" she returned. She told him of pillar flame and those about—the aiming of that roiling smoke finger.

"Warning—" he was beginning when Karla hurried through the door.

"Moon Daughter—we have found what we sought. Now we must prove it to those underground."

22

IN THE CHAMBER of the silver tree they found Oxyle holding some of the ash-colored leaves in a fan. The others crowded around him.

He looked at Twilla and Ylon, fires of excitement in his eyes.

"We know where Khargel bound the women! Now we can treat with this Chard!"

"A bespelling," Musseline said, "by such as Khargel—can it be broken? Is it not true that a spell of the second order—or of the third— as this may well be—can only be broken by the one who sets it? And Khargel has been gone for almost as many seasons as there are message leaves here."

"Did not Moon Daughter break Khargel's spell to release the undermen?" countered Oxyle. "At least we know now where our battlefield lies." He gave the leaves in his hand a little wave which set them fluttering.

"The seal to this heart hiding is broken," Vestel pointed out. "And that she-snake is free to come and go as she pleases. Can we set a barrier against her raiding here again? We do not know how much she had already thieved and what greater secrets she can find."

Ylon moved then. He had undoubtedly located Oxyle by his voice for he turned slightly in the direction of the forest lord.

"There is a lock with which even Lotis will not tamper." From within his jerkin he again produced the dagger. "This has been a key to gaining entrance, now let it prove itself a lock." His head swung as if he were seeking by scent or ear, and Twilla, guessing his purpose, took a handful of sleeve and drew him to face that still open way through which his iron had blasted them a path.

With the girl's aid Ylon crossed to the door, then went to his knees, measuring the opening from side to side with outflung hands. When he had at last satisfied himself on some point he leaned forward and drove the dagger, the quiver of his shoulders betraying the force he must use, into the beaten earth which floored this place, just a palm's width within the walls.

There came a murmur from the forest people. Oxyle, having surrendered his fan of leaves to Vestel, came up to them as Ylon arose again.

"You are clever, outlander. Yes, such will keep at bay whatever Lotis may wave toward our undoing while we remain herein. But what if her power be fueled by that of this outlander mage? He fears not iron."

"No," Ylon shook his head. "He would not fear iron. But there will be that which he will fear—being who and what he is. These priests fear and hate women. He is not easy, I will swear, with any partnership with Lotis. For to him she will appear to have every art his kind loathe. Therefore their linkage is already well-eaten by suspicion, and he will have no trust in her. If she strives to draw upon what he can command he will examine very well what pitfalls might lie in any such surrender or union."

"I trust you have the right of it. But it will be better for us if we be quickly about what we can do now," Oxyle said. "However, outlander, you have sealed us in here as effectively as you have sealed Lotis out and the door to what we seek lies elsewhere—"

"Easy enough to mend." Ylon stooped and wriggled the dagger a little, freeing it from its earthen sheath. "Your door is so unlatched, go through and leave to me the locking once again."

Those of the forest people went, sidling by at a good distance from where Ylon stood waiting, the dagger in hand. When they were all in the outer passage, Ylon followed.

Feeling once more about the portal he had earlier blasted he knelt again, stretched his arms a little within the room, and with both hands drove the dagger into the ground so that it stood upright, midcenter and well-lit by the pulsing of the silver tree.

Again they threaded passages but Oxyle, in the lead, appeared to have no doubts about direction and at last he came to a door in a hall which Twilla recognized. So had she and Ylon come from the lair of the great worm.

Choosing one leaf from the packet he had earlier held, the forest lord touched its tip carefully into the top of that intricate door pattern and drew it, following the lines from left to right. As the leaf passed so did the line it had touched begin to fade.

In the end there was a blank slab showing no markings. Oxyle stood facing that for a moment in the palid light, for though there were no mists swirling now, there seemed to be the faintest ghosts of such accompanying them.

Oxyle set hand to the door and it gave, not as it had for Ylon and Twilla, yielding to their bodies, but rather it swung away and they could look into the rough passage ahead.

As they started down that the faint light still held about them. For the first time the forest people produced tangible weapons in plain sight. Remembering the worm, Twilla hoped that those silver swords might have better effect against the hide of any crawler than Utin's blade had.

Stench wafted on a stir of air before them. It grew thicker as they reached the site of their battle. There had been drastic inroads upon the bulk of the crawler, in some places only a round of bones lay on the rock. What had come here to feast, and did such linger? Twilla brushed shoulder with Ylon as she steered him as close to the wall as she could, remembering those splashes of poison. As she did so, she warned the others.

They made their way by that obstruction and Oxyle kept to a swinging pace. It was plain that he wanted to accomplish what he could as soon as possible.

However, when they emerged into the underworld, he did not venture far from the exit. While the others crowded up behind him. They were being awaited.

Spread out in a line which might allow them to close in from both sides if those from the upper world came farther out were a number of the small warriors. Each bore unsheathed blades. Behind them was a scattering of others bending small bows, and the arrows set ready to those cords, Twilla was sure, were also headed with deadly iron.

From among his followers stepped Chard. Oxyle towered over him and yet there was a certainty of purpose, a suggestion of confidence in the smaller figure which matched the assurance of the upper forest leader.

Oxyle raised his right hand and wove a complicated pattern in the air. That showed in green lines, holding as firm as if he had produced a thread of real substance. In turn Chard steadied his boar-headed staff before him. From the eyes of that came thin lines of red reaching out, winding about the green, yet not touching. So for a long moment the air was aglow and then it winked out. Chard swung his staff and Oxyle also made a motion.

The under warriors drew back, those of the forest sheathed their silver weapons. Arrows were returned to quivers. Then Chard spoke:

"You weave the peace sign for us, over lord. But there is only one reason for us to welcome such as you into our ways—have you come to repair the evil wrought by your kind?"

"Khargel is long gone—and we hoped that his evil vanished with him. Yes, we shall do what we can to repair the weeping rift he left behind. But know this, Under Lord, this is again a time of ill will and worse. Not only do those from over mountain threaten, but there are those of forest blood who show the old taint." Oxyle's voice was grim, his expression dark, and Twilla could guess what effort it must be for him to admit this to one who was an ancient enemy.

"So we have heard," Chard replied. "That you speak the truth is in your favor, over lord. Release that which your kind have bound and then we can speak of other things—perhaps some which shall serve us both."

From his green jerkin Oxyle pulled one of the leaves. In this light the marking on it seemed so faded Twilla could barely distinguish that there had been lines at all.

"This we have found—in Khargel's sealed chamber. It points a way, but your ways are not ours and we cannot say where it lies." He held out the leaf.

Chard transfered his staff to his left hand to accept it. It appeared to fade even more. He uttered an exclamation and lowered the staff. Again the eye beams shone and what had been faint greenish lines on the leaf surface flared bodly red for an instant or two. Chard examined them eagerly.

Then he raised his head. There was a baffled expression on his face and Twilla believed an awakening of suspicion. The lines of the leaf had turned brown and the withered tissue of it was flaking away.

"This I do not know. Do you strive to pass off some mage work to win us, over lord? *Where are our women?*"

There was a growl. Once more the small warriors moved up, arrows were in land, put to cords.

His eyes were fierce, near as glowing as those of the boar staff. Oxyle held up both hands, palm out.

"Under Lord," he replied quietly, "your guards have in their hands what can send all of us to a torturous death. We play no games with you. If you do not know what that map held," he glanced for a moment to the fragments of the leaf lying between them, "then Khargel was the one playing games. Yet where we found it insured that for him at least it had meaning."

It was Chard's turn to look down at the fragments. Perhaps Oxyle had managed in a little to win through his rising suspicion. Suddenly, as if a new thought had struck him, he moved forward the butt of his staff.

Once Twilla had seen smith magic over mountain when a stone the smith declared had inward power brought to cling against it filings of iron. Now the shreds of ancient leaf moved in the same fashion. But what gathered about the end of the shaft was not a reassembled leaf, rather some crooked lines of fragments.

"Gogalar!" that guttural word had burst out of Utin who had crept closer to his lord. "Gogalar!" he shouted gutturally, stamping his foot against the rock, and his cry was taken up by all the others.

They broke lines, crowded in about Chard, while the forest people, very wary of the weapons being now shaken overhead and clashed together, drew back and away.

Chard having stared at that pattern now looked once more to Oxyle. "Mage power, Over Lord, but this makes good sense and we shall see how well it leads us. Those now suggest a way for which we must have a guide. Come, rest and wait until we can summon such."

They came to that hall which Twilla had seen deserted and then busy. However, Chard turned them aside before they entered saying that he well knew they wanted no near contact with what his smiths wrought. They settled instead in the open and the small-winged lizards came in a whirling flock to inspect them. Food was born forth from the hall and they ate. Twilla could hear whispering among the forest people commenting on a land so strange.

There appeared to be no shadow of night touching this land, still they waited. Twilla sat beside Ylon. She had described to him this inner country, and from his comments it sometimes seemed as if he did see what she pictured.

"We take but one step at a time," he said suddenly. "My father has summoned a weight of iron such as the forest people have never imagined. If indeed he has had promise of the land crawlers, then those are encased in iron. They shall be able to root into the forest and wrack their will as they wish."

"And will they?" she asked.

Ylon frowned. "Who can tell? These others may have still defenses we have not dreamed of. But," the hand resting on his knee curled into a fist, "it is folly! Those of the forest have no wish for the open fields. But people need not hack into the great trees. There is dead wood to be had—those of the woodlands do not touch such. If that could be offered to our people—"

"For what in return?" Twilla asked.

"I do not know. Perhaps so that there might be no reason to break the forest bonds."

"Payment to withhold raids upon their own land? Hulde had volumes of the old lore and never has such bargain ever been kept."

"Yes." There was a bleakness in that single word of his answer.

Twilla felt a light touch on her hand and saw that one of the flying lizards had alighted there, its small head held high as it eyed her.

"There is also the matter of the priest," she reminded him.

Ylon's mouth worked as if he would spit. "Yes. There is that. Perhaps we face more than we can hope to deal with."

"We?" she questioned. "Do you now range yourself against those of your blood?"

"I do not know. I bear with me always the hurt which the forest can deal. You, too, have seen the horror which our iron can bring to these people. And I cannot support the dealings with the Dandus beliefs!" he ended on a sharp note.

They were silent again and in time followed the example of their forest people who, except for Vestel, curled down into the long yellow grass and slept. There was everlasting activity about the hall yet no one came in their direction.

The spiraling notes of a horn vigorously blown brought them all alert. Chard, with an escort of warriors, had come out of the hall to head in their direction. Utin trotted beside him and within a few strides halted to again sound the horn he carried.

There was a billowing in the tall grass as if something stirred its way out of nothingness into the open. Then a great tusked head pushed forward and that boar, which had been Twilla's escort before, came into full view.

It swung its heavy head in the direction of the party from the upper reaches but gave no more than a snort as it passed them. Chard raised his staff in salute and the boar grunted, it might have been speaking in the manner of its kind.

Just as Chard could pass easily into the guttural speech of the dwarves so now his lips shaped a series of grunts Twilla could not distinguish from those of the animal, if she closed her eyes. Once more the creature looked toward the forest people who had now all gotten to their feet. Then it swung away, trotting at a pace unusually swift for the bulk of its body.

Chard broke into a fast stride behind it. As he passed the others he waved them on with his staff, while those of his own escort closed in behind. So they pushed their way through the tangled, straw-colored

grass of the land, coming out of that into a place of rocks, encircled
by a river-like stretch of gravel.

Twilla felt the knobbiness of the stone through her badly worn boots
and set her teeth. She must keep up, for Ylon depended upon her. His
hand rested on her shoulder as she twisted a way among those rocks.

There was a great warmth to the air and the dirt stirred up by their
passing stung. Clinging to some of the more rugged rocks along this
trail were patches of tough hair from which wafted the strong smell
of the boar—perhaps there was its chosen lair.

They came at last to the edge of a drop. What lay below was hidden
by a dank fog which arose only level with that lip where they stood.
The boar halted with a grunt and Chard moved slowly along that edge.

To risk descent into the unknown was a danger Twilla, for one, was
not willing to take, sure that she would not be able to aid Ylon if he
could not find his own hand or foothold. However, that was not to be
part of their testing. Instead Chard, the rest of them trailing behind
him, came to a place where there was a splitting off of that edge, the
promise of a way down. Twirling his staff before him, he unhesitat-
ingly took that path.

At least he had one aid. From the eyes of the boar staff there speared
out the joint beams which cut into the fog enough to show them that
what was here was a ramp, steep to be sure, but still better than any
other way to win into what lay below.

The fog was clammy against the skin, and there was that in it which
made Twilla cough. She slowed her pace a little so that most of the
forest people passed them, keeping up a flow of description about their
footing for Ylon.

Then the ramp became a flight of steps, luckily wide. And they
continued. The flare of Chard's light beckoning them on.

As suddenly, as if they had been lifted and dropped, they broke
through that corking of fog, though it clouded what lay around close
to the dark of night. More rock here, standing lines of it. Twilla remembered that farseeing she had tried to do for Chard. Just such a
pillar of rock appeared then in the mirror.

Chard halted at the edge of that stretch of ground. He was staring
out over the lines of standing stones, and he uttered a moaning cry
which was echoed by those of his guard. There was anger, fierce and
open on his face as he looked to Oxyle

"Give us back what you have taken!" He gestured to the dull ranks
of stones.

Oxyle stepped up beside the under lord and made a throwing gesture.
From his open hand there lifted that silvery dust which was the weapon

of forest ensorcelment. It hovered over the closest of those rocks, whirled down to encircle it, then was gone. But the rock remained.

"Give us back our women!" Chard's slender body was shaking now with rage.

Slowly Oxyle shook his head. "Khargel sealed them, our power cannot break through his set will. It is the law which rings us in, none of us may undo another's full spell."

"So. Then what—" Chard had half raised his staff in menace toward the upper lord when his gaze slid beyond and set on Twilla. He shouldered past Oxyle to come to her.

"You freed *us* from the holding put upon us, free now those who are dearest to us!"

"Then iron," she said, "touched—" and no sooner had she spoken those words when there was thrust into her hand Utin's own sword.

"Then use it again—now!"

She moved on to nearest of those waiting stones and tapped it with the iron. There was a ringing note through the pocket but the stone remained intact.

Helplessly she stepped back. The mirror swung as she moved. Ylon's hand was out and she passed the sword to him, raised the mirror and held it out to reflect the stone.

Words, she needed words! They jingled in her mind and she spoke then aloud:

> *"Be as were, truly be—*
> *Let this moonlight be the key.*
> *Return to life by mirror's will.*
> *Let right triumph over ill."*

The silver reflection blazed into life, the core of its beam enwrapped the stone, held but there was no change.

Twilla held the mirror steady, so tightly that its edges cut into her fingers. The light continued to play upon the stone, but it brought no answer. Still the mirror was alive, alive as it was when ready to answer her. There was something more, something she could not—

Swiftly she turned her head to Ylon.

"The iron! Bring the iron!"

By the guidance of her voice he came forward, touching her shoulder, he used that for a guide and, wavering a little, thrust the sword directly into the beam of that reflection. The blade blazed, a fire to equal that of the mirror—so brilliant Twilla hardly dared watch it.

23

YLON STUMBLED, CAUGHT himself, but the sword tip, awakened with the new light, touched the rock and now there was a change. The stone burst, shimmered, was gone and Twilla knew the one who stood in its place for she had seen her likeness.

"Catha!" Chard's cry was triumphant. He tossed the staff in Utin's direction and the warrior caught it. Chard was already clasping the woman, his head a little forward so that his face was buried in the crown of her hair.

It would be Twilla's labors for sure, even as it had been with those sealed in the fungi—save that this first prisoner released bore none of the signs of extreme aging the small warriors had shown. Each of the waiting pillars must be touched in turn. Whether the power of the mirror would last she had no assurance, she could only hope.

Explaining to Ylon what they must do she went on toward the next of the pillars, his hand on her shoulder for guidance Ylon matched step to hers. Again and again and again.

Tears gathered in her eyes tormented by those brilliant bursts of light as each imprisonment was brought to an end. The mirror appeared to grow heavier, or else her strength grew the less—but there seemed to be no end to the waiting pillars.

Those freed from bondage flowed past the two, women and children together, moving with cries of relief and joy toward those who waited at the end of this forsaken valley. Then—the last pillar shimmered into nothingness. Twilla nearly dropped the mirror as a great weight of fatigue enchained her arms. She staggered and heard the clang of metal against rock as Ylon dropped the sword and held her upright.

"They are all free," she said.

"And how is it with you, Healer? It seems that you ply your trade in more than one way."

Healer—it was a time since she had been called that. Healer—yes, what they two had done together here was healing.

She managed to slip the mirror cord once more about her neck. And became aware of a wind sweeping down upon them, a wind and that ruddy light which was a part of this buried world. She looked up. That fog which had sealed this foul valley was breaking up, crinkling in upon itself—it might have been composed of dried leaves now touched with fire.

Twilla drew a deep breath and then another. She felt that a burden had been lifted from her shoulders where Ylon's arm lay, holding her steady against his own body.

"I—I can manage now," she told him.

However, he made no move to loose that hold except to grope for the sword he had dropped. Rather he turned with her as they headed back across the now bare land toward that clamorous crowd where those released encircled Chard and the forest kin stood a little aside. By the time they reached the others Chard was awaiting them. The slender woman beside him, like him, showed a difference to the smaller women clustering around. She reached out hands to Twilla:

"Welcome, sister, life bearer, healer of old ills!" she said in a clear voice.

The other women, shorter, more thick bodied, sturdy of leg, fanned out behind her. There were the children also, though fewer than Twilla had thought to find, and they clung to their mothers, staring round-eyed at the strangers from the upper world.

"Has our promise been fulfilled?" Oxyle advanced a little from his people. Some of the women showed the shadow of fear on their broad faces and drew aside, sheltering their children behind them.

Chard had taken back his staff, now he struck it butt down against the rock three times, so that the low murmurs of the under people ceased.

"It has been fulfilled. But the doing was not yours, upper lord."

"Not so," Twilla spoke quickly. That Oxyle had failed to break the spell was none of his fault. "It is through the will of this Lord, and the knowledge of his people, that we came here. If forest spell cannot break forest spell—is that to be held against him? He brought hither me and Lord Ylon and if our power worked better against an evil locking, that is good fortune for all of us.''

"This healer speaks what is true," Catha said. "These would not be here," she motioned to Oxyle and his people, "if they wished us ill. I know not of what kin you are, Healer," she spoke directly to Twilla now. "However, if you say that what you have done here rests upon the work of others, then I believe that. Greetings to you of above, this moment you have undone what was of the dark—in one way or another.''

They tracked back across the lands through which the boar had guided them. Of that great beast there was no sign, but these he had led had no difficulty in finding the return path. Some of the warriors walked hand in hand with a woman. Two hoisted children to their shoulders, those broad faces under their helmets abeam.

The forest people kept aloof in their own small group, and Twilla and Ylon formed a third. Here they were neither forest nor underground, they might even remind those around them there was a new enemy. Though Twilla had seen no ill will in glances turned upon them from time to time.

At last they came to the great hall and there streamed forth more of the small men. There was joyous calling, women and children were caught in tight, rib-squeezing embraces and their babble raised to a small roar.

Keeping well aloof the forest people seated themselves in the tall grass and watched the restored families stream back into the hall. To all seeming they were forgotten. Shaking from weariness Twilla dropped to the ground and Ylon threw himself down beside her.

"Twilla," his voice was low, however, in spite of the clamor of the small people she could hear it easily, "what is now to be done?''

She sighed, she was so tired. Somehow at this moment she could not even begin to think ahead. "Who knows?" she asked.

She thought perhaps that the forest people might be ready to return to their upper land but they made no attempt to move, sitting quietly in a circle now, a murmur of speech running around. No words reached Twilla, and at that moment she did not greatly care.

At length weariness got the best of her and she slid down to lie full length in the beaten grass, her face turned up to the even light overhead, and she slept.

Ylon woke her at last. A crowd of under people had come forth from the hall carrying baskets cunningly fashioned of gold and silver with master smith's touch, as well as flagons and tankards. Once more they were fed bounteously.

While they were still satisfying their hunger Chard approached, Catha beside him. He went directly to the circle of forest people. Oxyle arose and inclined his head as he towered over the under lord.

"It has been done as we asked," Chard for a moment appeared uncertain, hunting for the right word, the right tone. "A grievous wrong has been righted. You have said that we now have a common enemy. There are those who seek and pry along the great river. We have seen their kind before but not in such numbers. For them we have an answer—as we shall show you."

He raised his staff and waved it twice in the air. There appeared at once at the door of the hall a group of the warriors. However, there was one among them who towered well above them in height. He shuffled in an odd, constrained gait and as they came closer it could be seen that he was entangled in a net of silver which bound his arms to his side, encased his limbs so that there was very little play allowing him to move.

He glared over the heads of his guard—his attention first for the forest people, and then, as he turned his head a little, his eyes widened at the sight of Ylon and Twilla.

His surprise changed to a look of disgust and Twilla saw those hands imprisoned among the mesh close into fists.

"It is a prisoner," Twilla explained to Ylon, "one of the over mountain men—a soldier, I believe." She went on to explain about the silver netting on his feet.

She did not know whether the guards would allow it but she steered Ylon toward the captive. The first disgust on that man's face gave way to a wariness. While the guard grunted and drew in tighter about their captive.

"What troop?" Ylon's voice rang out with the timber of an officer in full command.

The man scowled. At first Twilla thought he would refuse to answer but then he said harshly:

"I am second scout to Torlan's squad."

"So. By whose orders came you up river?"

"What's it to you, turncoat, un-man? I am not under *your* orders."

Twilla saw a faint flush rise under Ylon's sun-browned skin. The contempt of the other was plain. Still her companion made no other sign that he resented the other's taunts.

"Does Torlan try the river?"

The man spat. "I have nothing to say, turncoat."

Oxyle appeared suddenly beside Ylon. "The name of this one's officer has some meaning?" he asked.

"Yes. Torlan listens to Dandus' mouthings. He was bred in Sawash where the Dandus faith is strongest."

Oxyle favored Hahan with a bleak look. Then Chard came closer. Twilla believed that the captive—for all his harsh confrontation of Ylon was uneasy—as well he might be. Somehow that thought gave her satisfaction.

As the three stood silent, facing him, Twilla saw his shoulders twitch. He must be trying to loose himself from the bonds. But they held.

"You see," Chard spoke to Oxyle, "it is our forging which holds this one. Unless we loose it for him there is no escape."

"And how many of such can be forged?" the forest lord asked.

"Not enough to hold an army!" Those words were snapped by the captive. "Lord Harmond calls for such you cannot stand against— walking forts as never were in this land."

Ylon stirred. "He summons the field crawlers. But to get such over mountain will be a great task—"

Hahan sneered. "Not so great, un-man! Already they have passed the upper levels. They will indeed crawl and head straight for the forest!"

"They are sheathed in iron," Ylon said slowly, his head turning a fraction in the direction of Oxyle.

"This one is also sheathed in iron—after a fashion." Chard indicated the mailed shirt, the bowl helm Hahan still wore. He must have been in the act of drawing his sword when entangled, for the bared blade's hilt still was gripped by the hand now fast bound to his side. "Iron answers to the net—will even draw it for a short space." Chard spoke briskly, a craftsman testifying to the worth of his wares.

"If you are wise—un-man—" Hahan said, "you will tell these— these small fools they have no hope—"

"To every weapon there is a defense," Ylon returned. "Can you now walk free?"

Hahan writhed, making a great effort to break the fragile-seeming net. It held as he lost his balance in that battle and landed face down, only to be dragged upright again.

Ylon wore his listening face and Twilla knew that he strove to measure action by hearing. But she gave the message quickly:

"The web holds him fast."

"Well enough then—as least to take those who come spying."

Chard nodded vigorously. "Yes, this holds firm. Take the skulker away," he ordered.

"Lord—!" Hahan was once more struggling against his bonds,

looking to Ylon. "Will you let these earth-delving scum take a man? You are of the true blood—"

"No," Ylon replied with quiet emphasis. "You have already named me—un-man."

"What will these do to me?" Hahan had lost all his blustering courage.

"I do not know. You have come unbidden to spy on them—therefore your fate is for them to decide."

Chard brought the butt of his staff against the ground. "Take him—see that he remains safe."

Hahan was dragged away. Twilla dared to break the silence then:

"What will you do with him?"

Chard smiled. "We keep him—perhaps as bait."

"Guard him well," Ylon said. "He serves a leader who is touched with the Dandus evil. I do not know how strong that power has grown. Perhaps that one could even be a key to unlock your fortress were the dark mage learning be strong enough."

"I think not," Chard seemed satisfied. "But we are warned and be sure we shall be ready for any such invasion. We have safeguards—they have been activated. You have met with Aviral," he held a hand in salute to the boar's head on his staff. "Aviral is far more than the beast he appears.

"Now," he addressed Oxyle again, "we come to planning. Nets we can weave and under those anything weapon of iron is locked to its handler—until we wish otherwise. But what are these crawlers, outlander?" He looked to Ylon.

"They are moving fortresses of a sort, encased in iron for battle, moved by men within who are well-protected. Under such a cover these within can bring their walking fort to the walls of any keep."

"Here is no wall, only trees—" Oxyle observed.

"For that they have an answer also. If a keep is so attacked the men under the cover strike at the wall, bore into it with special weapons meant for the duty. With the forest trees they could well use the same bores—with enough purpose to kill the tree. While the crawlers are heavy enough to beat themselves a road, their mere weight bringing down all smaller growth. Though this much is true, I have never heard of them being used against such trees as grow above us here. The growth over mountain is never so massive."

"But—" Oxyle spoke to Chard again, "you can make nets—nets for the taking of men. Can you fashion them also to encase these crawlers? Since we cannot tell if their assault will bring down the great trees perhaps we shall have time to plan some trick of power if they are stopped beyond the fringe.''

"How large are these crawlers?''

Ylon turned to Twilla. "Guide me,'' he said without any show of shame.

He scuffed with one boot at the thick grass underfoot, plainly setting a mark. Utin moved quickly and drove his sword into the soil there, leaving it standing as a guide. With his hand on Twilla's shoulder Ylon marched forward, counting paces aloud. When he halted he turned though he could not see the path he had come. Another warrior marked that spot and one ran quickly with a line of thin rope drawing it taut between the two weapons.

"This is the best I can tell you,'' Ylon said. "As for width—it is the width of a goods wagon.''

The dwarf who had produced the line and knotted it carefully at the far end rolled it into a loop about his shoulders.

"Well enough,'' Chard agreed.

"So we shall use nets,'' Oxyle said slowly. "But there is still the matter of this smirching of the true power. Under Lord, will you return with us to the storehouse of Khargel? There is that we must learn. I do not know how far the rot has spread with my own kin—how much Lotis has stolen and uses wrongly. Our powers differ—it may be that yours can act as a check on what has happened.''

"Power I have but there is one greater than me,'' Chard beckoned and from among the gathering of the under worlders came Catha. "Will you go with these, Heartsworn? They search for the traces of the dark which Khargel loosed, or else something like to it.''

Slowly the small woman moved along the line of the forest people. She paused the longest before Karla and Musseline where they stood together and at them she smiled:

"Sister ones,'' she touched her hands to her forehead. Swiftly both of the forest women echoed that gesture. "Of old we wrought together. It was none of your belief who sent us to the stones. May we stand together now.''

She did not speak to any of the men, even Oxyle, though she looked up into their eyes, one after another, each for a long moment. Then she came to where Twilla and Ylon stood a little apart.

To Twilla she now spoke: "They call you Moon Daughter, do they not?''

Twilla wondered how this one had heard that name which Karla had first given her.

"Your power is also strange—but it shines moon bright and without a stain. We can work well together."

Then Catha fronted Ylon. "You have power also, Lord, and it is greater than you think. In time it will give you a great blessing. However, in the end your path lies apart."

Now she returned to Chard. He had rammed the butt of the staff into the earth so it stood upright and moved a little away from it, his hands outstretched. She laid hers within his grasp and he bent his head to kiss each in turn.

"Go you then, Heartholder. What can be done you shall do. And may Aviral stand at your side."

Thus with Catha now added to their number they left the place of the great hall and came back to the passage Twilla had taken twice before. The carcass of the worm was now near reduced to scraps of cartilage, and she wondered what kind of scavengers had eaten their fill here. They reached that door Utin had opened, and this time Catha was in the fore and gestured to that pendant boar's head so that the wall cracked and their entrance to the upper levels was open.

Now the forest men moved to the fore and though they made some haste they traveled by spurts—one after another of them scouting ahead.

The silver mists were still absent. Twilla took that to be a signal that Lotis's power had not diminished. She took comfort in the fact that Ylon, swinging along beside her, bore iron once more and held it in open sight. Around her neck Catha also wore a talisman—boar's head, and it, too, Twilla thought was of the same threatening metal.

At last they came to that doorway which Ylon had sealed at their going. Oxyle stopped them with an upflung hand. And Twilla could smell that betraying fragrance. Lotis must have been here. But if she had come she had not won past the iron barrier, nor had she restored any new one of her own—perhaps the iron prevented also.

Ylon knelt and jerked loose the dagger so that they could enter. Catha stopped before the tree of light. There was wonder in her eyes.

"Forest Heart," she said. "Once we, too, came to look upon you—before Khargel arose. Now I salute that which is the greatest of all!"

She knelt and bowed her head as did those with her. Even Twilla and Ylon did likewise.

24

DID THE FLAME tree answer? Twilla believed that it did, for the fire it contained appeared to race the faster and the light it disbursed brought out of shadows all of that room with its many chests of records. Catha arose and gazed at those shelves and all they bore.

"This is a mighty place of knowledge—" she murmured.

Karla moved to the side of the under woman. "In the elder times it was a knowledge our peoples shared," she said. "Let it be so again. You have the learning to read the First Tree script?"

Catha nodded. "We are close to the beginning, we whom Khargel sealed away. Before his meddling there was a flow of power between our peoples—your seekers came to us—ours to you. Perhaps," she smiled, "perhaps I stood here before—when we yet had friendship between us."

Oxyle swung on her. "That is the truth?"

"It is. My clan were always guardians of power. When we were yet younglings we were brought here and shown many things—"

She moved toward the nearest wall, reached out to touch one of the wooden boxes, running her fingers over the rough bark which surfaced it as if it were a script she could so read.

"Here lies the musing of Occant. *Your* ancient kin, Forest Lord." Her smile now had a mischievous quirk as if she in some way challenged him.

"Occant!" It was plain that Oxyle was indeed impressed. He ges-

tured toward the other shelves. "You be our guide, Lady. We have
tried to keep the remembrance of things but it has been from sapling
to tree long since any of us stood here."

Catha gave him a nod and walked along the shelves, pausing now
and then again to finger one or other of the storage boxes and each
time identifying the one she touched. Three such were eagerly taken
up by Karla and the others. Even Twilla began to feel this was indeed
a treasure hunt. They had reached the end of one set of shelves and
were confronting another when Catha stopped short.

Instead of reaching for a box she snatched her hand back. Oxyle
stood beside her. For the first time he was the one to reach for a box.
Like the lash of summer lightning the under woman responded, striking the container from his hold.

It struck the floor, splintered. Up from the broken wood fluttered
leaves. They might have been trying to escape—or attack. For, once
in the air, the script which was traced upon them smoldered, broke
into flame and they fluttered toward those nearby.

Nor did that fire consume them, the floating particles continued
to burn. While the fresh scent within the room was tainted with an
overtinge of scorching which caught at the throat.

Those about cowered away. Twilla saw a bit of floating drapery on
Karla's skirt take fire as one of the burning scraps touched it. And she
heard a cry of pain from one of the men who had brushed a similar
bit from the shoulder of his jerkin. The still burning, still unconsumed
leaves whirled in a faster circle, though they did not encroach on the
vicinity of the tree, rather circled outward. They might have been sen-
tient creatures in search of prey as they pushed the company back
against the walls.

Ylon! He could not see, dodge, as the others were doing. He had
remained by the door, sword in hand, to defend that entrance. Now
Twilla saw two of the leaves, like death pointed arrows—align themselves toward him.

"Ylon, down!" Twilla screamed that even as she threw herself forward. She stumbled against Fanna and went to her hands and knees,
then threw herself on until she struck against Ylon, bringing him down
with her.

However, the flame leaves were not to be so easily escaped. They
altered course to swoop lower. Twilla flung out the mirror as one might
hold a shield—though she had very little hope of that being of service.

The flames wavered, like birds fighting against a net. It was plain
that there was one power in battle with a second now. The leaves
which were nearest hit the mirror full center. Twilla was rocked by

the force of that. Something she would have believed had no weight now landed like the blow of a battled mace, driving the mirror down to strike against her.

There came another and another. Somehow Twilla managed to move the mirror away from them out onto the rock floor. Now the flames were coming faster and faster and the smell was chokingly noisome. Yet as each struck the plate it was swallowed as if it were a stone sinking into water.

Twilla felt dizzy, sick. Yet she could not turn her eyes away from that fall of flame—flames which struggled wildly now against their fate. There was something else, a sense of darkness which was not of the world she knew but beyond its borders. A darkness which hungered and now was raging with that hunger.

The last of the flames was gone. She squatted, afraid to touch her talisman. That there was true evil in that shower of ignited leaves Twilla had no doubts. What had they done to her mirror? She put her hand to the surface only to jerk it back.

Once more the reflecting disk had turned dull as of with a veiling of smoke.

Catha spoke first. "A trap, Over Lord, and *not* one of the older days. But the power which set it"—she put her fingers to her temples and closed her eyes—"that power was two in one and not of your past or ours."

"Lotis—" Oxyle breathed that name, his expression rock hard. "And what beside?"

He crossed to stand over Twilla. "We have you to thank, that such a trap did not close upon us all. There was—a summoning," he appeared to pick his words carefully, "which brought that box to me. And, Lady," he looked now to Catha, "what carried the alarm to you?"

"A summoning also—I was drawn and I knew that that drawing was not true."

Slowly Twilla advanced her hand once more and caught at the cord of the mirror drawing it toward her across the floor. The sick feeling of revulsion was still alive in her. Can good swallow evil entirely?

The disk lay in front of her knees now as she hunched still on the floor and she stared at its stained surface. There was no reflection of what was about them, the wonderous light of the tree brought no answer.

However, she leaned forward, her hands on either side of the mirror but not touching it. There was a swirling movement beginning at its center, ripples running out toward the rim. No true reflection was patterned so—this was inner nor outer. She made no effort to use her own will to attempt to clear it, though she shivered.

Now that center had become a core of light. Surely a light as belied the one time clean silver of its fashioning. Yellow-green-like the discharge of some foul disease feeding upon tormented flesh.

She was dimly aware that her vigil was being shared now. The others had drawn in, as intently watching as she.

A darker core in that poisonous yellow dab. Now the blot was taking on shape. A black hood encircling a head, the face within only a sliver of chin, the point of a beaked nose. But she knew it!

"The Dandus priest!" Twilla cried her recognition aloud.

Logic denied what she saw. She could be as certain as that she was alive, that that harbinger of evil had never been within this storehouse of knowledge. There were—memory stirred—Hulde had told tales in what now seemed the far past—power called upon power—like was drawn to like.

"Lotis!" Again Oxyle repeated that name. "How has she made common cause with this invader? Why?"

"Why?" Karla answered, "because the ancient, forbidden greediness is in her. We do not know what she has looted from here. As to how"—now she echoed Twilla's thought of a moment earlier—"like calls to like. Did we not sense, even when she was traveling over mountain, that Moon Daughter was coming into our land bringing strengths we could not access? Did we not send an anesgar to keep eye upon her? That she had rare gifts we guessed, though she was no threat to us. Was it not so decided until that pit-born daughter of foulness managed to change the minds of some?"

Then she turned upon Ylon who still knelt beside Twilla, his head turning from one speaker to another as if he must not miss a word which might make plainer his ever-darkened world.

"How powerful is this devil priest of yours?"

"No priest of mine," he denied hotly. "As for his powers I cannot begin to reckon them. The tales out of the past speak of dire action, blasting death. Fire is one of the great weapons—it is fire which struck here."

Twilla continued to stare at the mirror. That hooded head had shown clearly for no more than two breaths. It was gone, with that thickening of shadow covering true reflection.

A hand touched her cheek gently and she started in surprise, looking up to see Catha looking down at her.

"Wise One, draw this focus of yours closer to the Frosnost—for that is strong in life and stands against the dark."

Slowly Twilla arose, the mirror dangling from her hand by its cord. She had no wish yet to touch it directly. Hesitatingly she approached the tree, those about her clearing a path to it.

At last she raised the talisman with both hands and held its reflecting surface toward that ever flowing light which coursed through silver leaf and branch before her. Did this hold the same renewing she had found in the moon reflecting pool? She could only hope.

Now she did summon her will, staring at the flowing tree, then at the mirror, striving very hard to summon the one to unite with the other. The stain—surely it was growing less! She caught a glint of green silver and then another! Until, with a fast beating heart, she saw clear pictured the tree.

"Well done!" Karla stood on her other side as Catha already flanked her on the left.

The others were moving cautiously about the shelves of boxes, touching none, yet holding their hands close to each as they passed. Feeling for what Oxyle had called a summoning, Twilla guessed. But there was no need for her to join in that. The silver bright mirror once more lying on her breast, she edged back to Ylon watching that search.

In the end Oxyle, with Catha's help, sorted out four boxes. They had discovered no more set up as traps but they moved very warily. When they had these four he spoke:

"We need time to study. That which Khargel added lying here we must not touch, for it is already tainted. Of that there are four coffers missing. Lotis must have those. We must get to the outerways—and since she has broken the mists we must go on foot. Vestel," he spoke to the border guard, "and Fanna head now for the forest. We must know what is in progress there. Marse and Rogar," two of the other men stepped forward, "will scout how much of the castleways are held by Lotis' followers. Do not challenge them, yet." He tapped one of the four boxes, "we need to stand in full strength before we do."

"Lady," he spoke now to Catha, "do you fare with us or return to your kin?"

"For a time with you, Lord Oxyle. We must learn what dangers lie ahead, and I think that is best done from the upper land than the lower."

He nodded. "So, the rest of us will go to the place of close conference. Guards sent there should have held. And once there," he smiled at Ylon, "we have a guard which none of our blood will come against. Let us then move."

Thus their party split. Twilla walked with Ylon but he seemed to have withdrawn into his thoughts and she did not disturb him. They once more threaded the many passages, dim and bright, and though Twilla expected at any moment to come face to face with someone of Lotis's company scouting they all seemed deserted.

Oxyle had slowed pace when they advanced into the better lighted ways. He would halt for a moment or two from time to time with all the appearance of listening. There was no sign of the silver mists having returned, and there was a kind of echoing silence which Twilla found daunting. This was akin to the great hall of the under people when they had returned from their enforced imprisonment, as if no one any longer lived there.

It was apparent that the forest people were also finding something amiss in these surroundings. The two women drew together and Twilla saw that their lips were moving, though not even a murmur reached her. Now and then they gestured in the air, frowning as if what they did was not going according to what should be.

They were back in the treasure-lined corridors now and the gleam of metal and gems seemed cold, repelling.

Then Oxyle stopped so suddenly that Karla near ran into him. He stooped and picked something from the floor, looked down on it, his face grim set. Slowly he turned and held out his hand to Twilla.

Across his palm lay one of the asprites, a male, very still, its small head hanging across Oxyle's thumb at a fatal angle, its rainbow wings crumpled. Some great hand might have gathered it up in fury and squeezed the life out of it.

Twilla touched the small body lightly and shook her head. Even the mirror's power she was certain would fail here.

"An Asprite—who would dare?" Karla broke silence first.

Oxyle's rage was plain to be read. Still cradling the small dead flyer, he quickened step and the others fell in, now keeping together and often looking warily from side to side as they went.

Their journey did not end in the council chamber as Twilla expected but rather in a side room which bore resemblance to that forgotten chamber where Khargel's knowledge had been stored. Here again were boxes, though of polished, squared-off wood, and they lined shelves. While at the center there was a long table, stools by it.

"Will you guard this door—?" Oxyle did not address Ylon by name but he touched the other's arm.

"What I can do, I shall," the other returned.

Oxyle laid that small body on the table, straightening the limbs gently, smoothing the crumpled wings. He threw back his head then and uttered a sound which might have been a bird's trill. Those who

followed him gathered closely together, hand clasping hand in linkage.
Only Catha, Twilla, and Ylon stood apart.

Three times that achingly sweet cry arose. It was hard to believe
that the forest lord could voice such. Then he reached within his jerkin
and brought forth a small bag.

Twilla heard a gasping sound from Karla who was nearest. Out of
the bag he shook two rings, thick and broad, made to extend well up
to the first knuckle of the fingers he put them on. Having so settled
them he cupped his hands one at either side of the small body and
once more gave the keening cry.

He was holding, or else there existed now within the circle of his
flesh, a ball of glimmering silver covering the small body as it expanded. Then the ball turned faster and faster. It arose from the table,
where there no longer rested the dead, into the air.

So free borne it soared away, out of the door.

Oxyle stripped off the rings, returned them to hiding before he
spoke. "It is plain that there is a great rising of the dark. Our far kin
slain—" He hesitated. "For such a death there must be payment when
it can be taken. Now we have these—" he pointed to the boxes which
they had brought from the other storehouse which rested on the table
top.

"Do we do this fasting, Oxyle?" Karla demanded. "We have many
gifts and talents but to go for too long without food and drink is not
one of them."

"Well enough," he agreed. "But neither can we scatter to seek
those not here at this time."

Catha moved up to the table, carefully avoiding that portion where
the body of the asprite had lain. "Have all powers been rift from you?
Can you not summon what you need?"

Karla nodded. "Perhaps it is a time for testing. We can only know
when we try." She slipped around the table to the other side and then
leaning forward caught the hands Musseline stretched out to her. When
they had locked so together both women looked down upon the tabletop.

Twilla felt a faint warmth from the mirror. Power was being unleashed and her focus was answering in its own way.

There was a sudden curdling of the air—not of the moon-bright
mists she had seen before. These were tarnished and dull but still they
arrived in answer.

A flagon reared as a shadow and became substance. There was also
a platter of fruit. But these were not what she had seen at the feasting.
They were small, too ripe, the cakes were pale as if taken too soon

from the oven. When Karla and Musseline straightened up and dropped hands the food they had summoned was meager and flawed. But they ate and, though Twilla missed the fine flavor of that fare which had formed her first meal in the forest, she dutifully chewed and swallowed.

They each drank in turn from the flagon which was an awkward business but there were no goblets. The liquid she swallowed was more tart than sweet this time, yet Twilla felt restored and satisfied. She had seen that Ylon was served with his share. He had not left his place by the door and he held the fateful iron in full sight.

"Lotis would give us prisoner fare," remarked one of the men. "But at least her spells do not make us go empty."

Now they turned to the boxes they had brought with them. Karla and Musseline soon emptied the first and spread out the leaves it contained flat on the surface of the table. Once more Twilla could see that these were covered with what looked to be a raised and intricate green veining but which must be a script.

She could have no part in this. Though learned in two of the languages of ancient writing, she had nothing that Hulde had prepared her with to untangle this. She pulled a stool to the door and then went back for another.

"You can guard as well seated," she told Ylon. "Even Lotis will be wary of what you bear."

He hesitated for a moment and then sat down, but he had moved the stool sidewise so that he faced half room, half corridor. She pulled up her chosen seat beside him.

"What did Oxyle—the farewelling?" he asked in a low voice and Twilla described the ceremony of the rings. "But the asprite," she said with a flare of anger, "was killed—as if someone had squeezed the life from it. Would any, even a follower of Lotis, do that?"

"The rot has found a door and where it touches—there grows the foulness of its being." Ylon shifted his weight a little on the stool. "I do not know what now moves my father. A season ago I would have said that he tolerated the Dandus only because that was forced upon him. Now—perhaps he has joined—" Twilla saw his free hand clench. "But—to believe that—"

She understood. In spite of all which lay behind his maiming and the contemptuous attitude of his kin, there was a common heritage he found it hard to deny. He must have many memories which would call out against his severing all those ties. Hulde had not been blood kin but in her heart Hulde would always abide. Was that true for Ylon also?

YLON SAID NO more and Twilla felt shy about any intrusion now into his thoughts. She studied his face as he sat there, one hand locked about the weapon he had brought from the underworld. He was, she thought suddenly, like to a bowstring, taut and ready to send an arrow to the target. And what target was he seeing in his mind?

Lotis—it must be Lotis who could be the only one to remove the spell which maimed him. *Lotis*—

Her thought was echoed by a sudden cry of that name aloud. Oxyle had risen from the stool he had chosen. He brought his hand palm down on the untidy pile of reading leaves before him.

"So that is how—" He did not finish his sentence. His eyes held a hard gleam which reminded Twilla of those in Chard's boar-headed staff.

Those other searchers who had shared his quest among the records looked to him questioningly. If he had found some answer they had not. He turned to Karla:

"The moon sighting—she would not have dared—she has gone too far into the shadow for that to come to her service. It is the Dank Fire which she has drawn upon, the monster blood!"

The faces of his listeners betrayed shock, Musseline half rose from her stool, leaning across the table.

"But none travel that way!" she protested.

Oxyle's mouth moved to shape a grimmace far from a smile. "None? Did not Khargel?"

Now there was a soft cry from Catha, her hands up before her mouth—she might have been trying to so muffle some other denial.

"The Dank Fire—" Oxyle stated firmly once more, perhaps to impress it more strongly upon them.

"And to cut that tie," Karla said slowly, "needs blood, even as the setting of it must have such. We do not slay for power—if we do we become one with Lotis. Is that what you urge upon us now?"

Oxyle strode from the table, walking back and forth across the chamber, his head down, what Twilla could see of his face set in new harsh lines.

"We dare not feed it thus. But—where did she get the true wood for the first firing? If she has turned any of the trees we would have known—"

"There are the fallen ones," suggested one of the men.

Oxyle shook his head violently. "Dank Fire cannot rise from long-dead wood, it must be kindled from that which is still bleeding sap." His pacing had brought him very close to where Ylon had taken his position at the door. Now the forest lord stopped short, his attention for the blind man and his weapon.

"Iron, cold iron," he repeated softly, "cold to smother the Dank. There is no record of such ever being done—but iron is the enemy of our power, we cannot control it, we dare not touch it. The Dank Fire is unfortunately of the dark side of our learning. If we can find where that fire smolders perhaps your iron, outlander, will be the ending."

"Where lies this fire?" Ylon asked simply, getting to his feet.

"Ah—Karla!" Oxyle did not turn to the woman but there was the urgency of an order in the way he spoke her name.

She fingered the leaves that had been spread before him, piling them together and putting them to one side. Having so bared a space before her she placed both hands, slightly cupped, on the space. Musseline had caught up the flagon and shook it. They could hear a faint slosh from within, some drops must remain. And those, in a thin trickle, she poured into Karla's waiting hands.

For a long moment the older woman sat silent, peering down into the tiny puddles within her palms and then she spoke:

"Not within this heartland. Which is true, for such meddling would bring down all our lives. In the forest—and there is something—a promise of something—to come in support!"

"You know the site?" Oxyle demanded. "It is warded?"

"I know—it is. But the bespelling is of the forest—" she jerked her head in Ylon's direction. "He bears iron—no ward may hold against that!"

"Then let us go!" But again there were no mists of transportation to come to their aid. They must travel afoot as they had through all the maze of passages.

Only Catha did not start toward the doorway. "Time has come to threaten us." She held the boar's-head pendant close to her lips. "We of the under have our part in your struggle but that will come later. I must return to my own now that the hour draws near."

Oxyle bowed his head. "As you will, Lady. Remember this—the Dank Fire burns and so it builds. You are right, time may now be our final foe."

Leaving Catha to go her own way they came out of the castle on foot and down into the valley where was rooted the gemmed orchard. There were no asprites in the air, and over all the land there lay a kind of shadow, dimming the brilliance Twilla remembered.

Following a way she did not wholly remember they passed again through the giant tree and into a forest more of the nature she knew, she walking with Ylon as his guide. Once out in this world of the great trees she saw mists again. But these were forbidding, having the look of webbing. They swayed near, still never quite touching any of the party.

Karla was the foremost of them now and she wove a path in and out among the giant tree trunks, staring forward as one entranced, so that Oxyle pushed up to clear her way from dead branches, and small growth.

It was there that Fanna joined them, recklessly beating a way as if speed were the most important.

"The outlanders—they reach for power," he panted out. "They have cut to pieces one of the great trees, and they turn it to their purpose. Vestel says to tell that they play with wild fire—Dank Fire!"

Oxyle caught at Karla, gave her a small shake as if to rouse her out of that seeming trance. "How far?" he demanded.

She stared at him, through him, and he released her so that once more she forged ahead. Then rocks rose out of the ground before them. There was certainly the smell of burning, a smell which held none of the odor of leaves or wood, but something which turned the stomach.

Movement in the air caught Twilla's eye and she looked up. There was a sinuous black roll which looked more like a tentacle than any drift of smoke. It wove back and forth. Karla came to an abrupt stop, as if she had run against one of those rocks, though there was no obstruction before her. Though he strained forward Oxyle was not more free to advance than she.

He looked now toward Twilla and Ylon. "If these wards can be broken—then use the iron, outlander!"

Twilla steered Ylon on. She certainly met with no barrier nor did he. They scraped a way between two upstanding rocks far taller than their heads and looked down into a cup of valley. In the center there was a heap of branches sullenly smoldering, hardly seeming enough to account for the thick uprise of smoke. But—

Twilla cried out. There crouched also one of those monsters Lotis had set to pursue Wandi and her. And the thing—what it held!

A thin trilling, worse to hear than any scream of torment arose. The monster was swinging back and forth a stick grasped in one clawed paw. And fastened to that by a cord, crumpled of wing but still alive to suffer, was another asprite.

Swiftly Twilla reported what lay before. Ylon skidded down the side of the bowl, his blade out. The thing amusing itself while playing guardian to the fire threw the stick from it, reared. *An illusion?* Twilla could not tell. She fumbled for the mirror.

However, Ylon moved first. In spite of his blindness he brought down the blade he held in a swing which struck against what was indeed a solid body. So the thing was alive!

One clawed paw raked at him, but at the touch of iron it staggered back, clutching at the wound which kept on widening as if some keen edge continued to hack away and enlarge the wound. Throwing back its massive head it cried out a great scream of rage and fear. Ylon advanced a stride, caught his foot in the straggle of broken branches, went to one knee, but then threw himself toward the beast, blade straight out so that it pierced the lower belly of the creature who reared back and fell, its screaming growing ever more. Until Ylon, regaining his feet and guided by those outcries, plunged his weapon deep into the middle of the writhing creature.

Twilla attempting to keep away from the battle found her own action waiting. There was a rough cage and in it asprites crouched. Their thin trilling shrilled higher as she caught up the cumbersome cage and struck at the latching across the opening. Then she set the crude prison carefully down, the door to freedom open, while she edged around to where Ylon stood above his kill.

There was still the fire and tentacle of smoke twisting lower as if to net them in some noose. Twilla caught Ylon by the arm and faced him a little around. She had no idea how to deal with the fire she told him was there. It would seem that he could only use one form of action. To serve the fire as he had its guardian. He sent his weapon into the crackle of flames, twisting the length of steel around so that the piled branches scattered. Smoke rolled down upon them as a lash. They were choking as it twisted its great leaden coils about them.

Again and again Ylon, in spite of choking and gasping in the stifling smoke, stirred the fire. Instead of awakening the glowing wood to more fierce burning, his efforts acted as a masterful splash of water.

The smoke thinned, fell away from the hold about the two of them. Then it was gone and they stood by charred wood fast falling into gray ash.

Twilla felt a light touch on her cheek. One of the asprites hovered there. She remembered the one who had been bound in torment and found it easily enough for the others of its kind had gathered around and already had it freed from its bonds.

Gently Twilla raised the tiny being. There was the red burn of fire touch on the once perfect body. The hair of its head had been singed away, and she did not know if the crumpled wings could ever be straightened again.

Her healer's training made her long for her bag of herbs. Though whether those intended for human kind would serve for this little one she could not guess. Someone came up beside her. Karla.

"It is burned, and the wings—" Twilla said.

From a pouch at her belt the forest woman brought out a pad of what looked like green, fresh-picked leaves.

"Your mirror," she gestured. "Lay these atop."

Twilla instantly responded to that and now Karla was smoothing out two of those leaves, lying them flat on the surface of the mirror. At her direction Twilla deposited that small body as gently as she could on the stretch of green. Karla proceeded to lay two more leaves over the form and then she looked sharply to Twilla.

"Use healer skill now, Moon Daughter. Wish for return of health and strength, wish it with all your might!"

Twilla was carried away by the almost fierce note in the other's voice and concentrating her gaze all she could, she summoned her energy upon that bundle of leaves. She strove to see the asprite restored, free, the thing of beauty as it was meant to be.

Only dimly was she aware of others moving about her, that the forest people were circling the dead fire and chanting in such a way made her tingle in the wash of power.

She was still concentrating on what she held when she was steered by Karla back up the slope and into the woods. The stench of burning was gone, and now there whirled about them a breeze. The towering trees might have caught a light wind and somehow funneled it down to cleanse the air.

However, it was not the breeze which stirred the top leaf on the mirror she struggled to hold level. A small hand appeared, pushing that covering aside. Then the second top leaf followed, and she was looking down at the asprite.

The pale skin was no longer angry red from the lipping of the fire. And the wings were outstretched under the body uncrumpled. Though the fine hair was but a stubble on the tiny head.

There was a flash from the left and another of the small ones zoomed in from the side, grasping the edge of the mirror as anchorage. Twilla's charge sat up, held out her arms to the newcomer and was caught up in a close embrace. Together they turned their heads up to look at the girl. Then the male helped his companion to her feet, and she tested her wings with a flutter or two before rising directly before Twilla's face.

Those tiny hands were feather-tip light on her cheeks, as meaningful in this touch as an embrace such as she had just witnessed. Both of the asprites took to the air and now she saw they were flying with those liberated from the cage directly over the woods party.

Twilla tucked the discarded leaves in her tunic. She wanted time to study them if they were ever allowed time again for anything about meeting force with force, power with power.

Oxyle had not pushed on, instead he stood with his head high, staring to the right. The asprites gathered in a cloud about his head, circled twice, and sped on into the green gloom before the forest lord followed.

Twilla dropped back again to Ylon's side, once more to guide him as best she could. She noted that the faces of those around her showed a strain. If the failure of the Dank Fire had not given them any relief— she was tense within—what did lie ahead?

From among the trees came others of the forest people, a handful of men. These were armed with weapons which had the gleam of silver. Some were archers, and others held complicated meshs of the same silver netting as the under people looked upon for proper weapons—perhaps Chard's men had already began to supply them.

That murmuring of which she had always been aware in the forest was stilled. The great trees themselves might be listening, seeking—

The lines of those were beginning to thin. There were huddled shrubs here and there such as formed the out barriers of the fringe. And *now* there *was* something to be heard.

Voices—a mob might have been storming across the open toward the trees. Then, above that deep-throated growl, something else arose—chanting. Twilla shivered, clasped her mirror tighter.

This was no petition to any power she had been taught to serve. Though she did not understand those screeched words she felt them like blows, near heavy enough to make her sway as she went.

"Dandus rite!" Those words had been hissed by Ylon.

Odor followed sound. There was again something burning—wood—and with it other things—mind twisting herbs such as no sane healer ever harvested.

They came to a stop from which they could look out at what defaced the open land beyond. There was a fire here also! Surely only one of the forest giants could have provided such heavy billets of wood. From the peak of that pile arose a smoke as black and perilous as that of the fire Ylon had been able to quench.

The smoke was reaching—though Twilla felt no wind strong enough to blow in their direction. Now she could see that the hazy stuff was not entirely dark. Within it fiery bits were being carried on and out toward them.

Working with dogged haste the fire tenders—there were several of them—constantly drew up new loads of wood. But these workers were not alone. To the far right and left were drawn up Lord Harmond's fighters in full battle dress. They held their spears down across bodies, using them as staffs to push back the crowd, those who held no weapons.

The chanters marched in a circle about the fire, and their hooded and cloaked leader could not be any other than the Dandus priest. Now and then he brandished in the air a black rod from which hung a loop of heavy leather.

There were women to the fore among those guarded. In fact Twilla looking the closer she could make out that these women had been forced into a single mass, before them a double row of the guards. The chanting died away and the marching about the fire ended with the Dandus priest before the women.

He gave a flourish of his thonged rod and two of those who had followed him in his chanting wheel darted to one side, returning with a small body held between them. A child!

Twilla must have gasped that aloud for Ylon's face was working, rage warring with disgust.

"A blood fire!"

The child was dragged before the Dandus priest and, at some signal from him, that wheeling march about the ever growing fire began again. But the chanting did not rise high enough yet to drown out the screams. Those came not only from the vainly fighting child, but also from the women. There was a stirring in their massed group. Some struggle might be starting.

The priest paid no attention. Instead he strode behind the child and her guards and, with each stride, flogged at the captive with his rod whip. Each time that lash fell the child jerked and screamed, until, as the marks grew red about its bare body, it wilted and was dragged limply on.

But Twilla had seen enough when the prisoner had rounded the fire closest to the forest.

"Wandi!"

There was no one there quick enough to restrain her. She was out and running across the open. Above her the waves of smoke blotted out the sun, and there were small fires sprung up wherever one of those flaming bits of debris touched the earth.

More than the smoke threat was suddenly aimed at her. She ran into a wave of terror as thick as any wall, sent to bar her path. Only that strength which came from the mirror sent her plunging on through the tall grass.

There were cries arising from the crowd ahead, and above all the bellow of the Dandus priest. He had ceased his lashing of the unconscious child. Now he turned in Twilla's direction. His face was so deep in the hood of his robe that she could see nothing but the folds of black cloth.

He raised his rod-whip and sent the leash hissing through the air in her direction. She winced as a bite-like fire touched her. However, if he had meant to bring her down with that he had failed.

She could feel the heat of the fire. There were men moving in from either side, some of the soldiers detached to close on her and take her. Yet even if she would Twilla could not retreat now. Something so strong she could not control had taken possession of her, near all her mind, and certainly all of her body.

26

FIRE WAS CATCHING more and more in the tall grass, bursting upward unnaturally fast. The soldiers did not attempt to force a way through toward her now, rather they were angling off on either side. They must believe that she was only the first of a company come to confront them.

Again that rod lash dashed high in the air, the priest came forward a stride or two. Behind him two of his followers had Wandi in close grip, preparing to throw her into the sullen flames of the giant fire.

"Demon!" the roar of the priest's voice carried over the crackle of the flames, cries coming from the mass of people gathered to watch this horror.

Once more he was aiming that leash, more slowly, with greater care. The pressure of panic edged fear from his power was breaking down Twilla's defense.

The girl swung up the mirror—up and out—even as he aimed his next blow.

An answering twirl of pure rage-red fire shot from that leash. She braced herself.

Then that spear of flame touched the mirror. Twilla felt heat and pressure but she held with all her strength. The bolt he had launched against her, thickened as it was returned at equal speed toward him who had sent it.

He must have been very sure that his power would hold against any other for he made no attempt to dodge that returning spear of fire. It touched his breast. His dark cloak flared into flame.

In his hand the rod twisted, no longer a straight shaft but now writhing as might a serpent. He hurled it from him not seeming to notice that his garment was afire, that flames had followed up the folds of his cloak hood, peeling it back to show his death's head of a face.

There were flecks of spittle on his lips, he was plainly mouthing some spell. Twilla went on. The wriggling rod rose in her path, swaying as might a striking serpent preparing for attack, she did not pause.

Instead she found she was repeating words of her own now, singsonging them as she always did when she evoked the mirror.

> *"Dark to dark, flame to fire.*
> *Back to sender let it go.*
> *Even as the seasons flow.*
> *Let evil upon evil feed.*
> *Light cometh true where there is need."*

The serpent staff wavered before her. It thrust its thonged head out but did not touch her—yet. Behind its master shook himself and from a dark skinned body fell the rags left from the fire's touch, yet he showed no burns.

He was gesturing now and she did not doubt that he so called upon his full power.

"Let evil upon evil feed!" she raised her voice near to a scream, focusing through the mirror all the energy she felt within her.

Twisting upon the scorched ground, the serpent staff slewed around to face its master. Then it lunged up. That thong-loosed end caught him full about his bared throat with such force that Twilla herself was struck by a powerful echo of it.

Back into the reaching flames of his own fire that blow hurled him. She saw his face twist with agony. He strove to keep his feet, to clutch at the staff now weaving before him readying for another blow.

That came. His still fighting body was flung into the heart of the fire lit for his own purpose.

Twilla let the mirror thump down against her breast. She ran forward. Those who had been about to hurl Wandi into that same fire, dropped the child, scrambled hastily out of her path.

Now there sounded a roar—not born from the fury of the fire but from the people lined there under guard. As Twilla caught up Wandi she could see whirlpools of struggle within the ranks of the women. The guards, their attention sidetracked by the battle of the powers were taken by surprise. Men were downed by the sheer weight of women's bodies hurled against them.

Screams—screams of battle, not of fear now. Spears which had been wrested from the hands of guards were being used as clubs against their former owners. Beyond the embattled women, the men who had been ranked there, unarmed and under the same guard, came to swift life. A wild struggle was underway.

Twilla, nursing the child against her, saw mounted men drawing in, weapons out. However, the foremost of them were served no better. Being torn from their saddles and sinking into the hands of those they had held here only moments earlier.

Twilla glanced back toward the forest. There was still fire greedily feeding on the grass, creeping toward the trees. There, too, soldiers were circling in. She saw the face of the one shouting orders—Ustar! He seemed to have no fear of the fire, rather beat at any soldier near him, striving so to drive such unfortunates toward Twilla.

There was such a clamor that she could not hear the orders he was giving, but his mouth worked upon words. He kept sending glances in her direction as he struggled to get his men to close upon her.

It was plain she could not run for it, not with Wandi a dead weight in her arms. And the swirl of fighting was spreading out to soon engulf her.

"Healer!" She near staggered from the force of that grasp on her shoulder.

"Leela!" But how had the other recognized her since the change of face?

"That hound of the dead—you finished him! Here, give me the child. He swore that she was forest tainted and he needed her to raise power against those others—"

Twilla willingly released Wandi into the other's hold. There was a fierce scowl on the fishergirl's face.

"Take our children would he—that drinker of blood! He had us in his fist until he faced you, Healer. Be sure we shall not forget who broke his power. You—" a little of the rage faded from Leela's face, "Healer—you have healed yourself. You are as before the illness came upon you. May the One In Three be thanked. But get you away, we are your debt-held, but they will have out the rest of the guard swiftly."

Twilla pointed to the men Ustar was still sending in to block her return to the woods. Leela nodded. There was no need to explain. Instead she raised her voice in a great summoning cry and from the struggling mob now around the fire came others. Rutha, a great bruise on her cheek, but a broken spear haft in her hand, and women Twilla could not put name to.

Leela gestured to the hovering soldiers. The faces of the women were grim, set. Now that the bonds the Dandus priest had set upon them were broken they were minded to take payment for the horror which might have been. Children were precious, doubly so in this land. The Dandus priest had gone against all nature when he had taken Wandi.

Leela handed the limp body of the child to a woman just joining them, then she nodded to the others. They moved out, flanking Twilla on either side, though their course had to be a crooked one because of the patches of burning stubble.

"No!" Twilla saw only too well the expression on Ustar's face as he rode closer. His sword was bared and at his signal those others were losing their reluctance, moving forward with weapons ready. He could well cut down the women—

Then she saw Ustar brush his empty hand vigorously across his forehead, having dropped his reins. His horse gave an ear-splitting neigh and reared. Ustar kept his seat with difficulty, but he was not able to restrain the wild dash of his mount. And those of the other guards were acting as hysterical, two of them had thrown their riders.

Twilla saw small forms, their wings glinting in the air as they circled about. She spoke swiftly to Leela.

"Thank you, sister. But there comes now those who will see me safe."

She saw the fishergirl's mouth drop a little open as down flitted one of the asprites, seeming to dance at will upon nothingness. Then Twilla ran, weaving among the patches of fire, the asprites keeping pace with her as a small cloud overhead.

She staggered a little from the blasts of heat which continued to burst from those many small fires. Oddly the grass was not instantly consumed so they died from lack of fuel. Rather they continued to eat down into the ground, so that the earth itself glowed with rings of red and yellow.

Toward the wood those same rings moved determinedly. Twilla panted as she ran. There was still wild shouting behind, but she did not look back. She had thought that the black power would have died with the one who summoned it yet both the creeping fires and that pressure of fear upon her did not diminish.

A brush in the fringe burst into instant flame almost directly in her path. Twilla had to swerve to avoid that threat. The fire licked avidly at the shrub, withering leaf and branch in a second.

Now another farther in was catching though not as quickly. Twilla dodged that, hardly able to keep her feet now, to stagger on.

Arms closed about her and she collapsed against a solid body as sturdy as any of the great trees. Ylon, she did not need to look to know who supported her so.

For a long moment she leaned against him. The fires did not appear to eat so far into the woodlands. Above the crackle of the blazing brush behind she heard the trilling of the asprites as they now circled over both of them.

There were still cries from the outer fields but those were less violent. Leela, Rutha, the other women who had broken bonds when the priest went down, how would they fare now? If Lord Harmond turned the might of his soldiers against the land people it would end in blood and bitter death. For at least the women would stand firm if any again threatened a child.

Twilla was not aware that she had been gasping this out to Ylon until he spoke:

"The priest is gone—Karla had the far sight and told me. I do not know how deeply his evil has bitten. My father does not take kindly to any rising against his orders, but neither, I believe, will he take kindly to using weapons upon the women." He gave an odd sound like a laugh. "Has he not been working hard all these seasons to build up their numbers rather than cut them down? Dandus thinking can twist the thoughts, once that is removed who knows what will happen?"

"What was that one trying to do?"

"To bring destruction," Karla approached from behind them. "Within burned the Dank Fire, without burned that abomination, power feeding power. He would have unleashed upon us death fire had he been able to build all the strength he tried to harness."

"Lotis?"

Karla grimmaced. "Who knows? When the inner power failed, and then the outer, who can tell what that one will try to do?"

Twilla had shifted around in Ylon's hold so she could look out through the ragged frame of brush. Those fires spotting the land between the great fire and the forest still smoldered and spread, but slowly now as if the fierce strength was being drained with each passing moment.

She could see Oxyle and with him Vestel and others who might be the warders of the Edge. There were others there also, but their numbers were limited. Twilla had never known how many made up this tree-shadowed nation but she was sure that this gathering was but a small part of the numbering.

However, as she turned her head to see how many watched the fury without she saw something else. Along the shadowed aisles of the great trees gathered mists, those silvery mists, and those curled, and twisted as might flame blown by a full gale. Wind-laden with the sharp, clean scent of pine, riffled her mop of sweat-thickened hair.

There was a feeling of anticipation. A great beast might so crouch ready for the spring. This was no power of her species, nor she believed, of even the forest folk, it was the life of the trees themselves aroused to do battle.

The mists, flung like banners whipped by that wind, closed about them, so there was a fog, and then the silver ribbons reached out to where those bushes still smoldered stubbornly, enwrapping each as they reached it.

Instantly the fire was quenched. However, those mists did not venture beyond the brush fringe. The spots of fire on the open field were still alive, burnt to ground level but still agleam as might be evil eyes turned toward the Wood.

What came then was a sound to smother all the clamor of the struggle still in progress beyond. The great fire burned heavily. Out of its flames coiled limbs of smoke, like to those which had appeared at the Dank Fire. These reached for the sky, wavered, and then were sent streaming toward the Woods. As they passed over the spotted fires those showed new life.

Dandus Power? But the priest—he must be dead! Twilla had seen him sent back into his fire. Did power live on with none to order it?

The cries of those in struggle again sounded louder. She could see, even at this distance, that soldiers and the mob together were backing off, even now starting to run away. While the fire they had tended roared with a thunderous bellow.

Smoke coils touched tree tops. There was a spark of flame there in answer. The mists arose, encircled the threatened branches, quenched what strove to establish itself there.

Around Twilla the forest people were chanting. They had ringed around the threatened trees, their bodies pressed tight to the great trunks, their hands linked so each was enchained.

Now the girl saw something else. There was a quiver in the air, something hardly to be sighted—yet she was sure of it. That climbed steadily upward. Above the mists grew thicker; there was even a pattering of drops which struck lightly against her own upturned face.

One by one the smoke trails thinned and were gone. Now there arose

a full blast of wind among the tree tops. There were no storm clouds
aloft but this held all the force of a change-season tempest. Bits of
broken branch and tattered leaves floated down. The rage of that fury
which appeared to be confined to the crowns of the trees grew—
swept—outward.

The tempest struck, full on that great fire. Into the air flew brightly
blazing sections of wood near as large as the trunks of small trees.
The wind from the woods gathered these up, whirled them about. Instead of urging thus the fire to greater efforts as might be expected, it
was extinguishing, thrown charring logs wide over the open land.

Forest-born storm ate up the fire and it was gone. Now the tempest
scoured the blackened earth on which it had stood, so even ashes were
whirled off in a fog cloud which appeared to be also pursuing the
outlanders. There was nothing left at last but that black earth.

The wind died, there was no more clamor in the tree tops. Those
who had encircled the threatened growth dropped hands, moved away,
and the mists dipped to lap about them.

"So be it," Oxyle stood there. "Are your people now broken, outlander?" he asked Ylon. "Their own power is ended—at least for
now."

"They are not easily turned from what they would do," Ylon returned. "There will be those among them who will speak of a freak
storm, and others who will warn of fell mage work in that their priest
died. No, I do not believe that you shall see them inspanning their
teams to go back over mountain again."

"That is my thought also," the forest lord replied calmly. "You,
Moon Daughter—what would have of us? For it was your power
which ended that priest, even as his iron power ended the Dank Fire."
He gave a nod toward Ylon.

"Then you agree that we both deserve well from your hands?"
asked Twilla, already there stirred from the back of her mind that wish
which had been growing stronger with each day.

"There is none who can deny it!"

"Then—give back his sight!" She had caught Ylon's sleeve, pulled
him a little forward.

Slowly Oxyle shook his head. "Gladly would we do so—but it
remains—the fate Lotis called upon him only she can lift—so it has
always been."

"And Lotis has already tried to betray you all! How can you not
compel her to it?"

"Moon Daughter, each people live by certain rules set in them even
before their birth. The under men dig out metal, work it, keep the

underways of the forest clear of any troubles, even as we keep the outer. We serve the Great Ones," he gave a small gesture to the ranks of the trees. "You also must have limits upon your powers in one way or another. I would do this if I could, but it is denied me."

"And Lotis, does she go free?" demanded Twilla. Surely if they could take the woman into custody they might force from her the breaking of Ylon's ensorcellment.

"Lotis has gone—there are those who have been hunting her diligently and they can find no traces. She must be using things she learned from Khargel's lore to cover her tracks."

"And you leave it so?" Twilla was angry. Certainly Oxyle and those here with him who had suffered from Lotis's assumption of power were not just going to let her go free.

"We have warded against her every entrance to the heart. If she made any bond with that dark priest it did not serve her and he is gone. Our net will narrow until she is enchained."

Twilla realized that she could get nothing better from him in spite of his admission that he owed her, owed Ylon much. And with Lotis still free could they not expect further trouble?

However, whatever hold the woman had over the mists was now broken, once more they served Oxyle and his people. So leaving the wardens on watch the rest of them were enflooded by mist and came so into the great hall of the palace.

There was food and drink. Twilla sat beside Ylon this time and saw that he was provided with a full plate. However, beyond drinking from the goblet at his hand he made no effort to eat. Though his head was bent a little as if he were indeed regarding Twilla's selection. When he spoke his voice was stiff, he might have removed himself to a great distance.

"Tell me what happened!" That was an order. Twilla sipped her own drink. Not for the first time she realized he was a prisoner of his maiming.

Of that battle on the field about the fire he could only have gathered such information as those about him had shared. For a trained soldier such must have been hard to bear.

She sipped again and then as baldly as possible she described what she had seen and done, her own part in the struggle. When she spoke of the Dandus priest's torment of Wandi she saw his face harden, and the fingers of his hand by his plate curled into a fist.

"What has worked upon my father?" It was nearly a cry. "He is a fighting man but not one to descend to the torture of children! What has been done that he would allow this?"

She could not answer him but hurried on to that strange duel between rod and mirror. Now his hand shot out and fastened on her wrist in a punishing grip.

"What power are you able to summon, Healer? They tell of mages once, before the Dandus arose, who did wonders. But that was more seasons ago than any woman—or man—can number for a lifetime. If you held such power within your hands, why were you among the brides?"

"I did not know, I still do not understand what I can summon. When I am faced with the need I turn to the mirror—I have no other weapon. But I can only fight when battle is offered—heal when there are wounds—see when there is great need. Then—I am not sure of what I do to summon power—it moves in me and I know that I will have an answer—but even that answer I cannot foresee."

"You are then like a novice in the arms court who is not sure of her weapons. You must depend upon fortune in part—" he returned slowly. "Yet when you come into danger your strength answers. And whatever power the Dandus priest held must now be broke—"

She thought she knew what was in his mind and ventured to put it into words:

"They swear to me," her voice quavered, for she believed that with her words she was going to destroy his faint hope, "that your ensorcellment cannot be broken save through Lotis."

His lips twisted. "And she is far away for wishing me well. So be it."

He straightened a little, his shoulders squared, as one who had received an order dividing him from hope.

"It now matters concerning my father." Resolutely he put aside any other thought. "He will not take lightly the revolt of the landsworkers against his men. He prides himself on strict justice and obedience to authority—"

"No matter what the authority?" Twilla interrupted. "Perhaps though he was under some temporary bonds to the Dandus and those now be broken—"

He had taken up a cake, was crunching it between his teeth.

"If—and if and if—" he said. "Answers will come in time."

Someone paused beside Ylon—Fanna stood there.

"Outlander, Lord Oxyle would speak with you—it is of importance."

Twilla moved to rise also but Ylon flung out a hand. "Let me go without leading strings, Healer, I must learn to walk my own paths!" His voice was heated as he arose.

She watched him turn and go, and knew that he must resent also the touch which Fanna offered now and then to keep him in the proper way. She blinked and blinked again. She was a healer and part of the burden of such a calling was that one could understand another's pain—at least in part. Her presence to him now was a burden he could no longer stand.

TWILLA OPENED HER eyes to the curve of the petal overhead where she lay again in the flower bed. She had feared that sleep would bring dreams birthed by the trace of evil lingering in her memory. However, she brought none such shadows with her out of sleep.

There was no night or day here, but there was a comfort in seeing a wisp of the silver mist float within the room—that was at least an assurance that Lotis was not still making trouble here.

She went from the bed to the pool in the adjoining chamber, washing away the languors of that deep sleep. Folded across a stool she found waiting, not the bedraggled clothing she had shed, but a fine white chemise and a robe of the palest green—the green of newborn, first of the season's leaves. Standing were also the soft boots worn by the forest dwellers which molded themselves to foot and calf as another skin, and a girdle of silver mesh studded with pale green stones, buckled with a clasp which represented the living silver green Catha had hailed as the forest's heart.

There was a mirror on the wall, many times larger than the one she wore and Twilla stepped before that to study her reflection. Her features were no longer masked by the inflamed and puckered skin of her past disguise, but had a pallor she found strange. The loose hair trailing down to her shoulders also seemed—though that might be due to some flaw in the substance of the mirror—to have taken on another darker shade than the dull brown it had always been—now it was close in hue to the dusk of a summer evening.

Certainly she could not match the chiseled beauty of the forest women, but she was far from ill-looking. What would Ustar have done had she stood so at that lottery? Twilla gave a shiver—she was well out of that!

If—if there somehow could be peace between the forest and the open land—if Lord Harmond might be immobilized along with his men until they had a chance for defense. As Ylon she was counting ifs. Ylon—for him to remain in darkness—

Twilla's lips thinned. The struggle with Lotis was not over. And— she was a healer—she must hold that belief. For every ill, even rank ensorcellment, there *must* be antidote. Perhaps one lay in that treasure house of learning so long hidden.

Behind her the mist swirled thicker. She turned quickly to face Karla—and Catha.

"Well risen, Moon Daughter," Karla said. "Is all well for you?"

"Is all well for all of us?" Twilla countered. She had noted with surprise that three of the small-flying lizards were clinging to Catha's shoulders, while Karla carried a plump bag.

"You speak of 'us,' yet you are not forest blood."

Twilla could not guess what lay behind that.

"No," she answered slowly, "in that you are right—I am no kin."

Standing beside her Karla drew Twilla back to face the mirror. "Look deeply, with your heart also."

Twilla studied their two reflections. In the mirror there was no difference between the pallor of her own skin and that of Karla's, all the brown weathering had faded. But then she had been out of the sun since she entered the forest land. What else—did Karla suggest that they were alike in more than that and robes they wore?

"I do not understand," she admitted at last.

Karla laughed and Catha echoed her. "Ah, Moon Daughter, she you look upon is different. See!" She swept her hand across the wall mirror and the passage of that erased what Twilla studied.

Now—startled, she retreated a step, studying the new reflection. Yes, there was the weather-roughened skin and that cruel ugliness she had wished upon herself. The unkempt hair was much lighter in shade—like last season's hay.

"That face—I summoned and then dismissed. But—"

"You have eaten of the roots, drank the life blood of the great trees. Thus you have taken into your body what maintains us—becoming kin if not by birth. Even if you return to the outlands that tie remains."

Both Karla and Catha were watching her as if expecting some denial. However, as a healer Twilla could understand. What was eaten, drunk, absorbed into the body—yes, even among her own people that caused change.

"You find this hard to believe?" Karla prodded.

"This is true of Ylon also?"

"The outlander lording? Yes. Whether or not he believes it he is now a part of the forest. Now, Moon Daughter, tell us, what manner of women were those by the devil fire who stood and watched the little one near sent to her death?"

"You saw also they were under guard," Twilla's chin lifted a fraction. "They are women in bondage. Did they not rise against the soldiers when the priest died? I believed that I could leave Wandi with Leela—I learned to trust her when we were brought here unwillingly to be wed to men we had never seen."

"And why were you so constrained?" Catha asked sharply.

"They—those who ruled—discovered that if a man was wed he could not be ensorcelled by forest power—such as that Lotis used on Ylon."

To her surprise Karla laughed. "So, if a man had a wife for bedding he could not be bound? Yet these women were brought unwilling, is that not so? Can they now be contented with their lot?"

"I do not know. Those brought were of many different natures. Leela was a fishergirl and she was tied to one she seemed to find satisfactory, or so she said when she gave Ylon and me aid to reach here. I cannot tell how the others I know fared."

"Thus," it was Catha who took a part in the conversation, "there could be dissatisfaction—even dislike among these women, a secret wish for freedom?"

Odd that they were pressing her on this point as if they had some reason beside curiosity alone.

"And we saw," Karla continued, "that given the chance they turned even against armed men."

Twilla looked from Karla to Catha. "What do you want from me?" she asked a little sharply.

"This—here are women who have been forced into lives they have not chosen. I do not know how customs are over mountain," Karla replied. "But among our people there is always free choice, of either season partners or life bond. No woman of the kin would consent to mate against her will or desire—"

"With us below this is also true," Catha nodded vigorously.

"Perhaps some of those who came," Karla continued, "did find mates to their taste—by fortune's chance. However—if there exist among them a greater number who bear inner hate and fear—even as they attacked the soldiers at the fire could they not be induced to hinder all men's plans even in small ways?"

Again Catha nodded in agreement.

"Ylon," Karla went on, "has been with those of the council who remain loyal—for several followed Lotis and we know nothing of what she may be brewing, since she has strong wards. Now it is our thought, we women, above and below, that we must also prepare. Ylon has spoken of machines of war—iron—against which we might not be able to stand. Understand, Twilla, we do not war except to defend ourselves. We shall not storm their dwellings with the powers we can raise, unless they bring us to a bitter ending. We want nothing which they have—only peace."

"People fear what they do not understand," Twilla replied. "They speak of you as demons because they have seen the effects of such ensorcellment as was laid on Ylon, and what other evil seed their Dandus priest might have sowed—be sure he did."

"We need time," Karla said. "The under people labor at their forges without stopping, new smiths standing to take the places of those who are worn out. They fashion the nets, but perhaps those shall not be done soon enough. So—it is the outland women we hold in mind. You alone have knowledge of them—some of them. In what manner can we approach them?"

"For what reason?" Twilla demanded.

Karla stooped to pick up the bag she had put on the floor. She opened it and brought out something small, hidden in her fist. Then she looked to the under woman as if for support. Catha nodded. One of the flying lizards took wing and hovered over them.

"Lotis bound Ylon but that tie was of her will alone. Here is something else." Karla opened her hand. Resting in palm was a small locket-like artifact made of gold filigree and from it there came a faint wafting of perfume.

"Let a woman wear this and she can bend a man close to her will. Its power is not long lasting but if enough of these outland women have such and want peace, their mates will find it is not in *their* minds to draw weapons either."

Twilla's hands crossed on her own mirror. There was logic in this— even though a part of her shied away from such mage work. Perhaps Leela had found her fortune-sent husband to her taste. But Twilla was sure that many of those arbitrary matings had not been happy ones. It was true that the women, unarmed and alone, had risen against the soldiers—something she would not have believed possible had she not witnessed it.

"Are you offering me a task?" she asked.

"Yes," Karla said.

"This is a matter decided upon by Oxyle and the council?" Twilla persisted.

Karla glanced away so their eyes no longer met. "No—they speak of weapons and open war. We seek another means toward peace." She held out her hand as if willing what it held into Twilla's grasp.

Twilla found herself accepting the locket. It was a trinket which certainly appealed to the eye. Any woman would be attracted to it.

"This forms a binding such as that laid upon Ylon?" She must be sure of that.

"No," Catha's answer came quickly and emphatically. "It does not bind as does the power. Rather it will make men listen. They will heed the words of their mates."

Twilla believed that the under woman spoke the truth as she knew it. She glanced again at her reflection in the wall mirror. Leela, Rutha, the others who had ridden in the wagon with her would know her. However, those who had come earlier would not. Also she knew very little about the plainslands—would all the women, except those who had been in the village, be scattered once more to the farms? To travel to each—that was impossible. Leela might supply her with aid, that farm was closest to the forest and perhaps she could get news to help her do this. *Do this?* Had she already in her inner mind decided to play the part they were urging on her?

Let her be taken and she—her thoughts shuddered away from what might be her fate.

"Win us time," Catha urged softly. "You have," she pointed to the mirror Twilla wore, "a mighty weapon. Already you have proved that many times over—and you are one of the same blood as they. To you they might listen—"

Twilla looked again at her reflection. "I cannot go among them in these clothes."

"For that we also have the answer. When the outlanders first came and brought their axes of killing iron within the wood we met them with power. Some of them lost all memory of us and those we sent free into the open lands. Some, because of some fault of their natures, died. We have the supplies they abandoned and among those is extra clothing."

"Died?" Twilla centered in upon that portion of Karla's story. "Killed by your power?"

"Only because there was that in them which the power fed upon. Why some outlanders are so burdened we cannot tell. And that kind of power does not pass beyond the fringe of the forest—we cannot use it for open attack."

"You have stolen wits and memory." Twilla faced the other squarely. "Those you freed went out to become un-men—which is what their kind name them. They are held in aversion and hatred because of the mark you set upon them. Now you offer me this," she held up the locket. "Can you give blood oath that this will not strike in such a fashion?"

"Moon Daughter, it will do no more than we have told you—it will help the women to influence their men. All life will fight to protect their homes. We did no more than they would have done if they had had such powers."

"I am a healer," Twilla answered. "I will not carry any curses to those who have done you no wrong."

"Blood oath, Moon Daughter—" Karla brought out of her sash a silver-bladed knife, pricked her finger until a drop of blood gathered there. "By the blood which is life, I do swear to you that these amulets carry no more with them than we have said. Will you not give a chance to the women you know, one perhaps for freedom from fear?"

Belief had been forced upon her. Though Karla's mentioning of those who had succumbed to the power shook her.

What if, by some chance, some discovery made among the records Oxyle had found, they had or would find a way to use the blighting power beyond the forest's limit?

Yet—her thoughts strung together swiftly—that knowledge could also be put to use. That Lord Harmond would be sending against the forest all the forces he could raise she had no doubt. That he might be brought to any truce meeting she also doubted. But he was one man. And she still remembered very clearly that action of the aroused women against his guards.

"I will do this much," she promised. "I shall go to Leela—if she has returned to the farm. I will find out what I can—"

"And put to judgment what is the spirit of the women?"

"As far as I can, yes."

"Come—it is already dusk aloft and you would travel the easier by night!" Karla waved a hand and a coil of the mist curled through the air toward them, encompassing them, hiding all else from their sight.

Then they were standing in a room filled with chests and one of these Karla selected, pressing a spot upon its lid and then raising that.

Within were folded clothing which she shook out quickly and hung on other of the boxes.

Most of it was too large, made for brawny workmen. But the girl was able to sort out tight hose of dull brown made for some boy, a shirt of checkered brown and yellow somewhat faded, and last of all a leather jerkin which was a tolerable fit. She changed quickly, smoothing out the robe she so cherished and what went with it, sitting down to pull on calf-high boots which were an almost perfect fit.

The mirror was again hidden against her skin and Twilla tightened a belt from which hung an empty knife sheath and a small pouch.

"Good!" Karla eyed her transformation. "But to hide the hair," she groped in the chest again to bring out a knitted cap large enough to cover the hair Twilla bundled into it.

"You are as like to one of those tree killers," Karla commented, "as if you had appeared at the same birthing! Come!"

Again the mist served to deliver them to the very edge of the fringe. Out on the open fields before them there were still the blackened patches left by the fires which the forest winds had extinguished, and that bare scar where the great fire had burned. Twilla had no guide except memory—somewhere well beyond that scarring perhaps a little to the west—must lie the farm where she had sheltered with Ylon.

There was a flutter in the air, and something whirled about her head. By the reflected light of the mist which still hung behind her Twilla saw a small scaled body, a gap-jawed head.

"Sister in power—" Twilla started. She looked quickly around. Catha stood there and on one shoulder rode another of the small lizard flyers, her wrist supported the third.

"These little ones," the under woman said, "have a place in our plans. But they must learn what they shall face. Take them with you— no, do not think that they shall betray you by their strangeness," she said as Twilla started to shake her head. "They have their own ways of remaining unseen, save by the one they travel with. And you shall find them useful after their own fashion also."

Twilla was dubious but she did not doubt Catha believed in what she said.

"This is necessary?"

"For what we plan, yes," Catha assured her.

So under the shadows of the deepening night Twilla left the forest, not alone for the lizards soared over her or came to perch on her shoulders at intervals.

How far Leela's homestead lay she had no idea. All she remembered now was that it had taken her and Ylon a night's full travel to reach the forest. The moon tonight was the smallest slice in the sky, of little service for light. The cloaking darkness did not appear to bother her trio of small companions and she saw one deftly snatch a moth in flight, savoring its capture.

Then—from the forest at her back sounded that call she had heard in the past—on the over mountain road, outside her tower-room prison, from the sky when she and Ylon were near this same spot. She heard the flap of wings—wings so large that they blotted out for an instant that slice of moon. Her hands went to free the mirror her only hope of any defense against attack. Anisgar, Ylon had named it—but she did not know really what it might be or in what way it was tied to the forest. That it truly was she believed.

It flapped over her head and then was gone into the dark nor though she waited, it did not return. At last she trudged on but she listened for more than the small noises of the night.

She tramped without pausing. Oddly enough she had no desire for either food or rest tonight. The lizards fed richly on the insects her boots stirred into the air. Until, at length, they came to perch on her shoulders. The third's light weight settled on her cap, she felt its claws hook through the knitted wool into her hair.

The moon wore its way down. Though the night breeze was chill she felt too warm with constant exercise. Now the first palid streaks across the sky foretold day. Should she seek out a hiding place or was she close enough to Leela's holding to keep on? Twilla was debating that when she saw ahead one of those areas of hard-packed soil, which marked a field's boundary. She hurried her pace sure that she had found the outer limits of the place she sought.

The lizards once more took wing, flying a little before her. She caught the thick scent of sheep as she skirted the wall. Though she had seen or heard no dog on her former visit she wondered if one was kept for herding. The wind was in her face so her scent was not being carried to the farm. The lining of sun streaks on the horizon and the fresh light of early morning showed her there were indeed sheep moving in the field this earthen wall bounded. She guessed in what direction the home must lie.

Two more fields, one with a small saggy-coated horse hardly more than a pony in size and which snorted and jerked its fore feet from the ground as one of the lizards took off and skimmed closely over it as if drawn by curiosity.

The sound made by the pony brought two other draft animals away from a water trough where they had been drinking. These were surely plough horses, looking doubly tall as they trotted to their small companion, the three of them now staring in Twilla's direction.

She slipped around the corner of the field wall and came upon the lane which must lead to the house. On the other side of more walled but well-tended fields stretched the stubble of grain ragged on the ground.

The smell of smoke reached her. Not the clean odor of burning wood, but a nose-tickling assault which brought a hastily stifled sneeze out of her. There was the farmyard, its earth churned and cut by hooves and feet. At the farm-side stood what could only be the house, for the other two buildings to one side lacked the trim, well-kempt look of that third one.

Smoke rose lazily from the chimney. Twilla had just time to drop to the ground when the door swung open and out came Leela, a pail in hand. She went to the well and set about lowering its bucket for water.

But Leela's face! A dark bruise disfigured the cheek nearest to Twilla, and the fishergirl moved slowly, grunted a little when she had to empty the heavy bucket into her pail as if that action caused her pain. Had Leela been—beaten!

TWILLA HESITATED AND remained in hiding. If Leela's husband was in the house she had no intention of trying to reach the fishergirl. She watched Leela return, bearing her pails. The door closed behind her.

The three lizards had settled on a stone which helped to mark the entrance to the yard, and their coloring so matched the rock that she could hardly detect them. She had not made any plans, was merely following her desire to speak with Leela. Now she must adapt as best she could to what she found here. If Leela had suffered punishment for her part in the fighting about the fire she could well be in no mood to risk any chance of communication with Twilla.

Twilla started as the door of the house opened again with some force and a man stamped out. He was scowling as he turned and growled:

"Keep to your hearth, woman. If I have to pay any more fines for troubles you have a hand in, you'll pay in turn. See that you remember that!"

He slammed the door behind him with the same force with which he had thrown it open, and tramped heavily across the muddy yard toward one of the smaller buildings. Twilla remained crouched where she was. There was no other place of even partial concealment she could see.

The farmer came out of the building and started toward the field where she had seen the draft animals, a coil of harness across one shoulder. She watched him halter the two horses, lead them out and back toward the farmyard. Once there they were hitched to a two-wheeled wagon and left while he returned to the house.

He jerked open the door and his voice once more carried clearly:

"I go to Roamnors. Keep to your own tasks and look sharp at what you do."

If Leela answered, Twilla could not hear. The man shut the door once again and came to the cart, climbing in and turning the horses toward the gate. Twilla crouched smaller, wishing that she had the same ability as the lizards to fade into her surroundings.

She watched him down the lane, the horses plodding along at a slow pace which he did not try to hasten. Once she saw him look back over his shoulder, his scowl still plain to read, as if he suspected some disobedience to his orders.

He was out of sight before Twilla moved. She had made up her mind. If this man whom Leela had shown a liking for earlier turned sour in his manner toward her, then certainly she might be more ready to listen to Twilla.

The girl darted across the muddy yard and was at the door. Reaching out she rapped on it as hard as she could.

"Who comes?" Leela's voice was distorted by the barrier between them.

"One with a message," Twilla improvised.

The door opened, hardly wider than a space through which she could slip. But without a welcome she would not attempt that. Leela might have been so treated that she lost her former good standing with her husband.

"You!" Leela's recognition came quickly. "What are you trying, Healer? To get me whip-flayed?"

"They have beaten you?" Twilla swallowed. "What—"

Leela gave the door another push widening the opening.

"Lord Harmond lessoned us well—" She twitched her shoulders and then grimmaced. "His sergeant knows how to lay on the stripes—not enough that we cannot work, but well enough to make us mark his orders. Also he laid fines on our men and they repaid us for that."

"Because of the fight—"

"That—we mishandled his men and he did not take well to that—it shamed him—and them. And because we did not accept well what that shark priest would do. That priest had powers greater than even Lord Harmond—and the Lord resented that also. But—why did you come? If they nose you out you'll have to deal with more than a whip sore-back—Lord Harmond will have you to the stake doubtless."

Twilla felt the weight of the pouch she carried. Would Leela, any of the women listen to her? She knew no way of approaching the subject except baldly open.

"Your man bears you ill will?"

Leela grimaced again. "A fine sets not well on any man, nor does the ill will of his Lord. Johann believes that all those whose women fought back will be marked in Lord Harmond's memory as untrustworthy."

She had retreated further into the room and Twilla followed her, daring to close the door behind. At least Leela had not ordered her out and seemed willing to air her grievances.

"What of Wandi?"

Leela shrugged. "Her mam is dead or perhaps they would not have taken her so easily. Her da—well, he is in the punishment cells for resisting the priest's will."

"And she?"

Leela licked her lips. "Rutha took her and for that was shame-marched and beaten in the town square. Since the priest was dead now she dared to claim her and Rutha gives her house room."

"Why did they take her for sacrifice?"

"Why ask that, Healer? Was she not in the demon's lair and came forth unharmed? The priest claimed she was a spy for the forest."

"There are no demons in the forest," Twilla said slowly.

"So, Healer? You have been there—can one believe you? What if you are now so changed also?"

Leela had dropped down upon a stool, no longer looking at Twilla but staring sullenly at the small fire on the hearth.

"The priest is dead." Twilla tried another approach.

Leela looked up. "By your hand, that is what you would say?"

"I would rather say that evil met its just reward. You, Leela, cannot have me believe that you would willingly give any child to torment and death. Nor would have any of the women who stood with you at the fire. When his power was broke you proved that. Or is there another priest of darkness to tie you once more?"

Leela spat into the fire. "None, but there are those who still hold belief in his powers. And the Lord Harmond is disturbed because the Dandus was sent to him with certain orders. They think his power might well have given us the forest."

"There is no giving of the forest." Twilla felt free now to take another stool and drop her pouch on the table standing between them. "Those who live with the trees want nothing but to be left alone."

"Have they not sent blindness and wit-lack upon us?" Leela flared up.

"Only upon those who went within the boundaries of their land to take trees. Think, Leela, have there been any attacks upon the farms?"

"Wandi was taken—"

"And returned when it was discovered that one had broken forest law," answered Twilla. "Was she maimed or wit-blasted when she returned?"

Slowly the other shook her head. "That was why," she said, "the priest named her demon taken."

"What do you think of me, Leela? Do you judge me to be a demon under the skin? You cannot believe that the Dandus priest had a right to rule here—remember all we were taught in childhood about the evil they spread in the old days."

"Yes." Leela turned a little on her stool to face Twilla and once more met the other girl eye to eye. "Why are you here, Healer? If you are taken—you will face far worse than any lessoning by lash. No, we were not followers of the Dandus belief—but there are some who are and who would cry out for a like death for his slayer. Some of those are in high places. And Lord Harmond will not allow his rule to be questioned. What have you come to learn?"

Twilla drew a deep breath. "To learn the thoughts of the women. Over mountain would any husband allow his wife to be misused—add to that brutality of his own? Johann gave you that bruise, Leela, did he not?"

The fishergirl's hand went to her cheek. "He was angry that they took a third of his crops for a fine, and he had worked very hard to gather them. To him the fault was mine."

"How many women suffered beatings?" Twilla demanded.

"Ten of us, we who were well to the fore and the first to attack the guards."

"And none among the men protested?"

"Lord Harmond's wrath was great—they were unarmed—his soldiers could have cut them down with ease. And—"

"And some of them felt as Johann that their wives deserved what they received."

Leela twisted a little and then gasped as if she were in pain. "That, too," she agreed.

"The women need not be helpless," Twilla fingered the pouch. "They can put an end to this struggle. Those of the forest want only to be left alone—they have power and they will use it if they are pushed, but only if they are pushed. This I swear is the truth."

Leela sat silent for a long moment. "Wood is needed," she said slowly. "And there is the gold in the stream."

"There is also trade—not stealing," Twilla replied curtly. "No living tree may be taken, but with every wind there are storm-killed ones brought down. The gold—what if there could be an exchange of metal arranged?"

"They sent you here to say this?"

"Their women sent me."

"Their women—the witch ones who took our men! Why do they want our goodwill?"

"The men taken, as I have said, were invaders. Just as our people would capture any who ravaged your farms. The women send this as their message—let there be a truce between us wherein things may be spoken openly and answered in truth."

"Lord Harmond would say no to that."

"If Lord Harmond found that he had few followers how would he decide?"

"He has the right to call up all men for service. And that he has done—within twelve days Johann and the rest must report to him."

"The farms are scattered. What if the men on them did not appear? How could he round up such?"

Leela shook her head slowly. "It would be death for those who did not obey."

"Not if Lord Harmond were otherwise occupied. And I tell you the truth, Leela, do you think that a power strong enough to turn the Dandus priest's darkness back on him is going to allow Lord Harmond to do what he will without any check?"

"You have joined the demons!" Leela's voice held a grim note.

"I have joined no one, I am seeking peace. As a healer I cannot slay except when I am faced by the foul powers of the Dark as I was by the fire. No, I do not speak of my power but those of the forest have more than tangible weapons with which to defend themselves. And they will—if Lord Harmond brings destruction upon them.

"Leela," Twilla pulled at the thong which fastened the bag, "I have brought you a free gift from the forest women." She shook out one of the lockets. "She who wears this will have nothing to fear from any man who is close to her. He will listen to what she says, he will not lift hand to her, and what she wishes she can have."

Leela stared down at the locket. "This be mage dealings. What has any woman to do with such?"

"She can save lives, her home. I swear to you, Leela, that there is no dark work here. Men who are prone to violence can be brought to think better of it. Do you not want Johann to be as you thought him when last we met, or do you want him to continue as I have seen and heard him this day.''

Leela put out a finger very slowly but did not quite touch the locket. She raised her head to look again at Twilla and there were tears gathering in her blue eyes.

"We were—happy. Happy 'til that Dandus priest sent out the word. Yes, it is true, the women—most of them—were angry. We bear children to live not to die in torment. And he—I swear this, Twilla, that one took pleasure in what he did!''

"Such is the nature of the Dark," Twilla nodded.

"Johann protested when we women were herded like sheep but our men were also under guard. Then—then when the priest was gone and we got our freedom— We could only hold that for awhile. When they took us Lord Harmond singled out our men and told them to keep their women in order or suffer more fines—and we were beaten and shame marched.

"Johann—somehow he changed. Healer, when the priest went to whatever hell waited for him, could part of his spirit remain to touch men?''

Twilla's hands arose to her mirror. She shivered. That was something she had not thought of, if it were the truth then there was worse than she thought to come.

"I do not know," she replied slowly. "But, if it is true, then, Leela, this amulet will prove of double value to you. It will perhaps also allow you to free any shadow which has touched Johann.''

"Amulet—we had such for sea faring—there were the Eyes of Dood, the Nine Tailed Serpent. You wore them for luck." Her hand arose again to touch the swollen cheek. "If—if the dark has touched Johann, then I shall fight for him! And I shall try the worth of this." She reached out to take up the amulet.

Twilla sighed with relief. She had never been certain that she could do as Karla and Catha expected and get even this far with her persuasion.

"Leela," she leaned forward a little against the table edge, "there are more—more for women who have suffered the wrath of Lord Harmond and their own men." She shook the bag a little and it gave forth a jingle. "How may these be given to those who can use them best?''

"Market day—" Leela replied promptly. "Johann may try to leave me here but if this will help me do as you say, get him to listen to me, then I shall go in with him. There are those I think I can trust, to them I shall give these and the word. Twilla, I have trust in you and the truth you say you have told me. Let it be so!''

"It is so! Speak to Johann, tell the others to speak to their men—speak of a truce, a chance to bargain. Lord Harmond can have his soldiers but the will of the people may do much to delay any plans he has made.''

"What can be done I shall. If this gives me back the Johann I knew—then Twilla you have played healer well as I have seen you do so before!''

"So—and who are you who comes sneaking into a man's house?''

Twilla slued about on her stool. She heard Leela gasp. That door which had been slammed so hard before was now opened without a creak and they had been too immersed in their talk to hear it. There stood the man Twilla had seen, as she thought, out of sight earlier.

Now he strode over the threshold, scowling.

"Scalla favored me with remembering that I must have the coppers to pay for the feed,'' he continued. "So I catch you again in ill-doing, woman. And who is this lad you have brought to shame my house?''

Twilla was on her feet to face him, hand on mirror, though she had no desire to injure Johann.

"The hearthwife brings no shame upon you,'' she said swiftly. "I am a healer—''

"Paugh! There are no healers—not here. What farm have you run from?'' He approached her a sly twist to his mouth. "Your master will be out after you, and he'll be thankful to me for your taking.''

"Johann!''

His head swung toward Leela. "And you, woman. You have not yet learned your—'' His voice trailed off and the scowl lightened. Now he looked not only younger but oddly unsure of himself.

Leela had grasped the amulet in her hand and was holding it against her breast as if to give it greater power with all the strength of her body.

"Johann,'' she spoke his name again and came around the table to stand before him. "Why are you angry, Johann?''

His look was troubled and he brushed one hand shakily across his forehead. "I—I do not know. I have no quarrel—''

"No quarrel with me, Johann, is that not so?'' Leela now stood directly before him. She raised her other hand and touched his cheek gently. "There is no ill will between us, Johann—is that not so.''

He flashed a sudden grin and his hands went to Leela's shoulders, pulled her into a tight hug.

"It is so,'' he murmured into her hair as he held her. "I do not

know what dark one took my tongue. And—and I did this—'' He held
her a little away from him and put one hand under her chin lifting her
head a fraction before his fingers did not quite touch her bruised cheek.
"Leela, surely I was demon-led. I ask your pardon for you are Leela,
my own." Again he embraced her.

But Twilla was troubled. He had sworn by Scalla—and that was a
mark-name of power once shattered. Was Leela right in believing that
the death of the Dandus priest only scattered the wider the evil he
cherished?

"It is well, Johann." Leela stroked his cheek in turn. "There is no
ill between us now. I am sorry that you have suffered a fine, but I am
not sorry that I stood with the women for the sake of Wandi. A child
must never be tormented for another's gain."

"Yes," he nodded. "Why did any of us not rise to do the same as
you women did? We were demon-touched. If our lord demands a fine
for such then it is he who holds to darkness."

"Hush!" Leela's hand was instantly over his lips as he said that.
"Do not speak such thoughts—but do not lose them either. Now—"
She paused a little away from him, "This is in truth a healer—Twilla
by name. She has come to serve us as she can."

"But there are no women healers, Lord Harmond would not have
it so."

"Yet here she stands," continued Leela. "She serves man and beast,
even as do all healers over mountain. You started to Roamnors to get
help for the ewe—let Twilla look to the beast—"

He looked at Twilla, taking in her dress, and then staring at her face.
"Well enough, Healer. If you can serve my best ewe then be sure
I shall reward it."

His harsh anger of moments before seemed to have never existed
and Twilla no longer had any doubts over the efficiency of the amulet.
She followed him easily enough out to one of the sheds where there
lay panting a ewe with the fine fawn colored fleece of a superior
animal.

Straightway Twilla busied herself with the animal. She no longer
had her herb bag but she still had her knowledge and there was much
to be done. Johann knelt in the straw on the other side of the ewe and
watched her until at last there was a strong bleat from the sheep, which
raised its head and kicked with its legs, striving to stand again. He
aided it quickly.

Twilla studied a mess on the floor of the shed. "It has eaten samp
weed—look to your fields, Johann, such must be rooted out. Luckily
this one had not gotten much of it—samp weed kills."

"Yes?" He was steadying the ewe. "My thanks, Healer. I have only coppers but all in the money box is yours."

Twilla shook her head. "I need no pay, Johann. Leela is my friend from the past, I came to see how matters went with her. I found them not good, but I go knowing they will be better."

A flush darkened the weathered brown of his face. "Healer, I do not know what kind of good you have worked here, but that dark in me is gone also. It was evil and I was another man. But, healer, there are others of a like mind with me as I was, if you venture into the town—"

Twilla shook her head. "No, I am not for the town—I wander as healers are sworn to do when their aid is needed. But—tell me, Johann—you called upon Scalla—where did you learn that?"

His flush deepened. "Healer, there has been much talk in the market, in the ale house, at the mill. I—I listened because it was what was mostly what men talk of in these days. But—this do I swear, by the blood in me, Healer, I give no grain or lamb to the balefire! Nor shall I speak that name again!"

"I believe you speak the truth. However, it is unwise to call upon evil even in careless talk. I must be on my way now, Leela." She looked to the fishergirl standing at the door. "I am no longer needed here."

Leela reached out and caught her by the arm. "Healer, best indeed be on your way. And we give you hearty thanks, though some of our neighbors might not be so minded."

Johann nodded vigorously. "The next farm is Roamnor's—he—he paid tribute to the Dandus priest willingly."

"Thank you for the warning. Leela, guard yourself well, in times to come there may be more trouble."

They wanted her to take food, a well-woven blanket, but she refused. As she passed the gate the lizards took to wing and hovered over her. But she turned and waved vigorously to the two who now stood by the farmhouse door. If the amulets worked as well with the other women—surely they had a beginning even as Karla and Catha hoped.

29

THE SUN WAS already climbing and to Twilla, used now to the shadow ways of the forest, the land looked grimly bare. She hesitated about striking off directly toward the dark loom of the wood, sure that she could be easily sighted by any patrol which might exist.

As if they too were anxious, the lizards continued to wheel about her as she went, without settling again on her shoulders. Then, of a sudden, they bunched and flew directly down at her. She dodged but they returned in the same maneuver, sending her to her knees they swooped so low. Another pass and they had her nearly flat. There was the remains of another earthen fence neared and the constant swoops of the lizards drove Twilla into a washed-out portion of that wall.

The lizards dropped to the earth, straightway changing their color to the brown-red of the soil. Their actions she decided were in the nature of a warning. She crouched flatter. Then through her hands against the ground felt the vibration forerunning sound.

There came a jangle of gear, a snorting, and then a voice.

"Captain says keep clear of the patches—"

"Ain't none of us goin' there anyway."

Men's voices harsh and with the twang of that accent the mercenaires who had guarded the bride train over mountain used. Twilla tried to plaster herself against the earth. She could only hope that the drabness of her clothing was enough like the field earth that she not be easily sighted.

"They ain't showin' any," remarked the second voice. "And why should they?"

"They don't have to show," returned the other. "You was there when that demon sent His Mightiness into his own fire. An' didn't everyone swear as how *his* power was goin' to bring the demons right out of hiding to be cut down? Well who got it mid-center then?"

"You've got a big mouth, Rolf," said his companion. "Better close it before you tongue your way into the cells. His Lordship don't want any wild talkin' 'bout that dustup."

"It ain't wild talkin' when I seen it for my ownself," the other replied. "Got me a lump on the head to prove it, ain't I? That fool of a woman had a good swing—"

"Comes from hayin'. They learn that there when they has to scythe down a field. But the Lord learned 'em. They won't be tryin' such again. They got their public lashin's and then their men, they gave them what for, too. Don't take kindly to payin' fines, these dirt grubbers don't."

"Casper was talkin' funny last night," the voices had not drawn any nearer and Twilla believed that they had halted not too far away from her very-exposed hiding place.

"Casper's got the brains of a puddle hopper. You can take everythin' he says, swish it around, and maybe get one or two words of truth out of it. What's ridin' him this time?"

"He says as how that priest had him a friend in the forest. That he would never have tried that balefire if he hadn't had word that it was goin' to work."

"Well, it didn't. An' the one who gave him his comeuppance came from there. It was a woman too—wonder if they do the fightin' for the forest 'stead of the men. Now that *would* be somethin' to think about. Casper say where he heard this bit of news?"

"He was guard at the tower, the Lord and the priest talked some. But it was the captain as the priest was closest with. He an' the Lord ain't too friendly these days."

There followed a harsh laugh. "Now I wonder why? If my paw pushed me to wed an' bed that hag face I don't think I'd take kindly to the idea or to him either. I saw her plain when they pushed her out. Face was enough to turn a man's stomach it was. Good thing she and that demon-blasted Ylon got theirs in the river—good for the Captain that is. Ylon now, he was a good officer 'til the demons got him. Different from this one."

"The Lord, he's countin' on the crawlers. They're not too far from the town now. Run them up to that there woods and then just do some hackin' away where no demon is goin' to get at one. Maybe the Lord—he knows the priest's friend and got him secrets 'bout what is waitin' there. Well, we have our look-see here. I ain't goin' to ride no closer, got me a sore rump yet from when that horse dumped me yonder—''

"What made them go crazylike?"

There was no immediate answer to that and that demand came again:

"What made them go crazylike?"

The answering voice was lower as if the speaker did not expect to be believed.

"Flyin' things. They got to the horses—an' to men too— See them little marks here on my neck. Still showing but they ain't stingin' any more.''

"What kind of flying things?" the other pushed.

"Look here, I ain't goin' to get called up before the Captain for sayin' somethin' as he swore weren't true—though they got him too. Take it they were flyin' things an' they came from the Woods. Kept us from gettin' that demon as blew up the priest.''

"Flyin' things," repeated the other. "Well, whatever they were they sure did the business for the Captain's squad.''

The other grunted and then Twilla heard the horses moving off. She remained where she was until one of the lizards came to life, stretching its wings for a takeoff and she gathered that was now clear.

However, she studied the land ahead, trying to plan a passage which would not take her in plain sight. It must be near noontime, she scrubbed her face with her hand trying to beat off the midges which clung to the grass stems and seized upon her coming as an invitation to a banquet.

Reaching the site of the blasted fire Twilla made her way carefully around that dark scar. Even with the flames long gone she had no desire to come near where the Dandus priest had been working with dark powers. Was the friend he counted upon in the forest Lotis? Had the Dank Fire Ylon destroyed been in some way linked with this? Power called to power, Lotis might have set up a beacon of her own knowledge to attract that of the priest.

She came at last to the brush hedge and found a way through it. The cool of the forest was a balm after the heat of the outer lands. Twilla leaned against one of the great trees while the lizards plastered themselves against the trunk and were lost to sight.

Now she needed a guide back to the great tree—unless the lizards could supply that. But they were not moving on. Somehow she had expected Karla or Catha to be waiting but she might well have been alone in the mist-veiled shadows. There was no sign of any life.

She wished she knew the trick to the transportation mists but that was not within her range of power. There was nothing to do but plod ahead down an aisle between the massive trunks, hoping to meet one of the warders—but not such a beast as she had faced near the river.

Outside the sun had been heavy and bright, here was something close to twilight and it took some time for her to adjust to the change in light. The floating mists made it hard to mark a way very far ahead and she only hoped that she was on the right course.

The girl stopped short, head up, nostrils expanded to catch that faint scent. It was one she would never forget—Lotis's mark. She was no hound able to trace it to its source but she began to move again, very slowly, striving to measure the strength of that fragrance. At the same time she reached for her mirror. Lotis, she was sure, was making mischief and since the forest people could not apparently stop her—

Twilla ran her tongue over lips which seemed dry. Undoubtedly she was a fool if she thought that she could stand up to a mage who had earlier bested even her own kind. If she were wise she would go as far in the opposite direction as she could. Yet still she walked on steadily and as noiselessly as she could, while above her the lizards fluttered their way. They seemed to show no discomfort and certainly had not delivered such a warning as they had when they had sent her into hiding in the open.

The deep leaf mold on which she trod was changing. There were humps, growing larger between the trees and as Twilla went she saw that some of them had broken completely through the deposit of years to display crowns of round stone. These seemed to be aligned, leading onward with a narrow track between.

Twilla came to an abrupt halt. The scent of Lotis's fragrance still wafted about her but there was something else here—underlying that. Something which made her queasy. She had not entered that plainly marked trail ahead nor did she intend to. When dealing with powers it was best always to be wary.

The lizards had gathered in to her, their weight again on her shoulders and her capped head. It would appear that they had no more desire to advance than she had.

That hump-marked way was veiled from sight only a few lengths ahead. The mists—no—Twilla studied what hung there. And memory stirred. When Karla had come to her after Lotis had crippled the ways of the castle the mist which had brought her had had the same yellowish, curdled look.

Yet—the girl looked back over her shoulder. Yes, there were other drifts of the mist, silver untarnished, as fair as this stuff was foul. And foul it certainly was.

A ward—a barrier—?

Twilla was drawn in two directions—go on, mirror in hand and dare that—or retreat?

As she lingered trying to make up her mind that curdled mist billowed, twisted, something might be caught within its center. Twilla had the memory of a fly entangled in a web. *A captive?* She could not find herself able to turn away now.

Unslinging the mirror to hold before her, she took the first stride down that hump-marked path. The lizards soared. They did not dive at her in warning as they had beyond, rather they encircled her as she went.

Twilla noted that the murky web was not retreating and the bulging movement within it was growing more frantic. She swung up the mirror, focused it on the mist, but hesitated before she tried to call up any power. Would what or who was entangled there suffer if she blasted the mist?

Three cautious steps onward brought her between two stones more than waist high. These were glistening as if water washed over them and the stench of the thing ahead had smothered out all of Lotis's fragrance. Twilla studied the mist trying with all her might to see what was so engulfed. She only saw a shadow which moved as if some large hand waved from muck to treetop.

Then there reached her a thrust of fear—not her own but that of another. She dared not waste time. The thing entrapped was in a frenzy of terror.

Mirror held out before her Twilla edged closer. The lizards spun about her faster and faster, but none dived to warn her. She focused her will upon the plate in her hand.

A silvery haze arose from that, whirling about upon itself as it gathered strength and force as might one of those great windstorms of the outer lands. Then the last root of it separated from the mirror and it bored forward as if she had launched some giant, vaporous screw.

The tip touched the surface of that leperous barrier. Within, the movements became more and more frantic. From where that mirror-mist point had touched there ran lines, cracks. They deepened. The foul fog writhed with more than the movement of its captive now. It split, peeling away as that hardly seen form within must have launched itself forward.

Twilla faced what came through. It was a bird, not on wing but coming at a half waddle. But such a bird! Even as the trees around were giants of their kind, not to be seen elsewhere, so was this bird larger than any she had ever witnessed a-wing.

As it came it fanned pinions each near as long as a man was tall. And the body was equal in size to her own. Its beak gaped and she saw that the edges were serrated giving the appearance of toothed jaws. The head went up and a little back and it voiced the cry she had heard before—Anisgar!

Since it was coming straight toward her Twilla was forced into retreat, fearing that the thing might believe her responsible for its capture. The lizards broke the circle they had kept about her and flew on to hover above the giant creature which certainly could not take wing here where the close-knit trees would prevent such action.

The Anisgar halted. After that one loud cry it was silent. But its head, mounted on a long curve of the neck, stabbed forward with such speed Twilla could not avoid it. The strong, wickedly toothed bill touched the mirror surface with a lightness which surprised her.

For a long moment it stood so, beak against the mirror. Then its head raised higher and she was looking into great golden eyes in which there was a spark of flame red. It nodded its head several times and she thought she understood. The creature was too large to pass her, but it wanted freedom beyond where she stood.

Twilla backed away still keeping the mirror in sight, followed eagerly by the anisgar. She was beyond that hump-marked trail, back in the Wood. But still it could not take to wing here. Though its gait was not far removed from a waddle it went past her as she pressed herself back against a tree trunk. It was moving she was certain with a definite purpose.

Now she was curious enough to fall in behind as the anisgar continued on its way. They were not retracing the way Twilla had come, for the creature pushed off to her right almost as soon as they had left that hump-marked trail.

Somehow Twilla was not surprised when it led her to an open space where a storm long since had sent crashing to earth one of the trees. The anisgar gave a hop to the moss-carpeted top of the downed trunk to once more sound its sharp voiced call.

Mist whirled and out of that curtain Oxyle stepped, Karla close behind him.

"Hail Rittengan!" The forest lord called to the anisgar with words totally strange to Twilla. The bird lowered its head and he stroked the gray feathers there. Suddenly he withdrew his hand and sniffed at the fingers. He frowned.

Karla had already looked beyond the bulk of the bird and caught sight of Twilla.

"Moon Daughter!"

Oxyle's glance followed hers.

"Where—" he began and then paused before he continued. "This one was captive and is now free—your doing, Moon Daughter?"

Quickly Twilla spoke of the foul thick fog, of the whiffs of fragrance which had led her to it, and the action of the mirror.

"Lotis!" There was sheer loathing in Karla's voice.

"Lotis," Oxyle repeated more somberly. "She has gained more than we believed. Khargel's hoard of knowledge is closed to her—what other source—"

Twilla interrupted. "The Dandus priest. I overheard speech among the outlanders—he boasted of a 'friend' within the forest."

"The man is dead," countered Oxyle.

"But how much did she learn before that death?" demanded Karla. "We do not know. And those who follow the dark have their own way of shadowing what they learn so that they may seem far less than they are, until they are put to the test. She took your messenger—" the woman gestured toward the bird. "Had it not been for the smile of fortune that Moon Daughter came that way how would our plans have gone?"

Oxyle's mouth set in a grim line. He did not answer her but rather turned to the anisgar holding out one hand. The gray bird ducked its head to rest that on the palm of the man's hand while Oxyle stared full-eyed into its own eyes. So they were for a space of time, Karla and Twilla watching.

The anisgar threw up its head again with one of those cries. Then it sidled along the trunk of the tree, reaching the other end where the half-exposed roots tilted high. Oxyle motioned Twilla back. Karla had already retreated to the very edge of this clearing. The girl did likewise on the other side. The anisgar fanned its wings, ran at some speed a little way along the trunk and took off at an angle Twilla would not have thought possible, soaring upward toward the small visible slice of sky overhead. Then with a last cry from above it was gone.

Karla had already turned to Twilla. "What fortune did you have, Moon Daughter?"

Twilla reported her meeting with Leela, and that with Johann. Also that Leela was undertaking to see that the amulets would be distributed farther. Oxyle listening, was again frowning.

"What power have you set to work, Karla?"

"Upper world power, lower world united," she returned serenely.

"Catha was my aid. This is woman power, Oxyle, and it has its place—which is here and now."

"There shall be no meddling—" the forest lord began.

"Meddle!" Karla snapped. "We do what is needed. It is because no one 'meddled' that we struggle now against the sendings of that brain-darkened Lotis! She should have been brought to answer for *her* meddling long ago."

"There is the law." Oxyle looked uncomfortable as if he really could not summon a strong answer to that accusation.

"We abode by the law and we might have ended in a power-raised sleep. Lotis broke the law and now is a rottenness within our ranks when we should be facing the outlanders. Catha has her own powers and is not subject to the law of yours. While *I* think that it was broken long since and we need every weapon we can put hand on. Our amulets will cause no harm, rather they will win these outland women to more peaceful lives. Also their power is not everlasting, but it must serve until those invaders come to a better state of mind."

Oxyle did not look convinced. "You have taken this action upon yourself," he replied. "Upon you will rest the burden if it goes awry."

"And upon you—and the council," retorted Karla, "rest the burden of letting Lotis go her way. Has she not even dared to net your messenger, the anisgar? What if he had never been able to reach the nestings of his kind? Then all your plans would go for nothing."

He shrugged. "One error must not be balanced by another. Lotis is truly without the law. I would not have others take power to themselves. Perhaps these amulets will do as you promise, gain us some time, breed dissension in their ranks. We shall have to wait and see."

Having set the subject aside with a half warning he turned again to Twilla. "What news have they concerning these iron crawlers which Ylon says they will send against us?"

She repeated what she had heard from Johann and the two soldiers concerning the action to come.

The lizards had come to rest again on her, sitting with folded wings, small heads high as if they listened and understood everything she said.

When she had done Oxyle again held out his hand as he had to receive the head of the anisgar and the lizard playing ornament on her cap took flight, came to rest on the outstretched palm. Oxyle brought up his hand so that the creature's eyes were on a level with his own, and, as he had done with the anisgar, he stared at it.

With a sudden fan of wings the small flyer took to the air and, followed by its two companions disappeared down the nearest forest aisle. Twilla felt oddly deprived as they left her.

"Now let us see this trap for true power," Oxyle said. "We must make sure that it will not act again, for our forces will be about in the Woods very soon and we want no more entrapments."

Twilla guided them to the way marked by the buried and half-buried stones. The last traces of the curdled mist was gone. They could now see a circle of stones each shoulder high. The ground within that circle held no carpeting of dead leaves, rather it showed as slabs of the same stone flattened in an uneven flooring. In the middle of that was a jar of dull black, its open mouth pointed skyward.

Oxyle did not step within the circle. From his belt he drew a length of silver, slender and pointed like a throw dart. This he hurled at the jug. It struck fair and full on the round side of that and the container broke, broke and crumpled into coarse dust.

"So," Oxyle commented. "Another bit of the Dark learning—well removed. But now there must be a search made—for there may be other traps—perhaps even stronger."

30

TWILLA SAT AGAIN at the table in the castle hall. She felt overlooked as if dismissed from any action impending. There was a lot of coming and going but none spoke to her and of Karla and Oxyle there was no sign.

She was holding one of the goblets between her palms when she saw Ylon coming down the long room, his hand against one wall for guidance. Looking at him she could see those subtle changes which she had noted in herself. There was no longer any sign of beard on his gaunt face. His own weathered skin was leached to an uncommon pallor. In so much he resembled the forest men.

But none of them went sightless. And, watching his slow advance, Twilla's hands clasped the goblet with force as if she would leave an impress on the metal of its making. Then she was on her feet going to meet him.

He paused, his head turned a little, he might be studying her with those sightless eyes.

"Twilla?" That was not a question and she had not spoken to give him a clue, somehow he knew her.

"Yes."

"What is happening in the outlands?" He turned away from his guiding wall toward her and she was quick to touch his arm so he came with her to the table.

"Much." She poured from the standing flagon into another goblet and pushed that into his hand. Swiftly she retaled her visit to Leela, all she had learned from the fishergirl, and the scraps she had overheard the soldiers exchange.

His face was impassive as he listened to the end when she spoke of the entrapped anisgar and what had happened thereafter.

"A man may be dead," he said when she was done, "and yet poison he has poured remains. My father"—he hesitated—"my father has always been called a just man, keeping strictly to the letter of the laws by which he lives. But this matter of the priest, the child, the fire, and afterward the treatment of the women—those are the acts of hired mercenary, not of one of House blood. Yet he was always against dark teachings—"

Ylon frowned down at the table he could not see. "This country, perhaps the very air bespells a man for the worse. I say my father has been changed. There is more than one kind of blindness which can be set upon a man."

"He was not bespelled by the forest—he has not come here," protested the girl.

"No, it is the Dandus priest, to that I would swear." He drank from his goblet. "But the man is dead! Surely his influence can no longer entrap those he would have ruled!"

Twilla thought of Leela's words—"What if a priest, dead from his own spells, left behind him seeking thoughts to fasten to the minds of others? And if this has happened," she speculated, "will such soon fade?"

"We shall soon discover," he answered somberly.

"Ylon—what of Lotis?" Twilla asked suddenly.

He scowled. "I do not know whether it is because I am no longer of service to her, or if, in some way, I am freer in the forest. She can no longer summon me—though she has tried—oh, yes, she has tried!" His head went up and now his expression was that of the fighter he had once been.

If Lotis no longer bound him—what of his sight? Would that, too, return? Somehow Twilla dared not mention that. It was a subject too close, which always must lie in his own thoughts.

"The crawlers have reached the town," he said abruptly. "Oxyle's messenger has seen them. It cannot be long now before my father will move. There is this, you must understand, he sees himself as challenged and if he cannot outface that challenge he might well lose the support of his men."

"The nets?"

"The under men bring them even now. They are to be taken to the forest edge. Perhaps by sunrise tomorrow we shall be able to see whether power of mage thought can overturn power of armor's weight.''

"You have doubts?'' Twilla asked.

He shrugged. "There are no possibilities which cannot be met—if fortune takes a hand. But it seems that the nets have taken at least one river intruder and hold him well. Whether they can bring the crawlers under control—who knows?''

"Ylon, where do you stand in this battle, if battle it comes to be?'' she asked, her eyes intent upon his face.

He did not answer at once. Rather he drank again from the goblet setting it down carefully when he had finished.

"I am no longer Ylon, Harmond's son. By his will he cut me free of duty to blood ties. I do not like what has happened. That the foulness of the Dandus priest has besmirched my father. The forest, through Lotis, constrained me to bondage, but that is now also broken. I am free to choose. What I want''—he paused again, turning the goblet around and around on the tabletop—"is a fair peace. If my father strives to fasten his will upon the forest, in one way or another he will lose and that loss may be hard for all our race. If he can be persuaded to a truce talk—But to incline him so demands that he must be made to see that there are powers greater than he can summon, but powers which will not attack without provocation. I have spoken with Oxyle. He has promised me this—that if the crawlers are safely stopped, I shall be the one to state terms—''

"You believe that your father will listen?'' Twilla remembered only too clearly Ylon's outcast state in the village.

"If the nets do as promised he will have no other choice.''

What if they thought him a traitor? Twilla shivered. They could well cut him down before he had a chance to speak at all. Yet she knew that this was something Ylon had set himself to do, a way of proving that he was not un-man as they had labeled him.

Time flicked by as it did within the castle. She was never certain how fast hours sped within the forest boundaries, but Twilla was sure it was on a different scale from the accounting of the outer world. She sat with Ylon but they no longer spoke. Perhaps he was lost in his own thoughts. Lotis—again hot anger arose within her—Lotis had set him on this path, and, whatever would come in the end, could be laid to her sorcery. Twilla had known rage and hate before but that was pale against the emotion she now fought to control.

Where was Lotis? Did her own kin hunt her down, or were those stifling laws of theirs against such action? Truly Lotis had already proven traitor to those of her blood, surely they would not let her remain free to perhaps entangle and defeat what they now wished to do.

The traffic back and forth through the hall had thinned as time passed. Then of a sudden there came a small party through one of the doors, and Twilla recognized Chard to the fore of a detachment of armed under men. Over their heads fluttered a flock of the lizards and they marched in a line, bearing with them rolls with the gleam of fresh-worked silver. One party so burdened came on, to be followed by a second.

Mist swirled in and Oxyle stepped out.

The forest lord raised his hand in salute. "Well met, weapon smiths. And well timed your coming. These crawlers are already on their way. Come," he whirled out his hand and a coil of the mist circled up from the floor, wreathed the first party of the small men and their burdens and swept them away as another mist began to grow.

Ylon stood up. Twilla was quick to join him. When the second party from underground had been carried off Oxyle beckoned to the girl. She caught Ylon's nearest hand and urged him forward. Then there was mist about them also, and they entered those breathless seconds of transport.

As it cleared the duskiness about them was that of the shade of the great trees, while before them was the ragged fringe of brush which marked the edge of the forest domain.

Beyond that the sky was a streaked shell marked by the dawn. Oxyle advanced to the very edge of the brush. Throwing back his head, he sent shrilling into the air a sound so like the trumpeting of the anisgars that Twilla could almost believe he had taken on some of their nature.

There was the flapping of great wings in the air just beyond the brush. Then settled into the tall grass anisgars themselves. Twilla counted as they landed there, their long necks weaving back and forth, those saw edge bills open a little, twelve of them.

Oxyle did not go to them as they clustered together with any further sound. But there was sound coming from the open lands beyond. First merely a discordant creaking like a distant echo but growing stronger every moment.

There was a trilling above Twilla. She saw there not only the lizards, their skin wings widespread, but with them asprites. There was no signal given which Twilla could see, but that cloud of many wings flashed out from among the trees into the morning air and the ever-brightening light made them plain to see. They wheeled on toward the scars of the fire and Twilla somehow guessed that it was that landmark which must have been decided upon for a proper place to immobilize the strange war machines, if they could indeed be rendered harmless.

What part the small winged creatures had in the coming engagement she could not guess, unless they were set to play a similar game against mounted men as the asprites had done to her service before. They were now circling the burned patch, they venturing no farther than that.

That hollow creaking grew louder. Then a thin line of horsemen was plain to be seen, the high grass brushing their stirrups. At their coming the asprites and the lizards went into action.

Twilla heard the neighs of startled horses and the shouting of men. That long line began to draw together until the flyers apparently herded them into a more compact mass. The horses wild under such attack reared, strove to rid themselves of their riders and be gone.

What they had escorted into battle could be seen. None of the ripples of the prairie land were able to conceal the first vast bulk moving at what was indeed a crawl forward.

Behind that dark blur was its twin. Foot soldiers marched beside the crawlers. As the ponderous war machines advanced closer to the burned area there was a constant troubling of the air and Twilla, though she could not pick out any individual form, was sure that the lizards and the asprites were again at attack. There were shouts from the men and bared weapons flourished in the air as if to cut down some small foe entirely too fast to be struck.

What moved the crawlers Twilla could not guess. They were certainly not being horse drawn and they moved at hardly more than a slow walking pace. While the escorts, both mounted and afoot, were being driven in, herded toward one or other of the lumbering monsters.

The under men were on the move. Those bearing the first of the nets uncoiled them. A number of them acting together caught up their handiwork and sent it flying up over the brush, throwing with the same skill Twilla had seen fishermen use to spread out a net across as wide a span of water as possible.

Six of the anisgars arose from their squatting position and fanned around the net taking up position equally spaced. Almost as one they dipped their heads and their saw bills caught upon the edges of the net. Together they moved out farther, dragging the net among them. Then, with an effort but managing it, they took to the air carrying the silver strands now aglitter in the sun.

The second net was already being hurled outward and the remaining birds caught it as deftly as their fellows had done.

Out both small flocks wheeled and the brilliance of the nets caused a flashing which brought cries from the oncoming force. The anisgars having adjusted to the weight they supported moved purposefully at a speed which brought them over both the crawlers and the men mounted and on foot now clustered about them.

The huge birds began a circular maneuver while the men shouted and pointed upward. Twilla saw a flight of arrows but none came near the birds, instead those shafts sped toward the nets as a bit of iron might be drawn to a magnet, slapping themselves tightly to the strands.

Down swooped the anisgars, and without any command from Oxyle that Twilla could detect they loosed their burdens, which straightway fell. As the arrows had been drawn to the netting so was the netting in turn drawn to the crawlers and the men clustered around them. Then the nets touched both armored men and machine and held, drawing most of their outer captives against the bulk of the crawlers and seemingly binding them there.

Horses wandered loose but the forces sent against the forest were firmly entrapped. Shouts which began in rage turned to fear as those entrapped struggled unable to free themselves. Twilla heard the exultant voices of the under men, some of them patting each other on the back in the affirmation of a job well done.

Swiftly Twilla explained to Ylon what had happened.

"Who commands the force?" he asked in return.

She pushed forward a little. Then saw that leader plainly in a red surcoat meant to be a battle signal. "Ustar."

The guards captain was one of those fighting the strongest against his bonds. He cried aloud orders, none of which his followers might obey.

"Steer me," Ylon demanded. And Twilla caught his arm to aid. Then Oxyle and Chard joined the two and Ylon appeared to sense their coming.

"They may listen the better to me," he said.

The forest lord nodded. "Have your chance, Ylon. Though you may have less power with them than you think."

Ylon gave a small, bitter laugh. "I may have none at all, but one can always make trial." He moved toward the brush fringe and Twilla drew him toward a place which offered passage.

There was a steady clamor from the struggling men. But, though they fought their bonds none won freedom. While the crawlers seemed as tightly pinned as the bunched forces about them.

Ylon strode forward, Twilla fast beside him. She had one hand for his arm and the other raised so she fingered the mirror. Though from all she could see there was no danger of any of those ahead winning out of the net.

As the two from the forest approached the clamor of the men stilled. All of them were watching Ylon and Twilla. She could see Ustar very plainly now, his face was crimson with rage. He tried to lunge forward as if to throw himself at his brother, but such an action was impossible.

Ylon came to a halt at the edge of the seared ground where the balefire had burned.

"Ustar!" He raised his voice so all those beyond could hear.

The captain pursed his mouth and spat. "Demon lover. Traitor!" he answered hoarsely.

Ylon turned a fraction, guided by his brother's voice, to face him squarely.

"Where rides our father?" he asked.

"Father? You are no son to him, un-man. Are you walking wit-deprived again? Be sure you shall meet him at the proper time and it will not be a meeting you will take pleasure in. For this you shall pay dearly—"

"I think not," Ylon returned. "Again I ask—where is Lord Harmond?"

"Where he belongs and when he comes forth—"

"Ustar," Ylon's calmness was a rebuke to Ustar's anger-thickened voice, "believe this, you have come up against the first defense. There shall be others waiting. Though you shall not stir from where you are until Lord Harmond comes to treat—"

"To treat?" brayed Ustar. "He will come with fire and ax, mark that, traitor. Do you think he would speak with you, or with such as that demon whore beside you?"

Suddenly Ylon laughed and that sound seemed to react on Ustar as if a lash had been laid to his back. "Ustar, you should not speak such words of this lady. Lord Harmond himself offered her to you in marriage—"

Twilla saw Ustar's eyes go wide as he stared at her from head to foot and back again.

"So she was one with those—"

"Not so, she is what she said she was—a healer. And healing can make many changes. But this matter is not of importance now. If you or one of your men be freed, will you take a message to Lord Harmond?"

For the second time Ustar spat. "Free any of us, un-man, and we shall sword gut you, traitor that you are. My father will follow his own will."

Ylon shrugged. "So be it then. You and those with you shall have time to think. If you find one ready to serve as a messenger let it be known.''

He turned, Twilla with him. Behind them the cries of the netted men had turned to curses, delivered with the same force as they might have aimed sword blows. From sounds, Twilla did not turn her head to watch, they were again fighting the net strands.

Overhead fluttered the lizards and the asprites, the latter seeming to dance on the air. They circled Ylon and Twilla and then headed back toward the netted men. Twilla did not envy any who might catch their attention.

Un-man, Twilla thought. She had heard that word loud among the curses. Lotis—her anger stirred. If the curse of Lotis remained what life would Ylon have? He had served the forest people well, surely Oxyle could do something to break that spell. All their talk of laws and ancient oaths should not stand between Ylon and his eyes. Healer, she was supposed to be a healer and what could she do—except stand by his side, be his eyes when it was needful. *Un-man!* Surely no one had proved himself more than that than this *man* who strode beside her with the curses of his own people following him.

They came to the forest fringe and made their way through it. Oxyle and Chard waited.

Again it was as if Ylon could see them for he asked: "You heard?"

"We heard. Those will be left to consider what may be done to them. They may be less contentious later this day."

"Oxyle," Twilla repeated his name sharply as he was turning away. The forest lord looked at her.

"Lotis—" She did not know just how to begin a plea she knew she must make.

Then— The air shimmered and Twilla was aware once again of that near stifling fragrance. Ylon swung around to face that disturbance and Oxyle stood, his feet slightly apart, as one braces himself against an attack.

Lotis was there. Her beauty was in no way diminished and yet, when one looked into her green eyes, Twilla thought, one could see the deadly light kindled by the shadow powers she had been dealing with. She smiled.

"Ylon—come—" She crooked her finger at him.

He did not move. Lotis lost her sly smile, her lips thinned.

"Come!" She gave that second order loudly.

"I am no longer your bond man," he replied in a level voice.

"I have set my mark on you. You are mine!" She hissed like a cat warning off a rival.

"You set your mark on me and still I bear it," he returned evenly. "But you can no longer hold me."

"You—" she turned a face now rage flushed to Oxyle. "The law is broke—"

"The law has indeed been broken," the forest lord replied. "But by your own acts, Lotis, we shall—"

"You shall do nothing!" Her voice skittered up the scale into a screech. "I have powers you have not dreamed of. See what happens to this bond man who says he is no longer answerable to me!"

She lifted her hand but Twilla moved as quickly. Even as Lotis pointed a finger at Ylon and that finger began to blaze with a light beyond any true flesh, the girl swung up the mirror between Lotis and her prey.

A THRUST OF light like a spear sped from Lotis's finger. It struck full upon the mirror rather than Ylon's breast. Struck—and was reflected back in nearly the same instant toward the woman. She opened her mouth perhaps to utter some counter spell—or a scream.

For the light hit full upon her, struck and spread, enveloping her body as flames might have done. There came a sound—a wail which carried both rage and fear. For a long moment Lotis was so enveloped and then—

There was no woman. What reared at the foot of the tree behind where she had stood was a pillar of gray rock. Twilla backed away, the mirror in her hand falling to her side. She came up with a jolt as her shoulders struck against the trunk of another tree. There she stood, staring wide-eyed at that pillar which might have so reared here for an age.

Oxyle broke the silence first: "So be it. She has taken the brunt of her own spell. Nor will she be free of it—for only the spell layer can break such ensorcellment and a rock cannot find voice—"

Twilla was trembling, her free hand pressed against her lips. What had she done? When Lotis had been free there had always been a chance she might be forced to return Ylon's sight—now, she herself had destroyed that one small hope.

"She is—*not*," Ylon said slowly. "Always I could feel her thoughts seeking me. They are gone now." There was the lightness of relief in his voice. Perhaps, Twilla thought, he did not realize what this meant to him.

Twilla turned upon Oxyle. "She—she is impotent? There is no way to break her free?" she appealed.

The forest lord shook his head. "She is caught in her own bespelling, that we cannot break. But at least she is no longer a threat to what we would do."

"So—" Twilla's anger was as much for herself as for Oxyle, "she cannot return Ylon's sight now."

"That is so," he agreed.

"Lotis is—gone," it was Ylon who spoke. "There is nothingness. I have—" his voice dropped near to a mere murmur, "I have feared that she could once more bind me. What—what was done?"

"She sent a spell toward you, the Moon Daughter's mirror was a shield before you which reflected it back to her—trapping her in the fate she planned for you. Lotis is a—rock!"

Ylon gave a small, uncertain laugh. "A monument to her own evil thereby."

Their conversation was only meaningless words to Twilla, she was caught hard in her own dark spell. She had destroyed Ylon's last hope. He would remain an object of scorn for those of his blood. Perhaps— even to stand a rock might be better than a lifetime in the everlasting dark! She was a healer—and this was no healing—

"Twilla?" Ylon was holding out a hand, groping in the air as she was too far behind him for any touch. "Twilla, is all right with you?"

Her face twisted. She swallowed bitterness and guilt. She had doomed him and he worried concerning her.

"I was not harmed," she croaked, fighting furiously to keep tears well-bottled within.

"May the Three in One be praised!" He had located her by her voice and now he swung around and, with a stride, was before her— both his hands out now, running up and down her body as if he sought some wound she had kept secret.

His fingers came to rest on her shoulders and he drew her to him, enfolding her as she came.

"You have freed me, Healer. What is the matter?" he demanded a second later.

"I—your eyes—" she got out between small gasps. "Lotis cannot reverse the spell."

"Healer—Twilla—you saved a life. Keep that in mind."

"I—I will be your eyes—always!" she burst out.

He was smiling. "Make no promises, Healer. You have given me much already."

Ylon continued to hold her and she felt safe against his strength. Within her she vowed—not promised—that what she said was true. He would have her eyes as long as life allowed it so.

They stood up so still together as Oxyle summoned a carrier mist and brought them back to the castle hall. There were a number of the forest people gathered there. Many Twilla had never seen before. But they stood in two bodies separated by a space across which those in one stared straightly at the smaller group who seemed ill at ease. There were not many of those, three of the women, six of the men. And when Oxyle appeared they straightened tensely as if awaiting some judgment to be passed on them. Those who had followed Lotis Twilla surmised.

"We stand asunder," Oxyle greeted them all, "when it is the time for us to face another foe. Carwar." One of the men in that first row of the smaller group, looked to meet Oxyle's eyes.

"Lotis is ensnared for all time in a dead-spell she desired to set upon another," the forest lord continued. "She plundered the sealed knowledge yet there was a greater power to answer her. You gave aid to her, as did you, Ethera." One of the women started, her mouth opening as if to utter a protest and then closing. "Makcon, Alsida." One by one Oxyle named them.

"What promises did she make? Power for all of you greater than what the rest of us could summon? Yet that power failed. We have said that the outlanders act out of greed in their drive to despoil us. It seems that greed also lies here within our own fastness. Once before there was such greed—Khargel—"

Someone, perhaps in that shunned company drew a breath so sharp it was audible.

"Khargel," Oxyle repeated as if to impress that name upon their ears—their minds. "His greed near lost all to us—severed us from our small kin—turned us one against the other. Lotis strove to do the same. Look into your hearts. Were you serving the great trees or your own greed?"

Those he addressed stood silent. They no longer watched him, rather they were staring at the floor. Then the man Oxyle had first addressed spoke:

"There was other power—Lotis gained it from beyond the forest. She scried and found a source. It may still live."

"I think not. He who must have sent it is dead. Kin—" He took a step toward the group. "We fight now a battle for us all—against the outlanders. Do we stand divided so that they may gain from our weakness?''

"No!'' One of the women he had addressed answered. "Lotis led us promising great things, that we might use that from the storehouse of Khargel to turn back the invaders. She said that you were afraid to call upon what she could. But—and this true, Lord, we were uncertain and when she lighted the Dank Fire—'' The woman shivered. "Then we knew what fools we were and we scattered. Set us under binding, if you wish, we deserve no better.''

There was an assenting murmur from those standing around her.

"No binding,'' Oxyle replied. "We need all power for what we would do. By the learning of the under men the enemy have temporarily bond themselves and we are leaving them to think about their helplessness. Of this something may come in our favor.''

Neither Oxyle nor any of his people gave any other reproach to those who stood apart, and slowly they joined with their fellows. It was Oxyle now who gestured Twilla and Ylon forward and she guided the outlander to stand beside the forest lord.

"With whom do we bargain, outlander?'' asked Oxyle.

"Unless matters have greatly changed there is but one over lord—Lord Harmond. He was not with those you entrapped. It was his son who captained the force with the crawlers.''

"You are also his son,'' Oxyle replied.

Ylon slowly shook her head. "When Lotis took my eyes she took from me all that makes a man—in my father's opinion.''

Twilla shivered, with every word the burden she bore grew the heavier.

"Does kin blood mean so little among your kind?'' It was Karla who pushed forward a little to demand that.

"Lord Harmond,'' Ylon did not speak of him any longer as father, Twilla noted, "is first a warrior and a maimed man is of little worth among the ranks of any army. But I tell you this—only Lord Harmond can give the orders which will bring peace.''

"And if he is not among those we hold captive—can we believe that he will ride out to be also caught—even though our nets are all in use and that he does not know?'' That was Chard tapping the butt of his staff against the floor.

"Do you suggest then that some of us go to him? We would be as helpless as children. Our strength comes from the great trees—if we withdraw from them our power wanes,'' Vestel said sharply.

"We dare not even move to disarm those we have taken,'' Oxyle agreed. "They hold and wear iron. Only the under people can handle such without hurt and I do not send those in my place."

Chard rapped heavily with his boar's staff summoning the full attention of all who heard him. "We can call upon the tuskers—they will form a guard."

"One not immune to spears and swords," Oxyle straightway pointed out. "A messenger we need but—"

There was a sudden eruption of mist halfway down the hall and out of it stumbled, as he had been caught up while running and so delivered in mid-stride, Fanna.

"Lord," he gasped, pushing his way past Ylon and Twilla, "there comes another army—"

Twilla's grasp on Ylon's sleeve tightened. Another army and Chard had just said that there were no more nets!

"But—" Fanna was continuing, "these are not soldiers such as we have seen—they are women marching so, although they carry weapons—"

Women! Twilla looked to Karla and then to Catha.

It was Karla whose voice arose above the murmur of those listeners about them and she spoke directly to Twilla.

"Moon Daughter, perhaps our endeavors have brought forth fruit. Shall we see?"

Ylon and Twilla crowded up beside them. Mist gathered and the hall was hidden from sight. Then they stood before that fringe of brush looking out toward the tangle of men and crawlers. The captives were calling out to the women for aid as they tramped with purpose in lines which indeed had some resemblance to a half-trained force of recruits.

They stopped beside the netted crawlers and men but they did not approach closer those now shouting in growing rage for help.

Instead two of the women came on and Twilla knew them. There was Leela armed with a short-shafted spear and Rutha who held a bared sword. They passed the burned ground and came before the line of brush. It was Leela who called out in a voice loud enough to be heard above the clamor of the men:

"Healer—we would parley."

Twilla loosed her hold on Ylon. She glanced to Oxyle. "I will go," she said and was on her way before he could refuse even if he wished to.

Then she was under the hot sun of late afternoon, fronting those two who had shared her trip over mountain.

"I have come," she said.

Leela gave a quick glance over her sholder to where the crawlers had come to rest.

"They took our men—like plow beasts they use them to move those things. It grows very hotter within when the sun is full upon them. We would have them free."

"We have offered to treat," Twilla returned, "but that can only be with Lord Harmond and none among those netted would agree to take our message."

"So—" Rutha, too, looked back at the tangle of men whose voices arose even higher now. Where earlier they had pled now they were cursing and uttering threats. "I think you will not find a messenger there. But we also have voices and enough that Lord Harmond cannot close his ears to all. Our men have been pressed by the soldiers into this, we want them free. If to carry a message will aid in that we shall be glad to do so."

Leela nodded vehemently. "What is your message, Healer?"

"I am not the leader here, that I must discover. Wait."

Twilla pushed back through the brush and spoke directly to Oxyle. "Well, Lord, do you appoint a time for such a meeting?"

"At moonrise," he said. "Tell Lord Harmond to come himself at moonrise."

Would the lord listen to women no matter how demanding they were, she wondered. He had been so used to disposing of them for life in his shameful lottery. And he might still even have a portion of his guard who had not been sent on this mission. But the end must be left to fortune as always.

"Moonrise," she repeated and returned to the waiting women. "Tell Lord Harmond to come at moonrise, but until then his men remain prisoners. I am sorry for your men, sisters in bondage, but we dare not free them."

"That is so. But let our women remain. We two and another shall go."

Leela was frowning. "It is very hot in that thing of the devil. Our men will be spent by moonrise."

"I do not think so. They are strong and the sun is near down now. When that is gone it will be cooler."

"Come," Rutha pulled at Leela. "The sooner we find the lord and give him the message perhaps the sooner they will be free again. We shall do our best, Healer."

She turned abruptly and marched back toward the crowd of women. They had not approached the netted men too closely, but they were exchanging shouted messages back and forth.

Twilla remained where she was until she saw Rutha swing into the saddle of one of the loose horses which had been grazing and Leela helped herself to a second—then they were off, heading back for the town.

Twilla returned to the place she had left Ylon and swiftly she told him of the agreement of the women. He gave a low whistle.

"Indeed Lord Harmond will have to change his mind on several counts," was his comment.

Those within the wood could see the women now settled down in the tall grass, broken into small groups where each seemed to know well the others. Twilla watched them, suddenly a little wistful. She missed the quiet round of the old days when she had gone forth with Hulde and had had a measure of respect from those who called upon their aid. Though Hulde had been much bound up in her studies between calls on her skills they had often talked about many things and the wisewoman had always treated her as a peer. She had never had such a relationship with any women since she had come over mountain.

Karla and Catha had a place in her life, but the fact that they had sprung from very different roots always tinged their meetings. Leela, she thought, might have been the friend she longed for—or Rutha. But between them now stood the shadow of power and she did not believe that that would ever be swept away.

"Twilla?" Ylon's questing voice drew her. Again she knew the burden she must cheerfully bear from now on—never letting any know that it was not her first choice. If she only could have forced Lotis to undo the wrong she had done!

"I am here." Two steps took her to join him. The forest people were remaining where they were but there were baskets of fruit and their all satisfying cakes, as well as the sap-filled flagons appearing and they settled down under the spread of the trees to eat and drink.

Twilla swiftly took a portion from the nearest basket, chose a small flagon and brought them back to where Ylon waited, sharing out the provisions with him. After his calling of her name he was silent, only ate and drank with the air of one preparing himself for a future need.

When he had done, his hand went to the sword at his belt and he drew it, running his finger lightly down the edge of the blade. Twilla watched him with growing apprehension.

"Will they fight?" she demanded.

For a moment he did not reply and, when he did answer, there was troubled note in his voice. "I do not know what spirit rules my father now. He is a proud man, to admit himself defeated may be too bitter a mouthful for him to swallow. The under men have no more of their nets—if Lord Harmond has held back any force of men then—'' He shook his head.

"Would he agree and then play false?" she prodded.

Ylon frowned, his head forward so he might be regarding the sword he held.

"Before time I would have smashed such a lie back into the teeth of him who dared to utter it. All my father possessed when he was chosen by the king to come over mountain was his honor. And that he had cherished from his cradle. But why he allowed the Dandus priest to build the balefire—that was not the doing of the Lord Harmond I knew. Perhaps there has been some change over mountain— some command directly from the throne. If so—then—''

"Then any truce or understanding we might achieve here would be for nothing in the end," she said. She was tired, feeling her whole body ache with that tiredness. There never was any foreseeable end to the troubles now and ahead.

"That is the dark side of the matter. On the other hand my father may have been forced to accept that blood drinking priest and feels freedom with him gone. If that is the case he might well make very sure that no other such caller of the Dark gets a foothold here. There is this: In his youth my father was a sword brother of Arvanis, passing upward from novice to guardsman. He was recalled by the kin when his two elder brothers were drowned in a faring overseas. But the teaching of Arvanis has been his inner belief. He kept always a sword shrine in any house where he was quartered for long. If—if we can get him to swear the swordoath I do not think that even the king's own word can make him break it."

Twilla knew a little about the sword brothers. They were astute, dedicated men willing to serve any cause they knew was just. So incorruptable that any lord or king gave them absolute trust, but also so incorruptable that they took service with none whose cause they had not debated in open council and found to be good.

"That is why," Ylon was continuing, "it must be me who states the terms— Can you bring me to Oxyle?"

Twilla saw the forest lord at a distance. Chard was with him and Karla, Catha, and some of the forest men. They were talking earnestly together, each in turn, with the others carefully listening.

"Come," she was on her feet and reached down a hand to draw him up beside her.

32

TWILLA HAD LISTENED to their arguments for what seemed a long stretch of time. Ylon was fast set in his belief he would be the best spokesman to open any communication with Lord Harmond. Twilla wondered fully if he feared his father had in mind some surprise attack to center on the forest people. It seemed to her that Ylon himself was in doubt of where Lord Harmond now stood.

As the suggestion and counter suggestion dragged out she felt as if there was a wall growing between her and those engaged in such strong argument. She felt dull of wit, drowsy as one who had withdrawn in part from those about her. Her shoulders were supported by one of the giant trees, and she did not even feel the roughness of the bark through jerkin and shirt.

It was odd, this state into which she had passed so gradually that she was not aware of what was happening. Neither did she have any urge to break it, even if she could. Dimly she was aware of the woodland, of the forest people centering now about Ylon, of the floating mists. Certainly she was there.

However, she was also in another place and sometimes that sharpened enough to blot out her surroundings but never to the extent that she was not aware of where she truly was.

However, that other scene drew her, promised quiet, safety, removal of all need for struggle or action. She saw again the walls of Hulde's dwelling close about her. All the once-loved, familiar furnishings stood in their proper places. Twilla drew a deep breath and near tasted the freshness of the spicy, minted herbs she could strongly smell. There was the table even more crammed with retorts, phials, a brazier or two, and lord of all he surveyed, Greykin sat eyeing the clutter before him with his usual disdain.

There was safety here—that she knew and drew the vision about her as she might a winter cloak against the fury of a storm. She was seated on her familiar stool and she was busy with her set task, polishing the round of the ancient mirror. Though this time she did not hum the usual notes Hulde had first voiced for her.

No, she was singing something else, words out of nowhere so impressing themselves on her mind as they came one by one that she was sure she would never forget them:

> *"See not with the eye, but with the mind.*
> *Evil spell can no longer bind."*

Even through that half-sleep she grasped that, held to it. Round and round her fingers went on the surface of the mirror. She wore no pads to protect the flesh and the friction of that pressure caused pain. But the hurt was something far away, it had nothing to do with the here and now.

She polished on. Greykin yawned. A shadow moved. Twilla looked up eagerly—there was a flicker. She was back in the forest. Fiercely she fought to recapture that other half-seen world. She did so in time to front Hulde.

The Wisewoman was looking at her, smiling gently. She raised a hand to tuck one of her wandering gray locks under her cap as she said:

"A long way you have gone, Twilla. You have chosen and your path lies clear."

"I want to stay here!" There was a tree pushing its trunk from the wall behind Hulde and Twilla strove to thrust it away.

"One wants many things, child. Perhaps a growing plant wishes to be again a seed, sleeping deep in the earth. But such can never be. You have passed beyond these boundaries, Twilla, you must fashion your own heart place, dear child."

The walls grew dim, were gone. Greykin and his table throne vanished. For a moment Twilla fought to hold to Hulde. She felt a caressing touch on her forehead and looked out among aisles of trees. Catha was beside her, the under woman's small face somehow echoing the same smile Twilla had seen on Hulde's wrinkled countenance.

"You are prepared for battle then?" she asked softly and gestured to where Twilla's hands rested on her knees. The mirror was under them and one hand still lay upon its surface as if it had been halted in mid-swing. Twilla raised it to survey her fingers. They were reddened but the skin was not broken and, though they hurt, the pain was small and still seemed afar from her.

"I do not know—" Twilla answered, still half bemused. "Does it not depend upon the outlanders what we must do?"

"Your young lordling nurses fear. He has won his point with the upper lord. But there is trouble in that voice which will greet this leader from far away."

Twilla slung the mirror once more around her neck.

"Not alone," she said briefly.

Catha smiled again. "No, not alone, healer. I give you this to remember—when your heart tells you the moment—then heal as only you can. Be never doubtful, Moon Daughter. There are many things of power in the world, hidden and in use. But most of them pass by their own will and in doing so they shape the one who takes them."

"All I have learned has come by chance—"

"Not so. What you have learned lay within you to be awakened. And there will be more and more, as you will discover."

Twilla smiled uncertainly. "You give sustaining counsel, Catha."

"I give what is to be known. Now come, we break our fast again. Night's dusk is growing heavier and the moonrise follows thereafter."

The girl followed Catha and, passing among the forest people and the under men, she found Ylon. He sat with the bared sword balanced on his knees, running his hand up down the blade as if he polished it so, even as she had the mirror.

Twilla settled down beside him but did not speak. His head swung around so he was facing her.

"How far from moonrise?" he asked almost dully as if, having decided upon some act of duty, he discovered little hope in it.

"Not long. The messengers say that they still are enchained. But that the women wait with them."

"This whole matter rests somehow on women. Those of the forest defeated us in the beginning. Then—" he paused, "Twilla, you were unwilling to come over mountain, were those with you also?"

"Those I had speech with, yes."

"So we used women as weapons," he commented. "And yet, Twilla, you have already countered much of what was done and planned to be done.

"It is different within the forest. Yes, Lotis and some of the others fought, but in the beginning it was a fight to defend themselves. Here man and woman stand equal—each may have some powers open only to their sex. But those are weighed against each other and none is the lesser for it. Women have not fared well at our hands over mountain.''

"Each people has their own customs—"

"But," he said abruptly, "the wise learn the best wherever that is made plain. Ustar would have put you to raw shame to mend his own pride—"

Twilla laid a hand over one of those busy smoothing the sword. "Ustar is Ustar—I have Ylon to know and remember."

His forest-paled face suddenly flushed. "Healer—Lady—I am only half a man.''

"Here you have proved yourself complete!" she said sharply. That inner rage moving in her and with it the shame that she had destroyed his last chance of standing equal to his father and the men he had once commanded.

"Ylon—they come from the town!" Fanna stood beside them.

Ylon got easily to his feet and Twilla was instantly beside him. "Not you." He sheathed his sword and flung out a hand to form a barrier before her.

"Yes. You have said that this included women, Lord Ylon. Very well I stand with those of my own even as you front those of yours.''

The moon was indeed rising as they pushed their way back through the brush and stood at the edge of the open land. The captive men were silent but their women still kept their places not too far away and from the distance came the pounding of hooves, a handful of tall men rode into the fuller light.

At least one of their questions was answered, he had brought no large force with him, that straightbacked leader whose mount paced well before the rest. Most of his followers wore mail and went armed, but two huddled in the dull cloaks of townsmen. Behind a horse's length or two, rode others—women—so Twilla was sure Rutha and Leela had returned.

"They are here," Twilla said in a low voice, as that line drew up among the blackened spaces where the fire brands had left their scars.

Lord Harmond had still kept his place well to the fore, and now he raised his hands as his well-trained charger stood still and unlatched his helmet leaving his face bare in the moonlight. It was the same set countenance Twilla had seen at the lottery. This was not a man to be easily swayed though she had never believed that he would be.

She caught at the brush and pulled it away leaving an open path for

Ylon. He moved forward with the same determined stride that any soldier on the march would use.

Twilla followed him a space behind, standing. She was aware of other movement. Oxyle might have at last been won to allow Ylon to be spokesman but he was there and with him Karla, Catha, Chard, his boar's staff deep planted as he stood, both hands clasped tightly around it.

"I am here—" Lord Harmond's voice was as cold as Ustar's ravings had been heated by rage. "My men you hold in bondage."

Twilla saw a stir among that small group who had ridden here with him. Perhaps they wondered that their lord would admit so much.

"In bondage—not death!" Ylon's hand brushed his sword hilt. His head was raised and his father's voice was his guide so they spoke face to face.

"So speaks a traitor— Where is the commander who would talk with me?"

"He is captive to that whore before you—he speaks with her tongue!" The hoarse voice, worn by ranting came from the netted men, it could only be Ustar. "Do not deal with a traitor who bends to a woman's orders."

Ylon made no answer to the taunt.

"I have been given the right to treat," he returned calmly. "For I know what life lies in the outlands and what abides in the forest. You see your army in bonds, Lord Harmond, and I say to you that that is not the least of the defenses which can be brought against you."

"I speak only with leaders," the chill in his father's voice carried the arctic wind of mountain winter now. "No maimed man can treat with warriors. These have not given you back your eyes—perhaps they cannot. So there are limits to their powers. Make no mistake we shall search out such and use them."

"Do you swear that by Izearl?"

The name seemed to reecho across the open. There was sudden quiet from the captives. Lord Harmond sat statue still in the saddle.

His features remained as if chipped from stone and yet Twilla sensed something—a kind of wavering which lay now in the air about them. The moon was unusually brilliant tonight. Like to the moon she had seen in the pool where her powers had been restored.

"You speak a name—" Lord Harmond hesitated as if trying to find words.

"I speak a name which must be well known in the outlands. Was it for Izearl that your priest built a balefire and would burn a child?

Such was not the way of Arvanis. Have you bowed knee in Izearl's foul house?''

Lord Harmond's features twisted as if he could no longer control some tumult within.

''You speak of things you do not understand—''

One of the armed men behind him, his helmet well shadowing his face so he could not be well seen, moved forward.

''This has no bearing on what should be done here, my Lord. Let the un-man go and mouth his blasphemies in the Wood he has embraced. He is nothing—and he can do nothing—''

Twilla moved. She had no conscious bidding, but it was set upon her as much as if she were one of those soldiers under orders. She was behind Ylon now, mirror raised in both her hands. Standing on tiptoe she passed it over his head, bringing the reflective side down before his face.

In the brilliance of the moon his face was sharply defined, except for that mask of filmy silver across his eyes.

She spoke and her voice was meant for him alone but it carried.

> *"See not with eyes but with the mind.*
> *The evil spell cannot now bind."*

And she willed, willed him to do as he must do, look within himself for his cure. Lotis had laid the sorcery on him; Lotis was gone. But before her going he had already broken free of most of the spells she had set upon him.

Her voice arose, a little shrill. She was aware of nothing now but that reflection, of the need for turning within Ylon himself the key to freedom.

> *"See not with eyes, but with the mind*
> *The evil spell cannot now bind."*

And—she saw! Saw that misty strip lose substance become mere threads, and the threads themselves disappear.

And—she heard—heard Ylon's great cry from the innermost of his being.

''I see!''

There were answering cries from those watching him, even from the captive men. The women were on their feet and now they were shouting in turn.

''The healer! The healer heals—''

Through the line of mounted men moved Rutha and Leela.

Leela's horse shouldered away from that of the officer who had ridden out earlier.

"This is the healer," Rutha's voice was near as cold as Lord Harmond's had earlier been. "This is the healer your foul priest denied—that you denied, saying that nothing good comes of such wisewomen. Be sure of this, Lord, no more will you order us under the lash for saying your right is wrong. You shall not take our men to fight your battles."

She turned a little in the saddle to face those in line by the forest's fringe.

"Let there be peace—let mage craft go for good and not for ill. Is it your will also, you who are women?"

Twilla saw Karla, Musseline, Catha move forward.

"This is no affair for women!" The officer who had been pushed aside used his mount to come beside Rutha. "Keep to your hearths and your man's bed, woman!"

Lord Harmond had been staring at Ylon, even as his son was regarding him. Now he roused.

"Walthar, I am the king's voice here. If you think to speak for Izearl you are a voice alone.

"I have heard much of healers," he had urged his horse a step or two further ahead. "And much did I think was but idle talk. You have proved me wrong."

"No," Twilla shook her head. "It was your son's belief which returned his eyes. I was only the small means of opening the way. But this talk of Izearl—that is not for healers, my Lord. Nor"—she studied his face for a moment—"do I think it is for you either."

He raised his head high, and the moonlight turned his graying hair to silver.

"I listened to orders but the greater man chooses which orders he will harken to. I have come to parley and there is no secret thoughts to be held in hiding. Son," his face was no longer set, there was a wonder in it, and a kind of weariness as if he had carried far too long a burden he loathed, "let us speak with these tree rulers in peace. I will be grateful if they loose my men who have been so bond this day through."

Oxyle had come to Ylon's side. "It shall be so done, Lord—"

"Not yet!" Ylon interrupted. "Father, there are still those among your command who would follow another path. We have heard one even now spout forth his foulness. Give us Arvanis Sword Oath and we shall know that you are one in mind with us."

Lord Harmond frowned. His hand went to the hilt of his sword, but it would seem from his look that he would sooner cut down his outspoken son than yield. Then he sighed.

"How can I deny what you may think of me? If I stood where you stand I would ask such in return." He drew his sword and held it high by its blade.

"By the steel which is stainless I do swear that I have no thought of ill against these I would swear truce with, not shall any under my command show them ill. By the Great Smith who beats out the souls of men do I now swear this!" And he set his lips to the cross hilt of his sword.

He resheathed his sword and swung from the saddle, dropping the reins so the well-trained mount stood untethered. A gesture brought three other men to join him, one in armor—but not Walthar—and the other two in townsmen's drab wear. Together he led them forward.

"Release now my men," he said as he came to a halt but a sword's distance from Oxyle.

The forest lord gestured to Chard and that under leader held high the boar-headed staff. From its eyes shot rays of red gold, arching up and over the heads of the men, soaring into the night sky to bring a semblance of sun to counter match the moonlight.

As a fisher's line well cast could trouble the surface of a pool so did those rays touch the netting and from those points of contact ran light along each strand—leaving nothing behind so that men lurched free, stiff from their bondage. Then the tops of the crawlers arose and men pulled themselves out of those prisons. Toward them the women ran, brushing aside the soldiers, each seeking her own.

"Your men are free," Oxyle said. "Deed for oath. Now do we speak in truth, outland lord?"

"Yes."

Oxyle gestured and the brush parted so they could see the vast roots of one of the giants curling its upper length from the truth along the surface of the ground.

"Let us then sit in council."

Stiffly, Lord Harmond and those he had chosen came. The townsmen, Twilla thought, flinched when the shadow of the tree overcame them. But they seated themselves upon the roots and faced the forest dwellers and the under men staring curiously at both.

"You came unasked to this land," Oxyle spoke first. "What need have you for it—slavery? Have you no proper rooting of your stock elsewhere?"

"We needed food. There are many of us over mountain and the land—" Lord Harmond hesitated.

"The land?" it was Catha who prompted him. "What of your land? Can it not bear any growth then?"

"For many seasons we have ploughed it not for planting but for mining of what lay beneath—metal—"

It was as if Lord Harmond could answer them with nothing but the simple truth. Yet Twilla could detect nothing of bespelling. Even the silver mists had withdrawn to a distance so that they could barely be seen among the tree-walled aisles.

"Metal," it was Chard who spoke. "We, too, live by metal but we do not make it our master, rather it serves us. It would seem you have put yourself to slavery by your own wills."

"So you come here to grow food," Oxyle took up the confrontation. "Well, the land is rich, it will repay those who do not force themselves upon it as masters. But why do you trouble the forest?"

"In our own land wood forms our shelter, our heat to beat winter's chill."

"So you kill with the cursed iron. Even as you now seek metals for your use. Do you know no other way but that of force to take what you believe you need? We have met force with force and you name us demons and take strange precautions against us. What of the women you drag over mountain to be your shields? Are they, also, to be mastered and used as wood, as metal?"

"They shall not be so again," Karla said when there came no quick answer from Lord Harmond.

His eyes dropped under her probing. "Lady, until this hour I served my king, his orders were my will. You have broken that. I cannot foresee what will come."

"If you continue to provide this king of yours," Catha asked, "with the food his mine slaves need will he be moved to question how you rule here?"

"Lady, kings do not ask how one provides what they desire, they only hold interest in its arrival," Lord Harmond answered. "But I am honor broke—"

"Not so!" Ylon challenged from where he stood, neither with one of the parties or the other. "You have but given sword oath as an honorable swordsman. And I do not think that any of Izearl are those you will listen to. Give all peace and plenty and there will be an end. If the Dandus power rises, father, would you not rather stand with those of the light than those who go willingly into the dark?"

There was a silence. Lord Harmond did not look toward his son.

Strangely enough it was one of the townsmen who broke that silence first.

"Lord, we also are a part of this though we carry no arms. Sometimes a truce can end in a bargain—" his voice trailed away as if he were suddenly aware he had overstepped some rigid ruling.

"Bargain," Chard nodded. "Now you speak of what any can well understand. But it is well to remember in such bargaining that greed must not be fed. Over Lord," he addressed Oxyle with a little more formality than he had shown before. "These men speak of the need for wood. What if they are made free of that which died in its own time and not of that which lives. When the storm winds rage do not always some of the elders die, crash of their own weight to the ground. In doing so do not their heavy trunks blot out the lives of saplings which would have been great in their turn? Let the dead serve the living as is the way of life by the First Law."

"So we give our dead," there was a snap in Oxyle's voice. "And what give you, worker in metal—access for these to reach your cherished mines?"

"We can give a portion of ore if they wish," Chard replied simply.

"Any bargain has two sides," Karla spoke with a certain sharpness. "What have these earth grubbers, wearers of the cursed metal, would be rulers of all—what have they to offer us?"

Lord Harmond looked to the village man, "Well, Kather, what have we to bargain?"

The man spread his hands and shook his head slowly. "Lord, certainly all men have their needs. It is only that we find such—"

Oxyle frowned. "The forest gives us all—we have no needs such as you know."

"But," Twilla again did not know from where the words came or why it was her who must say them, "if both forest and land dwell in peace is that not a need you have reached for, my Lord? When we grow to know each other perhaps there will be more—perhaps even friendship though you are far from kin. If Lord Harmond holds this land, and so it has been promised him by the king, without any troubles thereafter, he will be serving the forest and the underworld also. For the king will be too pleased with the lack of trouble to ask the reason. I am a healer—and to my mind this is the beginning of a healing—"

She was suddenly aware of the warm weight of a strong arm about her waist, of being drawn closer to a support which to her was as tall and deeply rooted as any of the great trees.

"Do you doubt this healer?" Ylon's voice was firm.

Karla and Catha were both on their feet now. "Their is no doubt—this is a healing and let it be so!"

More slowly the men arose. Slowly, as if he believed his gesture might be without welcome. Lord Harmond held out his hand and Oxyle's flesh showed startlingly white against the hilt-calloused bronze.

Then Ylon had retreated, drawing Twilla with him. He made no move toward either party. Now his voice became a murmur for their ears alone.

"Healer, what will you do now?"

Twilla laid one hand on the mirror and with the other sought the green jerkin above his heart. The strong beat caught her own in rhythm. She looked into eyes which saw, not by her skill, but by his will—a will which was flowing into her and finding there a welcome.

"I follow my craft," she half whispered in turn. "And you, My Lord, do you again become Lord Harmond's heir, a man of war?"

"No. I have learned that there is far more in any world than a man can see, and that there is more he can see in the world than be easily believed. This rooting here will need nourishing—

"One," Twilla felt his other arm encompass her, "one who is of the land—both out and forest—and can speak to both. Welcome, healer, who has healed thrice over!"

She lifted her head a fraction and felt the touch of his lips. In time to come there might be many shadows rise but never one between the two of them.